rediscovering
Emily

AUTHORITATIVE

*We want to hear from you. Please visit **www.BKDell.com** and reach out.*

ISBN: 978-1982910631

Cover art by Amber_85

Ebook versions of this title are available.
For information please visit www.BKDell.com

Authoritative

Printed in the United States of America

This novel is dedicated to my beautiful wife Eleasha, the precious gift that God chose for me.

Rediscovering Emily
By B.K. Dell

PRELUDE

I always make it a point to drop the F-bomb during the first class of the year, especially in my Introduction to Philosophy course. I love this moment. I love the surprised look on their freshman faces. Their expressions freeze; they look from side to side, then back to me. They rewind the tape in their brains and question if they heard what they think they heard. Suddenly, the silence is replaced by laughter.

The students are thunderstruck, but those who think I'm just playing for effect vastly underestimate me.

No. I am grooming them.

The F-bomb is the most powerful word. With that one syllable, a message is sent: *lawlessness.* Your parents' rules aren't in force here. Their opinions no longer matter, and we are beyond their reach.

But it's more than that. It's a deliverance. I'm like a father whose children fear the monster in the closet. I walk boldly into the darkness in order to show them their fear is in vain.

No. It's still more than that. It's more like the moment after every revolution when the statue of the dictator is pulled down. I am the man with his hand on the chain.

I tread where they fear to tread. I tear down what they've been forced to worship their whole lives. I tear it all down. I become what every naïve adolescent loves: an iconoclast.

It's ironic; the time of life when we most seek individuality is actually the time in which we're the most homogenous. I like to call them Synchronized Nonconformists.

It's such a vulnerable age—an overweening need for validation combined with an abject ignorance of the ways of the world. It's such a splendid, vulnerable age.

What a difference a year makes, out of their parents' home and off their radar, alone for the first time, with no true sense of real life, facing with doe-eyed innocence the very things their parents shielded them from. The cord has been severed and these children float adrift, grasping desperately for something solid to grab on to.

I've never understood how eighteen is supposed to be the magical age of adulthood. As if they have powers of wisdom and discernment they lacked just one year ago. As if I couldn't tear through their defenses like wet tissue paper. As if they could ever be a match for me.

"This is no longer your parents' world." I like to make the same speech every year. "This is the real world. You are at long last beyond your parents' control. Don't underplay this moment. Celebrate it. Mark it. Embrace it. It is a freedom, a harrowing liberation. This is a time so momentous, it's a pity how many of you will waste it on drinking and sex." Again, there'd be laughter. "It's not just your body that has been set free, but your mind, your conscience, creativity, and intellect."

I *have* them now. I can always feel it—a current running through the room.

"Real mischief awaits the heart that is courageous… Real discovery rewards the mind that is unshackled." It's my favorite line. I pretend to compose my thoughts in the middle just to make it look extemporaneous. "True rebellion!" I loudly proclaim. "True rebellion, at last!"

And there it is—in one moment, I instantly become their favorite teacher. They will meet up with their friends later and say, "Dude, do you have any classes with Professor Larson? …Whoa."

Not favorite teacher, I become their favorite *person*. From day one, I launch myself into their thoughts, ahead of every parent, mentor, coach, pastor, priest, or rabbi. I suddenly have more power over their viewpoint, and therefore their hearts, and therefore their entire lives, than any one person.

I see it in the way they look at me. They unanimously make a subconscious pledge to themselves: they will do, think, or feel whatever it takes just to please me.

Yes, I know that look in their eyes—all sycophantic and clueless. It's idol worship devoid of shame. It fuels me up in a way I can't fully understand.

Chapter One

"Jesus saves." She sits up taller in her chair as if she had actually just said something. There is a natural blush on her naked face, and I can't help but notice her beauty one more time.

"Can you be a little more specific?" I say with practiced sarcasm. The charm of her beauty doesn't save her from the bite of my ego.

I study the flawless skin of her face. Flushed and florid, it stirs something ancient in me. And yes, something godless.

Of course, I am a predator, but it is not their bodies on which I prey. I have no interest in their bodies, when dominating their minds is so much more satisfying.

She continues, "Christ said, 'I am the way, the truth, and the life. No one comes to the Father except through me.'"

In one breath, she sums up her religion's greatest weakness, only she treats it as a selling point. A half-dozen flippant remarks fill my head, but I resist. I ask patiently, "But do you even know what you're saying?" It comes out as just a whisper. "Do you even know what that means?" Anger wells up inside me, and my voice gets stronger. "Do you even realize the *implications?*" Spittle flies from my lips as I make the word into like five syllables. "Do you understand that points to a God that no one should *ever* worship?"

The girl blushes more but says nothing.

"I mean, assuming I accept the awesome mantra, 'Jesus saves,' it begs the question, saves from what? Saves from *whom*? I think that's the one thing Christians like to forget. They chant 'Jesus saves, Jesus saves,' but don't often stop to reflect, *Saves from whom?*"

I leave the question open to anyone in the room to answer. No one does out loud.

"From God," I spit. "Jesus didn't gallantly save us from the wrath of the *Devil*, but from the wrath of *God*."

"Well… yeah," she says sheepishly.

I proceed, "So, God drops us into a maze, but you expect me to praise him for giving us a map? God throws us overboard, but you expect me to worship him for throwing us a life preserver?"

"No, it's not God who puts us in the maze; it's our sin. It's not God's wrath; it's God's justice."

I love it when they put up a fight. *Justice?* Nothing's more predictable. I could see that old trope coming since the time before the flood. "Are you telling me there is something we can do to avoid Hell?"

"Well, sure," she sputters.

"Romans 6:23 says the wages of sin is death," I proceed. "Are we given the choice not to sin and therefore not to die?"

"Of course. It's always a choice."

"Then we don't need Jesus?"

"Well, we need Jesus because we can't do it on our own. No human is capable of living a life without sin."

"But you just said we had that choice."

"We do."

Give me patience. "Can we choose to do something we are incapable of doing? And is it justice to punish someone for failing when success was never an option?"

"Um..."

I grin, but slowly my grin turns into a smirk. The last hint of good humor leaves my eyes and is replaced by all the temperance of a hungry lion. I head to my chalkboard.

When I feel the small white chalk between my index finger and thumb, I know that society routinely demonizes the wrong things. This small weapon I am holding is more fearsome than any gun. The ideas that begin on my chalkboard one generation, will be in the highest branches of government the next. And yes, they will be the ones to decide—more often than any gunman—who lives and who dies.

I begin, "How many people do you imagine have lived in the last hundred years? By my calculations it's somewhere around eleven billion. And what percentage of those were Christian? Well, about 1.8 billion people walked the earth in 1910, and about 600 million of them were Christian. Today the Earth's population is around seven billion, and over two billion of them are Christians. So, at least in the last century, Christians have accounted for about one-third the Earth. Congratulations.

"So, if there were eleven billion people who have lived in the last hundred years, that means somewhere around four billion will make it, or have made it, to Heaven. That means the number of people who have gone, or are going, to *Hell* is somewhere around..."

I turn to the chalkboard and draw a seven and a comma. Behind the comma, I draw a zero. I do this very slowly and deliberately, and I angle my body so that the class can monitor my progress in real time. I draw another zero and another. Then another comma. I draw another zero, then another, then another. Another comma. I draw another zero. I draw another zero. As I draw the final zero, my chalk comes around slowly to connect a perfect circle. I step back to see the number I have written and shake my head in horror and disgust. The number I have drawn looks like this:

7, 0 0 0, 0 0 0, 0 0 0.

"Keep in mind," I say somberly, "this is only one century. It doesn't account for the full six-thousand-year history of Earth."

A few clever students catch it and produce pockets of laughter. I push some of my long hair away from my eyes and grin.

I erase the last zero, and in its place, I draw a number one. I say flippantly, "That last change is because of me."

Again, the students laugh.

But I'm not finished yet. I pull out my cigarette lighter, which I always carry despite the fact I don't smoke. "Oh, but you shouldn't laugh," I rebuke the class. I raise my voice to where I'm almost shouting, and say angrily, "Because we are talking about seven billion souls from last century alone whose bodies will burn," I flick the lighter and hold my hand over the flame. "And the flame will never stop." I move my hand closer to the flame. It should be obvious to the students now that I am in significant pain. They can see it in my eyes, and they can hear it my voice. "And the pain never ends. And it is not just their hand." The pain from the flame makes it hard for me to speak. "And it is not just a lifetime. It is seven billion people who are burning from head to toe for all eternity. Because of God."

I turn to see the girl. She has tears in her eyes. Her skin no longer can be described as flushed but red and splotchy. There are tear tracks down both cheeks. She gathers her things to run out the door in dramatic and cowardly fashion.

I am a predator, but don't misunderstand; I have never laid a hand on a student, never delivered one inappropriate touch, sexual remark, or even a glance. Not once.

Sexual predators are taciturn loners with speech impediments and bad teeth. There are freshmen orientations, public service announcements, and special interest groups to raise awareness about the destruction they cause.

It's quite the opposite for me. I am well-paid and esteemed. I am feted and defended. I am educated, cultured, manicured, and eloquent.

And no one has a problem with what I do—not the parents, not the media, and certainly not the institution that employs me. In fact, I am revered. I am given unobstructed access to these children's minds, hearts, and souls, and the only obstacle that ever tries to block my path is currently fleeing the room.

"You have until the fifth of February to drop the class," I derisively call out to the back of her.

I hear the door slam behind her. I know I will never see her again.

Chapter Two

I believe a man must truly conquer the day before he has earned the right to sleep, or at least consume enough alcohol to feel the elation and self-esteem of a man who has conquered the day. Tonight, I haven't done either.

I am a sieve through which time passes but leaves nothing behind; aimless and lonely; wired, tired, uninspired. It's not the passing of time that bothers me, it's that I feel nothing strong about its passing. It's the feeling of taking too much Tylenol. It's the remnant fog of alcohol after the finicky elation has refused to come.

I can't get my mind off the girl's tears. She really threw me off my game today. I didn't even drop the F-word at any point. *First time in years.*

I down the last swallow of Scotch.

I decide to pour myself some more, but I remember it was my last bottle. I manage to make my way to the refrigerator and disinter one lonely can of beer from way in the back. She's still shackled with the yoke from which all her sisters had been loosed.

Yes, all alcohol is female. If I have to explain that to you, you either don't know alcohol or don't know females.

I crack open the last beer. It's not enough, but it's all I have left. Looks like I'll be up for fifteen more minutes. Perhaps I can somehow spend them without thinking about that girl.

Suddenly I remember one more bottle of alcohol in the house, one that I vowed never to drink. Not for the reasons you think. Not because it is forbidden or taboo in any cool, dangerous way. Not because it makes me *just go crazy,* makes my clothes fall off, or would cause me to drunk-text my ex. No, just because it's pedestrian, feeble, and *oh so* beneath me.

American absinthe.

A friend of mine had heard me brag about my experiences with the *La Fée Verte* in Paris. I admit I've found ways to bring up the story more than once, but people have always gotten a kick out of my lines, "Drinking absinthe is like discovering the meaning of life, and then forgetting it," and, "Absinthe makes the heart grow fonder." They've earned me the moniker, "The Absinthe-Minded Professor." Anyway, he thought that a bottle of absinthe would make a nice gift. Unfortunately, he was too simple to realize *real* absinthe can't be sold in the United States—ignorance of intoxicants of course denoting a perilous lack of sophistication.

It had to have been the most uncomfortable moment of my life. He'd gift-wrapped it and everything. I can only imagine what my face looked like.

Reluctantly, I unearth the bottle from the back of my cupboard and examine it. "Contains FD&C Yellow #5 and Blue #1." *Seriously?* The

Green Fairy needs food coloring? I think back to what my kindergarten teacher taught me: "Yellow and blue make green." Was that kindergarten or an old Ziploc commercial?

In traditional absinthe, the green color comes from the chlorophyll extracted from wormwood. The natural coloring is essential in absinthe aging, because the chlorophyll remains active. It can't be faked with Yellow #5 and Blue #1. Or at least it shouldn't be.

I ask myself if I am desperate enough, and the only answer my brain produces is the image of the young girl's tears. It's like a stain on my heart which only the right spirit could dissolve.

I decide to try the absinthe anyway.

I wake with a start. I feel bereft, as if I'd slept through an alarm, as if sleep had left me vulnerable to a problem that my mind had to rouse and address. I'm in my bed, in my pajamas. Did I oversleep? Did I forget an appointment? I search my memory. It's Tuesday; my first class of the day won't be until... until...

I check the time on my phone and discover my phone is gone. What's even more mysterious, there is someone else's phone in its place. The phone hasn't been left there casually, but plugged into the power strip by my bed, the way that I always charge my phone every night. I pick up the foreign phone and press the home button. The phone displays a beautiful young woman and it pricks my heart, the way photos of pretty girls always do. She has the cutest dimples I've ever seen on a woman, but I have no idea who she is. I do a quick search of the room. I impulsively long to smell coffee or hear a running shower.

But I'm all alone.

What a strange feeling. Could it be I underestimated American absinthe? How late was I up drinking? Did I finish the bottle? I don't even remember opening it. My eyes dart over to the trash can in my room. No bottle in the trash. I search my nightstand. No bottle anywhere. No glass. Okay, all right, so absence of evidence is not evidence of absinthe. Ha ha, philosopher's joke. That is to say, *drunken* philosopher's joke.

No time to be redundant now.

I realize that this can't be blamed on alcohol. There have certainly been nights when I couldn't remember lying down to sleep; I won't lie. Missing memory is the stuff of benders, and I have been on some pretty bad benders. But one thing is missing for that explanation to be plausible: my hangover. I have an unusual lack of any hangover, not even the one I'm rightfully due. In fact, my head feels clearer than it has in years.

Okay, someone's phone beside my bed is not altogether shocking, the shocking part is that someone must have brought it over, but I don't remember. Had someone else been here while I was sleeping? The thought chills me. How would they get in? Although the thought is absurd I quickly walk to my front door to examine the lock. The thought is absurd but no non-absurd explanation is forthcoming.

The lock's fine. I take a brief look through my living room. Nothing seems out of the ordinary.

The phone is strange, but I feel certain there'll be an explanation for it. When its owner and I swap stories, I can tell her about the bizarre feeling the mix-up had left me with. Perhaps if I play my cards right we can laugh about it together over drinks.

I try to discover the last thing I do remember as I trudge back to my bedroom. Mechanically, I raise my hand to stroke my chin. I feel a touch of smooth skin and I jump as if it had been a hot iron. It is the jolt one feels when they think they are taking a sip of Dr. Pepper and discover it's Coke. I instantly raise both hands to my cheeks. My beard is missing... Wait. My *beard* is missing? Someone stole my cell phone and my beard? *Diabolical!*

I continue to rub my bald face until it sinks in. Am I dreaming? I haven't felt my bare cheeks since my twenties. I'm a little freaked out here. Is this a practical joke? Is this Kevin's hand at work? How could he have shaved me without me waking up? *Shaved me? What am I even saying?*

I quickly step into the master bath to view my mirror. There I see a younger man, at least he somehow looks younger. He has my face, but his eyes are brighter. My beard is gone and so is my hair. What used to be long and flowing is now cut short and tight. I have a fat lip and my skin is tanned... in January.

I almost don't recognize myself. I can see the tops of my ears. It's as if my mind has been transferred to someone else's body. I look more deeply into the mirror. No, it's me all right. Just with a haircut and a shave and a tan.

In January.

Overnight.

While I slept.

I lean closer to the mirror to properly inspect this interloper. My skin is not only tanned, but I have a slight sunburn. I press a firm thumb into my cheek just to confirm it's not makeup or sprayed on or something. It stings. When I remove my thumb, there remains a white impression which quickly fades. Yep, definitely caused by the sun, but when? And how?

I also touch the cut on my fat lip. It's definitely a fresh wound. My nose feels a little funny, so I prod it with my finger. It produces instant pain and my eyes well up with tears. It doesn't appear to be broken, but something sure did a number on my face.

I have now passed from slightly confused to positively nonplussed. My stomach's beginning to tighten in fear. It isn't the fear of monsters with tooth and claw; it's the fear of ghosts or spirits, the incorporeal and the inexplicable, something beyond our reality, mysterious and unknown.

I confess I am scared. It's only my desperation that asks if I am dreaming. It feels nothing at all like a dream. And with a light on in every room in my brain, it feels more real than the majority of my life. Unlike most my mornings, life has my full attention just now.

I continue to stare at myself as I can come up with no other action to take.

I notice two pale lines on my skin, converging just below my collar, and I pull down my collar to investigate. There is a lighter imprint on my skin and I imagine that I had been wearing a necklace whenever I had acquired this sunburn. This is extra strange because I don't wear men's jewelry. I don't believe in it. I've never purchased a necklace that wasn't a gift; it's just not my style.

There is clearly something there where the two chain lines meet, the remaining hint of some sort of pendant, but I can't see the whole thing. I quickly open the top few buttons of my PJs and pull my shirt open wide.

I gasp out loud. The image is crystal clear, and yet I've never felt so unclear. The image is unmistakable, yet there must be some mistake.

It's a *cross*.

I turn on my faucet and wet my fingers so that I can rub it off. I grab a towel from the rack and smear on a dab of soap. But to no avail.

"What sort of trick?" I mutter as I scrub. Soon I have scrubbed so hard that my skin turns red and the cross is gone, at least for a second. I drop the towel and rub my eyes with both hands. I blink twice and study the red spot atop my chest. As the redness disperses and the tan lines come back into view, before my very eyes, an image of the cross redevelops on my half-baked skin.

I am definitely weirded out now. I have to call someone. I begin a frantic search of the house for my own phone. The search goes on for a quite a while. I forget about the shortness of my hair and the baldness of my cheeks. I forget about the cross. My single focus to find my phone degenerates into profanity. I ball my fists. There is not even a clear image in my head of who I would call, just a vague sense that my smart phone can save me. In any situation, my smart phone can save me.

Inspiration strikes; I can call my phone. Why didn't I think of it sooner? I can use the mystery phone to call my own. I am sure the owner won't mind. If she did, well she shouldn't've left it on my nightstand.

I dial my number, ready to listen for the ring…

"Please enter your password," a robotic voice commands. I stare at it dumbly, as my clear, Rocky Mountain inspiration pools into a murky mud puddle. How strange. I hang up.

The thought occurs to me I could just use the strange girl's phone to call whoever I wanted. Kevin, I say to myself and raise the phone again. Disappointment hits me again. I don't know Kevin's number. Why would I? I don't dial it. Further contemplation of my dilemma reveals that I don't know anyone's number. Not anyone. I am overcome with a feeling of loneliness. Without the address book in my phone, it's like I have no friends at all.

I lower myself down onto the edge of my bed and I have to steady myself with my arm. I feel like I'm sinking down a black, lonely drain. Tears sting my eyes. I'm drowning in helplessness.

I stare off like I'm thinking, but the gears in my head have ground to a halt. If there are any words to my thoughts at all, they would simply say, "Huh… strange." My mouth is open, my brow is furrowed and again my thoughts dully repeat, "Huh… strange."

The doorbell rings.

Stirred from my trance, I jump to my feet. The hairs on my neck stand up. My skin goose pimples and I feel both hot and cold. My palms are freezing straight through, but there is sweat under my collar. Odd that a doorbell should delight and terrify me. I realize that I am vulnerable. Vulnerable—that's the reason for my delight and terror, delight that a friend would come to save me, terror that an adversary would catch me so exposed.

I make my way over to the door and quickly redo the top buttons of my pajamas in order to hide my holy tan lines.

I can only make out a silhouette through the peephole, but I can't match it to anyone I know. I can see that my mystery visitor has long, lovely hair and an adorable svelte frame. It looks as though she might be carrying something. I continue to stare waiting for the silhouette to reveal more of its secrets, and I hear an impatient voice. "Open up! My arms are killing me."

The second I turn the knob even slightly, she knocks the door aside with a swift kick and me along with it. She storms in with the patience of a queen. I see right away that I was right about her hair and her figure, and so allow her impertinence.

As I watch her, I feel a warm air wafting in from the open doorway. I extend my hand past the threshold, confused. Seemingly, it's a balmy day outside.

She starts in on me at once, "I could hear you behind the door. I swear, James, you are so inconsiderate. You know this is why…" she stops herself from going any further and sets down her load.

I make my way over to the thermostat and am surprised to find the AC on, not the furnace.

Through the corner of my eye, I see her make an exhaling gesture with her hands. "I didn't come here to fight again," she says in a tone only slightly more civil.

Now I turn to see her face and gasp slightly. She is beautiful, but that isn't it. In incredulity, I raise the cell phone up between our faces and press the home button. *There's no mistaking those dimples.* It's her, the girl from the phone.

Immediately, she reaches out and pulls the phone down. "I don't want my picture taken."

"I wasn't... I..." I'm tongue tied.

"It's your stuff," she makes a nod with her pretty head. Her attitude is completely bridled now, and it's obvious that she's going to great lengths to appear... compassionate? Solicitous? Civil?

I am trying to read her face, and I wonder if she always wears this much makeup so early in the day. "What stuff?" I ask.

"All of it," she says. "I just wanted it gone." Her face twitches as she tries again to tapper her tone. With an obvious effort to look apologetic, she says, "Sorry. I... It's your stuff. You should have it back."

She stands here now, waiting. For what? It's obvious she knows me, which is strange enough. She obviously thinks nothing at all about having a conversation with me while still in my PJ's. And a quick peek into the box tells me that she has somehow acquired some of my things: some of my shirts, a lot of my books, one of my hats... As I puzzle all this, she is standing silent, with a slight tension in her face and tightness in her shoulders. It's a look that I know well on a woman. She wants something from me, but what? Absolution? Contrition? Did she hurt me or did I hurt her? What am I even saying? Finally, I blurt out the obvious, "I'm sorry, who are you?"

Her face collapses. Her eyes burn with anger. Her right hand raises to shoulder level, forms a finger, then a fist, then a finger. She's shaking. "Grow up!" she cries. She swiftly grabs her keys out of her pocket and turns to my front door.

"Wait, I mean it," I say as I move to block her path.

She rears back indignantly as I come even slightly close to her. "James," she growls out a warning.

I immediately step aside to pacify her the best I can.

Her hand, no longer equivocating, forms a long and angry finger. "I knew I shouldn't have come. I was just going to leave it on the porch. I knew you couldn't behave yourself."

With her path cleared, she steps toward the door again. I know I have to act fast. I have seen too many romantic comedies were the entire plot centered around one person's peculiar inability to ever tell the whole story, where if he'd have only spoken in detailed paragraphs instead of vague sentences, the entire misunderstanding would have been cleared up before the dark moment, maudlin ballad, and the flashback montage. *I refuse to live in a chick flick.*

I say, "Wait, please, stop. Please, I need your help. I woke up this morning and my beard is missing, my phone is missing, and I can't find an absinthe bottle. I am sunburned in January. I don't think it's January. So, I don't know if I time-traveled. Or if I was in a coma or am in a coma. Or

I'm dead somehow. Or if this is a prank. Or if my brain was uploaded to some computer... or something... or..." I wave all that off. "I don't know who you are. I promise. The first time I saw you was on this phone. Which I guess is yours. Then you show up here. And you're so pretty. I know this sounds crazy. Maybe I'm going crazy. Maybe I'm hallucinating. Maybe it's American absinthe. I don't know. But I am *not*... I am *not* lying!"

She's standing awfully still. I tried really hard just then to use the inflection in my voice to indicate I was done, but she's not saying anything. It's hard for me to read her face.

I sniff.

She still isn't saying anything. Her makeup is done really well. I didn't mean to imply earlier that she was wearing too much. She really knows how to apply it—looks professional, really.

Her eyebrow twitches slightly. Finally, she says, "That's not my phone."

"Oh." I say because I can't think of anything else.

"Yeah... I want to leave now," she says, giving no clues if she believes me or not, letting on to only one impulse in her mind; her face, her body language and her words all say the same thing: She wants to leave.

And she leaves.

She doesn't close the door behind her, and like a besotted sap, I watch her walk away without really knowing why.

Again, I feel bereft.

Chapter Three

I check the time on the phone. I haven't missed a class, but I don't have much time. I strip off my PJ's and find something to wear. Not much about my closet has changed and the familiar act of changing clothes brings me comfort; it's the only thing so far this morning that has felt monotonous and normal.

I choose a shirt I know will cover the cross on the top of my chest.

I grab my car keys, and just like my face, they feel different. There are far too many keys. I take a better look and identify at least two keys I can't account for.

When I get to my garage I discover that someone has smashed my car. The rear bumper is completely smashed, and a wash of anger sweeps over me. The anger is coupled with confusion because someone has parked their Jaguar right next to me. I don't know anyone who even drives a Jag. I've never seen the car before, but I check its front bumper just in case it could lend a clue to the state of my rear bumper.

Its bumper is fine, but I don't know what it's doing here. Unless we were in the middle of a hail storm, a guest to my home wouldn't likely park in the garage.

I actually consider the possibility of a hail storm, but it reminds me that I don't even know which season I'm in.

In desperation, I hop in my Prius, despite its severely smashed bumper. It adds a new ingredient to my current predicament of helplessness: embarrassment. I watch every face that passes me on the road, fearing that I might recognize a driver who might recognize me.

Finally, after a drive that felt five times as long, I arrive at Kevin's.

He opens the door, but stops it just past his temple, leaving his body fully behind it. *I don't have time for this.*

"I'm in sort of a bad situation here," I tell him. That should be enough for him to step out of the way and let me in, but he doesn't budge.

He takes a second to study my short hair and shaved face. "What are you doing here?"

"What do you mean? I told you, I'm in a bind."

"Listen," he says as he moves the door an inch in the wrong direction. "You can't just come by unannounced and…"

"I don't have my phone. I don't know your number."

"Look, I…"

"Kevin, why're you being weird? I need your help." The feeling hits me. He's in on it… or he's targeted too. He's affected. Or infected, or something. Whatever stunt, hoax, or strange magic this is, he's a part somehow. The Kevin in front of me is not the man I knew yesterday. I ask slowly, "Do you know who I am?"

He looks puzzled, then suddenly irritated. He snaps, "Don't kid yourself."

It's clear that he somehow took it rhetorically. I try again. "Kevin, are we friends?"

He frowns. There is real hurt there. "I don't know."

I'm searching my brain for some other line of inquiry, an attempt to discover which things about my old universe are still true in this strange new one. I ask, "How long have we known each other?" I wait for his answer and I realize that if my oldest friend says, "We met last week on Venus," it wouldn't surprise me at this point.

He steps aside and opens the door. Again, I guess he heard the question as rhetorical, although it truly wasn't meant to be.

When I enter his foyer I immediately smell coffee brewing. In the distance I hear the sound of his shower. The old dog; he's having the morning I first hoped I was having. At least I can guess one reason why he wouldn't let me in, but I have to know the others. I make my way to the barstools at the edge of his kitchen. That's where we always like to talk... or *liked*. I'm not sure. "Why did you say you didn't know if we are friends?"

He looks irritated again. "C'mon, James. You did this."

"Did what?"

He studies my face. "She left you, didn't she?"

"No... I mean... I don't know what you're talking about. Who left me?"

"Why did you come here?"

"I need help."

"Of course you do. Who punched you?"

I reach to feel my fat lip, but don't have an answer to give. I feel a renewed sense of urgency because I just heard the shower stop. "Something strange is going on here, Ke— Wait!" I hold up the phone. "Is this the girl you think left me?"

"Did you leave her?"

"Wait. You know this girl? Pretty brunette with dimples?"

"What... what are you—"

"You know this girl?" I press. "Please. I know this may sound crazy. But if our friendship means anything to you, please just indulge my stupid questions."

I can see from his face I just messed up. He is indignant. Of all the stupid things, his mind is stuck on the wording of my plea. "You know you've got a lot of nerve playing that card and—"

I desperately interrupt him. "Wait, please." *I've done a lot of begging today.* "Have you seen me since January?"

He narrows his eyes even more.

"The 16th; I went to bed on the 16th. It's not the 17th, is it?"

"No."

Okay. I am starting to rule out time travel, so I ask, "Have you seen me at any time after January the 16th?"

"Yes."

Not time travel then.

He reiterates, "The last time I saw you was that night."

"What night?" I shrug. "New Year's Eve?"

"No. You know what night."

I consider getting down on my knees. My face shows raw desperation. I look pathetic. "Please. I need to know when you last saw me. It wasn't New Year's Eve?"

"No. It was August 2. You should know that date; it wasn't the first birthday you ruined for me, by the way."

I'm trying to understand. "August 2 of this year?"

"Of course. What's the matter with you?"

I realize he doesn't trust my words. His mind is ruling out what I'm actually trying to say, because what I'm actually saying is crazy. I try to concentrate on being thorough. I say, "Last night I went to sleep, just like any other night. It was *January* 16. Today I wake up and it is summer. You're sure you've seen me after January 16?"

"Yes."

My story is weird enough now that I see some patience in his face.

The queen of bad timing enters the room. She's wearing only his shirt. She stiffens, surprised to see me. She hesitates, considers her attire, but decides to fully enter the room anyway.

I'm impressed with the caliber of woman in his home, but there's no time for that now.

"Who's your friend?" she asks him.

Before Kevin can answer, I stand up from my chair and extend my hand, "I'm James, but he doesn't know if we're friends."

She doesn't laugh.

"It's okay though, because I don't know anything at all today."

The two of them kiss a bit and she finds the coffee.

I know I have to turn her presence here to my advantage. I know he will be on his best behavior. I also know that I can't come off as crazy. I say, "I am so sorry that I've come to bother you two this morning." I turn to the legs and say, "We have known each other since right after high school, when we hung drywall together. And ever since those days, I've known that there is one man to whom I could always turn for help. This morning I've discovered that I must've done something to offend him, and I know it must've been something bad, but honestly, I don't remember." I let that part linger heavy in the air, until I realize neither are impressed. I realize there is a legitimate and commonplace reason for how that could happen, so I double down. "I don't know the reason, but I swear on my life that what I am telling you right now is true. I don't remember anything after January 16. From my vantage, January 16 was yesterday. *Was* January 16 yesterday?"

They both shake their heads.

I just needed to confirm it one more time. I continue, "I went to sleep that night, and I woke up today. Now, I've just recently ruled out time travel, but Kevin, I need you to tell me..." I can feel my face begin to flush with the intensity of my distress. I fear my eyes will pool up against my will. "...is this some sort of prank? I'm sorry for that time in Vegas. I'm sorry for the hoagie incident, but this is too much. I can't handle this. I feel I might go crazy. I feel I might break down. If this is a prank, please stop it and tell me now."

He shakes his head.

"You got me," I still insist. "You got me good. Real good. Too good, I promise. Just show me the cameras and please, please, let's all have a good laugh." I am coming undone. How pathetic I must look.

Again, he shakes his head. "No cameras. No trick." His tone is clearly trying to match the sincerity of my tone—which I appreciate. He continues, "Do you really think I would, or even could set up..." He trails off, not sure what he can admit to believe yet.

"Not think," I say glumly, "hoped. I hoped it was some sort of prank."

"You really think all this is happening to you?"

I want to object to the term *think,* but the simple truth is, I haven't ruled out that I am merely thinking it—either having the most elaborate dream ever or trapped in some Cartesian solipsism. I say wearily, "Prove to me that you exist when I can't perceive you," and smile wryly.

"Who won the Super Bowl?" she asks.

She thinks I'm lying. She is trying to trip me up and get me to expose myself. "I don't know," I tell her. It's not much of a test; only giving a correct response would prove anything. But who would be that stupid?

"Who won the first-round draft pick?"

Before I can answer, Kevin butts in, "He wouldn't know that either way."

Kevin likes to tease me. He isn't one of my philosophy friends; we didn't meet in a classroom, but on a construction site.

"I don't know," I insist. "I don't know anything that's happened between January 16 and today."

"Then you don't remember my birthday?" he asks.

"No. I'm sorry... for whatever it was I did." I frown. "Were you still okay with me on January 17? If someone had come to you on January 17 and asked you about me—asked you that daunting question I asked you earlier, are you and I friends? What would you have told them?"

Kevin nods somberly. "Yes, we were friends."

"*Are* friends," I correct him. "Because it is still somehow January 17 for me, no matter what the calendar says. I am still the man I was that day, and whatever happened to change me, or to come between us, has somehow *un*-happened in my mind. I am the man you cared for then, and I am bringing you a second chance for us."

This is the first time I've seen him smile since I arrived.

"Now, do you want to tell me what I did?"

He smiles again, a bit more somberly. "No. It's forgotten."

I smile at his phrasing. I might have hugged him here if we were alone. *Might have.* I ask, "Okay who is this girl on the phone?"

"I don't know her name. You two were dating."

"You don't know her name?"

"You only brought her by one time. She introduced herself..." He kind of trails off and shrugs.

"I didn't talk about her?"

"Not really. We haven't really talked much at all this year."

"Maybe she was taking up all of my time?"

Kevin shrugs. "Something was."

"How long were we dating?"

"Up until you and I parted ways."

"When did we meet?"

"In the beginning of the year. You hadn't met her by January 16?"

"No."

"Well, you would have met her soon after that, I think."

"She is pretty," I say. "Do you know how I met her?"

Again, he shrugs and I'm realizing I won't find my answers here.

I suddenly look at my watch. Crap. Kevin's reaction to seeing me had derailed me and I've forgotten about my class.

"I have to go," I confess. "I've got enough going on right now. I don't need to add trouble at school to the list."

I thank them kindly and make a quick exit.

Chapter Four

Not much about the university has changed, and with no mirrors around, things are starting to feel like normal. There's a certain feeling I get every time I step foot on campus. The imperious nature of the eighteenth-century architecture works its magic on me. I can't help but feel I'm a part of something regal—a task of superior importance. I climb the steps to the philosophy building and realize they've always made me feel a little puffed up. But more importantly, they've always made me feel safe.

No matter what problems face me in life, I always find peace in my studies. As if the accumulation of knowledge is… well, it's the *point*. It's the whole point. I wake each day, eager to imbibe more facts, and the greatest thrill in the world for me is to think about something in a new way. I know this might sound strange, but whenever I find my heart troubled, I just try to think about my books. I recount the last new theory I heard and run over the steps of its reasoning in my mind. I remember the last argument I won, how it felt, and where my opponent had misstepped.

The deepest memories I have in life are at this school. Not as the teacher, but as a student. My philosophy class was still being taught by my predecessor and I was eighteen years old.

It seems I should have weighty memories before that, and I do, but most of them aren't stories I could tell, just a few amorphous impressions, like the dusty smell of old books and the thrill of recording my thoughts on paper, my first time drunk on wine and a smattering of difficult bra straps, the impassive face of my mother and the back of my father's head as he'd run off to finish "his opus."

Funny how eighteen years of life seem to have produced less for me to truly hold onto than three credit hours at the feet of a great teacher, Dr. Davin Fowler.

I remember every word of that first lecture, after which I walked up to him uninvited and extended my hand. "I am James Larson," I said, as if informing him that it was a name to remember.

"James Larson?" he asked. I detected in his voice a tone of a challenge, as if he knew all that I had intended the introduction to mean. As if he knew and I didn't.

"That's right," I said defiantly.

"So, you've come here to learn about philosophy?" he asked, probing and mocking and taunting.

"Yes," I said with a childish insistence.

"And why do you wish to study philosophy?"

I felt certain in my young mind that this was clearly a test. He was trying to intimidate me, or feel me out, or… prepare me. Yes, prepare me, like the secret wisdom of the philosophers was a towering tsunami, and he was coyly asking me if I knew how to swim.

A thousand different answers filled my head. Finally, all I could think to say was, "Because I don't have wings to fly."

He looked at me like I was an idiot. It hadn't been a test at all, but yet somehow I still failed. Another student asked a question about his lecture and stole his face from me.

I slinked out of the room.

Yes, even *that* memory is somehow beautiful to me now. It was like an awkward first kiss shared with one you would later marry. It was like an irritating grain of sand in an oyster; it would later be covered by the exploration of new ideas, covered by the scouring of weighty tomes, covered with philosophical discussions that ran late into the night, until finally it would be a fine pearl.

I walk into my classroom now with a renewed assurance that things would be okay. My mind is no longer on the confusion of this morning. I am here now. I can just do what I do best.

A few of the students are already sitting at their desks. They look up as I enter. Their faces instantly force all traces of assurance out of me. Every face shows shock and they refuse to look away. They stare at me like I'm the Easter Bunny and I am filled with dread over what this might portend.

I look at them quizzically, but not one of them lends me the mercy of a smile. It demoralizes me somehow. When one is caught staring at a human, the polite response is to look away. These kids no longer see me as human. I am not the authority, the model, or mentor. I am certainly not their crazy, cool, new favorite professor.

My study of them studying me is interrupted by a voice.

"Excuse me, sir... Oh." It's Professor Nelson, and apparently it took him a second to recognize me with my new look. "Dr. Larson, what are you doing here?"

"What are you doing here?" I ask him in return.

"What are *you* doing here?"

"This is my Philosophy 101 class."

"This is *my* Philosophy 101 class."

I wonder for a second if the man is just repeating everything I say. Dumbly I say, "This is *my* Philosophy 101 class." *Great now I'm doing it.*

He brakes first and says curtly, "This *was* your Philosophy 101 class." Then, as if to negate this show of unbridled aggression, he quickly adds, "I don't want any trouble."

I frown. Effeminate philosophy teachers always annoy me.

"Maybe you should talk to Charlie," he says finally.

On the way to my dean's office, I wonder what all this might be about. Images of the way the students looked at me still run through my mind. Did they move the room my class is in? That seems strange.

No. Most likely I have been fired, but why?

When I reach the dean's office, there are two campus security officers standing in front of it. Looks like the effeminate professor phoned ahead. I walk straight through them. We are uncomfortably close, but none of us say a word. I step into the office and they step in behind me.

"What are you doing here?" asks the dean.

I am officially tired of that question. I am tempted to put on my best Jimmy Stewart and say, "Don'cha recognize me? It's me, George."

Instead I say nothing. By now I have figured out that I just come off as crazy when I blurt out every question that comes to mind—*Why is there someone else teaching my class? Why is campus security here?*

I have figured out there's about half a year of my life unaccounted for, and if what Kevin told me is correct, I participated in those months, but don't remember.

I piece together the clues. "I'm fired, right?"

He looks a little irritated, but at least he doesn't think I'm nuts. "Now Dr. Larson, you know you're not supposed to be here."

He used to call me James. "What did I do?"

"Dr. Larson, you know what you did."

Ugh. I will never answer a question indirectly again as long as I live. "I'm very sorry, but I don't actually know what I did."

"We've been through this, Dr. Larson." He keeps using my name, like a homeowner scolding a neighborhood kid, wanting to give evidence that she knows who his mother is. "Listen, nobody cares what you do in your personal life, but when you brought it to this school, you made it public."

"Brought what?"

"This debate is over. Our lawyers have instructed us not to engage with you. I'm sorry but I am going to have to ask you to leave." He makes an appreciative nod to his two goons, more for me to see than for the goons.

I consider employing my chosen tactic from this morning with Kevin and the mystery girl: lay it all out as fast as I can. But I decide I am too close to the psychology building, and I fear the university might have the power to lock me away somewhere.

I turn on my heels and leave.

As I walk back to my car, I get those same gawking stares I received from the students in my classroom… former classroom. I don't believe that me being followed by security is enough to explain their accusing eyes. After all, I'm not in handcuffs; they're not clutching me by both arms; but the students' expressions all look the same: shock by the first sight of me on campus, followed by a censorious disappointment.

I am a pariah. And deep-down I know I don't have the type of personality that can withstand being a pariah. Although I have spent much of my life bragging about being a pariah, and trying to become a greater pariah, I see now how phony that was. I never wanted to be an outcast. I was an outcast with one group in order to be accepted by another. I was no nonconformist. I bucked the conventions of one group, just so I could better conform to the other. I was no rebel. I only ever stood against the current, so I could be in step with someone else's current.

I always needed a group. No shame in that. The only shameful part is that it took me so long to admit it. The only shameful part is that I am only able to admit I need a home at the very moment I am being escorted out of it.

We reach my car and I open the door. I turn and take one last look at my beloved campus, the place where I always felt most safe. Then I get into the car and drive away.

Chapter Five

I'm a man without a home. I did something foolish on the way back from the university. I stopped at a liquor store and picked up some American absinthe. I am hoping it will complete the circle. I'm hoping it will seal the portal for good. Like a man who gets amnesia because of a blow to the head, but a second blow brings all his memories back, I am trying to orchestrate the second blow.

I remove the bottle from the brown liquor store bag and a white receipt falls out. I quickly pick it up to check the date; it says August 29. I am starting to accept the fact that it's not January 17. The warm weather was a big clue and one that would be quite hard to fake.

I pull out the mystery phone from my pocket. It too says August 29. *So, there you go.* I head to my bedroom and drop the phone into the top drawer of my nightstand.

My mind is running back over explanations that it had already considered. *Could this be a prank?* There are two problems with the prank hypothesis. First, it's way too elaborate: shaving my face, tanning my skin. They'd never be able to do that without my knowledge. Unless they drugged me. I look at my arms. I hadn't thought to do this before. If I'd been drugged, I might have a needle mark. There's nothing I can find.

The second reason it couldn't be a prank—and this is the clincher—no one loves me enough to go through this much trouble.

I scratch prank off my list.

I look back at the receipt. August 29. It's strangely comforting—just a little scrap of paper from an outside, disinterested source. It must be August 29. This receipt would simply have no reason to lie to me.

I pour a glass and raise it high like I'm giving a toast and I pause.

"Please. Please," I beg out loud.

I don't know what I'm saying. I don't believe in a God to whom I should beg, but I can't deny I am begging. I am holding a glass of fake-green alcohol and trembling in pitiful supplication, with no one to be supplicant to. I am wretched and I'm lost and I just want my old life back. "Please," I repeat aloud.

I drink the glass down, not admitting to myself what percentage of my brain really thinks it might work. I once was a man who would laugh at a plan as absurd as this. Look at me now.

I set the glass down quickly and close my eyes…

Nothing so far.

My eyes open and my legs start to move as a new idea strikes me. The receipt drove the idea home that all this—this great mystery—was caused by simple memory loss, not time travel, not a hoax, but memory loss. If that's the case, the solution seems so simple: I keep a journal.

I run to my nightstand and open the bottom drawer. That's where I keep my journals—hand written since I was in sixth grade. My heart leaps and I can see light at the end of the tunnel. I grab the top spiral with reverence because I know inside are the answers to all my questions. I am just about to find out what I did to Kevin on his birthday, who the mystery girl is, and just maybe, if I'm lucky, what caused the memory loss in the first place.

I turn open the back cover to view the last entry. I turn a few pages to find the entry's header. It reads "Nov. 2."

I place it down to search the pile for the newest one. It's not here. I'm trying not to panic. I run to the box in my closet where I keep past spirals. None of them are the most recent spiral. I run back to my bed and throw off the covers. I look under the bed and under all the pillows. I check the drawers of the nightstand. I can't find it. Frantically I remove the stack of spirals from the bottom drawer and pull the whole thing out to dump it. It's a big drawer and there is a chance that I didn't see it.

The contents of the drawer spill out onto my bed: the diaries, a few Moleskine sketchbooks, a Fisher Space Pen, and an old pocket watch. I don't see the missing spiral, but I notice something else. I used to keep a Bible in this drawer. *Yes, a Bible.* I once grabbed it from the hands of my mentor, and it seems to be missing as well.

I hear something roll off the bed and rattle to the ground. I search the floor but can't locate it. I drop to my hands and knees and can make out a large pill bottle that had rolled under the bed. I'm confused about what it could be, so I press my chest to the ground so I can reach it with my arm. With my face so close to the hardwood, I discover I apparently hadn't vacuumed in that missing seven-month period.

There's a loud banging at my door. Again, my heart pounds with anticipation and fear. What next? Who is it now? Friend or foe, or just another mysterious face? Someone to bring me hope or someone to squelch the little that I have?

He bangs again, at least I imagine it's a *he* by the force of the knock. I'm almost to the door when he bangs again. Whoever it is, he's impatient.

I look through the peek-hole-thingy. It's Kevin and he's brought his new lady friend. They are getting serious pretty quickly, I marvel. But I realize that's not fair; they could have been dating for seven months far as I know.

I turn the door knob slightly. He shouts, "We have it," as he nearly knocks me over bursting in. He is the second person to push through my door today.

She echoes, "We know what happened."

"That's impossible," I argue. "How could you know?" But in my heart, there's hope—an uncorked champagne bottle overflowing with sweet and intoxicating hope.

Kevin throws down the stapled printer paper he is carrying and shouts triumphantly, "The *Times*. We found it online."

"I found it online," she beams triumphantly.

I highly doubt they would print anything about my life in the paper. I say, "What the... How could..."

"You're not the first it's happened to."

Those words hit me with a strange sort of joy. I mean I am sorry about those others, but please tell me that this is some freak medical condition—*maybe caused by keeping cell phones on our person at all times. I knew it!* Tell me John Hopkins is working on it. Tell me they've already found a cure.

Before I say a word, he continues. "Read it."

I pick up the printout.

"Don't make him read it," she protests.

"It's all there," he says.

"It's three pages long," she says.

I put the printout down.

"You took Premocyl," she blurts out.

"I took... what?" I ask and impatiently pick the printout back up.

"People take it to forget."

"It causes memory loss."

I'm not buying it. My initial reaction is that their theory falls flat. "Why would a drug cause memory loss?"

"It was recalled!"

I am scanning the sheet... "...*Antidepressant drug, Premocyl... recalled after a disturbing discovery... extreme doses cause memory loss.*"

I shake my head. "I've never heard of it," I protest.

"Well, of course not, silly. It was news about four months ago," she says.

I like this girl. She's smart, and the *silly* was a bonus.

"But we missed it too," Kevin quickly adds. "A lot of people heard about the recall over a year ago, but no one who wasn't taking it cared too much. We hadn't heard of the second part until we found this article."

"What's the second part?"

"They recalled it, but some people held onto it. They offered everyone a full refund, but people soon discovered that they could get more money..." He pauses. "...by selling it on eBay."

I am starting to give credence to this theory. I have to sit down. "Wait, you're saying that I took the drug?" I ask.

"Well, no one knew what was happening at first," she explains. "Suddenly all sorts of people were reporting memory loss. Their doctors would ask them if they took any Premocyl and of course they would say no. Of course, they would. Just like you, they'd forgotten that they'd taken it. The drug covered its own tracks."

My eyes are still scanning and jump to where I spot the word, eBay. *"...before eBay promptly cracked down on the practice, which violated their terms of service, and canceled all offending accounts... it however can still be acquired elsewhere on the internet."*

I ask in disgust, "Why on Earth would somebody *want* memory loss?"

This time neither of them rush to answer. For the first time since they got here, my chatty friends are not talking over each other. In fact, they have suddenly become timid and fidgety.

I turn my eyes to the article instead. I scan until I reach the words, *"...heartbroken fools, aiming to forget their heartache..."*

I break the silence with a whispered, "Oh."

"It says that some people have been able to erase entire relationships from their minds... for good," she says.

I look over at the box that woman brought over, untouched since she left it.

"Only problem is, it erases everything else too," he says. I hear a lot of compassion in his voice.

I nod my head, somberly. "That it does."

We all stand silently at the graveside of my memories.

"Do the memories come back? Does it mention some way to reverse the effect?"

"No," they both say in unison.

Again silence.

Kevin adds, "There hasn't been a single recorded case of anyone getting any lost memories back."

"Any?" I bargain.

He shakes his head.

"So, that's it? I was stuck on some girl, so I drugged myself."

"That has to be it," she argues. "All the pieces fit."

Kevin is silent. He knows I'm already sold on the theory. The only thing I'm still questioning is my own... *cowardice? Reckless irresponsibility? Melodramatic, maudlin crap?*

I speak what he must be thinking, "I stole months from my life and potentially damaged my brain, for a *girl!*"

"Well, if you really loved her," she says.

Apparently, there is *one* romantic left in the room.

I stand abruptly when I think of yet another new idea and head to my office. I can see before I enter the room that there is an external hard drive resting on the edge of my computer chair, placed right there for me to see.

"You won't find anything," Kevin says, seeing where I was headed. "Your Facebook page has been deleted. We checked. And the email I sent you as a test this morning was bounced back to me."

I know he's right, but I jiggle my mouse anyway. A few clicks tell me that the hard drive, like my brain, has been freshly reformatted. "At least I did myself the favor of keeping some stuff," I say motioning to the hard drive on the chair.

"Well, you can be sure none of it will mention her. I'm sure your phone's been purged as well."

"I can't find it," I tell him. "Hey, can you call it?"

I'm not sure why I didn't think of that before. The truth is I've had more to worry about this morning than just my phone. But now that I am thinking about it, it delights me. I imagine all the answers my phone could possibly provide. There are past voicemails, past text messages, a photo album, notes, appointments, past internet searches. I couldn't have thought to wipe them all. My phone knows more about me than anyone.

My thoughts are interrupted as I hear my phone begin to ring. I jump from my chair filled with urgency and hope.

I make my way down the hall in a full-fledged run and triangulate the sound. It's coming from the top drawer of my nightstand. I pull the drawer open and see my phone.

Of course! People don't put pictures of themselves on their phones.

I figure it out the exact moment before I see it with my own eyes. My phone's in the top drawer. It has been there since I got home. I lift the phone with my unrequited love's face and answer. "I got it," I say disheartened.

"You wouldn't go to such lengths to forget her, just to have volumes of digital media around to remind you." I hear Kevin's voice, not on the phone, but in the threshold of my room. The girl appears there behind him. "I mean, it sure is bad luck that she came by this morning. You might have gotten away with the perfect crime."

"Not perfect," I say, holding the phone toward him. "I left one picture."

His brow tightens. "Now that is strange. Why would you…" I can see he's kind of bothered by this. "That's the first piece to all this that makes no sense at all."

His girl smiles. "No, it makes sense. It makes total sense," she says in a saccharine tone that implies she, in her girly wisdom, knows things that us boys are too boorish to comprehend.

"There you go again, the romantic," I say to her and add, "No, wait, the *silly* romantic."

She shrugs and fires back, "You're the one who couldn't bring himself to delete a girl's photo."

Touché.

I quickly check the phone. No text history. No call history. It's brand new, totally empty, and my old phone is long gone. I click to add that last call to my address book. "At least I got your number now." I say it with such a tone that is meant to imply I want to be alone and—what a great guy—he gets it.

"Call anytime," he says as he tugs on his lady friend's sleeve.

When they leave I try to remember what I was in the middle of before they came barging in with all their fateful news. I look at my bed. *Oh yeah.*

With a dull sense of obligation, I drop down and retrieve the bottle. Sure enough, it reads "Premocyl." And there is someone else's name on the label.

My heart begins to pound, but the beats feel forced and painful. It's so strange holding this bottle in my hand, knowing what it has done. Knowing what I have done.

I want to set it down, but I don't.

I know there's no point to search for my journal now. I make a mental note that I should search the bottom of my fireplace for it.

All this confusion and loss over a girl? Over a girl?!

It occurs to me that I don't even know her name.

I make my way, as if summoned, to the box she brought. Why did she have to come by? Why couldn't she have left it? To bring back my stupid junk? I can see a few hangers hanging out the top. Burn them. Burn them all. An extra toothbrush? Throw it out. I don't want to see it.

Yet my feet keep stepping.

It strikes me that *she* wanted to make sure I received what was rightfully mine, while I extended myself no such courtesy. She wanted to make sure I got a few books and DVDs back into my collection, but I blithely threw away seven months of my life. Seven months, one week, and six days of my life. Gone. What might I have learned in that time? I, who values knowledge so highly? What opinions might I have formed? How might I have grown as a person? I will never know.

The questions are filling my mind now, but one rises to the top. How did I come to hate myself? How did I come to disrespect my life and my mind so much that I'd be willing to throw away a piece of it? How did I have such contempt for myself as a human being that I would see myself as worthy of being drugged? The pills in the bottle rattle as I can't stop my hands from trembling. I put it down right next to the box. He did the deed and left me holding the bag. He did the crime and left me to do the time. Where is he now, the man who took those pills? That man is gone. He is gone and I'm stuck dealing with the consequences.

What could make me hate myself? What type of pain could be worth all this just to forget?

I look into the box now for the first time. Beside the clothes, beside the toothbrush, beside the books and DVDs, placed carelessly without distinction, is a small jewelry box. My trembling hands pick it up. I open it to see a diamond engagement ring.

Chapter Six

I wake up and it's just me. Just for a second, it's me. In this moment before I know where and when I am waking up, before I reclaim memories of what happened yesterday, and reclaim hope and fear of what can happen today. In this moment, I am simply me.

Now it's gone. Reality is quickly ushered into my conscience. I remember I was dumped by the woman I love. *Loved? I get the feeling tense will be hard for me for a while.* A split-second passes before the headache returns as well.

I can tell by the headache that I have not traveled through time. I open my eyes to find a bottle of American absinthe by my bed, nearly finished.

Okay, I've reached *tomorrow*. Now what?

I lie in bed for a moment and I realize I have no reason to get up. No job. No one to go see. No overarching purpose to life.

My collar is open and I reach to touch the center of my sternum. Now I have a reason to get out of bed: curiosity. I spring to my feet. I step to my bathroom mirror and examine my chest again. The cross is still there, but it's not as noticeable. I am slightly less red and the imprint that the cross left on me is fading away.

I stare at the short-haired me for an introspective moment. My beard is starting to grow back, too.

I can't stop thinking about the memories I've lost. Funny thing memories. I think most people sleep through life, waking only for a few choice moments of intense joy or intense distress. It's as if the mind only possesses its truest retentive ability while it's aroused from the haze.

Like with the death of my mentor, Dr. Davin Fowler.

My senior year, we learned that he'd been diagnosed with lung cancer. I rearranged my classes for my last semester so I would have time to visit him in the hospital. But the funny thing was, I didn't go. Not at first.

The reason was simple—reasons, actually: David and Fay. David and Fay were Davin Fowler's son and daughter-in-law, his beloved children whose names peppered every lecture.

It wasn't until I first feared losing him, my life going on without him, that I realized how much I loved him. I just couldn't bear to walk into that hospital and see him with the two of them. The idea of her doting on him and making him laugh provoked a sickening bitterness inside me. I could picture both their faces, simultaneously looking over their shoulders at me, not fully turning to greet me, but inspecting the intruder. "What are you doing here?" their faces would say. And, "Who do you think you are? These visiting hours are for family. You're just a student. This is family time. He never loved you. The school paid him to teach you. You were a job and now that job is done."

The moment I realized I loved Davin Fowler, I also realized I hated his son, hated him because he was born to the great professor and I wasn't. "Who are *you two*?" I fired back in my imagination. "What books have you read? What questions have you asked that made him raise his eyebrow? What theories have you posited that made him look up at the ceiling and stroke his chin? Who are you, David and Fay, who are you?"

I finally got up the nerve to visit the hospital, and I found him alone in his room. The nurse told me she wasn't sure if he was awake, and when I walked over to his bedside, I saw his wizened face resting without peace, agitated and irritable like the mind of a true philosopher.

"Professor Fowler?" I asked quietly.

There was no response, so I tried again.

"Professor Fowler?" I sat down by his bed.

Nothing.

"Davin?" I tried again.

His eyes lifted and acknowledgement filled them when they rested on my face.

He didn't say a word and the silence made me uncomfortable. "I thought David and Fay would be here," I said, wondering how much time we might have together.

He shut his eyes tight. He said, "They won't see me."

"What?"

"I haven't seen them in twenty years."

"But you're sick. You're…" I stumbled awkwardly, trying to avoid the word *dying*. "They won't come see you, even when you're sick?"

"They don't know."

"Well, they must know."

He shook his head. "For all they know, I died years ago."

"But, don't they care?"

"They have their own lives."

I couldn't believe it. I could feel the anger make my cheeks hotter. "What about Elaine?"

"She has her own life."

"But you were married for what? Seventeen years?"

"And divorced for ten."

"But you still talk."

"No," he said.

"Well, Julia then."

"She has her own life," he repeated.

"Veronica?"

He laughed. "That one I made up."

I thought back on the story of Veronica and suddenly realized I should have known. "Isn't there anyone?"

He smiled confidently and said, "I have everyone I need right here."

In that moment, my chest swelled. All my compassion for his sorry lot faded and my jealous heart overflowed with pride, until I saw him gesture over his shoulder.

I sat up taller and peered over his body to see a stack of books. I saw books by Kant, Popper, and Foucault. *Everyone he needs.* I forced a weak smile, but I could feel tears starting to sting my eyes.

"I'm sorry," I turned my head quickly and stood up from my chair. With my back already to him, I pointed at the clock on the wall and said, "I forgot an appointment... uh, I'll be back."

As far as I could discern, he had no reply.

My quick exit wasn't just to hide my tears from him. I had to get out of there. I had to leave right there and then because I had an idea. It was the type of idea that, once thought of, must instantly be acted out. It was a mission. I saw clearly I had one shot left to win this man's favor once and for all: I had to find his children and bring them there to him.

Chapter Seven

David and his wife, Fay lived in Edgewood at the time, which was a five-hour drive. I stepped out of the car and stretched my legs. Five hours was a long time for me to run over every possible scenario that could happen when I knock on that door. I hadn't intended it, but over four hours into the trip, I noticed that I hadn't even turned my radio on. I had been driving in complete silence, consumed by the possibilities.

I was somewhat surprised by the size of their house. It filled me with an extra bitter form of jealousy. But it also intimidated me. I had been seeing every aspect of not just our approaching confrontation, but our entire lives, as a competition, and this house was a trump card I hadn't expected. As I walked on my weary legs toward the front door, I saw the perfectly manicured lawn and sculpted bushes. The whole thing enraged me. The house was freshly painted with red brick and white trim. The white was as clean and bright as a fresh sheet of paper. I could feel my heart beginning to pound. What started as jealousy, and had moved to intimidation, turned into to rage, and had now become raw hatred.

It's just greed! I expostulated. *How dare they own a house this big? When others are suffering?*

I hated the man I was about to meet. And I wasn't entirely certain that I would be able to conceal that fact from him. After all, I was there to ask him a favor.

I rang the bell.

And waited.

I tried to control my breathing and put on my best attempt at a pleasant face. I think I was able at least to pull off indifferent. All of the twenty-plus intro statements I had composed on the car ride filled my head until I ended up with nothing at all. I was standing on my nemesis's porch waiting for his door to open any second, and I had absolutely nothing to say.

But it didn't open.

I rang the bell again. And waited again. Finally, I just walked back to my car.

I thought about what I could do, or where I could go, but eventually I just sat there in my car, as if on a stake out, and waited.

Finally, after ten o'clock that night, I saw a car round the corner. In the light of the street lamp I could see their faces. Their car slowed down as it approached their drive. It only took a second for me to identify him. He looked a lot like his father, but with none of the intelligence behind the eyes. I looked at the woman. Pain struck my heart again.

She was beautiful.

They eyed me suspiciously as they passed and disappeared through their solar powered gate.

I gave them a second to settle in before I walked up to the front door again. At that point my heart was pounding. I had only Tabasco in my veins. I wondered if I might just skip my intro statements and simply strike him in the face.

When he opened the door his face looked perturbed, even… *frightened*. Why? Had he seen the violence in my eyes? I looked down to check if my fists were balled. Remarkably they weren't.

"Yes?" he asked curtly.

"Are you David Fowler?" I asked.

He hesitated, like he was reluctant to give me his name. He seemed nervous. "Yes. Who are you?"

"You don't know me. I am friends with your father."

"One of his students?" he snapped.

"Friends," I insisted.

"What's this about?"

"He's dying."

His face didn't change.

"He's dying," I insisted.

"I don't…"

He stopped short, but I could guess what his statement would have been by the look on his face. "You don't believe me?" I pressed. "I wouldn't have driven five hours to get here just to make this up. He is dying."

"Where is he?" The insanely hot wife stepped out from the corner where she'd been hiding and into view.

David looked irritated as he turned to see her.

"Mercy Hospital," I told her. Looking back at David I said, "I know he wants to see you, despite whatever he might have said." I turned to the wife, "He wants to see you too, Fay."

For some reason, that seemed to spark David into action. He began to close the door right in my face. He said forcefully, "I am sorry, it's simply not a good time right now."

I couldn't tell if he meant that this hour wasn't a good time for my visit, or if the week was not a good time for his father to die. I pressed back on the door.

"Why don't you have him call me?" He tried to smile. "Just have him call me. We'll talk, okay?"

"You won't see him?" I accused, while maintaining enough pressure with my palm to keep the door open.

"I didn't say that. It's just… It's just not a good time now."

With that, he finally forced the door closed and I heard the deadbolt.

It was over. With more rage than ever, I turned back to my car.

Futilely, I kicked one of his bushes on the way, causing the whole thing to shake and a few of the leaves to fall off. *That'll learn 'em.*

On the way home, I couldn't get one detail out of my mind: the little hooks I saw lining the roof. The very hooks that come December would be used to suspend Christmas lights. Yup, he was Christian all right. I just knew it. Obviously Christian.

Hypocrite.

Later I saw a photograph of David and Fay. Of course, it wasn't the woman I had seen in his home.

Hypocrite.

Chapter Eight

I returned to the hospital with a heavy heart. I couldn't get his children to come see him and I resolved in the elevator not to even mention it. I had a rare copy of his book in my bag and I was determined to win his affection.

I knew what I wanted and realized how much I had always wanted it. I wanted him to see me as his heir. I wanted him to see me as his son.

The elevator dinged and my stomach lurched. My skin became clammy and my forehead became hot. The hospital hallway spoke of death and loss and *nonexistence.*

I pushed the door opened to his room, what I hoped was still his room. I rounded the corner and saw his motionless feet. His ankles were bare and so pale they were almost white. The hospital gown barely covered his spindly knees, which looked impossibly fragile. I didn't want to keep stepping, but I did.

When the rest of my mentor's body came into view, I gasped.

"What the…?" I snapped.

He looked up from the Bible he was reading, surprised.

"What are you doing?" My tone was harsh and scolding, no longer a student talking to his mentor, but a parent reprimanding a young child.

His face showed guilt and it did something peculiar to my callow heart. Suddenly, I wanted to be the master. I wanted to be on top.

"Life is too short for superstitions," I repeated back his old mantra to him. "You should understand that now more than ever."

"I'm a man with few comforts," he said, despondent.

I snatched the Bible from his hands, high on my newfound role. "There!" I pointed to the stack of books still on his table. "There is your comfort." I scolded him like a cat that peed on the carpet.

His dying eyes slowly rolled over to where I was pointing. "Yes, there," he whispered.

I sat down next to him, not wanting to try my luck. I got to play the mentor; he dutifully played the student. The scene was a success and now I didn't want to push it. I sat as low in my seat as possible, close to his level.

He said, "I guess I'm just afraid."

"Afraid of Hell?" My tone was still admonishing. I couldn't help it.

"No… dying."

Oh.

"…Nonexistence…" his fingers made a sad little dispersing motion.

My face fell. For this I had no words of comfort.

He saw how my face collapsed and said, "Oh it was easier when I was your age: 'I don't fear dying. We live and then we die. I personally don't want to live forever. I think seventy-five years is quite enough.'" He sighed. "It wasn't enough."

My face remained unchanged.

He continued, "Every day is painful. Still somehow, I want to live. I don't want to die. That the world is a without meaning and we're the products of random chance… used to be enough. But lying here now, it's not enough. So…" He took the Bible from my hands. "I just thought I'd see if there was anything I'd missed."

I smiled sweetly. I said, "You are a great mind. You are the greatest I, and perhaps the world, have ever known."

"Oh, come now."

"It's true. What better sign of your intellect than the fact you were unappreciated in your time? What better sign of real greatness than this unattended deathbed? With only me refined enough to see it." I tried to blush. "But you will note, I said you *are* a great mind, not you *have* a great mind. You are not a body, you are not a soul. You are a *mind*." I practically growled the word and made a clinching motion like I was clutching a fistful of pirate's treasure.

He nodded, and with that one nod I so greatly exceeded the role of rebuker to my rebuker, and became teacher to my teacher. I flew higher than I'd ever flown. The air was so thin I could hardly breathe. I grabbed back his Bible and said, "There is no life here, only death. For if you are a mind, then to stop reasoning is to stop living. *Nonexistence*. Let the souls of the weak-minded be saved. I don't want to save your soul but save your mind." I thumped the cover as if I were a Baptist, "For what does it profit my brother to save your soul, but lose the world? The world! The world of knowledge, the world of learning, and the world of reason." In history's best timing—a moment that unfolded like it were scripted, but I swear it's all true—I put down the Bible and pulled his book, *Absolutely Relative* from my bag. I saw the delight and surprise on his face when I revealed the rare text. I imagined it may have been a while since he himself had seen its cover. I said dramatically, "Great minds like you always live on."

He grasped at the frayed pages with his fingertips and then pulled it lovingly into his palms. His eyes got that far-off stare, and for a moment, they seemed less dead. He began, "What you said…" He smiled. "What you said…" His lips parted open and he examined me. Then he said four words that changed my life, four words that I had waited all my life to hear, four words that my own father never told me. He said, "You are so smart."

I wish it could have ended there. Sometimes I wish my life could've ended there. Why couldn't I have taken enough Premocyl to forget everything that ever happened after that second?

I was basically drunk. I was drunk on this crazy new energy and as usual, I took it too far. I pointed to the Bible and said, "Besides, the last Christian I encountered had obviously forgotten 'honor thy father and mother', and wouldn't even come to see—"

"What?" he snapped.

"David," I answered shaking my head.

"You saw David?" he snapped again.

I frowned, "He's a jerk. He claims to be so righteous, but he refused to see his own father. He's a hypocrite." At that point I realized he was staring at me, agitated. I couldn't bear his eyes, so I looked back down at the Bible. "You're better off without him. Trust me."

"How dare you!" he shouted.

My face shot up. *No, no, no, he had just been at peace.* I was completely blindsided.

"You had no right to... Who asked you to go see him?"

"He's not what you think. He's... *bourgeois.*" For the life of me, that was the only word I could come up with right then. It sounded just as lame when I said it aloud as it had in my head. But it didn't matter, because I doubt he heard it.

"Get out!" he shouted.

"I was trying to help!" I insisted.

"Get out of here and don't come back."

"Are you kidding me?" I shouted. "Look around you. I'm all you have!"

"Get out of here. You're not my family. You're not my son. Let's get that straight."

His words hit their mark. I screamed, "Fine! Fine, but I'm taking this." I grabbed the Bible. "You can thank me when we meet in Hell."

I stormed out of the room.

When I got home, I fell into my bed with my clothes still on. I curled up into a ball and wept. One fact tumbled over and over in my head, one simple truth that hurt me worst of all: *My mentor thinks I'm stupid, and I have no time left to prove to him otherwise.* Looking back now, I can't remember him ever saying I was stupid, or even implying it.

Nevertheless, I cried myself to sleep repeating it.

I couldn't stand to leave things like that, so I went back to apologize the next day. I offered his Bible back to him, but he refused to take it. He told me I was right. His exact words were, "You were right, my son."

When I left him for the last time, he was reading his own words, contemplating his own thoughts, and celebrating his own mind. He died that night with his own book clutched in his hands and his Bible on my passenger-side floor mat.

Chapter Nine

I decide to head over to Kevin's; I am anxious to show him the bottle of Premocyl I found.

At the last possible chance for me to do so, I remember to button the top button on my shirt. I don't want him to see the image of the cross on me. I don't want to be forced to hit play on that particular question I put on pause.

He opens his door and I barge right on in—why not? Everyone's been doing it to me. "I was going to propose to her," I announce. "Or did. Probably I already did. Probably that was the catalyst for me to take the Premocyl."

I walk to the kitchen where we like to talk. I don't see his girlfriend anywhere, and I'm happy we'll get to talk alone.

"How'd you figure this out?" Kevin asks as he takes his usual seat.

"I have the ring."

His shoulders slump. "Man, I'm sorry."

"I am losing my mind," I tell him. "I don't know where to find her. I don't have her phone number, her email. Do you realize I don't even know her name?"

"That's crazy."

"I can't stop thinking about her."

"Why?"

"Because I love her." I'm still standing. I couldn't possibly sit now.

"No, you don't. You don't even know her name."

"But, I did. I knew her name, and I loved her enough to ask her to marry me."

"Yes. Then. But not now. You don't know her now."

"But, I know I love her. Listen," I try to rephrase it, "I know that she is a woman I could love. Not just that. I know, secondhand, that she has all the qualities I love. I know secondhand that I love her."

"Dude, love is not a product of logic. You can't determine that you're in love like you're solving a word puzzle. You don't love her."

I completely ignore his sound wisdom and begin to frantically pace his kitchen floor. "I have to find her. I need your help to find her. Tell me everything you know about her."

"Me? I don't know anything."

"Well, surely I told you something about her. You said she came by one time. What do you remember from that night?"

"Yeah, okay..." he stares off.

"Think!" I insist.

"I remember she told this story..."

"Yeah?" I stop in my tracks to listen.

"One time, when she was in high school…"

"Yeah…"

"She brought home a stray cat and her parents let her keep it."

"Okay…"

"She named it Princess Wigglebottoms, but later found out it was actually a boy."

What? I hold out my palms. "How is that helpful?"

"You asked!"

"Okay," I try to smile as I begin pacing again, but less like a madman and more like a man on a mission. "Okay, what else?"

"Let me think."

"Something more relevant; does she live in a house or apartment? Does she have a roommate, a sister? Does she work? Does she go to yoga?"

"Let me think…" He snaps his fingers. "You told me she was good in bed."

I rub my face. "We *must* find her."

"Aren't you forgetting something?"

"Seven months of my life," I say flippantly.

"Something else. Something important for you moving forward."

"She rejected me? Is that what you're going to say? But why, Kevin? I have to find out *why*."

"You already did find out why, I'm sure. You asked her and she told you, and you didn't think the reason was sufficient, and you asked her for one more chance, and she said no. Something like that." He flicks his fingers to the side. "Besides, that wasn't what I was going to say."

"Then what am I forgetting?"

"It's simple. There is only one thing to even consider here, really. There is only one significant fact: you took Premocyl. Everything that you are trying so hard to unearth is the very thing that *you* worked so hard to cover up. So, what happens if you learn everything and then discover that you were better off not knowing? What then?"

"What then?" I grab the Premocyl bottle and give it a good shake. "Then I take the Premocyl again."

"Then you'll unearth it again!"

"No, this time I will leave a note."

"You left a note last time. Don't you see? Everything you did—it was a note. It was a crystal-clear note declaring, *you don't want to know!*"

"Lousy note. What type of suicide note leaves off *why?*" With this sad statement, I stop pacing. Suddenly I can sit. In fact, I only have the energy to sit.

"It wasn't a suicide," he says sincerely.

"I know. I know. And don't worry, I don't think I would take more

Premocyl. I'm not really saying I would. But I want the knowledge; you know why? Because I want it to be my choice. On the day that I know everything, then I will be the one to decide, not the one left in the dark. I will be the one to decide what pain I can bear. On that day, I will be the one to decide whether or not forgetting is worth the price."

"But don't you see? That day had already come. And on that day, you *were* the one to decide. It was you. If there is one person whose opinion you trust, shouldn't it be your own?"

"No. No, I will tell you why. Because it wasn't *me*. I would never choose that."

"You did." Kevin throws up his arms, stymied by my willful blindness.

"I have to know more," I say.

"No, you have to trust yourself. You want a note? Here's the note…" He actually grabs a sheet of paper and a pen from the counter and begins writing as he speaks. "This is what it says; it says: *Dear James, You would think just as I did. You would feel just as I felt. You would decide what I decided, if you just knew all the facts. You know how I know? Because you are me! Signed, James."* He tears the section from the bigger piece, folds it in half, and hands it to me.

I receive it mechanically but insist, "I have to try. I can't stand not knowing." He isn't being fair. He knows he'd do the same thing if the shoe were on the other foot. I try to persuade him, "She's my soulmate."

He smiles like he's got something up his sleeve. "Says who?"

"Says *me;* I asked her to marry me."

"Okay, well think about this one, the same you that wanted to marry her, is the same you that wanted to forget. You can't give credence to one of your decisions and ignore the other." He points to the pocket where I had slipped the note.

Wow. I hadn't thought of that. He's good. I shake my head and frown. "Love is not about logic," I explain.

He laughs.

The reality of everything that's happened hits me once more and I get very serious. "The truth is, I am not the same man who did this to me. I can't be. I don't feel like it's something I could go through. The whole idea is so repugnant to me… all I can say is, it must have been some kind of pain."

"I'm sorry I wasn't there for you," Kevin tells me sincerely. "I want to be here for you now. I want you to understand why you love her. You *do* love her; I know that. And I know why. It's not because of a bunch of facts about her you think you can deduce. You love her for the *one* fact you know about her."

"I don't know anything about her."

"Yes, you do."

"She's beautiful."

"That's not why you love her."

"It's a compelling case," I argue, grinning.

"Shanna's beautiful, but you don't love her."

"Who's Shanna?"

He looks at me disappointedly.

Oh, I guess that's his new girl's name. Yeah, she's pretty.

Kevin continues, "The one and only thing you know about this girl is that she *rejected you*. And unfortunately, that is all one person needs to know about another in order to love."

"That makes no sense."

"And it helps that she's pretty," he adds.

"No, that makes no sense."

"Do you love her?"

"Well, I feel like I should love her, and—"

"Do you want to be with her more than you've ever wanted to be with anyone?"

I look down. "Yes," I confess.

He frowns sympathetically. "Listen to me, James. It's not real. It's not what love is supposed to be about. When someone rejects you, it's like putting a big black mark on your heart. It's like getting a zero in one of your classes; it doesn't matter if you get a hundred on your next paper. That zero will not go away. It doesn't matter if you find love again, you will still be haunted by the equation: one person accepted me and another rejected me." He shrugs glumly. "Fifty percent! One grade of a hundred, another grade of zero. The zero is still there. And you know it will always be there.

"But a part of you knows it doesn't have to be! There is *one* person who can remove the black mark, erase the zero: the one who rejected you. Because when the one who rejected you returns, that black mark is no longer a *rejection*; it's merely a *misunderstanding*. And the one who said you were unacceptable suddenly thinks you're okay. And you need to know you're okay."

I nod, suddenly feeling worse than when I arrived. "I need to know I am acceptable," I confess.

"But, please, you need to find a way to feel okay without her. You need to find a way to feel acceptable even with the stain she put on your heart."

I shake my head. "I will never be happy as long as it's there. I will never get to feel like *me* again."

"You have to," he insists.

"With her," I plead.

"Without her."

"How? How?" I press. "Everything you say makes sense, but how

42

can I ever feel normal again without her?"

    Kevin thinks hard about it, then shakes his head. "I don't know."

Chapter Ten

It's been one day. It feels like one week. I have nowhere to go and no one to meet. I have nothing to do with my time except speculate on the depth of the heartache I *should* be feeling about a woman who I surely love, though I only met once and don't know her name.

I am a little drunk maybe. I finished the bottle of American absinthe, but it's not helping my mood any. I start the six-pack I have in the fridge, Pabst Blue Ribbon. Every wine-snob professor should keep PBR in their fridge just to play against type.

I clear off my kitchen table and arrange three items before me like a shrine: the bottle of Premocyl, the photo of the girl I can't remember, and the engagement ring I bought for the girl I can't remember. I continue to stare at them—first one, then the next—trying to get my mind to accept that this is my life now.

I left no way to get a hold of her. That is the bottom line. I play out scenarios, charming dialog and romantic ploys to win back her affection. But all the charm and ploys in the world can do no good if I simply do not know where to find her. I ask myself how I went wrong, and what's so bad about me that she would refuse to marry me. But all that too is a moot point if I can't find her.

Still, my mind races through it one more time.

I try to remove myself from the emotions of it all. At this point, there is only *one* path—that is if we rule out self-destruction. My path forward is easy. Drink tonight; start looking for a new job tomorrow. What choice do I have? Stay unemployed? Drink tonight; start trying to find love again tomorrow. What choice do I have? Remain lonely and broken?

Yes, I will drink tonight—not much choice in that either if you look at it. But tomorrow I will pick myself up and dust myself off and move on. Most likely my new job will force me to move a long way from here. Then I will start a new life, and the girl I can't remember will be nothing but a memory.

I hold up her photo on my phone and stare it down. Was I intimate with her? This feral beauty? Kevin seems to think I was. *Or was that a joke?* Is there a drug so powerful that it could pry *those* images from that special folder of my mind? I stare at her face, certain it will trigger something, certain that it will tell me what to do.

She buzzes.

I was so deep in silent thought that I jump. A note appears on the screen.

Tonight @ 7pm—Casimiro auction.

What? I slide off the reminder. After a second's worth of confusion, I open up the web browser and search the name, Casimiro. It doesn't take me long to discover some of his most famous paintings are being auctioned off tonight—and at the Baldovini Gallery, no less.

My first instinct is *too bad I can't make it*; I really love Casimiro. My next impulse is to ask, *were the tickets sold in advance?*

I wonder.

I quickly hop onto my bank's website to investigate my recent charges. I don't see any debit from Baldovini, but I do see what is obviously the diamond engagement ring. That one stung for so many reasons. I stare at the size of the withdrawal. I must've really loved her.

I also see a transfer to *Elite Jaguar and Land Rover.* Interesting.

I stick the phone in my pocket and get to my feet. Okay, if what Kevin says is right, I am the same man today as I was a week ago. I need only to ask myself, if I had bought tickets, where would I have put them?

I check my nightstand, my dresser, my desk… I can't find them which is really discouraging. Perhaps the theory doesn't hold water. I wander into the kitchen out of aimless desperation, and hiding in plain sight, I see two tickets sitting on the kitchen counter.

Hmm. It's obvious now that I left them where I would see them. I imagine that the reminder in my phone was left for the same reason. I feel a gentle elbow in my side telling me to get over my predicament, try to relax, try to have fun, and try to connect with the things which used to make me happy. For the first time since I woke up bereft, I am grateful to that man I was.

I check my watch—I only wish he had left me more time. Seriously? I mean I could've set that reminder to go off anytime today or even yesterday.

I run to my bathroom to turn on the shower. As the water is heating up, I go find the clothes I want to wear. I return to the bathroom and it hits me. I should check for other reminders I have set.

There aren't any.

I check for notes in the note app.

None.

I check for appointments in the calendar app.

None.

Really? A Casimiro auction? That's the only communication I bother sending over the abyss? The gratitude I had just felt for the *Premocyl Me* is gone again. I didn't leave any clues? I could've left a note. Kevin would argue that the wiped computer and deleted Facebook page *were* clues. They say, "Keep out! Cease and desist."

Then what about her face on my phone? Was that an oversight? Or also a clue?

A clue? I shake my head. I wouldn't have left a trail of

breadcrumbs; I'm not being monitored by the Secret Police. *Or am I?*

No, I would have left a long and bloviating note, defending my own actions to myself. None of this makes sense. Why did I leave myself desperately clinging to the few vestiges of my life that I didn't think to erase?

These are the thoughts in my head when I look up and see the fog on my glass shower. There is writing on the glass. It had obviously once been written in the fog and when the small bathroom steamed up again, the writing reappeared. It read "Emily + James" and both names, in schoolgirl fashion, were circled by a heart.

My jaw hangs open. "Emily, Emily, Emily." I repeat the name hoping for some sort of stimulation in my mind, two and a half carats worth of stimulation. But there is none.

There is hope, however. *Now I have her name!*

I still hold the phone in my hand, so I quickly snap a photo of the heart in order to show Kevin. I consider texting him but remember that I'm in a rush.

I shower with a new joy in my heart. It doesn't take me long to start singing the new song I just wrote, "E-M-I-L-Y… E-M-I-L-Y… E-M-I-L-Y… And Emily is her name-o."

The elation wears off fast and while driving to the event I can't stop thinking about the fact that I bought two tickets. How pathetic. And though I can now assume the Jaguar is mine, and one of the extra keys on my keychain must belong to it, I still take the damaged Prius. Pathetic.

When I arrive, I find the usual suspects: silver ponytails and tweed blazers; lawyers and professors, hippies and artists; the wingtips hobnobbing with the Birkenstocks. Undoubtedly, I'm the only one here who's ever installed plumbing.

Something strange is going on inside my head. I see them completely differently now. Men whose illustrious careers and academic pedigrees I once admired suddenly seem so phony.

I'm noticing what I never saw before, the look behind their eyes, the subtle tightness of the small muscles on their face. The lack of smiles. The lack of joy. As if the sole proof of the superiority of their worldview is that they look down on everything. They're frightened, every last one of them—just as frightened as I've always been.

They hide behind their diplomas and their philosophies. Philosophy? What a waste of time! A philosopher is a man who wants to feel smart but can't be bothered with experiments or computations. I know the system: exalt the name of some dead guy up to genius status, then quote all his unintelligible ideas. Each and every student is convinced they have found the royal road to hidden knowledge. But they never reach their destinations.

Philosophy is the largest collection of knowledge you can study without ever once encountering any true wisdom.

Philosophy is a bald peacock; it has no plumage, still it struts.

Philosophy is a man trying to explain an idea you could never make sense of but convinces you that it's your fault. Each year I led them blithely to the unemployment line, their minds to be poisoned, their parents' fortunes to be drained, all just so they can have the *second* most worthless degree on planet Earth.

Thank you, Woman's Studies.

Where is this coming from? I need a drink.

On the way to the bar, I see Clay Ingram, a mostly-friendly acquaintance of mine who works as an editor for a mid-size publishing house.

He's walking my way so I stop to shake his hand. He dutifully shakes my hand but does not stop his stride. "Well, how're you doing?" I toss out.

"Just fine," he replies stiffly, even though he has to turn back slightly to do it. In half a second, he is gone and I am staring at the back of his head. I watch him, puzzled, until he stops to greet someone else we both know. Stopped for him, not for me.

Looking around I notice Greg Park, who once begged me to co-write an article with him. I declined, but we stayed friends. I shoot him a quick wave, but he simply turns his head, his body language doing its best to insist that he hadn't just looked me in the eye.

What is going on?

Professor Bridges, who works with me—that is *used* to work with me—walks by in an animated conversation with someone I don't know. He intentionally casts his eyes away from me and even steers his comrade to walk as far from me as possible.

What is going on here?

After I hit the bar, use the restroom, and hit the bar again, I start to meander from painting to painting.

Fran Marco Ambrosio Casimiro is famous for what he calls the Casimiro Interruption. The Interruption is the name he's given to a line of raw canvas he leaves running through the center of his paintings. He would do this by painting the canvas different shades of the same color with a long piece of tape stuck to it. He'd then remove the tape after the paint had dried.

For as long as I've been aware of Casimiro, I have marveled at his Interruptions. I have collected newspaper articles and blog posts describing the audacity of leaving raw untouched canvas on an otherwise finished work. Talking to women in bars and coffee shops, I would make it a point to work my opinion of Casimiro's Interruptions into the conversation as often as possible.

The paint is usually thin enough that some creeps under the tape which is supposed to keep it at bay. This is often said to illustrate the human spirit's indomitable yearning for freedom. Others maintain it's representative of frustration, because a painter desiring a straight edge would so often—in this damnable world—remove the tape to find his clean edge sullied by the capricious and impudent paint. Some point to this and declare that the true thesis that runs through any Casimiro is the repudiation of quotidian drudgery.

The tape sometimes pulls chunks of dried paint with it from the positive side of the edge, leaving it jagged in spots. This is symbolic of the violence of oppression and the vituperative nature of the patriarch.

And then there is the raw canvas—all heretical and bold. *Courageous,* the newspapers write. *Courageous,* the blogs repeat. *Courageous,* I'd always say.

Casimiro's Interruptions are courageous. They're… They're… They're hard to wrap your mind around. It's more than rebellion. It's iconoclasm. They're godless, really.

Ah, they have the courage to be godless.

Yes.

Looking at the paintings now, standing so near to them, I feel different about them. It's not because I am seeing them in person; I've seen them in person before. I don't know what it is.

I am trying to remember the lofty things I once said about them. I'm trying to recapture that exalted emotion. But I don't feel exalted. I'm trying to grasp the metaphor, the symbolism, the innovation. I'm just *not getting it.* I'm repeating sentiments to myself that I so often droned on about to countless drunken bohemians. They no longer seem to ring true.

I look for the courage… but it's gone.

I look for any meaning at all. It's all gone.

What's happening?

I find myself standing alone. The lobby is full of different clusters of people, all in lively conversation, except me.

Then it hits me, I know where I've seen those same facial expressions—pity mixed with disgust, mixed with surprise—it was from my students… former students.

A phrase repeats in my mind that I hadn't considered before. My dean had said, "You made it public."

I am a semi-famous and semi-prominent professor. I mean I'm not a household name, but I'm no stranger to the public eye. It's been a while since I googled myself. I pull out my phone and fire up the web browser again. I type in my name and feel a moment's dread before I hit *search.*

All the old stuff is still there. My bio page at the university still shows that I work there. *C'mon guys, get it together.*

The Amazon page for my book is still up, but there doesn't seem to be any new activity. Eight five-star reviews, one two-star, and a one-

48

star. Same as it's been for two years.

I see a link to a YouTube video with my face in the thumbnail. My heart jumps because I see my beard is gone and my hair's cut short. This video must've been taken during the time I was *out*.

I click on the link.

It is a peculiar thing watching yourself from a time you don't remember, watching yourself as if a third party, saying words you don't remember saying.

I'm clearly in my classroom, all bald-faced and bright-eyed. The video seems to be shot by one of my students. The recording seems to cut in mid-sentence:

> "…is the real world. You are at long last beyond your parent's control. Don't underplay this moment. Celebrate it. Mark it. Embrace it. It is a freedom, a harrowing liberation. This is a season so momentous, it's a pity how many of you will waste it on drinking and sex. It's not just your body that has been set free, but your mind, your conscience, creativity, and intellect."

> I look different, but I am obviously giving the same speech.

> "Real mischief awaits the heart that is courageous. Real discovery rewards the mind that is unshackled. True Rebellion! True rebellion, at last!"

> I turn to the chalk board. "How many people do you imagine have lived in the last hundred years? By my calculations it's somewhere around eleven billion. And what percentage of those were Christian? Well, about 1.8 billion people walked the earth in 1910, and about 600 million of them were Christian…"

I'm mesmerized by watching myself—but a version of myself who looks quite different. Even still, I'm trying to decide how much of this I'm going to watch right here in the lobby. I look at the slider and see there's plenty of video left.

I quickly hit *pause* when something distracts me. An intoxicating fragrance fills my nostrils. I can't help but look up. A young woman in a formfitting little black dress has just passed me. I only catch a glimpse of her face, but I'd know it anywhere. It's the face I'd been staring at for thirty-six hours. It's Emily!

I shove the phone in my pocket.

Her pace is hurried, which makes me wonder if she had seen me while she passed. I know I can't let her get away again, so I call out, "Emily!"

I'm pretty sure she's close enough to hear me, but she shows no reaction to her name. It is obvious she is ignoring me and I think I detect the reason why. She is holding hands with a man.

Pain strikes my heart. *So soon?* She has found a new man so soon after… The idea comes to me, could this man have something to do with our relationship's demise? Is this the man who stole her from me? Had she been unfaithful? Cheated on me with this guy?

"Wait," I call again. Again, she shows no response.

I start after her, walking faster than eveningwear typically inspires. My shoulder collides hard with one of the bluebloods; I think it's Christopher Walters, but I don't care. I hear behind me that an overpriced drink has been spilled. A woman's shriek lets me know that an overpriced dress has been ruined.

I close on Emily and my rival. I grab her shoulder with my right hand and spin her around. I can tell right away that I've used *way* too much force. I could rationalize that it was the thrill of the chase. I could blame it all on the resentment and confusion that the last two days have brought me. I could blame it on the strange man's presence, and his face which seems to provoke aggression in me. I could blame it on the irritation I have suffered at the hands of my former colleagues. But the truth is not nearly so grand. I am drunk.

"What do you think you are doing?" I insist.

"James?" She feigns shock.

"How dare you bring him?" I shout.

"Who is this guy?" the squish asks her.

"Don't address her. What kind of a wuss are you? Your problem is with me. I just put a forceful hand on your date; you should have punched me by now. You're so unworthy of a woman like this." I pretend not to see that having just *deserved* the punch makes me less worthy.

Wuss doesn't have time to answer before a man in an ascot walks up and says, "Excuse me, but you just spilled vermouth down the front of my wife's dress."

"See this?" I turn to Wuss, "This is a man who can stand up for his woman." I turn back to the man in the scarf. "Good for you man, good for you."

"Who is this guy?" Wuss asks Emily *again*. Emily, not me.

"I'm Dr. James Larson." I'm irritated that my lips seem to have gone off teleprompter. I have no idea why they said *Doctor*. That couldn't possibly be what they and my brain agreed upon. "That's right, James Larson. I'm the one you stole her away from." I don't make the same mistake. I address only him, and I look him dead in the eye.

"Now, listen, I don't…" Wuss starts.

"James, don't do this here."

"Well, if you don't mind, we would like you to pay for the cleaning," the neckwear tries to interrupt.

I turn back to Emily. "To a Casimiro auction? If not for me, you wouldn't even know who Casimiro is!" I'm just speculating here. I only ever seem to date women who let me play a certain role in their lives: the teacher, the mentor, the professor. "And this clown sure doesn't know him," I add.

"...and I certainly feel an apology is in order," the fashionista is still talking to the side of my face.

"Oh c'mon, like you're the only one who's ever heard of Casimiro." Wuss pronounces his name wrong, putting the accent on the *CAS*, like everyone would expect. The correct way, or at least the more pretentious way, is to make it almost sound like two words and put the stress on the *MIR*.

I point a menacing finger in the phony's face and command, "You shut up."

He squirms a bit and tries to put on a defiant expression, but no words leave his lips.

I pause a moment, basking before the rival I just rendered mute.

The voice of the disgruntled man fills the void, "This is a civilized function after all, and..."

Okay, the initial respect I had for the man is lost and I point a finger in his face. "You shut up, too."

I'm on fire!

"Sir, you are drunk and I think you should leave." He raises his patrician chin a bit as he says it, but he shuffles a small step back.

I turn back to Emily. "I took Premocyl," I throw out as an accusation.

"You *are* drunk, aren't you?" accuses Emily.

"Yes! Yes, that's what us *self-important professors* do when we are dumped," I say it in the tone of a quote, but I have no idea if she's ever called me that. *Oh, they all do.* "We drink alcohol to make the pain stop. We take Premocyl to erase seven months of our lives." Apparently, *seven months* is my new trigger, because the moment I feel the words leaving my mouth, I surge with anger. "Seven months! That's what you took from me. That and my career, my friends, my pride." I am ranting too loud and standing too close. This will not end well. "That's what you took from me. And why? So you could be with *him*? So you could sleep with this loser?"

Finally, finally, the loser grabs me by the collar with one hand and punches me in the face with the other. The finger in his face must have had time to germinate.

Any cowardice he displayed before is made up for by the blow. It is a solid, respectable hit. And I go down.

The muscles of my abdomen tighten urgently while I impulsively try to get up, as if the boxing ref had just counted seven. I even make it to one knee before a painful lightheadedness overtakes me. It feels in this moment that the earth has only two feet of atmosphere and anything above knee level just can't support life. I feel like my head rose up, but all the blood that was in it stayed down.

My vision begins to darken and I collapse into a puddle of unemployed philosopher, staining the ground.

Chapter Eleven

When I come to, a kind man is tending to me. I jolt my head up, yelling, "Don't let her go. Don't let her go."

"Just try to stay calm," he says patiently.

I'm able to scan the area. There's no sight of Emily, just a bunch of gawking socialite nerds.

Reading my thoughts, my hero says to the crowds, "Folks, come on, the show's over. The auction's starting inside anyway. Let's give this man some room." No one moves, so he pushes, "Please, people, I know it's tempting to whisper and stare. Let's treat this man with some dignity. Please."

With the final *please,* most the people turn away. My Good Samaritan helps me to my feet and offers, "C'mon man, let's get you out of here. Let me take you home." This is an offer I'd instinctively refuse, but I can appreciate my need for help right now. And for perhaps the first time in my life, I just want to curl up behind someone, stay down, stay hurt, and let him be my shield.

"It's not courage, just raw canvas," is all I seem capable of saying.

I begin to let him lead me to the exit, but I can't seem to leave the night alone. I didn't come here to be stared at all night and humiliated. I can't accept it. I have to *do something.*

"I know what to do," I mumble as I pull away from his courteous grip.

"We really need to get you home," he pleads.

I wave him off. "I got this," I say.

I follow the sound of the auctioneer into the main room. I'm unaware of how horrific I look until I see it on the faces in the crowd. I notice my shirt is torn, but I can't really account for when that happened. I realize for the first time that I left my jacket in the bathroom and haven't had it for a good while now. I can feel warm blood on my face, but I am too much of a drama queen to wipe it off.

My collar is hanging open and I remember that I still have a faint cross on my chest. I reach up to button it, but the button is gone.

Everyone is looking at me, but the auctioneer is too much of a pro to stop. I try to make eye contact with every face I see, anxious to return their contemptuous glances.

The auctioneer clips on with no one minding him. "Five thousand, do I hear ten thousand. Ten thousand, ten thousand... Five thousand, do I hear ten thousand? This gentleman in the front has bid five thousand, do I hear ten thousand? Five thousand, do I hear eight thousand?"

I look up and I see that Interruption #57 is up for bids. It has always been one of my favorites.

"Five thousand, do I hear seven thousand? Five thousand, do I hear six thousand?"

The bids have stopped because the bidders are distracted by the *Larson Show*.

Finally, the young auctioneer breaks character. "Come on people. Five thousand dollars for a Casimiro masterpiece?"

Someone bids six thousand. It is followed by eight, then by ten. The room sinks back into the proper rhythm of an art auction.

"Twenty thousand!" I croak. My voice sounds awful.

The auctioneer is thrown off again. He doesn't know what to make of me.

He hasn't acknowledged my bid, so I repeat insistently, "Twenty thousand." I did a better job that time controlling my voice, and now I'm feeling pretty good about the scene.

The young man's gavel hangs teetering on his knuckle as he says, "Perhaps the gentleman is not in a state—"

The auctioneer is interrupted by a voice. I don't see the source, but I recognize it as Mr. Baldovini himself. He says, "We are always honored by Dr. Larson's participation, whenever he deems appropriate."

I search out Mr. Baldovini's face and I find him seated in the wings. Our eyes connect and I give a gracious nod.

Everyone in the room is watching to see what I will do next and one idiot even starts recording with his phone. *Great, so after tonight I will have two clips on YouTube.*

The pink-cheeked auctioneer, properly chastised, keeps his cool quite marvelously. He looks back to me and says, "Perhaps the gentleman might prefer to sit down."

This takes me a bit off guard. I don't want to sit down. I'm about to open my mouth with some suggestions of my own, but I hear someone shout, "Twelve thousand!"

The man stands up in the crowd to make sure I can see him. It's *him!* The loser. He is looking so smug, too, until I say, "Twelve thousand? I already said twenty thousand, you idiot!"

"Fine, then twenty-one thousand."

"No, wait, you just stood up all courageously and called out a number *less* than I had bid? Did that just happen? That is so funny!"

"Twenty-one thousand, to the gentleman on my left," the auctioneer moves things along, dutifully, "who is also standing."

"Thirty-four thousand," I call out instantly.

"Thirty-five thousand." Again, the guy only has the guts to up it by a thousand.

"Wuss," I can't help but say. I wasn't certain anyone would hear it, but there is so much marble in the room for even the smallest sound to bounce off of.

The crowd laughs.

Wuss immediately responds, "Thirty-six thousand!"

The crowd laughs again as he had just bid against himself.

I laugh too, enjoying the victory. "Sixty thousand. This guy doesn't even know the artist's first name."

"It's Fran," he replies. Then calls out, "*Seventy Thousand.* Where was he born?"

"Brooklyn, New York, to parents who had emigrated from Santiago, Chile," I say. "*Eighty thousand.* How many children does he have?"

"Five from four mothers," he answers. "*Ninety thousand!* How many paintings are in his Detritus series?"

"Eighteen," I answer. "*One hundred thousand!*"

"There are twenty," he says flatly. It is that stiff, excrement-eating tone of a man trying to say, "Checkmate" without sounding joyful.

I open my mouth to refute him, but remember that I had forgotten seven months, Casimiro must've added two more, recently. My face burns red. I can't let this loser best me again. I see no other way out. I shout at the top of my lungs, "Two hundred thousand dollars!"

The room is still.

The old boy with the gavel looks to Mr. Baldovini. Mr. Baldovini gives a pensive nod. The sepulchral silence is broken by his firm, professional voice, "Two hundred thousand, going once. Two hundred thousand going twice. Gone." He raps the gavel. "Sold to the man with the bloody face."

I turn on my heels, certain of my victory. I am surprised to see my knight in shining armor still waiting to give me a ride. If he has any reaction to what just happened, I can't read it on his face. I join him by the door without stopping my stride, forcing him to match mine. I say, "Now, that had to have meant something."

He helps me into his passenger seat and I slump over to the side. The vibration of the window is a comfort to the side of my wounded face, but I feel pretty certain I'm getting blood on his car. I also feel certain that I can no longer afford to reimburse him for the cleaning. I'm trying not to lose consciousness in this strange man's car, but I'm pretty sure I do.

I lift my head and ask, "Hey do you know where you're going?"

"Your place," he says although I can't remember telling him how to get there.

"Not my place," I say. "I just can't deal with my place tonight. Take me to Kevin's. I can tell you how to get there; it's not far."

Chapter Twelve

I am dreaming, mostly about my feet. I am focused on my feet and every stumbling step I take. I have consumed so much in real life that I am drunk in my dreams. I am trying to walk on what appears to be cobblestone, but my ankles are like Jell-O and I wobble.

I look up to discover I'm in a Venetian courtyard. There's a beautiful old building to my right and I see a woman on the balcony brushing her hair. No one else is around and the woman doesn't see me, so I stare.

She's dressed in a set of long white pajamas. Nothing sexy. Loose fitting and comfortable. She is beautiful.

She turns her face just far enough for me to see that it's the woman from my first day of class—my lachrymose darling, my sweet ingénue.

My mind still considers her outflow of tears to be a recent event, while in reality it was months ago, and something I wouldn't have otherwise been still thinking about, much less dreaming about.

I am excited to see her and I want to call out her name but realize I don't know it. I search my memory. I'm not sure I ever knew it.

I wave but she doesn't see me. After further *slow-witted* reflection, I decide to hide. I don't want her to have to face the feelings that my face would undoubtedly stir in her. I move back so that I can still see her, but she can't easily see me. I watch her. She looks so happy. More than happy; she looks like happiness is the simplest thing in the world for her, her undisturbed natural state. It is breathtaking to see such sincere, effortless joy.

Suddenly a shadow crosses over her. I reflexively look up to see what could be blocking the sun but see nothing. I look back just in time to see the shadow morph into a figure. There's now a man standing right behind her. He is dark and phantomlike. An amorphous shadow still shrouds him.

I yell without knowing why, just sensing danger, but the sound of my cry somehow doesn't reach her.

The man is moving in closer, but she doesn't see him. She continues to brush her hair. I can faintly hear her humming.

Futilely, I shout, "Get away from her!" I run a few steps forward, but I can't find a way to get up to her. I yell again, "Leave her alone!" The man doesn't flinch because my voice seems unable to travel.

He doesn't leave her alone. He reaches in to grab the sweet girl by her delicate wrist. She jumps when she feels his touch. She turns to see her attacker. She is too frightened to scream. She is paralyzed in fear.

All at once I am overcome with sensation. It isn't fear for the girl. I am surprised to find that it's indignation. I shout at the top of my lungs,

"How *dare* you touch her? Who are *you*? Who are you that you would aim to harm such a woman as this?"

The dark shadow slowly covers her white pajamas. Within a few seconds I can no longer see the girl, just a shadow.

I continue my useless shouting. "Not her. Not her! Leave her alone! She was happy. Why couldn't you have just left her alone?"

The shadow swallows up the man too, and in a second, they are both gone. Then the shadow is gone and I am all alone.

I wake up feeling nauseous.

I am in my own bed. I feel like I had been staying at Kevin's, but now I appear to be back home. I try to remember being over there, but I can't. *Oh well, I hope I didn't end our friendship again.*

The room kind of takes a tip to one side and I grab the covers so I don't fall off the bed. The room tips back and seems to stabilize for a second. I let out a miserable groan.

I think I hear knocking. It's probably what woke me from the dream in the first place. I look at my phone, then realize it is coming from the front door.

Cell phones don't knock.

I'm in no condition to receive company. I lay my head back down and slip immediately back into unconsciousness.

Chapter Thirteen

I'm thinking maybe I should go get the door. It's probably just Kevin, but I can't figure out if I heard the knocking a few minutes ago or a few hours ago. The room stopped spinning which is a good sign.

I listen for more knocking…

Nothing.

They probably gave up. I open my eyes to discover the room is pitch black. Plus, I am no longer on the bed, but the floor. I move back to the bed and feel around for my cell phone. I see it's nearly 3 a.m. I also see I missed a call from my editor. I have no idea what he wants, but he can wait.

My head is pounding. Maybe it was seeing my editor's number, but for some reason I think about my father and his book.

It was five years after I accepted the position at the university, and held the chair once held by my former mentor, that I heard from my actual father again.

I was alone in my home when the phone rang.

"Hello," I said with the quiet apathy of a scholar.

"Hello, James," the voice was trying too hard to be dramatic. *Yeah, must be my estranged father.*

"Dad, what do you wa—"

"It's finished," he interrupted me.

"What's finished?"

"It's finished," he stressed again.

I rolled my eyes. Neither of us said anything for a long time. Finally, I snapped, "So?!"

"So? … So? … So, it's the single greatest work of our time. That's what's so."

"Well, congratulations, now I have to—"

He could hear I was getting off the phone and his tone changed. "I need your help now, son." He had dropped the melodrama.

"With what?"

"With getting it published, of course."

"I can't help you with that. I don't know any publishers."

"But you know people who know publishers."

"I guess."

"I know you can help me."

"No, I can't."

"Can't or won't?"

"Can't."

"I know that you can."

"Fine. I *won't.*"

"Why won't you help me?"

"Why? Because…" I stopped myself. I couldn't say the words. *Couldn't or wouldn't?* I wouldn't. Not for his ears.

"James…" he sighed. "You know I did the best I could for you. I know I wasn't—"

"A father?"

"Now James. I was a father. I was a father. I… I never could get you to understand the importance of this work. But now that it's done…" His voice switched back to dramatic the moment he said the word *work*— just one of his triggers I know so well. "Now that it's done, maybe finally you will understand."

"Send it to me." It's hard to explain what possessed me. Curiosity was part of it. Martyrdom was part. Closure… maybe.

"What? You mean you'll—"

"Send it over, I'll read it tonight."

"Tonight, I, eh, uh… I'm all the way in Oregon, you know."

"Send me the file."

"I don't have uh… anything like that."

I shut my eyes, a slow-motion wince. "How do you have it?"

"It's typed."

"With a typewriter?"

"Well, yeah,"

"Okay." I breathed deep. "Okay. Mail it to me."

A month later it arrived in the mail, which meant he forgot about it for three weeks, or procrastinated the trip to the post office. The pages, as promised, were very nicely typed. There was no attempt at any binding. The pages were stacked in order and each page was numbered. The whole thing was wrapped in brown paper and tied with twine. It came to about 2 inches tall.

I looked at the page number of the last page. It read "1,362."

Every sheet smelled like ink and marijuana.

It was titled, "Reflections on the Empirical Proof from a Rational Imperative from Which We Must Induce the Paradigm of the Categorical and A Priori Existence of a god."

I was holding in my hands over 1,300 pages of one pothead's opinion of god with a lowercase g. And that pothead was my father.

It was agonizing.

The one thought I tried hardest to push back was, "For this, he neglected his family. For this, he wasn't around. For this." The harder I focused on not thinking those thoughts, the more they were repeated in my head, until nothing remained but a harsh rhythm: *For this. For this.*

In the next few weeks, I read it from the first page to the last. Over and over. Three times. I'm not sure why I read it three times. Perhaps I was hoping to find something I had missed the time before—some small piece of logic, or maybe an interesting perspective, or just a few lines that pointed to the profound humanity in the heart of the author. I would have even settled for some poetry. But there was nothing to be found. Nothing.

I would've even settled for a tall stinking pile of dog crap. At least that implies some order, something that creates some effect in the mind and demands a response, good or bad.

What I had instead was insipid pablum, page after page of wandering nothingness, where many words were used but nothing was said. No one part connected to the other. Premises were established just to never be used; conclusions were drawn from undefined maxims; and syllogisms were left incomplete. Page 158 was contradicted on page 869. Chapter 37 was plagiarized from an internet chain letter. The only consistent clear stance was the evil of capitalism. The grand total of my father's life's work was tantamount to three days' worth of chewing styrofoam.

With every page I read, my estimation of the man got smaller. Perhaps that's why I continued to suffer through it.

In the end, I felt nothing for him at all. In the end, all I felt for my own father was a hollow, sinking ambivalence which, like his screed, envied dog poop its potency.

I knew at once what I had to do. I had to lead by example. It wasn't enough to leave my father with no response, for that would fill him with the same unresolved emptiness his book had *thrice* left in my heart.

It was the next day that I called him.

"I read it," I told him. He didn't realize that I was mocking his dramatic flair.

"Yeah, and?"

"And, is this your only copy of the book?"

"Well, I have some first drafts and some notes, why?"

I was silent.

"Why... Why do you ask?" His tone was still jovial. It had that avuncular scratchiness that comes with old age and too many cigarettes.

I kept still.

"Wait now, James. Why do you ask?" His voice had changed, all panicky and serious. "Now, James, why did you ask that?"

I remained silent.

"Hello? Hello? James? James... why did you ask that, c'mon. James? Why did you ask that?"

I chuckled just barely, barely loud enough for him to hear.

His voice thinned to a wisp. "James, what have you done?"

"I burnt it father. I burnt the whole thing."

"You... You..."

"I rolled it up into a big fatty—actually, 1,362 of them! Then I smoked them all and sat on my butt, thinking about eternity and stuff."

"Now James, you twerp, this isn't funny."

"It isn't funny father. Because it's not a joke. You wasted your life. Your book was garbage and I did you a favor."

I hung up on the man. I threw my phone across the room. I knew I would never talk to the old stoner again.

I felt sad, but just a little. Mostly I felt pride. I did what I had to do. It stank what I did. Yes, it stank. But *hallelujah*, it was potent.

A few years after our last phone call, I saw my father's book available on Amazon. He had been able to recreate his wretched diatribe from his notes. And believe it or not, he was able to secure a publisher even without my help.

I ordered a copy of the book, out of curiosity alone. My father had managed to recreate a near perfect copy of the manuscript I still had.

Of course, I didn't really burn it.

But when it came time to write my own book, I couldn't help but think about my father.

It turns out I did know people who knew publishers. I was able to score a meeting with Browning and Redding, the largest publishing house of contemporary philosophical thought in the nation. It was the first time in a long time that I felt anything close to nerves. Along with the nerves came that persistent voice, which I've only been able to flee from, never able to kill. *You're a phony. You're a phony, just like your father.*

I was able to hide this well enough and the interview was going okay. We all sat down at a long conference table. I was on one side next to my agent and two men from B and R sat across from us.

The chairs seemed to have a limitless capacity to lean backward, and I almost capsized discovering that fact. I had to concentrate on sitting up straight.

The chairs were also too big and I felt a little bit like a young boy playing dress up in adult clothing.

The older of the two men began, "We can't tell you how happy we are to have the chance to publish a man who learned from Professor Fowler."

"Well, thank you. My work could never touch his of course, but I'll be happy if I can just maybe poke one small foot out from underneath his great shadow."

He smiled warmly at my false modesty and added, "I guess you really did have a hard time growing up."

I leaned back in my chair but was quickly reminded that I couldn't. I composed myself and asked, "How is that?"

"Well, you mentioned Davin Fowler's shadow, but there was also your father's. I mean, talk about big shoes to fill!"

I froze.

He misinterpreted the abject dejection on my face and tried to repair the damage, "I mean, not that we don't think you can fill them; we are very excited about what you've put together here."

"You know my father?" I asked, still in horrific disbelief.

They both laughed.

"Of course," the younger said. They looked at each other for an awkward moment.

"But he's only got like fifteen reviews on Amazon," I couldn't help but protest.

"Well, Dr. Fowler's book only has sixteen," the man said, genuinely confused.

My face went limp. I remembered what I had said to Davin Fowler, *What better sign of real greatness than this unattended deathbed?*

One of the men slapped the other's arm and laughed. "Look at this guy; he's all humble about his father."

I just stared off.

The older man continued, "Maybe you could tell us, bringing this back to your book, which we are very excited about…"

"Very excited," the other confirmed.

"Maybe you could tell us the ways in which your father's work has served to shape and inspire this book here."

The air froze. The man didn't realize what he had just done. It's simple: he had dashed all my dreams. When I had walked into this office, all I wanted was my book to be heralded, to be called the product of a great mind. But I didn't want my book to be praised, if my father's was as well. I didn't want to be considered a profound thinker if my father was as well. Suddenly, it all meant nothing. Suddenly, at the threshold of achieving my dreams, they crumbled in my hands.

I had a decision to make and not a lot of time to think it over. I didn't know what to do and had no grand principles to tell me. I didn't know the path to victory, but I knew that—against my will—my life was about to change. I knew that what I did next would be something I could never undo. I said, "I don't think it's possible to be a witness of true genius, and to share such propinquity with a great mind, without having it affect…" I paused dramatically. "…*everything.*"

I'd gladly trade half the memories I do have, if I could also forget that one.

Chapter Fourteen

I wake up with a start. I feel bereft. *Oh, please not again.* I try to remember last night. I can't. *Oh no. What have I done? What have I done?*

I look to see I still have my phone. *Good.* I hit the home button and see Emily's face. It sparks a memory. Did I see her? Did we speak? Why does my head hurt so bad? I sit up in bed and—

There it is.

It's huge. Six feet by ten feet. On the wall where I used to keep my dresser is the stupidest painting I've ever seen.

#57.

I remember now. I remember bits and pieces of the last three days, the longest bender I've ever been on. You don't always need Premocyl to mess with time.

I remember the auction, three days ago. I remember signing online to sell my cryptocurrency but discovering I had already sold it a few weeks ago. *That can't be right.* When I located the account to which I had moved the money, unexpectedly there was just enough in there—in USD—to settle with the auction house. *Whew.*

Either way, I am pretty cleaned out now. I suppose I could sell the mystery Jag, just so I could pay for... next month? October? November? How long can I last?

It's been a while since I made a budget and the idea doesn't excite me. I peruse the *empties* around the room and realize I've already blown through my alcohol allowance. Why is life so hard?

I remember that I was punched.

I grab my phone and use the camera feature like a mirror. The black eye he gave me is starting to heal, but it's ironic because my face was already damaged from before. The fresh bruises are on the right side of my nose, but you can still pretty much make out the old ones on the left. The fat lip I originally woke up with is nearly gone, but not fully. I look horrible. The only color in my face is the vibrant red of my bloodshot eyes. My gaunt skin seems too tight. My beard has grown back, and there are bags under my eyes. I am very pale and—I pull down my collar—the cross is gone. The cross is completely gone.

Whatever it meant, it's gone now.

I put down my phone and try to think.

I can always work on finding a buyer for the painting. Maybe I could go to Wuss and beg him to buy it. The thought instantly tightens my stomach and I regret having thought it.

I stare at the painting with a big courageous line of paint missing. I hate it. I wonder how many families could be fed for a year on that money. *Two in Manhattan. Eight in Texas. Forty-six in the Dominican Republic.*

I shoot up out of bed. Wearing just my boxers I make my way out to the garage. I see the dent in back of my old car. I'm going to be sick. I search the shelves and find an old can of paint. It reads "Interior High Gloss White." I can feel by the weight that it's not worth my effort. I find another can. "Interior Satin White." I lift the can and feel it's almost full.

I grab a paint roller and a crusty old tray.

When I return to the bedroom, I place my tools straight on the floor without first laying down any cover—I mean like a drop cloth, not gunfire. I try to pry the paint lid off with just my fingernails, but it doesn't work, so I head back to the garage to get a screwdriver.

It is on the way to the garage that I finally ask myself what I'm doing.

I am going to paint over the Casimiro.

I feel kind of strange. The news surprises me—both its content and the fact that I just seemed to have learned it as news.

I return with my trusty flathead and force it in the groove of the paint can. The lid pops right up. The paint fills the empty tray and I am stirred by how incredibly *white* it seems. I roll a thick layer onto my roller.

Wait, maybe I should think about this.

I feel strange. I really want to paint over it.

I really, really want to paint over it.

My mind goes back to the moment in my backyard. I created a fire in my barbeque grill. I thought it might be perfect for burning my father's magnum opus. I knew what I had to do, but I paused.

Like I said, I never burned it. No. I couldn't do it. Like it or not, I still have it. Should I be ashamed of that? Or somehow proud? Would I feel more ashamed if I had done it?

I stare at the painting. It's worse. It's worse. It deserves to die. I feel strange.

The doorbell rings.

Thank God.

I put the roller down onto the tray.

My mind is on the painting and its destruction when I open the door and discover Emily behind it.

She is holding a practiced sad smile and my heart quickens.

"What... um... what are you doing here?" I ask.

"I don't know," Emily says. She takes a quick look back at her car, as if contemplating an escape, or at least making sure it is still a feasible option. "I just didn't like how things were left. Are you going to invite me in?"

"Of course. Come in," I say as two truths reach my mind. First, I am in my boxers. Second, there is a large dresser in the middle of my living room.

"What's this doing here?" she asks.

"I... um, the painting," I mumble as I gesture to the bedroom.

Without being asked, she heads straight to my bedroom. She has a head start on me, so before I reach the threshold, I hear her gasp.

"What are you doing?" she snaps.

"I was going to paint over it," I answer as a disciplined child would to his mother.

"Are you nuts?" she scolds me as she heads to the bathroom. She comes out with a wad of toilet paper and uses it to clean the dripped paint off the floor.

My head's still fuzzy so I lie down on the bed. I hadn't noticed I dripped any paint on the floor.

She holds the toilet paper wet side up in her right hand and escorts it to the trash. Wasting no time, she seals the lid on the paint. She asks, "You weren't really going to paint over a two-hundred-thousand-dollar painting?"

"You ringing the doorbell interrupted me. If you hadn't come, I'd be finished by now."

She is having trouble with the paint on the floor and says, "It had time to dry, I need something to get it off."

"I have some all-purpose cleaner under the sink," I tell her.

"No," she says. "You're out of that."

"Oh..." I guess she would know. "There's some 409—"

Before I have time to finish, she heads to the kitchen and grabs the 409. Emily apparently has a pretty good inventory list of my cleaning supplies in her head, not sure why she asked me.

When she comes back, she has a roll of paper towels under her arm, 409 in one hand, and a pair of jeans in the other. She must have grabbed them from the dresser in the living room. She throws the pants at me.

She attacks the stain and I slip my pants on. "This feels nice," I can't help but say.

She shoots me a dirty look, but repeats her same sad smile. "You're a mess."

I watch her as she cleans up after me. I can only imagine how sappy my face must look. She walks the paint can into my guest bathroom and returns for the tray. The tray is full of white paint and the roller is fully loaded. She takes the whole thing into both her hands and looks around to consider her options. It isn't a long pause before she walks over to rest one end of the tray on my windowsill so she can open the window with one hand.

I watch in amazement as she dumps the entire thing out my window. She doesn't throw it, which might have left some chance it would land tray-first. No. She dumps it, allowing the paint to fall freely first, then tosses the roller and the tray.

I'm jolted from my googly-eyed reverie. "Did you just paint my grass?" I ask, indignant.

"Better your grass than this painting."

"That's debatable," I fire back. "Someone might actually find my yard beautiful."

She's staring at me puzzled now. She can't believe I just said that. Her stare changes from disbelief to disappointment, to sadness, to irritation. She lowers her body onto the edge of my bed. With her face in her hand she says gravely, "You can't keep doing this. Can't you see what you're doing to yourself?" She shakes it off and adds sweetly, "You said something at the auction, something about taking Premocyl…"

Great. I don't remember saying that. Now she knows the truth: I'm so obsessed with her I've resorted to self-harm. Chicks love that.

Her voice is tender. She adds, "So, I just wanted to make sure you're all right."

This is a breakthrough moment. It's the first sign Emily has given in the three times I've seen her that she cares at all. It's the first time she's dropped the *moving on without looking back* act and has confessed to her hard heart that we were recently in love.

"And obviously you're not," she adds curtly.

But that's okay. That's okay. I know an opportunity when I see one. I stand up and retrieve a shirt from my closet. Fully clothed and on my feet, I look determinedly into her eyes and strike the perfect tone—a balance of pathetic and firm. I say, "I am not all right. I have lost seven months of my life. I have lost *you.*"

"James, you and I can't—"

"Don't misunderstand me. I am not talking about anything you've done. When I got down on one knee and proposed… uh, I was on one knee right?"

She smirks a little and nods.

"When I got down on one knee, and you said *No,* that wasn't when I lost you. You clearly were the love of my life, and I did lose you. I lost you when I took the Premocyl. Before then, I had you. I had your face in my mind. I had your touch in my memory. I had your laughter, the warmth of your breath, and the warmth of your body. I had those things, and I lost them. I lost *you…* and I don't even know what happened…" I step aside and push the bedroom door fully open, silently inviting her to take this conversation out of my bedroom. "…but you do."

She looks at me, looks at the space where the door had been, and without saying a word, stands up to return to my living room.

I move around her and my dresser and lead her to my kitchen. The engagement ring is still on the counter where I had left it, so I snatch it up quickly.

"I shouldn't be here," she says, indicating that I hadn't snatched it quickly enough.

"No, please, sit down. I need you."

"Need me for what?"

"Isn't that obvious?"

She shrugs.

"I need you to tell me my story. Our story. I need you to give me *you* back." Her eyebrow shoots up, so I promptly add, "Nothing you didn't give before."

"And you shouldn't assume we slept together," she insists.

This remark surprises me. I can't tell if it's banter. *Yes, I had assumed we'd slept together, if we'd been dating long enough for me to propose.*

I force a smile. "That's why I need your help. I am only asking for your help to fill in some missing pieces."

"Like what?"

"How did we meet?"

She grins.

Oh, that felt good.

"We uh…" She stops and grins again.

I ease into a chair across the kitchen table from her.

She sits silently for a long time, it is obvious she is deliberating.

"Please," I say.

Finally, she says, "Okay I will tell you our story."

END PART ONE

PART TWO

Chapter Fifteen

"So, how did we meet?" I ask again.
"I hit you with my car," she says.
"What?" I ask, instinctively looking down at my legs.
She laughs. "I hit your car, actually. I rear-ended you."
"Seriously? That was *you*?"
"Yes. You told me I was—"
"Wait!" I interrupt. "Where was this?"
"14th and Hardin."
"What time of day was it?"
"I don't know. Evening."
"Okay. Go on."
"You said it was—"
"What color was the sky?"
"What color was— Do you want the story or not?" she asks
impatiently.
"The story? No. I want the *memory*."
"I'm not sure this is such a…"
"Please," I beg with the most imploring puppy-eyes I could make.
She sighs. "It was twilight. Um… the air was perfect, that's why I
had my windows down. It was our first warm front at the end of winter. It
must have been the weather that put me in such a good mood, because I
was singing." She gives a cute, embarrassed gesture, "I was singing along
with the radio."
"What song?"
"'Jesse's Girl.'"
"I love it."
"Anyway. You had stopped short. I saw you were going to cruise
through the yellow, and so was I. I looked away for a second and you
stopped short."
"Oh, I see, I stopped short?" I say playfully. "More like you
weren't paying attention. You were lost somewhere in 1985."
"No, you slammed your brake," she says irritated.
"No, you were too distracted with your singing," I keep prodding.
"You stopped short!" she snips.
"*Cruise through the yellow?* If I had cruised through the yellow,
you would have run the red."
She laughs a bit too hard, then makes a face I can't interpret.
"What?" I ask.
"It's just…" she smiles. "We've had this exact conversation

68

before."

I smile warmly. I say, "This is how we were, isn't it?"

She nods, smiling.

"This is how we teased. This is exactly what I wanted. You're so wonderful to..." I hold up both hands as if I am lifting and presenting her chin. "You're great. You're just so great." She looks down at the table and I frantically use both hands to wipe my statements away. "Forget it... please... please just go on with the story."

She straightens back up and says, "I stepped out of my car to look at the damage. My car was basically okay somehow, but your bumper was all banged up. By the time you got out of your car, I was already in tears. You rushed over to me and asked why I was crying." She laughs and insists, "You said it like the wreck hadn't just happened! I said, through my tears, 'I wrecked your fancy car.' You said, 'What? This piece of crap?' and then kicked another dent in your own bumper."

She laughs at the story and my heart swells.

She continues, "I laughed and you laughed and I was somehow still crying. Like at the same time! I didn't even know that was possible, but I was laughing and crying at the same time like I never had before. I pointed to the dent you made and said, 'My insurance isn't paying for that one!'"

I laugh, but it's a bittersweet laugh. All I can think is, *out of control emotions and a sharp wit—what a perfect woman.*

She smiles. "You told me later that you fell in love with me in that moment. You said you couldn't tell which tears were sadness and which tears were joy, but the only thing that mattered was how beautiful I looked with my face wet."

"Wow," I say, discovering that this story is genuinely true. "That's pretty much what I was just thinking."

"Yep, that's what you'd tell me." She turns her face away from me. I can tell she's seeing nothing in particular, but I detect an important ingredient in her long-off stare: sadness.

And my heart feels hope. "How did I ask you out?"

"You didn't."

"I don't understand."

"We traded insurance info and I left."

I'm confused. "Well, I must have done something, because the story doesn't end there."

"I saw you later at a book signing."

"We ran into each other randomly, *again?*"

She nods. "It was a pretty big coincidence, all right."

"Who's book?"

"Lefebvre," she says.

"Wow, of course." *Interesting. She likes philosophy.*

"But I somehow didn't see you there. Probably because I was in the back. When I was leaving, my car wouldn't start. I popped my hood, because that's what people do, but had no idea what I was looking at."

She continues, "So, I'm a girl with my hood popped open and my butt hanging out and no one from that stupid book signing stopped to help."

"That *is* surprising," I quip.

She shoots me a dirty look.

"Because…" I make haste to cover myself, "Because philosophy students are usually…" *Considerate? Kind? Civic-minded?*

"…male?" she finishes for me.

I smirk.

"I heard a voice behind me that said, 'What's the matter with your car? Rammed into too many innocent people?' I turned and it was you. I didn't have any tears in my eyes, so I guess you thought it was safe to tease me. I fired back, 'I think innocent is a bit of a stretch.' You said, 'Hey, I may fudge a little bit on my taxes, but that's no reason to plow into me with your car.' My mouth popped open in shock. 'I looked away for a second and you stopped short,' I insisted. 'Oh, I see, I stopped short?' you said playfully. 'More like you were distracted by your own singing,' you said. I was mortified that you had actually heard my singing but couldn't let you get away with it. I said, 'No, you slammed your brakes,' and you said… Well, you know how the rest went.

"You took a look at my engine and told me it's probably just the battery and went to grab your cables. You ignored me when I insisted I didn't want to be a bother and could just wait for roadside assistance. *My hero!*

"When you pulled your car up next to mine, I saw the rear of your car had the distinct impression of my front bumper and your right shoe."

"Nice detail," I laugh.

"Oh, and the sky was blue."

"Thanks for that."

"I said, 'Are you sure you really want to make me mobile again, what with so many innocent people on the road?' You smiled the most charming smile I'd ever seen and said, 'That was my fault. I stopped short.' I smiled. I admit I felt something in my heart right then."

She continues, "So, you got my car running and you disconnected the cables. My car had to be left running of course, and it really added tension to the whole scene. I felt like I had to get into my car and go, but I wanted you to ask me out. I thanked you, I fluttered my eyelashes, I pushed my chest out, I even put my hand on your arm, like this."

As she lists each of these things, she performs them. This time I feel something in *my* heart.

I clear my throat, "Well, I surely responded to that!"

She looks away, "No. No, you didn't."

"No?"

"You shook my hand and wished me, 'Good luck out on the road.'"

"What?"

"Then you got in your wounded car and drove off, leaving my wounded pride."

"Well when did I get your number? How did we connect? How did I ever get to see you again? Please tell me I didn't stalk you."

"How do you mean?"

"Well, I had the information from your insurance, right?"

She laughs. "Oh, you've thought of that this time. Well, you didn't before."

"I didn't think of that? That is strange. Did I think to nickname you *Dimples*?"

She rolls her eyes. "I was wondering how long it would take you to go there."

"I did? I knew it."

"Oh, don't act like you're so smart. That's probably the most obvious nickname a boy could give me."

She stays silent after she says it. It takes me a moment to figure out what she's doing. I say, "Oh really? Why is that?"

Still no smile; she's intentionally hiding her dimples from me. Very cruel.

Gravely serious with no joy in her voice, she says, "Because I have very large, cute dimples that are irresistible to men."

"Hmm," I say, also very serious. "That is interesting. However, I do not detect any dimples on your face at all." I gape at her face in fascination and wonder, which is sure to make her smile at least a little.

She doesn't. She is almost robotic when she reports, "They only appear when I smile."

"Hmm. Yes, I'm afraid I just can't seem to picture these dimples. Can you describe them?" This time, while trying to sound incredibly serious, I also sound a little bit British for some reason. This makes *me* laugh.

Which in turn makes her laugh.

"Never mind!" I shout. "Cancel the description. I see them now."

She continues to smile and even starts to blush.

I study her face and in the hammiest, most British accent I can muster, I say, "By Jove, those are bloody extraordinary! Irresistible, I say." I slap my knee. "Yes. Irresistible, indeed."

Chapter Sixteen

"I think I know how I finally got your number," I say to Emily. "You answered a personal ad online, and I answered a personal ad online. When we saw each other in person, we realized that we had been chatting to each other the whole time."

"No, that didn't happen," she says.

"I know, I was breaking into a house, and by total dumb luck it turned out to be yours. When you walked behind me with the baseball bat, I turned just in time to see you and yell, 'You again?' Then I took off my ski mask and you echoed, 'You again?' Oh, and we laughed and laughed."

"No. That didn't happen. Do you break into a lot of houses?" she laughs.

"No," I gesture to my bedroom where the painting is. "But I might have to start."

She laughs again. "Actually, I ran into you at a restaurant."

"You're kidding me."

"Not kidding."

"Wow," I shake my head in disbelief. "That's too big of a coincidence. Did I follow you?"

"That's what I asked. You said you didn't. You claimed you didn't know where I lived."

"But the insurance info."

She nods. "Yeah, I thought you might have been lying."

"Hmm…" Something occurs to me but I keep it to myself.

She interprets my *hmm* pretty well and says, "You were lying! Why would one you figure it out, but the other you not?"

"It could happen." *It didn't happen.*

"Oh my God, you were lying."

"I wasn't lying." *I was totally lying.*

"How would you know?"

"I just know. It was coincidence; it means we were meant to be together."

She looks down.

"Wait a minute!" I exclaim, completely overwhelmed. "It happened again!"

"What do you mean, it happened again?"

"We ran into each other. At the art auction, don't you see? Total coincidence. I definitely couldn't have orchestrated *that* one. Not after taking Premocyl."

"At the art auction," she whispers.

"Yes. How is it you didn't think of that? It happened again! What does that mean?"

She just stares off; the news really stirs something in her head and I can't interpret her eyes.

"What restaurant was it?" I ask to bring her back to the story.

"The Olive Garden."

"Okay." Now I definitely know I was lying because I never go to chain restaurants, but I don't let on. "Who were you with?"

"I was alone, reading my Bible."

"Your... what?"

"My Bible?"

"Wait, you're... Christian?"

She laughs. "Wow, that's the exact same thing you said to me that day." She laughs again. "That's even the same incredulous look you had on your face."

"What did I say about it?"

She looks off. "Let me think... I said, 'Yes, I'm Christian... *aren't you*?' Then you just smirked. You smirked like you knew something I didn't."

I am smirking now.

"You looked at me like I had been frozen for thousands of years and started babbling about Zeus the moment I was thawed—like if all the world had moved on and I was the only fool who hadn't gotten the memo."

"I'm sorry. I can be..."

"I know how you can be." She scowls. "But somehow I still love you."

The tense makes my heart skip, but she goes on talking as if she hadn't said it.

"You were taken off guard at first, but later on as we ate, you—"

"We are at the same table now?"

"Yes. You're very smooth."

"It was our first date," I smile triumphantly.

She smiles and corrects me, "It was the first time I told you I could never date you."

"Why?"

"Because you weren't Christian. The Bible says that we have to be equally yoked."

"I guess I told you I was atheist?"

"You did."

"And I'm sure I tried to debate you right then and there."

"No, actually. You completely moved on from the subject. You began to make me laugh. I'm not sure I've ever laughed as hard as I did that night."

"Brilliant," I say, impressed with myself as usual.

"Then at the end of the night, you asked me out. I replied, 'You're charming, but you're still atheist.' You continued to press and I continued to resist. Finally, you reasoned, 'Don't call it a date.'

"I could feel the connection grow between us as you waited for my response. It was as if we were both searching for a loophole for me to do what we both knew I wanted to do. I said yes.

"From that day on we began to see each other, despite my reservations. You continued to ask me out and I continued to say, 'Okay, but it's not a date. And please know I could never be with you.'

"The truth is, you challenged me; aside from making me laugh, you stimulated my mind. You were the first to ever get my brain really working, and I liked it.

"I was trying to get you to come to Christ, and you were trying to get me to forsake Him. No holds barred and may the best man win. That was our unspoken agreement it seemed.

"Soon, I was the one requesting to meet with you. I began to feel things with you that I'd never felt anywhere else. You would ask me questions, leading me, guiding me, and at the end you would show me that I'd just contradicted the very statement that I asserted in the beginning. But instead of feeling embarrassed, I would just marvel at your rhetorical skill. Before long it became clear that you were out of my league intellectually."

She looks at her watch. "That should do for now, I imagine. We have all the groundwork now. A foundation of story to build upon."

"What?" I gasp. "No. I mean, what happened next? You can't leave."

"I'm sorry, I've got to go."

"Well, when can I hear the rest?"

"I don't know."

"Well, can I get your number?"

"I'll call you."

"You can't go!" I'm almost trembling. I've never felt so helpless before a woman.

Maybe she sees the state I am in or maybe telling our story loosened her up because I see true caring in her eyes. She steps to me swiftly and kisses my cheek. She says, "I will let you hear the rest of the story. I promise."

Before I know it, she's out the door.

74

Chapter Seventeen

My phone pings. It reads:

Well, Mike flaked on me, so you might as well come over here so you can here more of our story.

It's Emily. My phone pings, again. Her follow-up text amends:

hear

I text back:

I don't know where you live. Lol

On the way to her place, I try to sort out the feelings in my head. What's the point of this little project? What's the point? *Mike flaked on me...* Why'd she have to add that part?
What am I doing?
I find her place using the address she had texted and ring the doorbell. I remember the 'first time' I met her and how she was so impatient on my doorstep.
I am starting to get impatient, too. I don't see any light through the small window, nor do I hear any noise. I double-check the address on my phone and while I'm looking down I hear the door open.
"Hello," I mumble.
"May as well come in," she says making an effort not to be cordial.
She hasn't bothered to turn on any lights in her entryway, but it appears that her hair is up and she's wearing a dress. She leads me to the kitchen, and when she turns the corner, the light hits her. She saunters through the bright kitchen in a tiny black dress and I...
Stare.
I stare at a meal prepared for someone else. I stare at a feast that I *both* have never tasted and will never taste again.
She catches me staring and says, "We had planned on going..."
She decides it's prudent to spare me the details.
"His loss," I say and regard her one more time.
I can't help but ask myself, *Could this girl have talked me into being Christian? Is that what the cross around my neck was all about? Or was I faking?* It dawns on me—that would explain so much. That is why I got rid of the cross and the Bible. I wanted to take the Premocyl to forget all about her and about Christ. But, I don't think I would fake such a thing—what a pathetic and short-term plan that would be. *And if I wasn't*

faking, would I turn my back on a Savior I believed in? Is any of this even possible? I look at her dress. Yes, I imagine while in that dress she could talk me into just about anything.

"Where did I leave off in our story?" she asks again.

"Um... You were about to convert me to Christianity," I say slyly.

She gives me a look I can't decipher. She says, "Well, I had pulled out my biggest gun. There was a festival at my church. It was one of those, *hey, bring your atheist friend under the guise of listening to live music, then we'll tell them about Jesus while his guard is down.*"

"You say this was at a church?"

"Yes."

"Then, I don't think my guard was down."

She smiles, "No, it wasn't."

"So, what did I hear?"

"Oh, you heard something all right!"

"Do tell."

"Well they had a number of speakers lined up, of course. Pretty typical, but... the crowd just had this energy. You could feel it throughout the room. People were excited. And there was a band." She squints her eyes like she is trying to recapture a distant image. "I just remember hearing people's love for Jesus. I don't remember any real thing that was said; I just remember thinking, 'Wow. It's not an act with these people. These people really love the Lord. I mean they really believe it.' I think everyone must have felt it, because the whole event kind of unraveled, but in a good way. People in the audience began to speak. There was a mic being passed around. I don't remember if it had been part of the plan for everyone to talk, but people started to bare their souls, and they were crying. They cried tears of sadness in one breath and tears of joy in the next. And it just felt like there was a healing. A healing. And it swept across the room.

"There was a little girl there, ten years old, whose friend had brought her. She called herself Christian but she wasn't really. Her parents were Christian when they got married and at the time they had her. They even named her after one of the female characters in the Old Testament. But..." Emily shrugs. "They stopped taking her to church after the divorce. So anyway, the pastor asked if anyone who didn't know Jesus wanted to come to the front." She pauses here. It is difficult to tell what is going through her mind, but she looks on the verge of tears. "So the little girl did." She sighs. "She was affected by the sense of peace and contentment in the air. She was impressed by the people's genuine love, not just for God, but for each other. So, the pastor prayed over her and stuff. And that little girl asked Jesus into her heart that day." She pauses to gather herself. "Her friend there asked her why she decided to come forward and she said simply, 'I saw your joy, and I wanted to be a part of it.'" Emily stares off into the distance for a second, then blinks every burgeoning tear away. She continues, "And you just weren't impressed."

I stay silent.

"But I knew that what I had to say *would* impress you, so I asked if I could not just borrow the mic, but in fact borrow the stage. I told them I had brought an atheist friend, and I thought it'd be a good idea to tell him and the crowd the story of my conversion."

"And they let you?"

She shrugs. "No Christian can resist a good conversion story. So anyway, I stood up and gave you a peck on the cheek. I was nervous, but I knew what I had to say. I climbed the stairs, grabbed the mic and said, 'I told the good pastor that I wanted to share the story of my conversion. And I think it is very important that I do so because… because…' I thought of that little ten-year-old girl who so trustingly accepted Jesus, and I spoke directly to her. '…because everything that has happened here tonight is a farce. It's nothing more than mass delusion. Their talk of morals and of hope is well-intentioned, but at the end of the day it is only wishful thinking.' I longingly imagined that little girl, like I wanted to help her avoid everything I'd been through, as if I had a time-machine and could prevent her from wasting too many years. 'They are just spreading lies. They are spreading false hope. And all their empty promises are ever going to accomplish is to set people up for a fall.'

"I continued, this time turning to the audience, 'Christ let me down. I've been searching for Him, but He's stayed hidden from me. I've needed answers and all I've received were riddles. I've knocked, but He hasn't opened. Not for me.' The crowd began to murmur. I spat, 'So, now I'm done with Him. I'm done with God. I'm done with the Bible. I'm done with—' They finally cut off my mic. I threw it to the ground like a vulgar comedian and shouted at the top of my lungs, 'And I'm done with all of you!' I jumped off the center of the stage and ran to you. The entire crowd had settled into a meek and impotent silence. You stood up where we had been sitting in the back and came to meet me halfway.

"And there, in a crowd full of Christians, two young atheists passionately embraced. We clung to each other like… like…" She laughs and shakes her head. "I guess I'm not the best storyteller."

I smile.

She says, "I just felt so close to you. I could feel your acceptance enfolding me, drawing me into you. I just felt so smart, like we were both so smart. We alone held the secret knowledge. We stood as the lone scientists in a world filled to the brim with superstition, the lone sophisticates in a world full of rubes, the lone intellectuals in a world filled with… *idiots!* It was like the whole world believed in fairy tales and we alone could see the truth. James, why can't they see?"

I shrug. "I don't know."

"I decided right then and there that I'd rather have respect from you than everyone in that room put together. I was prepared to be scorned by them—all of them, the whole world even—if it meant I could be admired by you. I needed you more than I ever needed Jesus.

"You were my savior.

"That's how I've always felt about you. Even from the beginning. Even when I thought I'd never see you again. Everything I did, I always thought, would this impress him? Would this please him? If I could just let him know somehow, would he think I was smart, finally smart?"

I have no idea what to say. There was a lot to unpack there, a lot that she said with her words, even more that she said with her body language. The air between us feels different and I know I have an opening. I say, "Tell me about our first kiss."

"It was that night."

"I thought it might have been."

"You drove me home. The sky was black—the type of black that inspires the things blue just won't allow."

I smile at the sound of that. "Home to my place or home to yours?"

"Mine. We were right here."

"What were you wearing?"

"Well I... I guess I was wearing this dress."

"You wore that dress to a Christian event?"

She smiles naughtily.

"Sacrilege," I say.

"You asked me to pour some Scotch."

"I did?"

"Yes."

"Gee, I wonder what I was after..."

"Well, you ended up getting it," she smiles coquettishly.

"No way." I blurt out too quickly, sounding a bit like a teenager. I quickly get back into character—*suave and sophisticated*—and add coyly, "You know, I could really go for some Scotch right now."

"No," she says with too much relish. "Don't even think about it."

"Okay," I say, although I count the number of times her eyes dart to the kitchen. Three. I consider my next move. *Should I let it go? And miss an opportunity? Should I gently push?* No. Frankly it'd be overkill. *Wait. Yeah, just wait.*

I sit here saying nothing. It soon becomes obvious that I'm not going to be the one to put the derailed conversation back on track. If someone's going to pick a new topic, it will have to be her. Only she can't do it because she can't get her mind off the two matching highballs waiting in the cupboard.

Finally, she says, "Fine," pretending to be put out.

She pours herself some first and takes a quick sip. She says, "You know what would go well with this? Drambuie."

"No way. You're joking, right?"

"What do you mean?" she asks.

"That's my drink!" I tell her.

"No, it isn't."

"C'mon I mentioned that, right?"

"No. You never mentioned it."

"I never mentioned liking Rusty Nails?"

Her jaw falls open and her eyes pop. "No way!" she screams. She can't believe I know the name of the arcane recipe. I guess she thought I was messing with her up until now. Shock is replaced with intimacy in her eyes. Her whole face takes on this puppy dog look, as if liking the same drink was pure kismet.

I like that look on her face. I'd like to see more of it. She finishes pouring the drinks and I hold one up to toast. I say, "To Rusty Nails."

She repeats, "To Rusty Nails." But I pull my glass out of the way just in time.

"Wait." That isn't good enough. I amend, "To more still left to discover."

She gives me a reluctant look, nods and says, "To more still left to discover."

I take the first sip and feel the warmth radiate through my chest. "What did I toast to that night?"

She strains her brain. "I think you said something pretentious like, 'To reason.'"

I laugh.

"Where did we take our drinks?"

She motions to the couch and sits down first.

I hesitate. "Wish side was I on?" Yes, I just said *wish*. I don't think the alcohol has hit me this fast. I think it's Freudian; you see, I *am* currently making a wish.

She doesn't seem to have noticed my slur. "On the right," she says.

"Was I sitting a few feet from you so I could look at your beautiful face while we talked? Or was I sitting beside you like this," I move in close, "so I could feel the heat of your body?"

"Feel the heat," she breathes more than whispers.

"What was my move?"

"Your move?"

"Yeah, you say that we..." I chuckle. "So, what was my move?"

She looks off into the distance, trying to think.

"Oh, surely you remember my move?"

"Well, you were very bold; you must've known I wanted you to take charge."

"I can be good at reading people sometimes."

"Well, I wasn't very subtle. I pressed my thigh into your thigh like this."

"Yeah, that's…" I struggle to keep my breathing calm. "…effective."

"There's more. I casually let my hair down," she says as she reaches to her up-do. She quickly removes a couple of pins and the whole thing comes cascading down in locks of beautiful flowing hair. As good as her word, she does it all casually, as if every move *weren't* irresistible.

"Then," she continues, "under the guise of setting my drink down on the coffee table, I leaned forward like this, and *stretched* here in front of you…" When she says the word stretched, she seductively enacts the posture she is describing. She looks back to me from the corner of her eyes, over her feminine shoulder, past her vexing hair. "…and allowed you to admire the slope of my back."

Does she really understand what she does to me? *She cannot understand. Not fully.* I say, "At this point I have no choice but to run my hand along the slope of that back." As I say this, of course, I do just that. "I thought you said I took charge. Seems like you were the one pulling the strings."

"Oh, you took charge all right." She turns her face away from me, pulls all of her hair over one shoulder and exposes her long, alluring neck. Without looking back, she says, "Before we could finish our conversation, before we had finished half a glass, before we ever even kissed, you grabbed the zipper of my dress and slowly unzipped it all the way down."

Feeling about as in charge as a marionette, I anxiously obey.

Chapter Eighteen

I wake up.

I feel content. I smell Emily's hair and realize her delicate body is still in my arms.

She is beautiful, but I realize that this glow I feel isn't from the sex. It is victory. It's my former mentor's death bed confession, "You're so smart." It's the title of professor, a greater title, a truer title than one university could ever bestow or revoke. It's the look in her eyes when she looked up to me and said, "You alone are the intellectual in a world full of fools."

Is that how she said it? I wish I could remember exactly how she said it.

Emily is the reward for excellence. Intellectual supremacy. Reason assumes its throne on the most high. And *she* is the proof. Emily is greater than any crown of life. Emily is greater than an imaginary infinity. Emily is paradise in this bed and eternal life in this moment. She is my sweet reward—a visible, tangible reward the world can't deny. Let all who see her covet her. Let all who see her wrap her enticing arms around me know how great the conquests of the mind and how irrefutable the value of sophistry.

Emily is my muse and I her teacher.

She twitches beside me.

I lean in and whisper, "Good morning, Dimples."

She coos.

"You're beautiful," I tell her.

"Dan coo," she mutters.

"But I know you've been lying to me."

"What?" She lifts her head up. I think I see panic in her eyes.

"I know you didn't drink Rusty Nails before you met me."

She smiles and flops her head back down. "Yeah, busted." She lifts her finger, but not her head. "But I was already a fan of Casimiro. I am a bigger fan than you."

"Yeah, but you don't own one of his paintings!" I inform her haughtily.

She laughs, mostly at the remembered scene.

I decide to quickly change the topic. "Why did you make the speech you made?"

I think a part of her mind may still be asleep; I always have the worst timing with things. She utters, "Muh?"

"I talked you out of Christianity, right?"

"Yes."

"But the speech you made… it wasn't about making an argument, it was kind of—"

She interrupts me, "I don't know." She yawns. "I had a better speech all planned out in my head. It was about ten minutes long. I timed it. But when I got up there, that's just what came to me." She closes her eyes again. "What time is it? Still early?"

"Hmm. Yeah," I say. "Public speaking is hard. The first time I taught class, I had a whole lecture prepared, every word, but I got nervous, strayed from the script, and accidentally used the F-word." I laugh. "I was so worried I'd get in trouble. I had only ever worked construction jobs up to that point. I soon found out there was just as much cussing in the university as the construction site."

She laughs and says, "One group uses it to prove they're sophisticated, the other to prove they ain't."

I blush because that's the exact thing I was about to say.

She says, "Yeah. You've told me this before."

I nod and smile. I feel like I've known her forever, and by forever, I mean last night. I consider saying that line out loud, then veto it.

Propping herself up on her elbows, she adds, "In fact, you've given me the whole first-day speech." She mimics my voice and says rather self-importantly, "Real mischief awaits the heart that is courageous. Real discovery rewards the mind that is unshackled."

I smile. She thinks she's picking on me, but she gave the line verbatim—one of the best compliments I've ever received. I pretend to be offended and playfully fire back, "Well, I'm sorry I don't have a line as good as, 'Two young atheists clung to each other like... um... uh... hold on...'"

She hits me.

She lays her head back down on the pillow, and as if just to let me admire her, she closes her eyes. I do admire her; I make the most of it. I gently stroke her hair, over and over, until I realize that at some point she had fallen back asleep.

I am overwhelmed by this moment. I have an urge to write in my journal when I get home, but remember it's missing. I touch the part of my chest where the image of a cross once had been and remember I forgot to ask about it. How strange. It doesn't seem to fit with the story as she has left it. If we both ended up as co-atheists, then why was I at one point wearing a cross?

I have never been religious. I have a lot of atheist friends who grew up Christian, in fact most of them. But not me. We never mentioned God or Christ or Heaven in my house. My parents never said anything good or bad either way.

The closest I'd ever come to religion was one day when I was ten years old. Yes, I do remember it.

My mom had loaded me in the car and she didn't say why. When I asked where we were going, she said the store. When I asked why she had all her possessions packed in the back, she didn't answer at all.

We headed east through our neighborhood. It wasn't long before we passed the store and I protested, "Mom, we just passed the store."

"We're not going to the store."

"Where are we going?" She didn't answer, and ten-year-olds don't have much tact. "Mom, where are we going? Where are we going?" She wouldn't answer so of course I turned it into a song, "Mom, where are we going? Mom, where are we going? Mom, where—"

"Stop it. Stop it!" she yelled. "We're going for a drive."

"Mom, are you leaving Dad?"

"Yes."

I sat very still.

"Mom, does that mean *I'm* leaving Dad?"

"Your father doesn't want you."

"Yes, he does."

She didn't reply.

We drove for thirty more minutes in complete silence. I put my head against the window like a cold, hard pillow and started to cry. I wasn't sobbing, and I tried hard not to let my mom hear me crying, but when she clicked on the radio, I'd guessed she had.

She drove until the traffic fell away and the highway narrowed to just one lane. Two hours outside of town, driving through a map-dot whose name I can't remember, our car blew a tire.

My mom got out of the car to investigate it. Wasting no time with self-pity, she promptly popped the trunk and pulled out the spare. But when she dug back into the trunk to find the jack, she realized she didn't have one.

Meanwhile, I was listening to the cuss words echoing in our large trunk and staring out the window at a quaint blue church. I had never seen a church painted blue like that. And I had never seen one so small. It seemed like just a model of a church, like what would be made into a child's toy meant to represent a church.

My pondering was interrupted by a man's voice. I couldn't hear what he was saying, but I heard him use the word *jack*. I watched him and my mom talking in the side mirror. Then I heard another voice, female. She was standing right outside my window so I could hear her clearly. She said, "It's cold. Why don't you two come inside while Paul changes the tire?"

I knew my mother would object to her assumption that the man should do the work. She said, "Oh, it's okay, I'm perfectly capab—"

"Nonsense," the woman said. "We've got the heat running nice and warm. Come on in and bring your boy; take yourself a breather."

I could tell this was torture for my mother. She wasn't the type for uncomfortable situations. She forced a cordial smile and quickly gestured for me to follow. We were both led into the church. My mother was stiff with her arms glued close to her sides and I was doing my best to be proper for her sake.

Once inside, the nice lady offered me some milk. Before I could answer, my mom refused. It was only then that I noticed the woman was more pregnant than I'd ever seen a woman before in my young life.

She began to make small talk with Mom in the foyer and my eyes kept going to the entrance of the sanctuary. My mom was struggling hard to be pleasant, so I was able to slip away without notice.

The lights weren't on in the sanctuary, but dim light eased in through the stained-glass windows on both sides. The sun was in the exact right position to stream in through the small, round stained-glass window high behind the altar.

When I stepped into the aisle, I could feel the warm breeze from the furnace. I could feel the tension in my muscles start to relax. The tears had dried from my eyes, and for a moment, I didn't remember that I was being stolen away from my father and my home; this could've been a road trip we were on. I felt a thrill of adventure as I stepped further into the dark sanctuary. I approached the streaming light—red and blue and yellow— and dipped my hand into it, feeling a child's wonder.

I didn't know how to pray. I've never prayed. But I remember talking to God. I wondered if He could stop what my mom was doing. I wondered if He had the power to bring my family back together. I knew that I didn't.

I stepped forward until the beautiful light shone on my face. I said, "Make her turn around."

And then I felt at peace.

It didn't take long for the nice man to change the tire, and my mom came to find me. She thanked the nice couple, told me to get in the car, and pulled back out onto the street.

My mom would wear a face for the sake of company, which would always take a while to wear off. We had just gone through the town's only stop light, when her façade faded and my mother began to cry.

"What's the matter, Mom?"

She didn't answer.

"Mom, why are you crying?"

She still didn't answer.

"Mom, it's okay. Everything's all right, Mom."

Suddenly I was pulled away from her. I was thrust into the passenger side door as she flung the car into a fierce U-turn. There was no crossover and our tires sprayed dirt and gravel into the air as she left tire tracks through the median of the small country highway.

I grabbed the door to steady myself, saying, "Whoa!" I got my bearings and sat up to look around. There was a cloud of dust behind us, our home and my father somewhere ahead. I realized what had just happened and screamed, "Way to go, Mom!"

She thought I was cheering on the reckless driving, but that's okay.

I was cheering because I somehow understood, even then, the courage it took her to turn around. I was cheering because my prayer had been answered.

A week later, I was helping mother with the laundry. I told my mom about the prayer and asked her if it had been God working in her heart.

She snapped, "Don't ever mention that day again. We don't talk about that day."

I looked down, trying to bury my chin into my chest. I could feel my cheeks redden.

She forcefully hoisted the basket of clothes up onto her hip and added, "It wasn't God."

When I think back now, I know how silly I was being. It was the flat tire that changed my mother's mind. It was luck. When she got the flat tire and was unable to fix it, it made her feel helpless and dependent. And dependent people always run back to their mire. It is only when women feel singularly independent that they flee.

Perhaps it was God who caused the flat tire, you may suggest. But that makes no sense because why then would God have let us leave in the first place? If God were to do something to change my mother's heart, why didn't he do it before we made it that far? If God is so adept at changing hearts, why didn't he change my father's heart and maybe he would have treated mom better? And if having her turn around was the right course of action, why didn't he just do it himself? Why was he waiting on a set of orders given by a ten-year-old boy?

But what about the peace that had come over me in the sanctuary? you ask. Simple. It was nothing more than the effect of coming in from the cold—not just the cold, but really a break from my mom, too. The car ride was obviously tense. That's a lot of drama for a ten-year-old boy to absorb. Then there was the beauty of the lights mixed with the catharsis of having already cried out every tear.

That's all it was.

Chapter Nineteen

Again, I sit before my unholy trinity; I'm alone in my kitchen pondering the bottle of Premocyl, the only photo I have of Emily, and a rather large engagement ring. None of them hurt me quite like they did before.

I am slowly getting her back. And by getting back, I mean reclaiming the story. Reclaiming the touch of her skin and the taste of her lips. And of course, reclaiming the hurt of her rejection, owning the pain that is rightfully mine to own. It's a peculiar urge in a man to know precisely that which he is missing.

The doorbell rings. I know it's Emily because I am expecting her this evening. In fact, she's right on time. I stand up and hide the Premocyl in the cupboard; I slip my phone into my pocket, but the ring I place strategically behind a box of tissues.

I walk to the door with some trepidation. I have sufficiently prepared myself to hear about her regrets, that she didn't *mean* to sleep with me, and she shouldn't have led me on when things are so complicated already. I take a deep breath and fix my most affable smile on my face.

When I open the door, she throws her arms around me. The kiss on my neck is so natural that I almost don't feel it, at least not on my neck. I feel it with all of my insides and all of my heart.

"Hello, Dimples," I practically purr.

Emily slips her slender body around me and into my home as if she lives here. I follow her to the kitchen.

"Where did we leave off?" she asks as she opens my refrigerator and helps herself to a bottle of water.

"We slept together," I tell her.

"Yes, of course, but I meant the story." She is joking.

"Yes, that's what happened in the story. I appreciate the illustration by the way. You *are* a master storyteller," I laugh.

She blushes.

"You had just rejected Christ," I tell her.

She smiles.

I pull out one of the high-back chairs in my kitchen for her. They're comfortable enough to settle in for a long conversation; plus, they're tactically close to the ring and the tissue box.

We sit down, and she continues her story, "It was an exciting time. I remember you holding me in your arms the next morning. You were careful to get my attention like you had something important to tell me. You looked me in the eye and with the tone of a wise teacher said, 'There's something you have to understand about the choice you've made. Everything for which you have always praised God, all the success in your life and everything good that you've obtained, wasn't done by God at all; it was done by *you*. You. You deserve the praise. You are the master of your own destiny, writer of your own book, and captain of your own ship. You are the only one you can ever count on and you are the only one who can save you.' Whoa." She tilts her head back and repeats, "Whoa. Those words thrilled me. It was like a new liberation.

"Then you took me to one of your parties, thrown right here." She looks around the kitchen nostalgically. "You had champagne flutes and even a string quartet. I had never been to a party like that before. You invited all your atheist friends. There were reporters and columnists, artists and novelists, and professors of course. I had to stop and take it all in. It was in this room that it hit me for the first time... I had heard once that 95% of the world believes in a deity of some kind."

"That stat's no longer true," I insert ruefully.

"I discovered in that moment," she continues, "that I was surrounded by the top 5% smartest people in the world. More than that, I was *part of* the top 5% smartest people in the world." Then she laughs. She shoots her hand up over her mouth and says, "Then we all got crazy drunk!"

I shrug, palms up.

"It was a great night. I was so nervous in the beginning, but by the end of the night we were all just like old drinking buddies. In fact, half the men there came on to me—and one of the women. People whose articles I had read in the paper were suddenly hitting on me."

I grin, "But you remembered to save the last dance for me, right?"

She grins back, "Yes. By the end of the night, we wouldn't leave each other's side. For some reason, we had all climbed up onto your roof. You lay on your back and I laid my head on your chest. The only people left at the party were Brittany Mason and one of the professors you work with."

"George Hampton?" I suggest. I don't correct her tense.

"That's it. The conversation turned to God and they asked me what I thought. I had been Christian all my life and the idea of actually saying harsh things about God still felt strange. I turned and looked up at the sky as I considered my answer. It was a clear night and out here where you live, you can see so many stars. You can't see them like that at my place. I felt in that moment you had brought the stars to me. Like you owned them. You had brought me the most intelligent people in the world and you had brought me the stars in the sky. I lay there completely overwhelmed by the vastness and the mystery of the universe. I said, 'I believe there is only one savior of all mankind, and it is *reason*. I believe that the human ability to think will one day deliver us from poverty, deliver us from racism, sexism, and hate, deliver us even from climate change, which is to say save us from ourselves.' I sat inspired by my own words. 'Yes, *reason* has the power to save us from ourselves, if only religion would stop getting in the way.'"

"Wow," I tell her.

She smiles proudly, "Prof. Hampton asked me to marry him."

I laugh. "Well, that makes two of us."

She laughs, a bit uncomfortably.

My eyes dart over to the Kleenex box.

"Then I fell asleep, or maybe passed out, either way I woke up and I was on a rooftop, overwhelmed by the strongest vertigo I'd ever felt in my life. My whole body spasmed and I grabbed you with both hands. I could feel your strong arm behind me and I heard you telling me it's all right. Then we just laughed." Her eyes begin to get a bit misty. "We laughed. I thought I was falling, but you were there to catch me."

I smile also. "Things seemed to be going so well..." I prod.

She nods but looks away.

"...hard to believe I know how it ends."

"Maybe it hasn't ended," she mumbles.

"What was that?" I ask, although I heard her.

She shakes her head. "I guess I was scared. Scared of falling. Just a really intense, sudden flash of vertigo, that's the only way I can explain it." She adds, "I never felt so smart and so special as when I was with you."

"Not even with Mike?" I jab.

She laughs out loud. "There is no more Mike." She makes a dismissive gesture. "Really there never was."

That's all I need to hear. I move in. I place a gentle hand on her shoulder, then against the side of her face. It causes her to tremble.

She whispers, "It was always you. Even before I crashed into you, it was you. Even when I thought it was Jesus..." She pauses. Her eyes are filling with tears. "...it was *you*."

The tears don't actually leave her eyes, but I am not sure if I will get a better window than this. I chivalrously reach and grab the box of tissues, leaving visible the box containing her ring. I grab the first tissue quickly but pause, pretending to have just noticed that her engagement ring was now rudely confronting us both.

"I'm so sorry, I..." I reach for the ring box to slip it out of sight, but pause to give her a sincere, confused, conflicted look. I place the box on the counter and say, "I think I am ready to hear the story of how I proposed."

She shakes her head. "I'm not ready to tell it."

So, I wait. The two of us sit in weary, sweet, agonizing silence.

Finally, she says, "I confess it was the last thing I expected. I did love you and I had given you every indication that I wanted to marry you. Yes, it was soon, but everything had just been going so well..."

"Where were we?" I ask.

"We were right here."

"Right here?"

"Yes, right here."

"That's not very romantic."

"Oh, but it was. It was! You said you hadn't planned it here, it just... the feeling overpowered you."

"Hmm," I say not quite convinced.

"You know what it's like to just be overpowered by an urge. It was an itch you needed to scratch. That's what made it romantic, that spontaneous urge, that desperate need."

I nod.

But Emily takes it up a notch, "Can you imagine: neither of us woke up that morning believing we would be engaged that night?" She is looking deep into my eyes. "Can you imagine a world where wonderful things happen, even when no one is expecting them?"

My heart is pounding. "Where were we exactly?" I whisper.

"I was sitting in this very seat. And you were sitting exactly where you are now."

Tears are forming in her eyes. I can see her starting to breathe harder and there is a small tremble in her voice. I look over to where the ring is waiting and she catches me doing so. "What was I wearing?" I ask, testing her.

"You were wearing blue jeans and a light blue button up shirt." I am wearing jeans and a light blue shirt.

"What were you wearing?" I test her again, almost breathless.

It's impressive that she doesn't look down. She keeps eye contact with me and says, "I had a red top covering a white spaghetti string tank top, blue jeans, and red pumps."

It's a perfect description of what she's currently wearing.

I let out a laugh. It sounds like a sob. It may have been. All the tension and all the confusion that had built up in me since I woke up bereft is leaving my body in a paroxysm of emotion. I somehow manage to ask, "What color was the sky?"

Emily turns to look out the large windows in my kitchen and is surprised by a splendid sunset. She whimpers at the sight of it, releases one sweet feminine sigh and says, "Oh, it was immaculate."

When she turns, she finds me already on one knee. I have the ring box in my hand.

Tears jump down both her cheeks and she tries to continue with our little game, "You got down on one knee, and held up the box."

I jump in, too, "I was overcome with the moment, an invincible desire, a perfect hunger. I was overcome with your beauty. It was the happiest I'd ever felt. It *is* the best day of my life." I crack open the box, and two months of my former salary shines before her face. I can actually see the large rock reflected in her eyes.

"You took my hand," her voice trembles openly now, unguarded. "I was so afraid of rejection, but I just didn't care."

"I was so afraid of happiness, but I wouldn't let that ruin things, not this time." She squeezes my hand until it hurts and gasps, "No, James, not this time!"

"My voice was scratchy," I say with a scratchy voice. "But I summoned the strength to say, 'Dimples, I love you. I love you like I've never loved anyone else before. I don't ever want to spend another minute without you. I never again want to wake up when you're not there. Don't be afraid; if you fall, I will catch you. Dimples, will you marry me?'" Through my tears I see her already beginning to nod. I plead, "Take this stain off my heart. Please, please, please marry me, Emily."

At the speed at which a bullet leaves a barrel, her hand shoots out from mine. I'm startled by the sudden movement, like a warm blanket being jerked off my body or the air being jerked from my lungs.

"What did you call me?" angry spittle slips through her lips as she hisses.

Panic strikes me as fast as an arrow, but realization washes over me as slow as cold honey. "Em...ily?" I say stupidly.

Her eyes are full of naked anger and she is now a truer color of red than I have ever seen a human face. She gets up so fast that she knocks over the chair she was on and runs to my door.

"Wait!" I call out.

She struggles in her panic to open my front door, but only for a second. As she rushes out the threshold, I can hear her desperate sobs.

I run out of my house to catch her. Amazingly, she has already made it to her car. Still a few yards away, I hear her engine start.

I reach her passenger-side window and I dip my head down to see her face. With my face near the glass I frantically pound. "Emily, Emily, wait," I cry out in clumsy, stupid desperation.

"That's not my name!" she shouts with venom.

Okay, yes, I got that. I try to make my way to her driver-side window, but it involves crossing the front of her car. She hits the gas. I slam both my hands on her hood and jump backward, so she stops.

I am standing frozen with both palms on her hood. I can't currently tell you where the diamond ring has landed. We stare at each other through the front windshield as she contemplates crippling me for life. This is the first time she has made eye contact since I used the name *Emily* but I can't verify that there's anything human in there looking back.

Her eyes frighten me deep within and I make haste to exit the path of her wheels. Her front bumper barely misses my shin and I stumble to the pavement.

I can smell the pungent odor of burnt rubber as I am left crumpled in the middle of the street.

Chapter Twenty

I have to go see Kevin.

"What is it, now?" he greets me warmly. "Wait. Do you know what day it is?"

"Saturday."

"The date, I mean."

I roll my eyes, but a big part of me doesn't really want to get on about reporting what I'd come here to report, so I play along. "The first."

"Of what month?"

"September."

"Okay."

"1996."

He laughs hard from the belly. I confess it makes me feel good.

"So, tell me the news."

"I proposed to her."

"You what? Why did you do that?"

"Same reason all men do—because I thought, with 100% certitude, she'd say yes."

"But she didn't?"

"Well... things went a little... things didn't go as planned."

"What happened?"

"I called her Emily. I said, 'Will you marry me, Emily.'"

"So?"

"So, that's not her name!"

His hand shoots up to his mouth. He's trying hard to suppress a laugh.

"You can laugh," I sigh.

"I wasn't going to laugh," he says while laughing. "I thought Emily was her name."

"No."

"Well, then what the heck *is* her name?"

My shoulders slump. "I don't know!" I say it with such perfect pathetic exhaustion that I force myself to laugh.

He laughs more, and on the happiest, saddest, most absurd day of my life, I find myself giddy, laughing with a great old friend.

"Then whose name is written on your shower?"

"I don't know," I exaggerate the irritation, if that were possible, and tickle myself again.

He laughs harder. "But wait. It was written on the *inside* of your shower... so that means."

"I understand the implications," I snap again, placing my face in both my hands.

"Whoa," he says, "you dog."

I groan. "Whoever she is, she cost me the woman I love... again. I said, 'Will you marry me, Emily!' Her face changed so fast it looked like the film was missing some frames. It was like the artless edit of an old B-movie. Her happy face, her wonderful joyous happy face, was instantly and abruptly replaced with some horrible... rictus of... horribleness."

"That sounds horrible," he says flatly. "Did she seem happy though, I mean, before you called her another girl's name?"

"She was crying."

"Whoa. Tears of joy?"

"Yeah."

"Whoa. Hey, then maybe you can fix this."

"No."

"No really, bro, this is an easy one. You just have to find a way to slip her one pill of Premocyl."

"Not funny." I shake my head humorlessly.

"I thought of a clever way to slip it to her."

"How's that?"

"Hold her nose until she opens her mouth, stick the pill in and hold her mouth shut until she swallows."

"Subtle."

"Then you say, *I just slipped you Premocyl. You won't remember this tomorrow, and by the way, I've lied every time I've complimented your cooking.*"

I don't laugh. "It's very clever; can we stay focused please?"

He smiles. "I really do think you can fix it. Just explain to her what happened. I mean you didn't do anything wrong."

"I took half a bottle of Premocyl."

"Well that's sick and reprehensible, but you haven't done anything to *her.*"

"I called her by another girl's name."

"A steamy shower-girl's name."

I don't laugh. My giddiness from a moment before is long gone.

"Did she ever introduce herself to you? Did she ever say, 'Hello, my name is So-n-so'?"

"No." I stroke my beard and consider this.

"Well, there you go. She knows you took the Premocyl. Your mind's confused. There's a lot for you to sort out."

"How do I explain where I got the name Emily?"

He shrugs nonchalantly. "Simple. Just tell her you..."

I wait.

Nothing.

Dang. Thought he had something there for a second. I say, "There are... other things."

92

"What do you mean other things?"

"Well," I hesitate. "There's another little detail I might've left out."

"What's that?"

"When I woke up, I had a sunburn."

"And a bruised face," Kevin interrupts. "Did you ever find out who did a number on your face?"

I shake my head. "But that's not even the strange part."

"The fat lip and a busted nose is not the strange part?"

"I had a sunburn, and on my chest was an imprint of a cross necklace, as if I had been wearing a cross when I got burned."

"A cross as in... *the* cross? That's weird." He laughs. "Okay, that's the strange part! I mean I can picture someone wanting to smash your face; I can't picture you wearing... Do you even own a cross necklace?"

"No," I scoff. "Wait, yes I do. I do own a cross." How come I didn't think of it before? "One of my students gave it to me."

"Trying to convert you?"

"No, quite the opposite." I'm trying to remember what that cross looked like. *Could that have been the one on my chest?*

"But why would you be wearing it?"

"Well, yeah, that's the question. Nothing really fits perfectly. Another example, she told me that we saw each other at a Lefebvre book signing, but Lefebvre doesn't have any new books out, I checked."

"I have no idea who that is."

"Also, I have an extra mystery key on my keychain. That's weird. Then of course there's the painting."

"What about it?"

"I hate it."

"Why'd you buy it?"

"Never mind that. Didn't you hear me? I said I hate it. I hate all of Casimiro's work now. I looked online. I looked at everything he's ever done, and Kevin, I hate *all of it*."

"Are you serious?"

"I don't have to tell you how strange that is."

He nods. Kevin has always given me a hard time about Casimiro. He has always hated him and could never understand my devotion. At least he's mature enough not to say I told you so.

"I hear voices in my head," I continue layering it on.

"You do? What kind of voices?"

I shrug.

"What do they sound like?"

"They sound like me... they just sound like thoughts."

"Well, are you sure they're not... you know... thoughts?"

"You tell me; they told me to paint over the Casimiro."

"Good thing you didn't listen."

"I almost did. I went to the garage and found some white paint."

"No way."

"I had a roller out and everything."

"That's insane."

"Maybe, but it just felt right. It still seems like a good idea. Even when I look at it now, I can't describe to you how much I hate it. And I still hear the voices. It's like, I know that it's simply paint on a canvas, but the voices tell me it represents something destructive in our society, something pernicious. They tell me it's a threat. They tell me the painting mocks everything that's sacred, and..." I narrow my eyes and listen within. "...and the mocking is so weak, and the sacred so strong... and the words and the laughter, they just bounce right off. Until one day, the sacred is weak, and the mocking is strong. And none of us know how it happened, but the *something* was destroyed by the *nothing*, the solid was collapsed by the hollow, and everything great was dismantled by everything meaningless. And it is all so clearly depicted in that painting. It's the image of saints being marched into Hell."

Kevin breathes deep. His face shows concern now, but he remains calm. "The sacred? No, that doesn't sound like how you think. That doesn't sound like you talking at all. Maybe it's a lingering side effect from the drug."

"I don't know. It sure feels strong. I just want the pieces to fit, you know. Why didn't I delete her photo?"

"I've been thinking about that one too. Here's what I think: you just plain forgot. You bought the Premocyl, just as a comfort. You swore you'd never use it. Then one night, *while drinking,* you decide to take it after all. You dotted a lot of I's and crossed a lot of T's late into the night, but you missed one. That's all."

"Maybe. But why is there an entirely different girl's name in my shower? Why was there a cross on my chest? How did I get fired?"

His head perks up. "Two of those questions might have the same answer; did you have a girl in your class named Emily?"

I see where he's going. I try to remember. It's too common a name. It's the type that slips right through your memory. "There was an Emily in my Nineteenth Century Philosophers class two years ago—or was it three?—but I would never touch a student. You know that."

"What if she was no longer a student?"

"But then I'd no longer get fired for it." I tilt my head. "I think she might have been an Emma, actually."

"Hmm."

"I'm so confused." I sigh. "Do you think I should be pursuing this woman before I find out who Emily is?"

"I think a botched proposal is a pretty good time to take a break."

94

I'm proud of him; he said it with zero hint of sarcasm. Still I say, "You know you're not real helpful sometimes."

"Sorry." It sounds sincere. "Hey, what about that Christian guy who drove you home? Did you know him?"

"What?" I ask, confused.

"After your YouTube clip."

"Oh." It irritates me that he chooses to call it my YouTube clip, instead of the night of the Casimiro auction or something. "What makes you think he's Christian? He was at an art auction."

"Christians can like art."

"I guess."

"His car had a bumper sticker that read 'Cornerstone Church.'"

"How'd you see his bumper sticker?"

"You were throwing up in my yard a few feet from it."

"Oh." Okay, so our Good Samaritan is Christian. That's cool. "Why do you think he can help?"

"He said he'd call you later just to check in. I thought he was someone you know."

"He said he'd call me?"

"I guess he didn't."

This is strange. I argue, "I didn't give him my number. Why did he think he knew it? That man was a total stranger."

"Dude, so was the girl you just proposed to."

"Hmm." I think back to the way he showed so much concern for me that night. I just assumed he was nice. Did he use my name? No, but he didn't ask for my name either. Could he have known me? "So, it looks like we have one lead. Did he leave his number?"

"No."

"Then I have no way to find him." *So much for our one lead.*

"Well… maybe. Long shot, but we know where he might be tomorrow morning."

I'm intrigued. "Where?"

"Dude, you are so slow tonight!" he says, a bit harshly to a guy who's just been rejected, but I digress. He adds, "I'd ask if you are taking stupid pills, but I don't want to give you any ideas."

I'm still digressing.

"Cornerstone Church?" he insists.

Oh! Oh yeah… Interesting.

As soon as I get home, I look for the sole cross I've ever owned. It was given to me in the first year of my career. It was the last day of the semester and a beautiful young brunette came to me after class. She'd specifically hung back until all the other students had left, which was hard to do because so many of them wanted one more chance to tell me how much they admired me.

No longer given the option of playing it cool, she walked straight up to me and extended a pinched hand. It was obvious she was holding something, so I opened my hand and she dropped her offering into it. It was a gold necklace with a cross pendant.

"What's this?" I asked.

"I want you to have it."

"Why?"

"Because I don't need it anymore." Her other hand, which had been near her face nervously twirling a tendril of hair, stopped mid-twirl, and I was seduced by the look in her eyes—that strange type of pride, desperate for praise, begging for attention, and shamelessly proffering oneself over to another. I can't remember a single detail about her face, but I remember the look. It was the first time I'd seen it from a student but wasn't the last.

She told me she had walked away from her faith, and that my lectures had been responsible.

I haven't thought about her in a while. I was a young man in those days, ten years ago. Our ages were not so scandalously far apart, and yes, she made it clear what she was offering me. I say I was seduced, but I never touched her. She had already given me that which I craved most. I admit I went to bed alone that night thinking about that look in her eyes.

I saved her cross. I kept it as a trophy, as if her faith were my first kill, and certainly not my last.

There's a small box in my dresser where I keep it, along with some cufflinks, and a tie clip—the extent of my jewelry collection.

I open that box and I'm only partially surprised to find the cross is missing. The tie clip and cufflinks are there—I haven't been robbed—but no cross.

And even more mysterious than what's missing is what's new: a thing I don't recognize, a woman's Claddagh ring.

This has me confused for a moment, but I think I figure it out. I grab the engagement ring to compare the two. They are the exact same size.

So obviously I swiped this ring from Emily because I knew she wore it on her ring finger. I took it to the jeweler and that's how I knew her ring size.

Only her name's not Emily.

Right.

Chapter Twenty-One

Of course, I'm running late. Of course, I am. This is only perhaps the most important thing in my life right now. This is the one lead I have that could possibly bring me answers. *Real* answers.

I am still sorting through everything that Emi... I mean *what's-her-name* told me. I don't know which parts to believe. Could she really have lied to me? And about what? I can't dismiss all those stories and all those details just because a few parts don't line up, can I? I at least know she must have rear-ended me because I have the proof on my back bumper.

I check the time again. I had looked up the time for this church's service on the internet, but I guess what I should have looked up is traffic. There is some sort of accident jamming up traffic and every second I spend in this car unable to move is making my chest tighten with rage.

Of course, I didn't want to sit through the sermon. It was my intention to arrive just as everyone was leaving and do my best to spot the mystery man in the crowd. Now the idea that I would have to wait another full week in suspense is sending me into a full-fledged panic.

I finally pull into the parking lot and am pleased to discover it's filled with cars. Before exiting my car, I check my hair in my rearview mirror—I'm not sure why. The moment just feels too important for messy hair, I guess. I eye the front doors of the church. There's a chance that all the answers I'm looking for are on the other side of those doors. I feel like I might be sick, and I have to force myself to get out of the car. I boldly open the doors to the lobby and... there is no lobby.

It's a small church and I open the doors directly into the back of the sanctuary. I'm interrupting the sermon. I hear the pastor stop mid-sentence and I see every face turn toward me.

It's already pretty embarrassing, but the silence is filled by impassioned whispers. The whispering grows stronger and I can't understand. I feel like I have done something scandalous. I just opened the door, after all. *What's wrong with you people?*

Finally, a woman stands up. She is young with bright red hair and sort of pretty. She puts her hand on the shoulder of the young man beside her as she tries to squeeze past his knees and out of the pew. All eyes are on her as she walks sheepishly over to me.

As she gets close, I search for words to say to her, "I... uh..." but it is already too late. She steps into my space and wraps both arms around me.

I wasn't expecting that.

Next, I see a nice looking middle-aged couple moving in my direction. He appears to be of moderate means, but she looks like a rich man's wife. I am taking all this in when they both hug me as well.

Is this some sort of Christian thing?

Behind them are two young twins. Female. They both hug me at the same time. I'm not sure if it makes things more or less surprising when I hear one of them whisper my first name.

Am I supposed to know these people?

I see the man who helped me that night. He gives me a hug, too. My eyes light up and I whisper to him, "You're the one I need to talk to."

Before he can answer, I see a young blonde up front. It's *her*.

Her.

She is standing at the end of the aisle, making no move to come closer. Our eyes connect and everyone sees it.

They seem to step back, as if on cue. The crowd parts like the Red Sea. They clear a lane, straight down the center aisle, leading me to her. She has tears streaking down both cheeks. I recognize her tears instantly. They are the tears that haunt my dreams. It's the girl who stormed out of class. My sweet ingénue.

I step toward her slowly. She continues to silently cry. When I reach the front, I extend both my arms in a sheepish questioning gesture. I've received so many hugs here today, it only seems right. She neither submits nor retreats, but I throw both arms around her. She's stiff at first, then returns my embrace. The second her arms are around me I know, I feel like I've always known.

I say, "Hello, Emily."

She says, "Hello, James." James, not Professor Larson.

I let go after a socially acceptable welcome, but she holds on for one last squeeze. She lets go and takes a small step away from me.

I pick up on this subtlety and ask, "Can we speak in private please?"

Her face shows fear, maybe intimidation. She says, "N-no."

The pastor steps into the space right beside her. I know that positioning. If this were a bar, the next line would be, "Is this man bothering you?" Maybe I'm imagining it.

He says instead, "Hello, Dr. Larson. Welcome back." He's clearly aiming for sincere and he's a pro. With one greeting, delivered with such an endearing tone, his *sincerity* tank is entirely empty.

We shake hands.

I turn back to Emily. "Please, may we speak alone? Please."

She considers it then shakes her head somberly. "Not now."

I sigh. If it has to be here, then very well, let it be here in front of everyone. I begin, "It's not what you think." Truth is, I have no idea what she thinks. "There's this drug called Premocyl. Have you heard of Premocyl?"

She shakes her head. But I see the pastor's eyebrows shoot up.

"It's an antidepressant, or *was*. They recalled it because, if taken improperly, it can cause severe memory loss."

She is puzzled, but I have her attention.

See? Told ya it's not what you think. "They recalled the drug, but a sort of black market arose. People began to purposely take the drug... in order to forget. They began to take it specifically for the side effect."

"Why?" she asks tremulously. New tears spring up in her eyes.

"Well, usually to escape heartache. They hope to completely forget—"

"No," says the pastor. "She means, why did *you* take it?"

It stings me that she can follow my thoughts so well, but I can interpret hers so poorly. I suppose that's what forgetting seven months gets you. It also grates a little that the pastor picked up on it. I reflexively check for a ring on his finger. *Married. Good.*

I say, "I am not fully sure why I took it. I have been on a long and painful path trying to put together the pieces that the drug has left." My *sincerity* tank is now empty too. I look at both her and the pastor and say, "My journey seeking answers has led me to this church." And my *manipulation* tank is low.

Emily says nothing, but the Pastor speaks up. "I know all about Premocyl. I think I can help."

When he says he can help, I find that I believe him.

He turns to Emily and in a solicitous tone asks, "I would like to take this conversation to another room. Would you like to join us, just us three?"

She nods, and I am happy to get away from the crowd.

As we exit the sanctuary, I hear the church band start to play. The three of us enter a room which looks like a small auditorium. There are rows of seats and a center aisle, but it appears there is a Jacuzzi where the stage should be.

No one says anything at first. I can feel the pastor watching my face intently. "Well?" he finally says.

"Well what?"

"Do you remember me?"

"No," I say. "I take it we've met?"

"Yes, sir."

"And you were important to me?"

He shrugs. "You were very important to us."

"Why would you screen our calls?" asks Emily. The thought just occurred to her and now she doesn't know what to believe. "I mean, if you didn't know who we were, then you wouldn't know which calls to screen."

I'm quick to defend myself, "I didn't screen your calls. I wouldn't even know it was you calling." She's not picturing this.

"Yeah, I know. So, if you took Premocyl, how could you have screened our calls?"

"I didn't!" I contend. "I haven't really been getting any calls."

"Every one of my calls went to voicemail. Sophie too. Brandon too," she insists. There is real pain in her voice.

"Perhaps his phone never rang," the pastor steps in. "If he had set his phone to block your numbers."

"I didn't block them," I plead. "I wouldn't."

"You don't *remember* blocking them," the pastor offers. "You had to have done it before taking the drug."

I want to object, but what do I know? I squint. "I can't think of why I would do that."

"You wanted to cut us out of your life," she accuses.

"No… I… I didn't even know you were in my life."

"What about the note I left?" she asks.

"What note?"

"I left a note on your door. I went by to check on you. You know, because *everyone* was worried. But you weren't home so I left a note on your door."

She still can't hide the pain in her voice and I notice that she didn't want to take personal ownership for the visit. "Wait, did you knock or ring the bell?"

She shoots me an impatient look. "I don't know."

"I never got a note."

"Knocked, I guess."

"I… I…" I'm struggling here.

"Do you remember this place?" The pastor asks and I am happy for the interruption.

I look around. The room has a peaceful feel to it. The colors are gentle and everything is exceptionally clean. The air is cool and dry and has a faint smell of chlorine.

I notice Emily's face soften and I can't explain why. Her tears start flowing again. She surprises all three of us when she reaches out to squeeze the fingers of my hand.

I look back to the pastor and shake my head. "No… should I?"

He sighs. "I was hoping you might. I was hoping this room in particular might have jogged some memory."

"Why? Have I been here before?"

He nods gravely and says, "This is where I baptized you."

I feel a chill travel the entire length of my body.

END PART TWO

PART THREE

Chapter Twenty-Two

When I arrive home from the church, my head is still spinning. I have spent my entire life building a code to live by, and that code had only one rule: logic is king. Logic was the only demand I asked from the world. But now, suddenly, nothing at all makes any sense. Suddenly all is illogical.

I instinctively stagger over to the fridge. I eye the remaining beer, but it seems to offer no comfort. I close the fridge and eye the liquor bottles on top of it. To my surprise they aren't calling my name. I listen closely. They are silent.

I walk, adrift, into the living room and discover one more peculiar thing: I'm not depressed. *Confused—you bet!* But there's no hint of the depression I've been ignoring for as long as I can remember. It was just yesterday I was turned down for a marriage proposal for the second time by the same woman. Yet somehow, I feel fine. Better than fine, there seems to be a small balloon in my chest and it's filled with helium. No, better, it's filled with… what's lighter than helium? It's lifting my heart and my mood, and I'm not sure why or how.

She held my hand. That's what it is. She reached over and took my hand into hers. My face and my neck are growing warm and I can't help but smile. It's odd, but I feel a greater joy from just the touch of this one's hand than I felt holding the other naked in my arms. How marvelous.

I remember her note. I run to my front door and check the outside of it. Nothing there. I check the porch and the walkway for where it might have fallen. I don't see anything.

I head back in and look around. I step through my own house as if I'm retracing steps. I see the painting on my bedroom wall and I see the white paint stains on the floor that refused to come up fully. I walk over to the bathroom and inspect the trashcan.

I see a pile of wadded up paper towels with spots of dried paint. I grab the can and dump the contents onto the floor. As I sift through them, I see nothing but the paper towels, the toilet paper she tried to use first, and a few empty beer cans from that particular bender.

I don't know whether I am disappointed or relieved. I glance back into the can and I see a tiny flash of orange. There appears to be two things still stuck to the liner: a wad of toilet paper with dried bits of white paint and a crumpled up Post-it note. The small note had been folded up inside the toilet paper.

My heart races. *Her.* Whatever her name is, she hid my note.

I franticly unfold the note and it reads "We're worried about you.

Everyone misses you. Especially me. If there's a problem, let us help you."

The note hits me in a visceral way. And for a brief second, wait… yep, I hear the whiskey calling. I ignore it and lower myself down onto the bed.

I read the note again and again. I try to hear Emily's voice reading it, but sadly I don't really know her voice. First, I try to read it as words written by a love interest. Then, I try to read it as words written by someone who feels it's their Christian duty to fight for my soul.

Both work. I'm not sure what to think.

My thoughts go back to my journal and the service it could have provided to me in a moment like this. I know for certain, if I didn't before, that moment I took the Premocyl was an act of sheer hatred. Self-hatred. Everyone likes to always remark how in love with myself I am—they don't mean it kindly—but here's their evidence to the contrary. I hate myself, always have.

I read the note again. *Why would she hide it from me?* Was she trying to keep me from reconnecting with these people? Why would she do that? *But then again, why would I do that?* I was the one who blocked all their numbers. Maybe they're destructive somehow. They didn't strike me as destructive while they were hugging me. He said I was baptized. *That's… That's just…* I don't know what to do with that.

I look in my phone and find the setting to block numbers. There are several listed there. I conclude one of them is Emily's but I don't know which one. Why would I block Emily's number? Emily, the woman who reached so gently for my hand?

Hmmm…

Pain pricks my heart and I open my drawer to find the Premocyl bottle. I read the name on the side, Juliet Klein, the lady it was originally prescribed to. *Juliet Klein.* The whole time I was searching for leads, people who played a role in my missing story, I was neglecting one right under my nose. I pull out my phone and do a quick internet search. In no time at all I am able to find her address—just twenty-five minutes away in White Sparrow—and her phone number. I consider grabbing my keys and heading over there, but before I make a decision I find myself dialing.

I barely have time to think because she picks up so fast.

"Hello?"

"Hi, uh, this is, uh… You don't know me. I, um, that is I don't think you know me. I…"

"Who are you?" There is only curiosity in her voice, not impatience.

"My name is Dr. James Larson, and I… I'm holding a half empty bottle of Premocyl and it has your name on the side."

There is silence.

I continue, "Listen, I know that you sold your old prescription illegally, but I am honestly not concerned about that. I... I will spare you the details of the hell I've been through. Suffice it to say that I am in a bad spot and I have very few people who can help. I have a lot of questions and very few people who can offer any answers."

There is still silence.

"Listen, I am not upset with you. I really don't care where the Premocyl came from, but obviously I can't remember, and... I need your help. I am asking, no, *begging* for your help. Will you help me?"

There is still no answer so I look at the phone.

Crap, I miss dial tones.

I had no way of detecting the point at which she hung up. I look at the call log and it shows:

(308) 555-4217
Outgoing call
12:06pm 6 seconds

Six seconds? She must've hung up right when I said Premocyl. I suddenly wish I had not introduced myself as *Doctor* Larson. Of course, I call back, and of course it goes straight to voicemail. I leave the same rambling speech I just made, this time being recorded, this time more desperate and pleading, and hang up.

I've always hated this moment: waiting. *The ball's in her court,* I say to myself, but before I can even finish, I start to text her:

I don't care what you did. I really need help. Listen to your voicemail, please.

Nothing. Waiting again. I stand like a statue watching the phone. Each second like a vice is tightening on my eyes. I'm not sure a full second has passed before I try again:

Did you sell your old Premocyl to this man?

I hit the camera icon and snap a quick photo of myself. It's pure stimulus response, but I actually smile for the lens in front of me. I hit send. I quickly add:

I may or may not have had the beard at the time.

I hit send. Again, I'm waiting. I can't sit still so I begin to pace. The painting only makes me more irritable, so I walk out of the bedroom.

I can't wait until I'm able to sell that thing. I know I'll never get back a fraction of what I paid for it. The same thing goes for the Jag. I will have to sell it as used, despite the fact that I've only driven it... I don't know how many times I've driven it. I'm not sure I've driven it at all—off the lot perhaps. I could also sell the engagement ring. How depressing.

The balloon from Emily's touch can't be felt anymore and it feels like my whole life depends on the response from some timid woman in White Sparrow.

My heart rejoices because my phone goes *ping*. Thank God! Thank God! It reads:

No.

My fingers have never moved so fast in all my life as I type:

Did yoyh sell Prekmocyl to this woman?

I fumble to attach the photo from my welcome screen, the very face that first greeted me that fateful morning. I hit send.

I watch the screen. The typos irritate me, but she can still make out the question. I pace and I clench my fist. I squeeze the phone so hard, I fear it will break.

I begin to scream at the phone, mostly obscenities.

I stop pacing. My legs and hands are trembling. I shut my eyes tight and bring both my hands, and my phone, to my forehead. Almost like a prayer. I try to stop my brain. I try to focus.

Why am I so frantic now?

Because I need answers.

The girl who rear ended me?

That's all my mind says and I'm confused.

The girl who left Christ for me. The girl I made love to. The one I proposed to twice. The love of my life...

Yes, her.

Just what kind of answer are you waiting on?

Now I see it clearly. If the answer is no, then I've learned nothing and am even more confused. If it is yes, then I have been duped, violated, all my recent happiness is flushed down the toilet and everything I think I know is a lie.

With my eyes still closed, I hear a *ping*.

Okay, I understand now clearly. I know I would rather have answers. I would rather be put out of my misery. I would rather hear the answer that I dread most than to be left in doubt. With a determined heart, I open my eyes.

It reads: *Yes*

Chapter Twenty-Three

I'm behind the wheel of my car, trying to stay awake. Don't worry, the car is parked. I'm parked on *what's-her-name's* street. I strategically found a spot behind a large truck parked on the street a few doors down.

I'm waiting for her to leave the house and I confess, I don't even know where or when she works. But it's Monday morning so it's statistically probable that she'll be heading to work soon.

My only hope to avoid detection is to see which direction she turns for work. If she goes left out her driveway, then I'm in business. If she goes right, I'm busted. She will see my car and the plan will fail. Left takes her over to the interstate, so it seems far more likely she will go left. But right leads to Hwy 28, a major road and the main connection to Morganville, the town directly north.

So, fifty-fifty.

I yawn. Yesterday I found out I had been drugged by the woman that I had proposed to… oh and baptized into Christianity. Needless to say, I didn't sleep well after that.

Wait… I don't even know for sure that I proposed to her the first time. I think I should just assume I still don't really know anything. I think I need to play it safe and question everything she ever told me.

I can now see the clues she intentionally left for me to find: the photo on my phone, and the tickets to the Casimiro auction where she could *happen* to run into me. That wasn't just another coincidence. She even brought a little prop with her to make me jealous. She's a criminal mastermind.

Then there's the way she returned the engagement ring for me to find on the very morning after I first woke up confused. *But why?*

I remember how well her makeup was done that morning. She knew it would be the "first" time I ever saw her. So, was she trying to attract me? All the while pretending to push me away? Was she trying to attract me *by* pushing me away? I look back on everything that happened, and everything I've learned, from the moment that girl was a perfect stranger to me, to the moment I loved her like I've never loved another. *Mike flaked on me?* She even had me show up at her place to find her in *that dress*. She likely never had plans with him that night. Step by step, she led me right where she wanted me. A more perfect ruse could not have been scripted.

Kevin had said the main reason I was attracted to her was in fact *because* she dumped me. Was that what she was counting on? Do all women just naturally understand that concept?

Probably.

But where did the engagement ring come from? I had to have been the one who bought it; I saw the debit in my account. And an engagement ring can only mean one thing, right? I think discovering her Claddagh ring in the exact same size supports the theory that I did at least intend to propose. But why would she turn down my marriage proposal just to try to… what? Win me back? And if she did say yes… then why? Why? What was it *she* wanted me to forget? Did I even get a chance to propose? Did I leave her? I'd have to have a good reason to leave a girl like her.

And if she was lying, how did she do it so well? She told an intricate story; surely she didn't make it all up.

I finally see her. She is backing out now. My heart rejoices when I see that she turns left toward the interstate.

I wait about ten minutes, then get out of my car. I walk down her block at a gingerly pace. My eyes slowly pan the neighborhood, the cars, and the windows of nearby houses. I try my best to not give the appearance of looking over both shoulders. *Do people still watch their neighbors' houses?*

I stroll onto her doorstep with the same nonchalance I used to promenade through the neighborhood. I already have the mystery key from my keychain ready in hand. I hold my breath and… of course it fits the lock. I step in and shut the door behind me. I push the curtain on her front window aside. No activity in the street.

As soon as I decide I've made it in undetected, I consciously switch my pace, no more slow and listless, suddenly quick and urgent. I head straight to her bedroom. I'm struck by the fact that the house is such a wreck. Her bed is not made. Her nightstand is cluttered. I see a basket of clean laundry waiting to be put away. I wonder how long she has lived out of that basket, bypassing the need for dresser or hanger.

I wanted to have a game plan before I stepped into her home, so I defined what it is exactly I would be looking for: *whatever she is hiding.*

I start my search with the usual suspects, the back shelves of closets, the backs of bottom drawers. I search her walls and shelves. I don't see anything incriminating. I head to her nightstand, and as I open the top drawer my heart skips a beat. She has a gun.

I wasn't expecting that. I pick it up gently. My first impulse is to see if it's loaded, but then I remember that I am a philosophy professor and therefore know nothing about firearms. I have to think, so I scratch my head with the tip of the barrel. No, I'm just kidding.

I choose to believe that she most likely doesn't have aims to kill me. The gun was placed in the front of the drawer where it would be handy during a break-in. If she had bought this gun to be used solely as a murder weapon, she would most likely treat it as such from the moment she bought it. She would keep it hidden from the start.

I conclude she's just one of the 42% of American households who owns a gun and that it probably has nothing at all to do with me, or our situation. Probably.

Just as I come to a comforting resolution on the gun situation, I hear the front door. She's back! Trying not to panic, I quietly push the top drawer of the nightstand closed and I run to the closet.

I pull the closet door closed slowly, fearing that she will enter the room in time to see it closing. But also fearing that bringing the door closed with too much speed is liable to produce a squeak from its hinges, or worse, it will produce a gust of wind that will knock a small object off her vanity or a picture frame from her wall. With equal and opposite, unbearable impulses in me, I pull the door closed at the exact perfect speed. I see a shadow pass through the light in the crack and I know she has entered the room.

My heart is pounding; it's simply not cut out for these cloak and dagger scenarios. To make things worse, I realize I am still holding the gun. I can only imagine her dread when she opens this small wooden door and discovers a man behind it holding a gun. Will her mind have time to realize she knows me before her heart goes into full cardiac arrest? Will it even matter that she knows me, and has just spurned me, if I am discovered hiding in her closet with a gun? How comforting will it really be to call out, "It's only me!" when the *me* is a jilted lover, unemployed, with nothing to lose?

I quickly place the gun into an empty cubby hole meant for shoes. It produces a loud clank as it makes contact. *I'm such an idiot.* I failed to do it at the perfect speed.

I listen to determine if she heard anything. I can't detect where she is. I lean my head closer to the crack of the door. Still nothing.

Finally, I hear her place something down on the bathroom counter. It doesn't sound frantic.

But my heart is only pacified for a second because I spot her dresser drawer. It is open and some of her panties are on top of the dresser. *Oh no! Did I leave that open?* She didn't see it as she walked in, but she will surely see it when she walks out. She will know someone's in the house. She will rush to her gun. The gun won't be there and she will know someone is in her house with her gun. She will panic. Let's hope she only has one gun.

I know I have to close that drawer, which means I have to leave this closet.

Wait, did I leave that drawer open, or did she? Maybe she did it. Maybe she will step out of the bathroom and discover that the drawer she opened had been closed behind her. I try to think. *Did I leave the drawer open?* I can't focus. *Why is it so hard to think?!* My heart is pounding in my ears.

I hear her turn on the water. That's my shot and I just go. I open the door—perfect speed—run to the drawer, snatch the panties because it's faster and close the drawer—perfect speed again.

The water stops and I don't feel confident I can make it back to the other side of the room, so I duck behind her bed.

My heart's pounding like never before and I'm drunk on adrenaline I haven't tasted since Junior High. I am trying to control my breathing lest that give me away too. *I've got to get in better shape.* I am gasping so hard I'm certain to get caught.

Now I am a man hiding behind her bed, breathing heavy, and holding her panties. *Great.*

Finally, I hear the front door open and close.

It takes me another ten minutes to convince myself that most people have very few occasions to open a door and then close it without stepping through. Most likely she is gone.

I put the panties and the gun away. I double-check my surroundings for any clues I might have left that I was ever here. At this point I just want to abandon my mission and leave.

I step from her bedroom and walk down the hall. Out of the corner of my eye, I see an assortment of items strewn across the bed in the guest room. I distinctly remember this door being closed the one time I was in her home. I walk quietly into the room. The bed is made, but not pristinely so. It clearly hasn't been used as a bed in a long time but does seem to have been used as a seat—there was an indent in the pillow where someone had obviously been leaning her back against the headboard. There's a clear lane through the clutter for her legs to stretch out. One side is littered with small pieces of torn paper and crumpled tissues, as if someone had a bad cold or had been crying. There is an empty pint of ice cream, scraped clean. Then I see it. I gasp when I find the incriminating piece: my notebook, *my journal!* It's lying next to a cardboard box containing a Bible, *Prof. Fowler's Bible.* I pan the room further. On a small table by the bed, I spy my old phone and its charger. When I go to grab them, I see my former student's cross necklace there too.

I scoop everything up into the cardboard box and rush out the door.

Chapter Twenty-Four

In the security of my own home, I lock the front door, imagine she probably has a key, then turn the deadbolt.

I first head to my bedroom, but the painting disturbs me so much I can't relax. In the kitchen, I grab a bottle of water and sit at the table.

The first thing I do is plug in my old phone. I know it will tell a less detailed story, but we live in an AV world and screens are our first go-to.

I open up the photo library. I start with photos I remember taking, last fall. Then I see some that are foreign to me. Most of it is pretty random: a screenshot I took of some order confirmation number, a screenshot of a song I liked on Pandora and whose name I wanted to remember, a screenshot of a project on Kickstarter I wanted to keep an eye on. There was a photograph I took of my own hand holding a can of tomato paste for some reason.

My first indication that I was dating someone is a photo I had snapped of a rainbow. It is a beautiful sky and anyone who doesn't look at it and feel moved has no heart at all, but I simply wouldn't have snapped a photo unless I wanted to text it to a girl. A few more finger swipes and I come upon a photo of what's-her-name, a joint selfie, if that's not an oxymoron. Our cheeks are pressed together and she has her arms around me. In this photo she looks drunk, but I am still reminded of how beautiful she is. She's giving the phone a seductive glance, one that she has perfected even while drunk.

I scroll a few more and I see a lot more of her. A lot more. But only one photo.

I continue to scroll and am surprised to see, not one, but several images of my damaged bumper from all angles. They are obviously taken to send over to my insurance adjuster. But I would have sent those soon after the accident and that didn't fit the timeline what's-her-name gave me. Supposedly that was the moment we met, but I had images of her before then. *What is going on here?*

After the bumper are a few screenshots of customer reviews on the Jaguar XF. Nothing is making sense.

I keep flipping.

Then I see her. Emily. It isn't a selfie. Someone else took it. It's just the two of us standing side by side. She may have her arm across my back, or I hers, but I can't tell from the photo. I look at this one for a long time. It's my first appearance in this album with my beard shaved and my hair cut. There are balloons behind us and we both look so happy.

The next photo is of a whole group standing shoulder to shoulder. Most of them I recognize from yesterday in the aisle at the church. They go on and on in different combinations. It seems like everyone wanted to get in a photo with me. It seems like there's a lot of them. Most the people seem to be our age, or more like her age. She was an older student when in my class; by my best guess, we're ten years apart. There are some my age and a few even older than me. There is also a larger collection of babies than I am used to seeing at social gatherings.

The only constant I notice in every photo is me and Emily. I wonder if Christians typically throw parties after baptisms—I note that my hair's not wet in the photo—or maybe just in honor of baptisms.

That seems to be the end of the album. There was only one photo that contained just me and Emily. I select that photo and attempt to text it to myself.

No service.

Of course, there is no service, because my SIM card is in my new phone.

I ponder this for a second, then I hold the two phones a foot from each other and photograph the second one with the first. The picture quality comes out less than ideal, but that doesn't stop me from making it my new welcome screen.

I head over to the text messages and am surprised to find a conversation between me and Emily on August 28, the day before I woke up, the night I was poisoned, exactly nine days ago. My last text to her read "I was faking the whole time."

I scroll up to read the rest of the conversation. I imagine we had been talking on the phone, and then only finished our conversation in text, because there's not quite enough info to go on:

Thu, Aug 28, 8:11 pm
She says she wants to come back over

Why?!

She says she feels bad for losing her cool

It's late

She sounded pretty calm

What'd you tell her?

I said yes

I just feel bad for her

I want to make sure she's going to be okay

It will just be for a minute, then I'll kick her out

Hello?

Please don't be mad

Hmmm... I'm really finding my overdependence on pronouns to be frustrating. It was over four hours after that exchange, in the middle of the night that I texted Emily again:

Thu, Aug 28, 1:36 am
This was all a mistake. Please don't ever call me again

I was faking the whole time

I decide to investigate the rest of the box. There are two items in there I've never seen before. A t-shirt that reads "Honduras Mission Group," with a Bible verse on it, and a book called *Seasoned with Salt*. A quick flip through its pages tells me it's not a cookbook. I would naturally assume these items aren't mine, but the book is signed by the author and addressed "To James."

Knowing that none of this will fill in the gaps quite like my journal, I grab the spiral and settle in.

Chapter Twenty-Five

I open my journal and turn to the first entry I don't remember writing, two days after my last memory:

January 18

She did show up for the next class, the girl I said I'd never see again. No one who has ever walked out of my class the first day has ever come back. No one who I have ever made cry has stood up to face me again.

I couldn't believe it, but there she was. She made eye contact with me once and quickly turned her face away. Her eyes were red around the rims as if she had spent the whole morning crying.

She put her book bag down on her desk but didn't sit. She stood with her back to me, motionless for what seemed like a very long time. Finally, she turned around and walked straight toward me. She kept her head down as she walked, raising it only at the last second. She stood a few short feet away from me, now suddenly *in* the moment for which she had preemptively shed all those tears. Her hands shook slightly before she folded them into her arms in front of her, protectively.

She delivered the lines she had composed, though her voice was quivering. "You are powerful, and I am powerless. You are learned, and I am naïve. You are an institution and I'm just an individual. You're a man, and I'm just a girl. You are wise and I'm foolish." She squared her shoulders. "But God sent the foolish to confound the wise."

"First Corinthians chapter one," I said casually.

She tried to keep the surprise from her face. Her shoulders deflated a bit, and she gave a slight nod. As she returned to her seat, I watched the delicate muscles in her pale young legs. In that moment I was… put in my place? A little bit. Humbled? Definitely not. It's more like I was… oh heck, I was in love.

She sat her slender body down into the chair and proceeded to execute part two of her awful plan. She pulled out her Bible. That's all. Just like that. She pulled out her Bible and started to read silently. I stood waiting for a recitation of a specific verse, or an argument she was prepared to lob at me from behind the Good Book's protection. She didn't. It took me a minute to realize that reading the Bible during my class *was* the plan.

I chose to ignore it. If she was expecting a reaction, she would just have to be disappointed.

But as the minutes ticked on, I couldn't stop glancing back at her. Occasionally, we would all hear the gentle wisp of a thin, gold-gilded page. Like a grain of sand between my toes, it began to itch, but I ignored it and continued on with my lesson.

I was my usual self, charming and witty. Soon I noticed that every laugh line I delivered produced laughter from everyone in the class but her. I immediately made it my mission to be funnier than I've ever been in my life. I was on a roll and every reaction I got from the class I counted as a victory. I relished the chance to remind a poor, pious Christian that she was the one left out, as always.

My eyes couldn't stop darting back over to her. I tried to stop it and I couldn't. She never once laughed with the other students or even smiled. She never once looked up from her pages of scripture.

Soon I noticed myself stuttering a bit—stuttering about a subject I knew by heart. The stuttering was followed by long pauses. I would begin a sentence and suddenly find myself lost, ignorant of where I was going, and unable to identify the last three words that had left my mouth. The itching had grown into irritation and the irritation was becoming unbearable.

Love? How could I have just felt that I loved this girl? She is vile. She is loathsome. I confess what I felt in that moment was *hate.* Is it my class, or isn't it? I finally spoke, "If you don't listen to the lectures, you won't understand the material."

She had the gall to pretend I wasn't talking to her. I could feel the hatred rising. I quickly shined my laser pointer on the pages beneath her gaze, and her head promptly snapped up. This actually brought me a small jolt of pleasure which helped ease back the rage.

"You." I don't know her name. I repeated, "If you don't listen in class, you won't know the material."

She stayed calm and asked, "Do you grade on class participation, Dr. Larson?"

The urge in me to lie was immeasurable. "No," I said. "But If you don't hear the lecture, there's a lot you won't understand," I repeated for the third time.

"I'm prepared to take that chance." If you can believe she delivered this line with no hint of sass or sarcasm, I'm telling you she did.

"It's very rude," I told her bluntly.

She gave me a sweet frown and even nodded. She said, "I'm sorry, sir," then she went right back to reading.

Exasperated, I said, "This is my classroom, and I am telling you that you must put away your Bible." I didn't accidentally say, *asking you,* and I didn't make the mistake of saying *ordering you,* and I hit the word *must* with just the right amount of emphasis, but I wish I would have said *reading material,* instead of *Bible.*

Every eye in the class was on her. Her eyes were on me. She said, "No."

I stood there like an idiot. I swear maybe an hour passed. I had no idea what to do. Visions of me grabbing her by the ear and marching her out of my classroom filled my mind. I also considered a few quips that could save face and laugh the whole thing off. But in the end, I did nothing. No response at all. I just turned back to my chalkboard and continued the lesson.

January 20

So, Emily's plan to humiliate me thickens.
That's her name. Emily.
She was late today; I had hoped she wouldn't come at all. I watched the other chairs fill up and repeatedly checked the clock on the wall. At 9 o'clock, my heart was light and I began my lesson. But when I heard the door, I knew exactly who it was.
She walked in and said, "I'm sorry I'm late, Dr. Larson."
It sounded sincere, and I had no choice but to respond, "Apology accepted," just as sincerely. It made me want to puke, all this civility.
So, she sat down and started to read her Bible again and I continued to ignore her, but then two minutes before the end of class, she closed her Bible and quietly slid it into her bag. Then without getting up, without making a sound, she folded her hands and started to pray.
I mean, what was she trying to pull?
I started talking louder. I did so without thinking, then suddenly felt childish.
She mouthed the word, *amen,* then checked her watch.
I had no idea if I had finished what I was saying, but dutifully blurted, "Fine, that's all for today," then told them what to have read by the next class. I actually said the word *fine.* What's wrong with me? Why does this woman continue to get to me?

January 23

Today I got smart, I knew she would try that praying stunt again, so I waited until I saw her put her Bible away and announced, "That's all for today. Class dismissed."
The room became filled with the sounds of students rising from their desks, gathering their stuff, and beginning conversations with each other.
She was the only one who didn't rise. Again, I kept her isolated. She stayed in her seat to finish her prayer amongst all the noise and commotion.
Eventually, no one in the room was left besides her and me. She was praying and I was glowering at her. I knew she was currently praying

114

for my soul and I couldn't stand it. I was attempting to actually melt her skull with my stare.

She mouthed *amen* and began to gather her things. She said, "Have a great day, Dr. Larson," and left.

I didn't respond.

January 25

I tried the same thing today. I waited for her to begin praying and dismissed the class. She must have had a lot to say to God, because she remained an extra-long time.

Again, it ended up being just the two of us. She sat with head bowed and hands folded, and I didn't take my eyes off of her for a second. I was convinced she could feel every second of my stare and I didn't want to give her one moment's relief.

Time ticked on and I was certain she'd crack from the pressure.

Finally, I did. I said loudly, "Don't pray for my soul. I don't want you to!" She didn't move a single muscle, not even around her eyes, not even around her mouth. So, I continued to heckle, "Don't pray for my sins, I don't want them to be forgiven!"

No response.

Finally, I watched her stupid, pretty mouth whisper *amen* and she stood up to face me. She said, "I'm not praying to upset you."

"Yeah, right."

"I want to thank you for not trying to stop me. It's obvious you must treasure our religious liberties as much as I do, Dr. Larson, and I really respect that about you."

God help me, I almost said *thank you.* I held my tongue for a second, then eloquently blurted out, "Just go."

January 27

She one-upped me again. Today was a very bad day.

Why do I let her get to me? Why can't I stop thinking about her?

Anyway, halfway through my class I saw her put her Bible away. I instantly checked my watch. It wasn't time. What was she doing?

She started praying right then, but my lecture wasn't anywhere near over.

I paused. I stuttered. I choked. I couldn't dismiss the class, I had more to tell them. It wouldn't be fair to truncate their lesson just because of one troublemaker.

I wanted to scream. *Stop it. Stop praying to your invisible God. Open your eyes. What's the matter with you?"*

But I didn't.

When I ultimately did dismiss the class, she looked at me as she gathered her stuff and said, "Again, Dr. Larson, I'm sorry if the free expression of my faith troubles you in any way. Thank you for protecting our sacred rights."

"Oh, shut up," I sassed.

March 3rd

Today was the day that my 101 class had to turn in their first paper. It was to be written on Immanuel Kant. When I finally got home, I pulled them out of my brief case, put on Dylan's *Basement Tapes* and poured myself a Tanqueray and tonic.

No, I didn't read Emily's first. I actually picked a paper at random to read first… then I read hers. I'm not sure what that proved. It was kind of silly after all. Now that I think about it, it may have proved the very notion I was hoping to dispel.

I took in each word slowly, conscious of the fact that I would never again get to read it for the first time. I read it like it was War and Peace, like it was a Shakespearean sonnet. And with each word, an unnamed feeling of suspense welled within me. I had been telling myself I wanted to give her a big fat F. I found out by the second page that wasn't true.

Each word sparked an inaudible rejoice—my mind's salute to her mind, finer than I imagined, more nuanced than she cares to let on. Each word confirmed my burgeoning suspicion that she was a worthy adversary, despite her superstitions, despite her tear ducts. Hers was a mind curious enough to find, and vast enough to hold, the weighty but elusive gems hidden in great texts.

I followed her thoughts as they twisted from one way to the next, and before long I could've sworn I could hear her voice, carrying each word, cradling them like they cradled the subject matter, that great, venerable subject matter that challenges the human mind and exalts the human heart. She even had me seeing Kant's genius in a new light, looking at it, after twenty years of study, as if it were the first time.

When I reached the end, my head was filled with discovery, about Kant, about her, about me. I knew once again that I loved her. But she closed her great exegesis with the single line of its own paragraph:

"But I think it's all horse spit."

I laughed. I laughed and I read the whole thing again. And when I got to the end again, I laughed again. And a part of me, a part that was becoming less and less concealed, wished she could have been beside me to hear me laugh.

March 15

Something strange happened today. I say it *happened*, rather than I did it. It's strange but I just felt like it happened.

Emily began praying smack dab in the middle of class, just as before. And I stopped. I stopped my lecture mid-sentence. I waited for her to say *amen* and then promptly continued my lecture. I didn't do it to psych her out. I'm really not sure why I did it. I just stopped speaking and allowed her to pray in peace.

I watched with my eyes but did not try to melt her skull. My face was as patient as a butler, and I simply waited.

When she finished praying, I returned to my lecture as if it were all such a natural occurrence inside a university classroom.

April 5

It's now become our routine for me to pause my lecture as Emily prays. And of course, she still reads her Bible in my class every day.

I can't help but wonder if she is only pretending to read the Bible, because sometimes she will laugh spontaneously. I have read the Bible; there aren't many jokes between its pages.

Naturally, of course, I think she is laughing at me—either at something I said that she was pretending not to listen to, or at a thought that had tickled her from a separate and secret dialog in her head, though probably still about me.

She doesn't laugh out loud, just bursts into a reckless smile, at which point her fingers shoot up in a subconscious attempt to hide it.

Then of course, maybe she is actually reading and has just come across a description of sin that fits me to the letter. Perhaps in Romans 1, but so many places, really. She usually smiles two or three times a class.

The rest of the time she is statue still. Her head slightly bowed, the left side of her hair tucked behind her ear. Sometimes I stop to just watch her. She doesn't react. She doesn't look up to see why the talking has stopped, although at least fifty other heads do.

They realize who I'm staring at, though I doubt many of them could guess the reason, I mean with us so clearly being rivals.

Today, I ran into one of my star students in the cafeteria. He was reading a book for Hampton's class so I said, "You know Dr. Hampton considers you his favorite."

He smiled modestly and shot back, "Yeah, I was kind of hoping to also be your favorite, but I guess I couldn't compete."

I tilted my head slightly and asked, "With Greg Barrett?" Another one of my star students, with the best grade in the class.

The kid just laughed and said, "No, not with Greg."

I laughed too, as if I were in on the joke. I made a display out of checking my watch and quickly ran off. I told myself later that perhaps I misunderstood. *Not with Greg.* The student wasn't contradicting me but agreeing. Of course, Greg Barrett is a great student and of course he couldn't compete—*not with Greg.* But there was a look in the kid's eyes, a playful mocking telling me that explanation wasn't true.

He is a man too, after all. Perhaps he has noticed that smile at the tips of her fingers. Perhaps he doesn't fault me one bit for staring.

April 17

Something wonderful happened to me today. I was grocery shopping when a beautiful woman came up to me and started hitting on me. *No really, I swear it happened!*

She said she had been a student of mine, but it must've been too long ago for me to remember. I was embarrassed that I couldn't remember her so I tried to play it cool. I asked, "How is it you would even remember me?"

She said, "Of course I remember a professor like you; after all, we're both atheist."

Well, this got my attention.

It was obvious this woman was throwing herself at me and, I've got to be honest, it felt nice when she gave me her phone number.

This was the first moment in a long time that I didn't think about Emily. In fact, Emily simply can't compete with this new girl. I think she's just the thing I need to finally put all this Emily business behind me. And it couldn't happen soon enough.

I mean c'mon, an atheist with a beautiful smile and adorable dimples! I think this will be just the girl to make me forget all about Emily.

I put the journal down.
I did not just read that! I have to laugh to keep from crying.
I pick the journal back up:

May 12

Today was the last day of class. I, of course, have been obsessing about this day for months. But to be more accurate, it wasn't today I have been obsessing over, but tomorrow. Tomorrow is the day for me to face one fact: I will never see her again. Tomorrow is what I fear; I had actually thought very little about what would happen today.

That was until I drove to class. The thought of not seeing her, as I said, had been weighing on my mind for weeks. It had become such a dreaded prospect that I actually began—out of desperation—to entertain ideas of how I could save myself from such a fate. If I just had some sort of plans to see her again! I wasn't going to ask her out, really. I just wanted some sort of plan. If I only had her number. If only I knew I could call her one day and say, "Hey, it's Prof. Larson. Do you feel like talking? Just talking?"

The problem was of course, how do I pull that off as her professor? I've always considered any romantic relationship between a professor and a student unethical, but after today she's no longer my student. It's a gray area I'm not comfortable with, but Emily is an exceptional girl, so I would make an exception. But how do I get her to say yes, and am I prepared to risk my job and my reputation just to have her say no?

Various scenarios ran through my head. All of them ended with me stuttering and mumbling, or sounding completely moronic, or putting my foot in my mouth. There wasn't actually going to be any "class" today; students were just going to turn in their papers and leave. There was a chance I might catch her alone, or at least semi-alone.

I told myself to accept that she didn't feel the same way for me. Every reason for me stay silent repeated in my thoughts. My mind explored all the different ways it could go wrong. But none of them could silence the voice that repeated, *If you do nothing, you will never see her again*. I hadn't reached a single conclusion, nor come up with a single plan when the students began to arrive.

When the clock struck nine, I still hadn't seen her. Was she late again? As every student turned their papers in and slowly filtered out, I still hadn't seen her. I was all alone in my class, facing a turn of events I did not expect, a bleak, grim turn of events.

My heart leapt when I heard the door. But I looked up to see that it was not her. Some girl I had never seen in my life walked in holding a small stack of papers.

She asked, "Are you Prof. Larson?" At this point I worried that I was being served a legal complaint.

I said, "Y— Yes."

She said, "Emily asked me to bring this to you; it's her final paper for your class."

Like a love-struck fool, I lowered my eyes in pathetic and demonstrative grief, but said nothing.

She said, "She's sorry she couldn't make it herself, but she wanted me to thank you."

"Thank me for what?"

She shrugged. "She didn't say."

"Oh… oh, okay…"

I took the paper, and the girl turned to leave.

I said, "So, she couldn't be here?"

The girl half turned and repeated, "She said she was sorry she couldn't come."

"Oh. Okay."

The girl continued to walk out.

Like a desperate dweeb I said, "So, you're her friend, like, you know her?"

The girl turned and looked straight at me, straight into me. She knew everything but said nothing.

I continued, "Like if I give you a message, you could…"

She frowned at me, shook her head forcefully, and said, "She just wanted to say thank you."

"Oh…" I looked down pathetically again and said, "Then just tell her you're welcome. Tha- That was the message I was talking about. Just say… just say you're welcome."

It was awkward because I met up with Dimples later. Of course, I said nothing to her about Emily. I hid every hurt, hid every thought of what I didn't and couldn't have.

It's strange: she's by far the most beautiful woman I've ever been with—she totally puts Emily to shame—but then how come I've spent all my time thinking about Emily? Have I even written much in here about the woman I'm actually dating? Did I even write about how we met? I think I did.

Anyway, my girlfriend could tell something was wrong but she didn't ask any questions. She just dutifully and masterfully helped me to forget. And now she is lying naked beside me, and I'm writing this beneath a small LED book light. Seriously, there's a beautiful girl only two feet from me, soft and toned, resplendent and perfect, and I am writing about another woman.

She made love to me tonight like a woman who's searching, like if she imagined all the answers were contained in her climax. And to be completely honest, I've always viewed sex the same way. I want intercourse to save me. I want the touch of a woman and image of her body to lift me up out of this hollow existence and ease my every pain. I want that and am always able to convince myself it will work.

After the first time we had sex, I caught her crying silently in bed. She wouldn't roll over because she was trying to conceal it from me. I let her pretend I couldn't tell. I have no idea what that was about.

But not tonight. Maybe tonight she actually found a few of those answers. Maybe she did. I truly hope so… because there she is sleeping peacefully and here I am still searching.

Chapter Twenty-Six

May 31

You'll never believe what happened to me today while driving to the post office. I was approaching 14th and Hardin and I stopped short at a yellow light. I probably could have gone through, and as a matter of fact I had planned to, but something made me decide to hit my breaks.

Sure enough—Bam! The car behind me hit me. I immediately stepped out of my car to make sure everyone's all right and who did I see getting out of her car?

Emily.

The woman I can't stop thinking about.

I put down the journal. I didn't see that coming. *It was Emily who ran into me?* As a liar myself, it doesn't take me long to figure out what Dimples had done. Now I know how she was able to make up so many detailed stories about us; she had obviously read this journal, and all the best lies borrow heavily from reality. *Clever girl.* I'm starting to see the whole thing. She didn't tell me her own story, because that story had failed to move me before. No, she told me the story that made me fall in love. *Clever girl.*

I read on:

Emily saw me and started crying. I was totally confused and I asked her why she was crying. I thought maybe it's because she didn't want to see me.

In between sobs, she shrieked, "Oh Prof. Larson, I'm so sorry! I tried to stop in time and I didn't come to your last day of class and…"

I could barely understand her, I said, "Honey, calm down, it's all right. Now what is it you're saying? Why are you crying like this?" I didn't mean to call her honey; it was 90% in response to her crying, but I think it was okay.

She sobbed, "Because I wrecked your nice car."

"That's okay," I said jovially. "It's not that nice."

I must have really nailed the timing because she laughed, although she was still crying.

It felt really good, so I got carried away. I said, "See, watch, it's just a hunk of junk," and proceeded to kick a new dent in the already smashed bumper.

She laughed again—still crying—and I was in heaven. She said, "My insurance isn't paying for that one."

I knew in that second! At last, I knew for certain what I had spent so long trying to hide. I was finally clear on what I spent so long trying to obfuscate. I really do love her. I love her in a way that goes beyond infatuation, goes beyond our rivalry, and goes beyond her physical beauty.

I couldn't tell which tears were sadness and which tears were joy, but the only thing that mattered was how beautiful she looked with her face wet.

I couldn't control myself. I felt overwhelmed. I mumbled, "I knew it."

"Knew what?"

"That you're the perfect girl."

Of course, in that moment her crying and laughing both seemed to become magically under control and she stood there completely silent.

That should have stopped me but it didn't. I couldn't stop. I said, "And smart."

She looked down, feeling uncomfortable.

I couldn't stop. I barreled on, recklessly, "...and kind."

Her face grew even more uncomfortable.

I couldn't stop. My brakes were out. "...and so... so..." At this point, even the blades of grass around us were begging me to stop. The voices in both our heads, the cars, the sky, the entire universe was in one accord that I should leave it alone. "...so *beau—ti—ful.*" The word slid up the entire length of my esophagus as if I was drunk. Was I?

She said, "Prof. Larson."

"Call me James."

"Prof. Larson, I think we should exchange insurance information."

"Yes," I said subdued. "Yes, of course."

After the formalities, I threw a Hail Mary. I knew it was futile, but I blundered through it anyway. I said, "Would you like to go out with me sometime?"

"No." The response came back so quickly, it nearly preceded the question.

My mind gummed up. The awkwardness and the rejection made it hard for me to think straight. I just didn't want her to leave. In desperation, I motioned to the wreck and I insisted, "But don't you think that maybe it was your God who brought us together?" I thought maybe I could make it sound a shade less obnoxious than I heard it in my head.

Her facial expression let me know I failed.

"What if..." I pressed her. "What if God wants me in your life?"

It was a classless move, and she was actually more upset here than I'd ever seen her before, but she tried to hide it. She gave a fake smile and said, "If God wants you in my life, He'll make it happen. And there's nothing anyone could do to stop it."

She got into her car and started the engine. I walked over to the driver side window, hoping she would want to add one more thing, just to ease the sting I was feeling, but she just stared straight ahead and kept the window rolled up.

"I'll hold you to that," I called after her as she quickly sped off.

Good going, Professor.

Chapter Twenty-Seven

June 6

I got a check from my insurance company. They said the car was totaled. I thought that was strange because I always thought totaled meant un-drivable. How could a car be totaled if it drives just fine? Anyway, they paid me the replacement value of the car, minus what I could get for it at a scrap dealer.

I've found a new car I like, but I don't want to just scrap the old one. What if there's some poor wretch who needs a car to get to work, someone who doesn't care what the bumper looks like? I'd hate to turn it into junk metal if there's a chance it can do someone some good.

But that's not what's really on my mind.

I'm still thinking about Emily. I don't know why I can't let this one go. I'm obviously never going to see her again. I can't stop thinking about the speed with which she turned me down and the expression on her face when I called her beautiful. Then of course there was the girl she sent to turn in her final paper. These all seem to be culminating into some sort of theme: she just ain't into me. I guess I have to accept it.

It was fantastic luck that she ran into my bumper. It was luck that gave me a few brief moments with her. And I did get her to laugh. It was nice for me to have heard the sound of her laughter. But now I must lock that away, hold onto the memory of those sounds, and just be grateful for that fleeting moment of bliss.

It kind of reminds me of Dostoyevsky's White Nights. It's a story of a lovesick man who spends a few brief nights with some young, glorious creature. After she leaves him for someone else, he reflects on his one *moment of bliss,* and ends the book with the declaration, "One moment of bliss… Why, isn't that enough to last a lifetime?"

Only, I'm so melodramatic that the story made me cry, and with tears blurring my vision, I failed to see the comma. "One moment of bliss… Why isn't that enough to last a lifetime?" So, I thought the character was demanding to know why it wasn't enough. Which is fantastic, because just to ask such a question, the reader can imagine that for all the character's life he was told by overly romantic stories that it *should* be enough. And now here's this poor sap discovering, in the worst way, that the poets had lied to him.

It wasn't until I reread it in a different translation that I realized my mistake. I realized that the story itself *was* the romantic tripe and that Dostoyevsky *was* the perfidious poet.

I confess, it was a letdown.

Chapter Twenty-Eight

June 18

I've been finding excuses to be in the area of 14th and Hardin around twilight, but I haven't spotted her car yet.

That's okay. I've figured this out. I have a plan! I kept thinking about the last thing she said to me, "If God wants you in my life, He'll make it happen."

It was never meant to be a ruse. I brought up God's providence because I was heavy on desperation and light on class. I never thought it could open up such a perfect opportunity later—that is, providing I manage to see her again.

So, I did a search for Christian concerts that were coming to town and bought tickets to one. There's a number of musicians who'll be playing. I have no idea who they are, but I downloaded most their stuff, and they all sound pretty good. It wasn't quite what I expected.

Okay, if you're thinking that I'm going to this concert because I think I might bump into her there, you are underestimating me. No, I bought two tickets!

The next time I "happen" to run into her, I am going to ask her to come with me. I am going to tell her that I just happen to have an extra ticket to a Christian concert and I want her to come. It will be the last thing she expects. It will blow her mind.

But if you think I am just waiting around to run into her, you underestimate me again. I've decided to be proactive. I don't believe in fate. I don't believe in gnomes or Puck. I don't believe in the watchmaker God, much less the matchmaker God. I had the good fortune to have a single chance encounter, but I am now taking it into my own hands.

And after what she said, how could she explain the fact that we've mysteriously run into each other twice? She would just have to conclude it's God. Then what choice would she have, deny the Lord's promptings? Or however she'd put it.

There simply aren't that many Christians in this college town. If I go to enough events where only the hard-core Christians go, it is statistically probable I run into her. *Statistically probable,* not fate, luck, or God.

I've made a calendar of upcoming Christian events in this area. *For my sins,* I plan to hit them all.

Chapter Twenty-Nine

June 23

Today was the first event of my plan, a Christian book signing. I had hoped I would see Emily there which would spare me from attending the other events on my list, but my luck apparently isn't that good.

The book signing wasn't quite what I thought it would be. The author seemed likable enough and he wasn't as idiotic as I had anticipated. Some of what he said made sense in its own tooth fairy kind of way.

I did bail a little early since Emily wasn't there. When I got out to the parking lot, I noticed a young lady bending over her car's engine with the hood up. Naturally I went over to help.

When I asked if everything was okay, an attractive young lady with dark hair and green eyes turned to look at me, taken off guard. Just then another dark-haired girl with green eyes emerged from inside the car—her twin, literally. She said, "Yeah, we think it's just the battery."

"No problem," I said, "Let me get my cables."

The sisters made the standard protestations about not putting me out, but I ignored them and drove my car to the spot right beside them.

The event seemed to let out shortly after I had left, and as the people trickled out, it seemed like nearly all of them asked us if we needed help.

"Got it under control. Thanks!"

"Just the battery. Thanks!"

"No thank you. I think we've got it."

I swear it took us twice as long with all the interruptions. Actually, it was quite impressive. But so what? I never said Christians aren't nice, I've just said they're wrong.

Sherry and Kerry (the twins) thanked me appropriately and then both gave me a hug. Before I was about to enter my car and leave, Kerry (or possibly Sherry) asked, "Did you just come from the book signing?"

I figured this might have been a roundabout way of determining if I was Christian. "Yes," I answered the question as it was literally asked.

"We have a friend who's putting on a fundraiser next week at such and such church." They didn't say such and such, but I can't remember what they said. I have it written down.

"What is she raising funds for?"

"*He* is raising funds for a school in Honduras."

My mind started working. "Will there be a lot of people there?"

"Yes, he's been in contact with a lot of churches here locally. He's really trying to get everyone he can, so we're hoping for a large turnout."

That sounded perfect. "That sounds perfect," I said.

They wrote the address down for me and then both hugged me again.

Chapter Thirty

June 28

I did end up going to the fundraiser, but I'll spare you the suspense, Emily wasn't there. That's okay; I am prepared for this plan to take some time.

Interestingly enough, Sherry and Karen (the ones who invited me) weren't there either. But there seemed to be a pretty good crowd anyway. It was actually a lot of fun. It wasn't quite what I expected. There were bounce houses, cotton candy, face painting, and even a photo booth.

After a moving presentation—about a school which did tell unsuspecting kids all about Jesus, but also fed them, got them off the streets, away from the gangs, and probably saved their young lives—I was able to meet John and his wife, Lauren. I thanked them for what they were doing and told them I had been sent by Sherry and Kerry.

They looked at me strange for a minute before we were able to untangle it. It turns out their names are Sherry and Karen. I don't know where I got Kerry. I don't know why I think all female twins must have rhyming names.

Anyway, I asked them how I could donate. They told me about the tickets they were selling and the mugs and t-shirts.

"What if I just want to write a check?" I asked.

They pointed to two different tables, but also indicated I could give it straight to them. So, I pulled out my checkbook and wrote them a check for five grand.

There was a voice inside me that wanted to tell them it was an atheist giving them money, or that it was money made by teaching godless philosophy, but mostly I just wanted them to be successful in what they were doing. Mostly I just wanted to help some children who needed help.

They both hugged me, yes, even the dude. They grabbed a t-shirt for me and insisted I take it. Then they asked if I would hop into the photo booth with them.

I refused ten times before they were able to convince me. Ultimately, they got their photo—she with the oversized glasses, he with the huge afro, and I with the hot pink wig.

The entire ride home I felt good. It wasn't until I got home that I remembered why I had gone in the first place—to run into Emily—and I had to remind myself that the evening was a failure.

Chapter Thirty-One

July 2

The concert was amazing. It really wasn't at all what I expected. I didn't see a single tambourine. The moment I got home, I bought every song I could remember. In fact, I am listening now.

Oh yeah, I will spare you the suspense, Emily wasn't there. And I obviously didn't run into her beforehand to offer her the ticket. Oh well; I ended up making good use of it after all.

I was wandering around the parking lot, trying to search every face hoping to find Emily. I came upon a young girl crying. She was in her early twenties and she had bright red hair, not red like orange rind, but red like a fire engine. And her clothes were modest, almost old-fashioned. I thought it made a fun combination. Plus, she was crying, so this girl was hard to miss.

She had a group of friends around her, trying their best to comfort her. But all their faces showed worry too.

I walked over to her and asked the obvious, "What's the matter?"

"I lost my ticket," she said. "We've looked everywhere."

I laughed. I quickly produced the envelope which contained my two tickets and said, "Oh, well I'm so glad I found you. I was walking from my car and I found this ticket on the ground." I handed it to her. "I guess you just dropped it; that's all."

She looked askance at the ticket, looked at the envelope it came from and then looked at the man beside her. I hadn't noticed yet that they were holding hands. She said, "This isn't my ticket. We were in the balcony. This says floor."

I said, "Well, floor is much closer! It must have upgraded when it fell."

The group laughed.

I grabbed the ticket back from her and put it in my envelope. I said, "Tell you what, I don't want you to have to watch the show without your boyfriend. Why don't you two take these, then I can have the one you've got left?"

"We couldn't." she said, but reflexively grabbed the envelope that was handed to her.

"Look at it this way, I am excited to get to know the rest of your group here. If I were to keep these two tickets, I'd be left sitting all by myself."

The girl smiled. The boyfriend handed me his ticket. They both thanked me, then one of the girls in their group grabbed my hand and said, "Looks like you're with us, then. Let's go."

Really, she grabbed my hand. It was so simple, but it was the most unguarded thing I've seen a person do, possibly ever. I just felt accepted by them, not because of anything I did or did not do, but because their default setting was just to accept people. It was nice.

The three left in the group were Brandon, Alyssa, and Sophie. I originally assumed that Brandon and Alyssa were together, but I found out they weren't. In fact, when we took our seats they insisted I sit in the middle so I wouldn't feel excluded.

Religion never came up. I guess they might have assumed I was Christian, because I was at a Christian concert, and felt no need to try to convert me. We spent most the time before the show talking about music. I went on and on about Bebo Norman, my new favorite, but I discovered that Alyssa also likes Bob Dylan. Brandon however didn't know who he was. What's wrong with this next generation?

Still we had fun. Brandon said he liked art so I told him all about Casimiro. Without understanding why, I invited him to the auction coming up. A voice in my head said it was all about the plan and that I didn't actually want the guy's company. But that explanation made no sense.

Chapter Thirty-Two

July 3

My life is getting weird.

My girlfriend showed up unannounced tonight—my *atheist* girlfriend—and I was wearing a t-shirt that quoted Isaiah 6:8.

"What are you wearing?" she asked in a tone like she had caught me dressing in drag.

"It's... um... laundry day."

She stepped into my living room. "What are you listening to?"

I had put together a Christian music playlist, and though some songs are more Christian than others, she unfortunately happened to walk in right in the middle of *How Great Thou Art*.

"It's *Elvis*," I reasoned.

Of course, she walked into my kitchen and of course the book I had just been reading was lying open. *Yup. Max Lucado*. Highlighted paragraphs and everything.

She picked it up, excited to see what I was studying—after all she had once been my student. She used her thumb to hold my place while she swung it around to read the back cover.

Her face shifted.

I shrugged.

She looked around at my place. "Did I drive to the right address?"

I laughed. I realized of course that I'm *not* busted, but rather a grown man who can read, listen to, and wear what I want. I flashed her a charming smile, at least I think it came off as charming, and said, "Didn't I tell you? I'm Christian now."

She laughed, displaying her unfathomable dimples. "Yeah right! Did someone give you a lobotomy?"

I thought that sounded rather harsh and not really all that funny. I wanted to rebuke her for it, but then I realized something, something I thought I had detected in her before but wasn't sure: when she makes jokes like that, she's doing it for my sake. She's saying what she thinks I want her to say. That makes me sad. She hasn't moved past the roles of I as her teacher and she as my student. I wish she would.

She obviously saw this inner dialog on my face because she asked what was wrong. I gave a placating laugh, but it was too late.

She huffed and asked, "Where are we going to watch the fireworks tomorrow?"

Again, she saw discord on my face. I had already told Sophie I'd meet her and the gang I met at the concert yesterday. They said people from their church meet up to watch fireworks on the roof of their church building, and they invited me to come. What a homerun if I "happen" to run into Emily on Independence Day—heat, sweat, hotdogs, and fireworks!

But what a fool I was to think my girlfriend of over two months wouldn't consider the Fourth an assumed date night?

"Um... actually, I have other plans," I told her.

She froze.

"Um... with... Kevin." This was the worst lie I ever told. I could not have said it less convincingly. I practically added a question mark at the end.

"Well, then I can just tag along." This was less of her inviting herself as it was just trying to challenge my lie.

"No, because he wants to... talk about... guy stuff." Another horrible lie. At this point she's convinced I'm cheating on her, and I wished I hadn't already used the *I'm suddenly Christian* line.

She gave me a disgusted look, then turned to leave. "You're acting weird tonight. I think I'm just going to talk to you later."

"You don't have to leave," I told her, but made no real effort to stop her.

July 4

I was getting ready to go see fireworks with the people I met at the concert. When I stepped out of the shower, I went to my phone to select my Christian playlist to pipe through my speakers and I noticed an email from Lauren and John. The subject line read "Thank you for your generous support of our Honduras ministry." I laughed. It's like I've entered a parallel universe.

I clicked on the email and it was telling all about how good I should feel because I am helping them bring impoverished children the Gospel. She included "Last week's photos from our missionaries in Honduras."

Why not? I clicked on them.

It was a lot of what I expected: white adults with brown students, everyone clustered around simple desks in a mostly-bare classroom, pretty young girls with Honduran kids hanging on them affectionately. I thought I saw something interesting in one, so I zoomed in. In the background of the photo, among the children of Honduras, was one of the palest white girls I'd ever seen. It was Emily.

Unbelievable!

I scroll through more photos and I don't see her. Frantically, I scroll through them all. She was in two of them. No mistaking her.

You've got to be kidding me!

I have spent the whole month going to every single Christian event

I could find just to run into this girl, and she's in another country? *Argh!* Impulsively, I clicked off Bebo Norman and, out of rebellion, downloaded some Marilyn Manson.

Honduras?

I'm thinking about buying a plane ticket. Not really. Though it would be bold.

I say it's unbelievable, but it isn't really. I knew from the offset that if I immersed myself in their world, it'd be statistically probable I'd find her. I just thought it'd be in the actual United States.

After considering my options, I hit reply on the email and typed, "This is amazing. How long do the missionaries typically stay before returning home?"

I hit send.

All alone, I remembered that I was still supposed to be getting ready. I had to leave in about an hour.

I watched the clock. Why? Why go if I knew Emily would not be there? It's not like I *wanted* to go. It was just part of the ruse. It was just to make Emily think that God was trying to get us together. Now she is gone and I will likely never see her again.

I know some groups go on missions for, like, two years. Or is that just the Mormons? I'm not sure.

But still I watched the clock. Surprisingly, I hadn't ruled out going from my mind, but I couldn't justify it. It's not like I wanted to go, I repeated. I had to remind myself that she was the only reason I'd ever hang out with those people. If there's no chance I'll see her, then...

I left the option open that I might actually go until the last second. At which point, I started drinking.

I drank and I hit refresh on my email. Every time I took a swig, I was supposed to hit refresh. Or every time I hit refresh, I was supposed to take a swig. I had gotten mixed up; honestly, I've played better drinking games.

Outside I heard distant fireworks. I told myself I didn't care. It's not like I haven't seen fireworks before. Or tasted hotdogs. All I did was spare myself the effort of having to be friendly to people I had zero in common with. That's all.

Finally, I got Lauren's reply. It made me smile. She said that people typically only stay for two weeks. She had described the photos as from "last week," so I knew Emily would be back anytime.

I quickly typed out "thabkso much!" and hit send.

Chapter Thirty-Three

July 18

So, Emily's back from Honduras. Don't ask how I know.

This whole time I was trying to find her, I had her address from her insurance info, but so what? I couldn't just show up at her house and try to play it off as serendipitous, could I?

Although I did think about it.

You know: I was coincidentally driving in the neighborhood when my car breaks down. I knock on the nearest door and say, "Excuse me miss, but… wait a minute! This is *your* house?"

Great minds don't have better ideas, they simply have *more* ideas and an effective system to filter out the bad ones. Yeah, that one got filtered out.

So anyway, I showed up at the Olive Garden and asked for a specific table for two by the window. It was 7:50 on a Thursday. I waited patiently for ten minutes until I noticed the hostess lead an attractive woman to the table right beside mine. It's Emily.

I had to look over my shoulder to glance at them, but I could see that Emily had spotted me and was considering asking for a new table. Finally, she sat down and the hostess left us sitting back to back.

I'd picked the seat closest to where Emily usually sits. We were inches apart, practically touching. The way I orchestrated it, our backs were to each other. The other seat would've been facing her, but it was over six feet away, and anyway it would've been facing her back.

As soon as the hostess left, Emily turned toward me and whispered, "You're following me!" It was more of a hiss than a whisper.

I turned my head. We were still back-to-back, so we were talking over our shoulders to each other. I could see her leg begin to vibrate up and down with nervous energy. "I am not following you," I said in a loud mock-whisper. "And this is not a library."

"It's too unlikely for me to run into you twice; you must be following me," she said in a more normal voice.

Here was my chance to say, *God did it,* but I remembered the look on her face last time I tried it. I said, "I'm not following you. Besides, where would I be following you *from?* That implies I could find you in the first place."

Her face didn't relax and I was beginning to fear she was actually upset. She said, "The insurance information I gave you had my address."

"Okay, do you *live* at the Olive Garden?"

"You went to my house and followed me here."

"And arrived first?"

She thought about this and almost seemed like she was about to concede. She said, "You've *been* following me. You know I come to this table to read the Bible on Thursday nights."

And Monday nights. That's exactly what I did. I said, "That's absurd. Do you hear how crazy that sounds? I'd never even be able to think up something like that."

At least not right away.

She said, "Um. Okay."

"Okay," I said.

"Okay," she said.

I turned around more in my chair to look at her. In a firm friendly voice, I said, "Why did you have someone turn in your last paper for you?"

She didn't answer right away. A waitress came by and Emily told her she wanted a water and that she needed more time to look at the menu.

"Why did you have someone turn in your last paper for you?" I repeated once the waitress was gone.

"Because I didn't want you to ask me out." Her leg stopped shaking. She sat very still. It was hard to make out what she was thinking because I could only see the edge of her jaw. It's such a pretty jaw.

"I understand," I said. "Do you want me to ask the hostess to find me another table?"

Long pause. "No." Now she'd gone back to whispering, and her leg started shaking again.

"Will you come over to my table and eat with me?"

"No!"

"Can I come over to your side and sit with you?"

"No!"

"Okay. Well, then can I just ask one more question?"

"Fine."

"Did you avoid me on the last day of class because you didn't want to reject me, or because you didn't want to accept?"

Her leg stopped again. She said, "Reject you," but she said it a bit too quickly.

"Emily..." I tried to get her to turn around to look at me. "Emily..."

"You said that was your last question."

"This is not a question."

She begrudgingly turned around.

I looked her straight in the eye and said, "I'm sorry."

"For what?"

"I'm sorry for making you cry that first day."

She didn't respond, but her eyes jerked away. She didn't turn her shoulders back though. She remained open. Her gaze was not back toward her water, but to the side.

I got to see her perfect, beautiful profile as I continued, "My philosophy teacher was the first one to ever call me smart, despite the fact that I had always been rather smart. I always had the ability to read a text and understand its meaning right away. Plus, I have the freakish ability to retain it, a photographic memory. I had one talent, yet it never seemed to be enough. Not for my parents. Not for any girls. Then suddenly I was made a professor, at a pretty young age, where my only job all day was to sit and act smart. Then they gave me an audience. You've seen my room, it's even built like an auditorium. It has stadium seating for the love of Pete! And I'm on center stage. It was like I could make up for lost time. They put me on stage and the play is to act smart, and the students eat it up. They encourage me; you have no idea how they encourage me. When I act obnoxious, they eat it up. When I go on and on like a jackass, 999 days out of 1000 I will get nothing but laughs. And it just feels so good. And I just get carried away. On the thousandth day, I got tears. And I'm sorry. I'm sorry I got carried away and I'm very sorry those tears were yours."

She still didn't look at me. She said, "I accept your apology." No whisper this time; her voice was firm and strong.

I got up from where I sat, walked over to the empty seat across from her and sat down without asking. I said, "Now I want desperately to tell you there's another side of me, but I think you already know. I think maybe you've caught glimpses of it."

She nodded.

"All I'm asking is for the chance to show you more of that side. Just for the length of one meal. Will you give me that chance?"

This was where she was supposed to blush and nod submissively, but I must've forgotten who I was dealing with. "On one condition," she said.

"What's that?"

"You promise me you didn't follow me."

"I swear," I lied.

I could see she was satisfied. She believed me and I instantly knew she was a greater woman than I had even thought. The most honest people are always the easiest to fool. Emily could never tell such an effortless lie and act so casual about it; so in her mind she projects that inability onto me as well.

We had a great conversation after that. It may have been the best date I've ever been on. I asked her for her number, which I already technically had, and she said no. I asked her on a date and she said no. Actually, I am having a hard time remembering right now what was so great about it…

Oh yeah. She agreed to see me again. She insisted that it wasn't a date and she may have a case; it is a three-year-old's birthday party. But I will get to see her again!

I didn't use the God line. Not once. I didn't remind her that she had said, "If God wants you in my life, there's nothing anyone could do to stop it." But I'm pretty sure she remembered. She had to be thinking about it.

I'm thinking about it too. I'm thinking what exquisite proof this is that God is *not* in control, and what a perfect metaphor this is about how to get things done. I tried to leave things up to chance (God). It got me nowhere. I got nowhere until I took the power into my own hands, came up with a plan, and made it happen. Self-serve. No omnipotent deity required.

Consider the month I've had. I ran into two women who needed help outside of the bookstore. Surely if there were a God coordinating all of this, it would have been Emily that I saved with my mighty jumper cables. How romantic would that have been! Or surely, I would have jumped in a photo booth with Emily at that fundraiser. Surely Emily would have been outside the gate of the concert, ticketless and crying. And let's not forget that particular concert ticket was purchased for her. I had hoped and even tried to run into her before the concert, but I didn't. And that was my best plan at the time. Now instead of going to listen to live music, we are going to some toddler's birthday party. It's not ideal, but it's more than I got while *waiting on the Lord.*

So, let this mark the end of a wasted month. I tried *giving it to God*, now I'm going to handle it. Last week I did it His way and it got me absolutely nothing. She wasn't even in the country. Now I'm doing it my way, and I can't wait to watch what happens!

Chapter Thirty-Four

July 21

    I just reread my last entry. I honestly don't know what to think, but that's the least of my problems.

    Okay. I went to pick her up for the party and texted her on the way to ask where *exactly* her house was, because I couldn't seem to find it. Do you get it? Because if I couldn't find her house, it would mean I've never been there before, and I've never followed her. Also, it broke the barrier of me contacting her via her ill-gotten phone number—but just for expedience while in a bind.

    I thought that was pretty smart.

    The car ride was weird. I could tell from the moment she answered the door that she wished she hadn't invited me. Really, I got the feeling from her that she wasn't even comfortable with me approaching her doorstep.

    That is such a tough moment for a man—butting up against the impenetrable wall of female unpredictability. When she doesn't laugh at your first joke, you're fine. Just keep joking. But when it comes to your third or fourth and you can just *feel* the date imploding, what do you do? Keep acting breezy? Act *more* breezy. That's the killer. That right there. She doesn't laugh at your joke, so you start to make more jokes. Soon you are just saying any joke that comes to your mind, and so obviously the jokes are getting worse, and you're wearing a big neon sign that says, *Just please give me some positive feedback. Laugh at me, look at me, love me. Why won't you love me!?*

    And it's like quicksand. The more you struggle; the deeper you get. But guess what? If you stop struggling, you're still sinking. Is not like quitting gets you out of it. You're still sinking if you remain perfectly still. That's the thing. So—what?—I should've done nothing and let myself sink? No. I'm going to struggle, of course I am.

    It makes me sick just remembering it.

    Anyway, things started looking up the second we got there. In fact, everything changed. Everything. I must say it was the greatest, strangest moment of my life so far.

    We walked into a medium-sized house for a three-year-old's birthday party. The second we walked into the room, I heard someone shout, "Oh, thank God James is here; now I don't have to worry about not getting home."

    I turned to look, and it's Sherry. Or Karen.

    She came over and hugged me. Emily asked her if we know each other, but she didn't hear her because she was busy calling her twin over.

Both twins hugged me and one of them said to Emily, "You didn't tell me you know James." I couldn't help but notice she said it in a *you-dirty-girl-you* kind of way.

Emily began to say, "Well, we're—"

I felt certain this was to be followed by *just friends* so I immediately inserted, "We're on a date," just so I could see the twins react. They didn't disappoint; they ooh-ed and aww-ed like they were twelve.

Then from over my right shoulder we heard another voice. He said, "Oh wow, Dr. Larson. Why, last time I saw you, you had a pink wig on."

It was John and Lauren. Lauren rushed over ahead of her husband and greeted me with a huge hug. While I was shaking John's hand, I could hear Lauren asking Emily, "How do you two know each other?"

I quickly turned my head and insisted, "We're on a date."

Before Emily could answer, Lauren said, "Well you've got yourself a real keeper here, let me tell you."

"Oh, well, we…" Emily stuttered and asked, "Do I?" She smiled as she said it, and did a good job not sounding too surprised.

Lauren began to speak, but we were interrupted again.

It was Brandon and Alyssa. She said, "Oh wow, I didn't know you would be here," then out the side of her mouth added, "Quick, somebody put on *Blood on the Tracks*!" Behind her was Daniel and Paige—they were the couple I gave my tickets to. Sophie wasn't at the party yet, but she showed up later.

Emily had finally had enough. Completely blown away, she turned to me and asked, "What is going on here?"

I swear to you, I couldn't even answer. I couldn't stop grinning. How cheesy I must've looked. It was partially because of the sick, imploding place I was just in moments before, watching our date fall apart. Then suddenly I was showered with hugs and praise, and I was able to see her whole demeanor change. No longer in fear of what I might say to a room full of Christians, she was proud. I could see it, she was proud she brought me. But there was more. It was the sheer exhilaration of… what? Christians would call it the answer to a prayer. Providence, maybe. God's hand at work. It was the real-time, front seat, firsthand spectacle of a deep and desperate prayer being answered.

If I believed that.

I don't.

I don't believe it, but I have to confess, this was *not* statistically probable.

Anyway, so as the night went on, I was on fire. It's amazing what a few compliments will do for me. They fuel me. And I was burning hot. Every word out of my mouth was winsome and assertive and funny. The girl I couldn't get to laugh in the car ride over was holding her sides, close to tears, at least two times that I can remember.

Everyone kept asking me if I had enough soda, or if I wanted more cake, or if I thought it would be a good time to open presents. I even led the crowd in happy birthday. It was so weird. I was like the guest of honor or something. A few times I forgot it wasn't my birthday.

At one point, Lauren even pulled the photo booth strip of us from her purse. There I was, *Professor James Larson,* wearing a hot pink wig, seducing the camera with a duck face and a power-to-the-people fist. They showed it to Emily and she almost wet her pants laughing. I pretended to be embarrassed, but I know it scored me major points; it humanized me in her eyes.

At the end of the night, the crowd had thinned out. People had splintered off into different groups. Emily told me she would be right back and it was obvious she was heading to the restroom, so I walked out the front door.

I found an out-of-the-way spot on a porch swing.

When she finally stepped out, she said, "There you are."

I replied vaguely, "It's a nice night."

I was hoping that she would sit next to me without me asking, and she did. I was hoping that she would reach for my hand before I reached for hers, and she did. Her touch fueled me more and I blurted out, "I'm crazy about you."

After just a second's hesitation she replied, "I'm crazy about you." Only hers sounded sad.

"But?" I foolishly, foolishly asked.

"But... you're atheist."

I wanted to keep the mood light, so I immediately shhh-ed her and pretended to look back at the house. "They'll hear you!"

She wanted to laugh, but a tired smile was the closest she got.

I said lightly, "Ya' know, I've been thinking that over, and I've reached a conclusion."

"And what's your conclusion?"

"It doesn't matter." I shrugged. "It doesn't matter."

She sighed weakly. "It matters."

I petulantly snatched my hand away. That breezy act took more energy than I realized, and I abruptly reached the end of it.

She sat up and placed both her hands on my arm. She said, "Listen. I like you. A lot. I think you are funny and sexy, and you're obviously smart. I like you. But I think that dating should only be for discovering the man you want to marry. And I could never marry an atheist."

Wait, she called me sexy?

I wanted this. I saw a way it could work. It was a way I feared she wouldn't like, but in my mind, I saw it working. I saw her happy. I said, "What if I could persuade you?"

This time she withdrew her hands. She said, "There are two ways I could choose to interpret that, and I don't like either of them."

"Let me ask you something," I began. The sun was setting and the spot we were in just got a few degrees cooler. "Do you think you need God to be happy?"

"Yes," she said simply.

I frowned. "That's…" I was smart enough not to finish this sentence. "Let me ask you something else; if I could prove that God doesn't exist—really prove it beyond any doubt—would you stop believing in Him?"

"N—" she began but stopped herself. Her eyes got a bit misty and she said emphatically, "I wouldn't want you to do that… Why would *you* want to do that? Why would you want to do that to me?"

Time seemed frozen. We could not understand each other at all. The two of us, agape, seemed to study each other the way a philosophy professor studies a broken car engine.

Then a strange thing happened, the girl I had been spending all my time thinking about, just dropped out of my mind. Somehow, she was gone. Gone in a flash. And the girl beside me was just some young, silly girl.

It was heartbreaking.

The drive back to her place was too quiet, so I tried in vain to make a joke. I could feel the car imploding.

We got to her place and I realized there was still one thing I *had* to do. Wow, it always seems to be bad timing with this girl. I said, "You're about to step out of this car, but I'm not prepared to never see you again. I was hoping I could get your number."

"You already have it."

I nod. "I have it, but you didn't give it to me. I guess what I'm really asking for is permission. I already have your number; may I use it to call you sometime?"

"You already texted me."

I shrugged amiably. "And you survived it."

"No." She didn't laugh. "I'd rather you didn't call me. Or text me." Brutal.

Nothing left to do now but pull the final ripcord. I said, "But… you said, 'If God wants you in my life, there's nothing anyone could do to stop it.' Those were your words. Don't you remember saying that? With everything we saw tonight… Don't you think, maybe your God is trying to get us together?" I am not sure what percentage of this was manipulation and what percentage was my own brain trying to work through all of it.

She frowned. Perhaps I shouldn't have used the word *your*. She said, "I do believe in a God who sometimes interferes with human lives. And I do believe He is up to something. But I don't think He's trying to get us together."

I made an *ah, c'mon!* face. "Then what?" I pleaded.

"I think He's knocking on your door. I think He wants your attention on Him... not on me." She smiled. "I already have your attention." As she said it, she reached to push a strand of her hair behind her ear, the little minx, the confident, deserving little temptress. She went on, "I think He is trying to get your attention for Himself. I think he's using me to get to you."

Argh. I couldn't think of anything to say to that. I sat there silently, knowing she was courteously waiting for a break in the conversation to step out of the car and out of my life. I knew I had to say something, anything to prevent that from happening. The pressure was unbearable.

I saw her hand reach out and grab the door handle, but she did not pull it. I panicked.

Not a second too soon, inspiration struck. I said, "If God wants me Christian, and you are my best hope of becoming so... then aren't you obligated to let me take you out again? I mean Great Commission and all that?"

She thought about it. Her hand slid off the handle. I could tell she was considering it. Finally, she said, "You have Moses and all the prophets," then grabbed the handle and mercilessly opened the door.

It was as if she had opened the door of an airplane at 35,000 feet. My heart became depressurized and all my hope was being sucked out the cabin amidst screams and flailing oxygen masks.

She saw the hurt on my face and regretted the curt way she'd said it. She leaned in tenderly and gave me a peck on one side of my face. On the other side, she placed the tips of her perfect, heavenly fingers.

I said lugubriously, "Luke chapter 16."

She gave me that same look of surprise and admiration I'd seen before, then stepped out of my car forever.

Chapter Thirty-Five

July 27

This week was hard since the last time I saw Emily, but on Wednesday I got a call from Sophie. She said they were having a BBQ and wanted me to come. I'm glad it was a phone call because I couldn't hide the goofy smile on my face.

It wasn't as dramatic as a car wreck. It wasn't an improbable coincidence. And it certainly wasn't a sign from God, but I know I will see Emily again. I will take it.

I'm sure I can convince this girl. Most Christians are simply born into their beliefs. They imbibe it with their mother's milk. But elected reason has always been more powerful than forced indoctrination.

I have to admire her though; she will be a tough nut to crack. I am going to have to do more than my usual technique: beat students into a mental coma with the Open-Minded Playbook. This technique is so pervasive that most freshman these days come to me already scholars of the Open-Minded Playbook and will say the most blatantly dishonest stuff just to maintain the façade of tolerance and acceptance.

This is especially pathetic when those students are Christians. They claim to worship Christ but forsake him with the first hint of any ridicule.

No, ridicule won't work with Emily. With her voice shaking, her nerves shot, and her face wet with tears, she had still refused to back down. This won't be easy at all.

I keep going back to our last conversation. I asked, "If I could disprove God, would you stop believing in Him?" And she said *N.* She didn't actually say *No,* but she got out the letter *N.*

The reason she can never accept the truth is because the lie gives her hope. So, to bring her over to my side is simple, I would have to crush that hope. I would have to get her to let go of her nostrums and come to grips with the simple truth: belief in the Bible does not offer any hope. Not really.

Christ is a crutch and she will not need a crutch when her leg gets better. I only have to find out what's wrong with her leg and heal it. I know I can heal it. Our love can heal it.

She will no longer need Christ; she will have me.

I am physical. I am real. She would come to thing that's ever happened to me. If in fact—

Wait, what? I flip over the spiral to start that line again.

She would come to thing that's ever happened to me.

Huh? I open the spiral and lay it flat so I can see the beginning of the sentence at the end of one page, and the end of it at the beginning of the next.

She would come to… thing that's ever happened to me.

Nope, it's not me. That sentence makes no sense. I scratch my head for a second, then notice something caught in the spiral. My mind knows right away what it is: tiny scraps of paper. They're the remnants of a page which was torn out. A page or two? Or three? Four? I examine them but have no way of knowing.

Crap. Just when I was settling down into a nice warm bath of answers, I'm thwarted by this cruel bucket of ice water.

I remember the torn pieces of paper I saw on what's-her-name's guest bed. Right there next to used tissues. I should've seen it coming. I should've known it then. Again, I feel violated. I'm right back where I was.

But only for a moment.

I tell myself to put the missing page or pages out of my mind and focus on the ones I have. I continued reading.

…thing that's ever happened to me. If in fact God has forgotten my sins, why can't you?"

Her face was stone. "I don't want to have this discussion," is all she said.

"You like me, right?"

She didn't answer, just squirmed.

"You don't have to say it; I already know you like me, or else you wouldn't have… So, if by some miracle, and maybe it is a miracle—it felt like a miracle—I became Christian, then you'd have no problem dating me, right?"

She said nothing.

"I mean Christ separated me from my sins as far as the East from the West, and you're what? Saying that's too close, the East to the West? Too close for your comfort?"

She said, "You're not going to convince me with Bible verses, I already know you know the Bible. You've always known the Bible, even as an atheist. So really it proves nothing."

"Wait, what am I trying to *prove*?"

She didn't answer.

"Wait, wait, what do you mean by *convince you*? Convince you to go out with me? Or…"

144

Her lips were tight. Her eyes were hard. She said, "I mean prove to me that you are what you say. I mean, convince me that you are a Christian."

Wait, did she just say I was a Christian? Did I write that she said I said I was Christian? That would certainly fit in with the rumors of my baptism... *but still.*

I read on:

She said, "Convince me you are Christian. It just seems so..." She trailed off.
"What?" I quipped. "Miraculous? Providential? Just seems so impossible, even for God?"
"*Convenient.*"
And that's where things are now. She doesn't believe me. I admit, it's unbelievable.
I asked her to dance. There were only a few other couples out on the floor and I led her to a spot far away from any of them.
I worried about holding her too close for a Christian function, but she wasn't worried at all. She allowed me to hold her. She allowed me to feel her soft breath on my neck. And when I squeezed her in my arms, she squeezed back.
I pulled away from her slowly because I wanted to see her face.
No, that doesn't quite describe it. It's not that I wanted to see her face, it's that I was overwhelmed by a burning desire to see her face in just that second. Like my heart was on fire and her face was the water.
I smiled; just the image of her face calms my nerves.
She smiled back and I saw something I hadn't before, one delicate wrinkle by her young eyes. But far from detracting from her looks, it exalts them. It's like the first step of a long, but glorious, process has begun.
I said, "You're going to be beautiful even when you're old. You will never spend a day of your life that you're not beautiful."
Her face flushed red. She has a superhuman blush, taking her face from nearly white to solid red. It's the most alluring thing I've ever seen. It has always had the power to undo me, but this time I saw something different in it, something I missed as an atheist: reflected light. I'm reminded that we have a beautiful and attractive God. I'm reminded that God is a masterful artist.
I said, "God knows what He's doing. If you want to take your time, take your time. But don't underestimate Him; I made that mistake myself for far too long."
She began, "I *want* to believe—"
I interrupted her, "No, that's on me; that's not on you. It is up to

me to convince you, and that's exactly what I plan to do."

Chapter Thirty-Six

August 16

Fortunately, our next event was a bonfire. John owns some property out past the city line. The stars were out and it was a cool crisp night for August. There were even fireflies. I can't remember the last time I saw fireflies.

It was the perfect night to be in love. It was the perfect night to believe in God.

I brought a copy of my book, *Potissimum*. I waited for the perfect moment and then tapped a pen on the edge of my soda bottle. When everyone turned to listen to me, I began my speech.

"As many of you know, I have been a college professor for ten years, and as such, I have been given unique access to the minds of our young children. This is a stewardship I never deserved. This is a role I didn't treat with proper respect. In fact, I abused it.

"I hated God. And I taught many of my students to hate God." I wanted to state it as clearly as possible, without equivocation. Dropping such a confession before this group caused my voice to shake. I forced myself forward, "Very few stood up to me, most capitulated. Many turned their backs on their Savior. I robbed them of their innocence through philosophy and vain deceit. I robbed them of their salvation. I despoiled them of their eternal life. I tried to do it to this woman here, but by God's grace she was too anchored.

"So now I have a legacy of nihilism. Bodies in my wake. Lost souls. I wish I could go back to speak to them. I would tell them to run. I would tell their parents to better guard their young treasures. I would tell them to challenge me. *Stop listening! Don't buy into it. Take me on, I fold rather quickly.*

"I wish I could apologize to all of them today, but there are too many." I closed my eyes. "But I pray for them.

"I am obviously going to change the way I teach my class, and I can honestly say that I am not likely to hold onto my position much longer. But there is something I can do now, here tonight."

I pulled out my book. "If I could tell you the blood, sweat, and tears that went into trying to get this work written and published you wouldn't believe me. If I could convince you of the life I put on hold just to finish it, followed by brown-nosing my agent and editors, followed by the obsessive checking of my Amazon page just to see if anyone had left a new review in the past few hours, you could never understand why someone would torture themselves in this way.

"It's so strange to love something with all your heart one moment and then later feel..." I looked at the book. "...nothing for it. Nothing but dull sadness.

"This book epitomized all the filth I inflicted on young minds for a decade. This book is the culmination of every lie the devil ever told. Even though the book never once mentions Jesus, I see clearly now that when I attacked truth, I attacked Christ. So, with that in mind, I confess..." I stepped closer to the fire. "...it *is* hard for me to kick against the goads."

I threw the book in. I was kind of hoping that the crowd would cheer, but they didn't.

I turned to look at Emily. She said loud and sarcastically, "Well, I'm convinced."

There were a few stray comments from the group that sided with me. "Ah c'mon," and, "Just trust the guy." That felt good; it made up for the lack of applause.

Emily didn't respond to them but looked at me. She sassed, "Your publisher just made the one copy then?"

"Six actually," I said dryly.

She laughed.

I smiled and gave her my standard *you laughed, so I won* face. Then I turned away from her and back to the crowd. I said loudly over the crackle of the logs, "But I have just cashed out all my investments. I've gathered together all the money I have and plan to buy the print rights from my publisher so I can make sure it is never printed again!" I said it in a rousing tone, the type of peroration that is naturally followed by raucous applause.

Again, they were silent.

Emily looked at me concerned—she will make a great mom one day—and said, "What about you? What will you live on?"

I responded quickly, "Don't the pagans themselves chase after such things?"

"Matthew chapter 6," she said quickly before I had the chance to.

I said, "Man cannot live on bread alone, but on every word from the mouth of God. Matthew Chap—"

"No, I'm serious!" she snapped. "What will you do?"

I shrugged. "I'm serious, too." Then I looked straight into her eyes and said with full sincerity, "Sometimes you just have to take a chance, even if you're scared. Sometimes you just have to leave things up to God."

Then there was a cheer. Finally. Through the cheering, we heard one person yell, "Go on, kiss him."

She didn't. She slowly turned, then walked over and switched the music back on.

I put the spiral down. I just have to take a breather from it. I look up at the $200,000 painting and hate it. I guess the negotiations with my publisher were interrupted.

After a moment, I pick the journal back up:

I wanted to pursue her then, but my book was still burning. It's hard to explain, but I felt like it was somehow my duty to watch it burn.

I watched my book burn until it was gone. I couldn't help but think about my father. I hated everything about his book, the writing, the time he spent writing; I even hated the cover his publisher had used. But I never saw it for what it was: a vain attempt to find life outside of Christ. All my father ever wanted was love, but he never knew where to search for love. He never knew the Source.

I despised him, then later became him. I searched for love in the same stagnant places. We both sought life where there was no life to be found. That's what all the sophistry was ever about. Nothing more.

I could have at least been sympathetic. I was the one person in the world who should have had the most sympathy for him. What he struggled with, I struggled with. The lies he believed, I believed also. With no Christ in my heart at the time, I could have at least given him my love. But I didn't. I didn't honor him when I still had the chance. And I'm so sorry.

Emily found me later that night, she stood with her arms folded an arm's length away from me. She asked, "What were you trying to do?"

A number of different ways to answer this question filled my mind. Finally, I said, "What was I trying to do? The same thing I'm always trying to do these days, get you to believe me."

She didn't smile. Her face remained impassive.

I said, "Aw, c'mon, what do you want? I gave up my book for you!"

"You gave up your book for me, or for Christ?"

"Well, of course for Christ."

She nodded. "I *want* to believe you…"

"Seriously?!" I snapped. "Didn't you see it burn? What will it take?"

She didn't answer.

A voice in my head told me to shut up. Not another word. I liked that question—*what will it take?* It so perfectly summed up my whole attitude toward her. I wanted to know what I could do. I wanted her to know I would do anything. I repeated, "What will it take?"

Her eyes drifted away and it appeared she was thinking. I was excited that I might get a real answer.

An impish grin overcame her face. She said, "Get baptized."

Chapter Thirty-Seven

I turn the page. I turn it back. That's all there is. "Get baptized." That is the end. The date of that entry is August 16, almost two weeks before I woke with no memory.

I close the journal.

There were no entries after that. They were not torn out; they were never written. Sometimes I let things lapse, even for weeks. I didn't know I'd ever be in this position or trust me, I would've written every day.

So, I still have questions.

There was surprisingly little about Dimples, not even just her name. Every encounter with Emily was recorded, but my entire relationship with Dimples was barely mentioned. *That's messed up!* There was nothing in there describing how or when I broke things off with her. That no doubt happened during the torn-out pages, which is obviously why she tore them to shreds.

It also didn't describe what happened between Kevin and me, but his description—alcohol and my big mouth—is probably enough to go on. Kevin's birthday was within the dates of the missing pages, so I imagine all of this could have fallen to pieces all on the same drunken night. And perhaps that perfect storm of ugliness was the catalyst for my conversion. Or one of them.

There is nothing describing exactly where I left things with Emily. I didn't even have time to detail my own baptism. But I get the sense that one happened just recently.

It is astonishing to me that I could ever be Christian. It doesn't seem real. I've been lied to so much recently that I am reluctant to believe even my own words in my own handwriting.

I get up from my seat and go to find where I tossed the note Kevin wrote for me. I find it and read it one more time:

Dear James,

You would think just as I did. You would feel just as I felt. You would decide what I decided, if you just knew all the facts. You know how I know? Because you are me!

– James

I chose God. Somehow or other, I chose Him once. I was reading their books, but I forgot every word I read. I was listening to their music but forgot every note.

I still need more answers, so I go back to my old phone. I stare at Emily's photo for a second, then I go to her texts. Her texts were saved to my phone even without the SIM card, which means her number was saved even without the SIM card. I hit the CALL button.

Oh yeah, no service. I thought that was too easy.

I type in her number to my new phone and call her. Of course, she doesn't answer.

I immediately text her:

> *I did not send you that last text from me.*

Who did?

> *It's a long story. There's an explanation for everything. Nothing's as it seems right now.*

There was no answer. I quickly add:

> *I did not block your numbers. Someone else did. I never screened your calls. I never got any messages or texts, because your number was blocked, but I did not block it.*

Again, there was no answer. I typed:

> *I'd like to speak with you face to face.*

I don't know.

> *Please.*

I'm at Alyssa's party. You were invited, but you don't remember.

> *Perfect. Where is it?*

Alyssa's house.

> *If I once knew where that was, I don't now.*

I've never been so anxious for a text and she's really taking her time. Finally, I get the address, throw my shoes on, and hit the door. I sit down in my driver's seat but decide to run back into the house. I head into the bathroom and shave off my beard. I'm clean-shaven now, just like the man I'd been while with her.

The drive feels strange. It's still Monday. I read the full story in one night. It feels like it's been weeks since I stole the spiral back, but it was this morning. I read it all without what's-her-name probably realizing it was gone.

I walk into the party and, just as in the church yesterday, everyone hugs me. This time I know a couple of their names.

Brandon and Alyssa greet me with affection. I know my Good Samaritan's name now because my journal says I invited Brandon to the Casimiro auction. I assume that's Alyssa beside him. Brandon asks cautiously, "Are you all right?" The tone of his question makes me believe my Premocyl problem had been the topic of conversation at this party before I arrived. The confused look on his face when I say, "Hello Brandon," confirms it.

Sophie is also surprised that I know her name, but that one is a lucky guess; she just looks like a Sophie.

Sherry and Karen are pretty easy to spot, but I call Karen Sherry. Dang, 50% chance and I blow it. But really, that could've happened even without the Premocyl.

Paige really stands out because she has bright red hair.

And Emily.

She holds back and lets everyone greet me. Finally, I step to her and gesture for a hug. She is good enough to grant it to me. When I feel her arms around me, my heart swells like I'm twelve years old again. I can't believe it.

I ask her if we can speak alone and again she refuses.

Fine. "Then I can say it in front of everyone." All eyes are on me. "As I guess a lot of you already know, I was poisoned with Premocyl."

Emily's eyebrows shoot up. This wasn't what I had told her just yesterday.

I push the issue. "I originally thought I had taken it myself the way that some people use the drug to forget all about heartache. But it turns out that isn't the case. I was poisoned. I don't know how because I don't remember how.

"I am now left to pick up the pieces of a broken life, or well, at least an interrupted life. I thought I had been dumped, because I learned that's why people take Premocyl. I want to be clear. I did not decide to take the drug. I never screened any of your calls. Your numbers were entered into my new phone for the sole purpose of me never hearing from you, but I wasn't the one to block them, I don't think. It's still confusing, but this I do know: The drug caused me to forget every second I ever spent with everyone in this room. It caused me to forget about falling madly for Emily. It caused me to forget my own baptism."

I have their attention now. I double down. "I went to bed atheist and woke up Christian. Also, I have an engagement ring, which evidently I had purchased myself, but I have no idea who I bought the ring for." Karen puts both hands up to cover her gaping mouth. Apparently, she believes she knows who the ring was bought for.

I hold up the Claddagh ring and allow Emily to see it. I wait until I see recognition in her eyes, then say, "And this strange ring was in my dresser, which I obviously nabbed in order to give the correct size to the jeweler. So, it stands to reason that whoever this ring belongs to, is also the girl I had hoped to one day marry."

I don't bother asking. I step into Emily's space, grab her hand and attempt to slide the Claddagh ring onto her ring finger.

She begins to cry. She's either one of those girls who falls apart at any mention of being a bride, or she's a huge fan of Cinderella. Or perhaps she really does love me.

I get the ring all the way onto her finger, look straight into her misty eyes and say, "Perfect fit."

Turning back to the crowd, I say, "The good news is I found my journal... and everyone here is in it. I've just recently read the different stories of how we all met. Don't worry, the journal spoke highly of all of you, but as many of you can imagine, it spoke most highly of this woman here.

"And to my utter amazement, it spoke highly of J-Jesus Christ." I pause. The name seems to stick in my throat. Everyone just heard it. I have always been the type to deal with embarrassment by naming it. I say, "I am an atheist. That I had a personal relationship with Christ is a hard thing for me to even say, much less consider."

As I speak I can see my beloved's face turning. I know if I continue talking this way, she will run out of the room crying as she did on day one.

I act fast. "Emily, I want you to know that the whole time I was telling you I was a Christian, I was also telling my journal. I've kept a journal for twenty-three years and I've never lied to it. A man typically has no reason to lie to his own journal. When I told you I was Christian, I truly was."

Someone in the room mumbles sadly, "Was?"

I breathe in deep. I look only at Emily but motion to the room. "This is why I need your help. There were pages missing from my journal. It was torn out by the woman who drugged me. And it happened to contain the... my... uh... my conversion."

"So?" Emily asks.

"So, I am missing information. I am prepared to trust myself. I want to be with you. I want to accept Je—" *Dang it. Name got caught again.*

"Jesus," she says impatiently.

"I am missing information," I insist. "I don't know the full story. Just tell me what you said to me."

"What do you mean?"

"Tell me what you said to convert me."

"I didn't say anything."

"Well you had to have told me something."

She sighs. "Are you prepared to change your entire life if you find out I won a debate with you?"

"N-n—" I say boldly.

"It never happened," she assures me. "I could never win a debate with you."

Although I'm 90% sure that's an insult, I choose to cling to the 10% chance it's a compliment. I press, "But there has to have been a reason. There has to be something I heard, something I read, or something one of you said, maybe…" I gesture pleadingly to the room. "There has to be some new piece of datum, something I didn't know, or maybe misunderstood, perhaps something I never considered before, or something I had thought of, but just barely missed it. Please! I must have told you what it was. I must have shared with you this new thinking. This precious new thinking." I open my arms to the room, ready to receive anything they can offer.

Emily's face is changing. She's starting to understand just what it is I need from her. She whispers, "You've got it all wrong," and shakes her head slowly. "In all my years as a Christian, I have seen and heard of a lot of converts. But I've never seen or heard of anyone who was converted by a clever argument."

"No, there must've been something. There must have! Think."

"No." Even as I become frantic, she remains calm.

"Well, I, uh, you mean I didn't tell you what triggered it? That aha moment? I was atheist one minute and Christian the next; there had to have been an epiphany."

"There was."

"And if I had an epiphany, something had to have triggered it."

"Something triggered it." She is being vague here and it's a bit frustrating.

"And did I tell you what it was?"

"You did."

"Well…" I hold out my hands in supplication. Another minute of suspense and I will be on my knees. I plead, "Well, what was it?"

"We kissed."

The room is silent. I don't mean for my face to show disappointment. It's so hard for my mind to shift gears. While this is obviously exciting news, I'm trying to deal with the heartbreak of not finding what I came to find, and worse finding that it may not even exist.

Everyone waits for my response.

I smile and say, "Well, we could kiss again." I'm only half-kidding. I pucker my lips and lean toward her.

Like a ninja, her two fingers are instantly covering my lips. She commands, "Wait!" Now it's my smile beneath her fingertips. I can't help but smile right now. "You've read about our time together from your own words." She pulls her finger off my lips and I instantly miss her touch. She continues, "You've heard the story. You must've heard you were happy."

"I sounded happy," I nod.

"You must have heard you had a home."

"I had a home," I nod.

"You want to force your mind to decide. You want me to show you evidence so incontrovertible that you simply *must* believe. You don't *want* it to be a choice."

I narrow my eyes, tilt my head, and ask, "Is it a choice?"

"It's a choice if you kiss me. It is a choice if you walk out that door forever. You don't want it to be a choice. You've made an idol out of reason. It has crushed you. You have chosen to serve reason, not God, and now you are its slave."

"Reason's slave?"

"It has robbed you of your choice, like a tyrant."

"No."

"Then choose; you know what your heart wants to choose."

"I can't."

She smiles haughtily and begins to speak, "You—"

"Wait," I interrupt. "I choose you. I choose all of you. And, yes— okay?— Yes, I choose God. I just don't know if I fully..."

"...believe in him," she finishes for me.

I shrug and frown.

She shrugs, "Okay then, kiss me."

"Really?" I say too much like a schoolboy.

"Yes."

I can't believe it. I remember the joyous balloon in my chest that came just with the touch of her hand. Before me stands a woman who can excite me with just a smile at her fingertips, just a wisp of her hair, and just a blush. Now she is asking me to kiss her lips. I tremble.

I step to her and take her in my arms. It is strange with everyone watching us, but it also feels right. It feels like I am home again. Our faces draw in close and I pause. I pull back far enough to look into her eyes and say, "You know what this is? This is our *second* first kiss."

We kiss.

As I pull away awkwardly, the disappointment on my face is evident.

She sees this and scrunches her brow.

I say, "Hmm... Maybe our *first second* kiss might work."

"What?" She slaps me—pretty hard actually—but there is laughter in her eyes.

I say, "Babe, I've been atheist all my life, it's going to take a better kiss than that."

She reaches to slap me again, but I catch her hand and use it to pull her in closer. I can't stop smiling. With my face close to hers, I say, "This is how we were?" I smile, *slaphappy*. "This is how we were, isn't it?"

She rolls her eyes. "This is how *you* were. This is what I had to put up with."

I laugh.

Finally, she grabs the back of my head and kisses me properly. It is a great kiss and it lasts—despite the people there—a long time. When we pull free the crowd applauds. They are always a great audience when I need them most.

She takes my hand and walks me to the other side of the room. "Show's over, folks," she says to her friends and they eventually start talking again amongst themselves.

We are alone now. She's finally granting me the private conversation I've been asking for. With great trepidation she asks, "Well?"

"Well," I laugh. "Did I turn into a prince? It's not magic." I smile.

"I know," she says, but in such a tone that implies she does not know. "Did anything…"

"Come to me? Yes. I learned through great, tender, sweet-as-honey revelation that I love you." My tone is light and my face is joyful, but it changes slightly when I see the look on hers. With a little ironic laughter in my voice I say, "Oh, we haven't said that to each other yet, huh?"

The blush is spreading in patches on her skin like dye on fabric.

"Oops," I smile.

"Oops," she whispers.

"Well, I do love you. So it should be said. I … love… you. And, isn't that enough?" I grab her chin and raise it to look at me. I am being so dramatic. With all the weight and meaning and deep-felt conviction of a perfidious poet, I insist, "Isn't that enough?"

Why, isn't that enough to last a lifetime?

Tears fill her eyes once more, she shakes her head and whispers, "No. That isn't enough."

Just saying the words makes her cry more. A tipping point in her tear ducts has been reached, her cheeks and neck are transitioning from splotchy-red to solid and I can tell she can't handle this. I know she's a mere moment away from walking out.

"Wait. Wait." I can see what a precarious moment this is, and I advance oh so gently. "Wait. I got baptized. I read the whole story. That was real. That happened. You waited for me. You did everything right. Then after my baptism, you finally believed me. You finally could date me." My words are firm, but my tone and my facial expressions indicate that there was some question there at the end.

"Yes," she says. "That's how it happened."

I can see my gentleness is working. She's remembering the good times and that our story did have a happy ending. "Yes, and that was real. That was a decision I made freely, perhaps the last decision I made freely, because ever since I was drugged, nothing's been real. Can you possibly imagine how strange this has been and what I have been through?"

She nods. "But you said you're no longer Christian?"

I try to come up with a way to explain this to her. "Do you remember the first day in my class, the day I made you…"

She nods quickly—*with kindness and mercy*—both affirming that she remembers and granting me permission to not finish that sentence.

"Well, that day from my vantage point was nine days ago."

Her face changes as she is considering the immense scope of all that means.

"I didn't choose to be atheist again. I didn't backslide. I simply forgot… or was made to forget."

She stares off, blinking away tears. *She's so pretty.* She turns her face to me and asks me directly, "Do you want to become Christian?"

I don't have a clue. I really don't know, but I think I loved this girl from the moment I saw her and—this is interesting—I don't think I can actually hate God and love her. If the goodness I see in her is God, then I have been wrong about God all this time. *That's good. I'll go with that.* I say, "I think I have been wrong about God this whole time."

She smiles. "But do you want to become Christian?"

Right now, I am prepared to say anything to get her to stay. "Yes." I don't think it's a lie. "I walked into this party, asking for… well, really, asking for just that." I motion back to the spot where this all happened. "I was asking for help to become Christian."

"It's not going to be an argument," she says.

I shrug insouciantly. "Okay, but it will happen. It happened once; it will happen again."

I can see on her face how badly she wants this, so I go in to close the deal. I place my hand on top of hers and squeeze. I say, "I will be Christian again."

She breathes in deep and I watch her exquisite frame expand. She says, "I want to believe you."

I quip, "Listen, if I were going to lie, I wouldn't have told you I'm still atheist. If I were going to lie, I would have shown up here with a Bible and a tambourine, singing *Jesus loves me this I know*."

I can see that was too flippant for her, so I immediately go in for some damage control.

I say, "I followed you to Olive Garden. I want you to know. I looked up your address from the insurance and followed you around town until I knew where you'd be when."

She laughs. "Yeah, you already confessed to that one… right

before your baptism."

I smile. I often impress myself, but not usually with my honesty. *Perhaps she had really made me into a better man.* I say, "But the reason I'm telling you now is because it's the only lie I ever told you. I've read it in my journal, you can read it too if you want. The whole time I was saying I was Christian, and you didn't believe me, that whole time I was telling the truth."

She nods. "I know."

"Okay," I say. "I understand why you didn't believe me then, but I'm begging you to believe me now."

She nods again. "Okay."

"Okay?"

She nods. "Okay."

"Okay, what?" I ask anxiously.

"Okay... let's do it." She reaches out with the hand I am not holding to grab my other hand. "Let's give this another try."

My heart sings. I squeeze both her hands so tight.

She adds, "But..."

No. No but.

"I've spent so much time unsure," she says.

"I know," I tell her.

"You have to promise me something. You have to promise never to lie to me."

"I promise," I insist too quickly, but both my hands instantly go slack.

She feels it and looks at me inquisitively.

I slowly pull them both away from hers. We are no longer touching. *Uh-oh! I think I'm about to impress myself with my honesty again... Dammit.* "There's one more thing."

I see her face change and I beg my mouth to stop.

"I want to tell you everything, because I want to show you I'm never going to lie, not even by omission."

No, don't do this.

"What is it?" she asks impatiently.

"Well, I told you after I was drugged... everything that happened then... it wasn't real."

No, seriously dude, don't do this.

"What happened?" she pushes.

"If you remember the man I was... I was terrible. I was wretched... I didn't have God. I didn't have you..."

"What did you do?" Her voice is hard as jade.

"She told me your story, the girl who drugged me. Really, I thought she was you. She told me our exact story, only she played the heroine. She told me about the car crash, and the restaurant... but in her version, I won. So... so... we were both atheists. We had no promise to God, no moral-based proscriptions. And... and I didn't even know you existed, really." There's one thing I can safely assume about Emily; since she's unmarried, she's untouched. She'll make a slightly older bride, especially for her community. That's a long time to wait, but I'm certain she has. How can I confess this now? How can I tell her the act she's regarded as sacred her whole life, I treated as commonplace? I can't, not to her. What I could mention so casually to Kevin, I can't even breathe to her. I can see the impatience growing on her virgin face. I look for some mercy or compassion. *No, don't see any.* "We were atheists," I insist. "And atheist don't wear purity rings..." She knows now. I continue to stumble, "I thought I loved her..."

Emily says nothing. Far from out-of-control tears, her face is calcified with disappointment. I reach out to her but she recoils back. She takes a step further away from me, her dry eyes looking into mine.

"I'm so sorry," I beg. "It was all so confusing. I was drugged. I was lied to..."

She's not listening.

In one last gesture of unmistakable symbolism and cruel finality, she pulls the Claddagh ring off her finger and presses it hard into my palm. She turns to walk out of the room, heading to one of the bedrooms in the back of the house.

I move to follow her, but Sophie—from out of nowhere—steps into my way and dutifully raises a hand to stop me. She says, "We've just got to give her time."

I accept this, although my heart is breaking. I let her see me nod.

With nothing left to do but leave myself, I head out the door without saying goodbye to any of them. But Sophie follows fast on my heels. I feel her beside me and she speaks in kind, comforting tones, "Please don't blame Emily. Put yourself in her shoes. She liked you so much, and waited for you for so long. And all the while, she felt she couldn't be with you. Then you convert, but she doesn't believe you." She shrugs. "She was just scared. Finally, you get baptized and finally she is free and clear to give her entire heart to you, to love you without fear. And that's the exact moment you send her a rude text and stop answering her calls. You ignore the note she left on your door and then we all hear this strange story about you and a painting..."

The things she's saying bother me more than I can explain and anger creeps up my throat. I hadn't been able to picture Emily's side— from lack of info, not lack of empathy—and now that I'm hearing it, I see that she too has been a victim of that dimpled witch. "I couldn't help it," I say as I stride, not slowing.

"Whatever the reason," Sophie stresses. "It happened and she can't just bounce back like it didn't." Most of what Sophie is saying, she's only saying because she hasn't yet heard the bombshell I dropped on Emily just now.

I'm too distraught to carry on with the conversation, so I slip into my car without another word and close the door rudely behind me.

Sophie is undaunted. She bangs on my window and yells through the glass, "She cried for three days straight!"

My engine starts up and I hit the gas.

I still hear her as I go, "She cried for three solid days!"

Chapter Thirty-Eight

I'm outside the home I grew up in. I didn't come here seeking answers from the sight of the property, and no one from my past still lives here. Looking at the house now, I feel next to nothing. The new owners have painted it yellow and they have had my favorite tree removed. It makes me a little sad, but not in any real way.

But like I said, I am seeking no answers from the house. No, I came here for a starting point. I head east out of my driveway, through the old neighborhood where I grew up. I am heading toward the grocery store where my mother used to shop, but I pass it. I drive until the traffic falls away and the highway narrows to just one lane.

I'm setting off in search of a small blue church.

About 2 hours outside of town, I am convinced I've passed it. I am convinced that I don't have enough information from my young memory to recreate the journey. I wonder if the church would still look the same, or if it exists at all. After twenty-eight years, it could have been sold and turned into a day-spa. They may have ditched the comforting blue façade and replaced it with something trendy, bright colors and neon. Or maybe it's been demolished. How sad.

I am sure I missed it. I'm sure I've gone too far.

I don't know why I've driven all this way. I have no clue what I expect to find here. This is the only place I've ever felt God, or at least felt *something*. This is the place where I witnessed a miracle. Perhaps not a miracle, perhaps just an answered prayer. But what's the difference really? It was a miracle to me.

My car slows down as I consider my next move: keep going, backtrack, or give up altogether. I crest the hill and can see a gas station in the distance. I could use a fill-up, so I pull in.

I decide to go inside to pay, but really, I want to ask the attendant here about the church. She's an older lady with blond hair and gray roots that are starting to show. And honestly, she doesn't seem all that nice. I hand her a bill. "Twenty dollars on pump one," I say, despite the fact that mine's the only car there.

She stabs some buttons on her machine and the beeping it produces is my only response.

I begin, "Say, I was through this way a long time ago and I remember seeing a blue church." Her face definitely changes, but I can't quite read her expression. "I was looking for it, traveling east." I point. "Have I passed it, or do I need to keep heading that way?"

I can read the look now, and it is irritation. She says brusquely, "You passed it."

"Thank you," I tell her, then pump my gas and get into my car.

When I pull up to the street, I feel certain I should keep driving forward. This lady's mistaken. There is no way I could have passed a blue church. I deliberate, then finally I side with the unhappy lady and turn back the way I came.

I drive slowly, searching for anything that might look like the church. It could be half-covered in trees now. It could look very different than I see it in my childhood memory. I could've even been wrong—at ten—about the side of the street it was on.

I carefully scan both sides, then see it. It least I *think* I see it. I pull my car to a sad stop outside the building and get out.

The church has been abandoned, left to the weeds. The joyous blue paint has faded. Layers of dirt and grime, plus UV rays from the sun, have left the walls a non-descript sepia tone. The sickening color makes the whole building just look exhausted. The glass has long since broken away and the openings in the windows have been recommissioned by spiders. Shattered glass still lies on the ground, dangerous to any child who might come by, yet no one has bothered to clean it up.

My heart sinks.

The front door is cracked open about six inches, so I walk inside. There is more broken glass inside the lobby area, plus a few piles of dead leaves from the big oak outside. I hear something from inside the sanctuary and I wonder if I'm not alone. I step into the doorway to the main room and take in the full scene. What I first thought might have been the squeak of a door hinge, was most likely a rat.

No one's here. I am all alone in the sanctuary, perhaps more alone than I've ever been. The place, once so beautiful and inspiring is now completely desecrated. There's garbage and rat droppings all along the walls. I feel a crush of disappointment and it makes me weak. I try to breathe in strength, but the smell of mold, wet wood, and rodents only helps to reinforce my feelings of disgust.

The soiled carpet is so worn, it's hard as cement. When I walk in further, I hear an unnerving crunch beneath my shoes. I watch my feet to avoid stepping on the dead cockroaches.

The stained-glass windows, which had once so inspired me, are now shattered and lie mostly on the floor. There's dirt and dead flies all along the window sills. The broken glass of these works of art is mixed in with broken glass from beer and whiskey bottles.

The silence, which comforted and cradled my heart, is disgraced by the sickening sound of rats scurrying through the walls. Wind and cars can be heard through the missing windows. A broken gutter clanks outside as the wind pushes it repeatedly against the wall, like a passing bell for the beauty that was lost.

The pews, which had been so polished, are covered in dirt. The brass ornamentation along the arms of the pews once shone bright and proud but are green and tarnished now. The vaulted ceiling had once made the place feel open. Now the shocking number of cobwebs covering the rafters give it a haunted look.

The warm breeze of the furnace once stroked my skin so gently, it produced a moment I remembered for twenty-eight years. But now the air is stagnant, thick, and heavy. It is hard to breathe and I feel like it's choking me. The eerie stillness reminds me of death.

The round stained-glass window above the altar, whose light I had dipped my hand into while I spoke with God, now has a broken tree branch protruding through it.

A filthy sleeping bag in one corner is giving off a faint smell of urine, and it makes me angry. There are cigarette burns on the pew and a pile of butts. I notice a discarded condom in the aisle, and both my fists clench tight. I can't quite read the words spray-painted in graffiti behind the pulpit and I know I'm better off if I don't try. The large wooden cross at the front is still in one piece, but a terrible crack runs straight through it.

I stagger down the aisle, crestfallen, like it had been my home or something, like I was returning to my own house after a fire or a flood.

I lower my body down onto one of the pews. Someone had carved three words into it with a knife. Surrounded by all this blight, I can't decide if the carving was the taunting graffiti of a secular vandal, or the desperate plea of a half-hearted believer. It reads "Where is God?"

Overwhelmed by a feeling I don't fully understand, I lower my head and close my eyes. I know there was something beautiful here once, and it jars me that it could be violated by those who…who *knew not what they do*. I think about that young girl, and how I took what I wanted from her. I didn't see the beauty and the majesty of a life. I used her body like a thing while I was in love with someone else. I used her body *because* I was in love with someone else.

I force my head back up and force myself to open my eyes. I know one thing for certain now. I know what happened here. The vandalism, the desecration and neglect—I did it. It was me.

It was me. It was me. Tears begin streaming down my face. I lean forward and rest my forehead on the back of the pew like a drunk who's about to pass out. And I weep.

I sob uncontrollably. Like a child. Like an addict. My body shakes in heaves and in that forsaken church, I am face to face with the demon from my youth: I am unloved.

I had forgotten what it felt like, that feeling of being *unloved*. I thought I had escaped it. I ran so hard for so long. Then one day I could no longer see it behind me and thought it was finally gone, but still I ran twice as long, twice as fast. Then I ran some more until I was convinced there was no possible way these feelings could ever catch up.

But the first time I stop, here they are, waiting close by the whole time. And I hate myself. I hate everything I've ever done. I hate pictures of me. I hate to see me on video and I hate my voice on tape. I hate my brain. I hate my thoughts that keep coming and coming and coming and won't let me rest.

I'm not trying to make a choice.

But I cry out.

In that rat-infested church, I cry out. Amidst the urine and the feces, I cry out. Beside the graffiti and broken glass, I cry out.

"Help me!"

I don't mean to say it; I don't think, but the words spring forth from the depths of my pain, "Help me! I need you..."

My mind adds one word and forces my heart to say it, "...Emily."

As if I were addressing the whole thing to her.

I try to wipe the flood of tears, but they keep coming and I wail, "Help me, Emily. I can't do this on my own; I'm completely dependent on you. Only you can make me happy. Only you can take away this hurt. Remove the black mark on my heart and make me whole again. I'm so sorry for what I did. I'm sorry for everything I've ever done. I was always so proud. I was always such a fool. I rebelled against you. My heart was black. Please forgive me. Please forgive me... Emily."

END PART THREE

PART FOUR

Chapter Thirty-Nine

It's day two of my pity party. I haven't done any drinking, but I've done a whole lot of thinking. Perhaps the drinking would have been a more sensible choice.

Bottom line: my life is out of control. I lost my job, which is devastating for a man—no fun for a woman but devastating for a man. Also, I don't know if I would want it back. That's more painful than it sounds. I think knowing what I want and not being able to have it would be preferable to having no idea what I want, or even who I *am*.

And of course, I'm powerless over that whole situation.

I'm in love with a woman who definitely hates me—possibly still loves me but definitely hates me. And even if she does still love me, we can't be together because I don't believe in her God. I feel powerless there too.

The first day was the worst day. I called her in the morning and left a voicemail begging for forgiveness. Every hour I didn't hear from her, I lost ten IQ points—a strange phenomenon, but very real. By eleven o'clock that night, I called her, hung up on her voicemail, called her again, hung up on her voicemail, called her again, hung up on her voicemail... I waited ten minutes to give her a chance to call back. *After all, I'm not pathetic.* Then I called her again, hung up on her voicemail, called her again, hung up on her voicemail, then called her again, hung up on her voicemail, and called her again. *What have I become?*

Shortly after that, I received a text from her friend, Sophie. It read:

Just give her time

I stared at the text for a long time. It didn't say "Get a life," or "Leave my friend alone, you creep." There was kindness in it. There was acknowledgement that I was hurting too. I appreciated that.

That was yesterday. Since then, I've been lying in bed and closing my eyes and trying to convince myself there is a God. But you can't choose your own beliefs. This one insuperable objection keeps repeating in my mind: *you cannot choose your own beliefs.*

Beliefs are the products of reason applied to observation. They're not things we make up at random. I envision it like seeing my pillow on the bed beside me but telling myself it isn't there. Or the blanket, or my clothes. I feel my clothes on my body, I see them, and I remember putting them on. It's not a process of free will that makes me believe I'm clothed. I escape into my mind and tell myself, despite all that, I believe I'm naked. I focus so hard. I concentrate like a Jedi Master, summoning all the power of my will, nearly popping all the blood vessels in my head. But it doesn't work.

I plead with her in my heart. *This isn't fair. We cannot choose our beliefs. I will do anything you ask of me. Anything possible! I can't do what you're asking me. I want to, but it isn't possible!*

I have no more resistance. I need her here. I need her to come to this lonesome room. Come to me and save me. Take away this pain. I just need her here.

She said I was a slave to my logic. I can hear my old retorts—booby traps that I keep rigged in my mind twenty-four hours a day, seven days a week, just waiting for some Christian to wander in by chance and trip them: *"I am a slave to logic, like I am a slave to what's real. Guilty! I am confined in what I believe is real by the cruel despot, reality."*

But I can no longer recite them with the same zeal, because I no longer care what is real. For the first time in my life, I am prepared to say, *You want me to deny reality? Very well! I will. Without hesitation, I will. But please Emily, show me how.*

At one point, I convince myself that walking into the shower with my clothes on would be the final proof of *mind over despotism,* will over reason. I can do this. I can be set free! Our minds are so powerful. And mine is more powerful than most, so I've always argued. I once convinced myself that Casimiro was a brilliant man of indispensable talent; I can surely do *this*.

I stand and watch the water run, picturing the moment that I step in, letting the water cover my bare chest. How good it will feel to know that I had broken the chains of logic's tyranny and that I am in control. Then I can have her. Then I can have God and hope, and a Savior and eternal life. I can be happy then. I can finally *rest.*

I hesitate. The water is warming up nicely now. The glass walls of the shower are starting to fog and I get a bit of unexpected encouragement: "Emily + James." I tell myself it's a sign from God, although I don't believe it.

Yes, I do believe it and I am naked. It's time now and I take one step into the shower. I feel my pant legs shift.

No, I don't.

I walk into the shower with all my clothes on. Water darkens the fabric quickly and the weight pulls down on my shoulders—heavy as my depression.

I feel stupid. I know it's not a victory. I never once doubted my clothes. I didn't once even come close, and I will never once believe in God or Jesus or Heaven or any of it. Never once, *again.*

Sopping wet, I have proven my determination. I have proven my love for this girl and the fact that I will do anything for her. Anything possible.

I step out and I change into something dry. My movements are slow because I want to postpone the inevitable: the moment in which I have to ask, *what do I do now?* I can't keep up this binge-thinking. It's produced nothing more than a set of wet clothes.

I feel like 100% of my problems have no answer.

I look at my books on my bookshelf. In my former life, just perusing the spines would bring me solace. "There's your comfort," I had once reprimanded my own mentor. But they bring me no comfort now. They are a poor substitute for love.

I decide to try prayer. I feel silly but I get down on both knees beside my bed. I fold my hands, and bow my head, and I pray.

The prayer is rather hostile. I say, "Listen God, if You're real, You already know who I am, and You already know what I'm going through. So, help me. Just tell me what to do. Tell me what to do, God; I'm listening."

Here I wait.

"I'm listening, God."

I wait some more.

"Okay… okay…" I say, half smug and self-righteous, half genuinely disappointed. "I didn't think so."

I stretch out across the bed, depressed. I grab a pillow and place it underneath my wet head and something overcomes me. It isn't an answer from God, it's just a thought that popped into my head out of nowhere. It's insane. Yes, yes, it's clearly insane, but it's an urge that's so strong, and I know it's just what I need right now.

I instantly grab my wallet and my keys, and head out the door. As I drive, the idea grows stronger in my mind; I'm starting to think I just might do it. I pull up to a hardware store and head straight to the paint aisle. Standing before the wall of color swatches, I pull a few out and evaluate them. They aren't quite right and I shuffle a bit to my left to investigate a few more. There's a woman in my way and I try to force a smile. The smile must look as awkward as it feels because the lady decides to leave. *Good.* I step into the spot she vacated and find the absolute perfect color. *This one must be it.* The color still affects me. It is vibrant without being too exciting; it is tranquil and welcoming. Just as I remember.

I read the label on the swatch: "Azure Blue."

I load up my basket with paint rollers, trays, brushes, drop cloths, tape, scrubbing brushes, cleaning supplies, rat traps, brass polish, some towels, a broom, a dustpan, a hammer, a crowbar, and some work gloves. That's all I can think of right now. I'm sure I'll have to come back.

I put it all on my Lowes card, having no idea when I will be able to pay it off.

I'm driving to the old dilapidated church with my car filled with supplies and I have no idea why. I don't know what I'm doing, but I know that I am actually doing *something*. I don't know why I am doing this, but I know I *can* do it.

Perhaps I have just found a way to put off that annoying question: *What now?* I tell myself this should at least buy me three weeks, a month? Only God knows.

I pull up to the front of the church, park my car, and decide to immediately get to work. But before I do, I pull out my earbuds and my old phone. I investigate my old, new playlists—music I've never seen before, but Kevin told me I could trust myself.

The only name I recognize is Bebo Norman because I mentioned him in my journal twice. So, now's the chance to test Kevin's theory, I guess. I select my *Bebo* playlist and hit play.

Chapter Forty

I start out by removing all the weeds, vines, and debris from the outside of the church. I clear up the broken glass and do a general cleaning of the outside walls to see what repairs I need to make on the siding. Despite its sad appearance, it seems to have maintained its structural integrity.

I repair the soffits and fascia along the roofline and remove a few broken window frames.

I'm staring up at the progress of the work and I'm feeling pretty good for the first time in a long time. The muscles I haven't used since I worked my way through school are all screaming at me, but it's a pleasant sort of pain. The weather's beautiful and I'm impatient to start painting. I know the color which once made such an impression on me in my youth will keep my spirits up and fortify my morale. Plus, there's no electricity, *so painting it is then.*

I started on the left side of the building and am working my way to the right.

I haven't checked my watch in forever—seems like such a gainfully-employed thing to do—but my stomach tells me it's close to dinnertime when I hear the sound of tires on gravel behind me. I turn my head to see a police car. My interest is piqued, I guess, but not enough for me to stop working.

I hear a car door followed by footsteps. I glance over to see a portly policeman in a beige uniform approaching. He doesn't see me watching him because he is evaluating the state of the building.

I turn back to focus on my work without greeting him. The footsteps get closer, close enough for him to be sure that I know he's here, even with my headphones in, but I still don't turn to meet him.

"Looks like you're fixing up the ol' church." The voice is folksy and friendly and I give him extra points for not leading with, *What are you doing?*

"Yes, sir," I answer, although I know he wants more.

"Looks like you're doing a great job," he says and I hear his feet shuffle even closer. I can now see his shadow cast onto the wall beside my own.

"Thank you, sir." I still offer nothing.

"Is it just you here?"

"Just me, sir."

"What company are you with?"

"No company."

"You work for yourself?"

"Actually, I'm unemployed."

"Unemployed from what?"

"Professor of philosophy," I say as I dip my paintbrush into more paint. *Now it should be clear.*

I see the shadow of a hand scratching the shadow of a head.

He says, "Sir, did anyone *ask* you to do this?"

I put down my brush. I turn around to look him full in the face for the first time. "No." I shake my head and my whole body shimmies in a confused shrug. "To be completely honest with you sir, I have no idea why I'm fixing this church." I look him dead in the eye.

He has the chance to say something and he doesn't.

"But I know it needs fixing. And frankly, not a whole lot in my life has made sense for a while, but this does. Nothing I've tried to do has worked out, but this is working."

He looks up at the job I've been doing and I'm pretty sure I see approval. Suddenly we are just two men, looking at a job that was done either correctly, or incorrectly. He lets me see him nod, but still asks, "Do you know whose property this is?"

I look at the building one more time. With all the sincerity I can muster, I say, "Sir, all I know is… is…" *What do I know? I don't know anything.* My heart is constricted. He is going to make me stop. I can't let that happen, but I have no words. "is… that…" *I can do this; I am an erudite and… something college professor whose vocabulary is… something.* I take a deep breath. "All I know is that this side," I point to the left, "looks better than that side," I point to the right. "All I know is, it'd be a crying shame if you asked me to stop."

The cop looks at the church and he looks at me. And maybe he likes drama, or maybe country people just take their time, but he sure is slow to answer. Finally, he says, "I'm pretty sure the owner won't mind at all," then turns to head back to his car.

That prompts me to ask him, "You know who this church belongs to?"

"Yes, sir."

"Who does it belong to?" I ask.

He says one word before getting back into his car, unfortunately I don't catch it. As I pick up my paintbrush and get back to work, I'm pleased with how our exchange had gone, but my mind is still working to figure out his one-syllable parting.

Oh… It finally dawns on me: *God.* He must've said God. This makes me smile more than I would've expected, and I get back to work.

Chapter Forty-One

I am driving home at the end of the day. I can't keep my mind off Emily. I want to call her of course, but I can't. I pretty much eliminated that option the day I called her seven times in a row. Or was it eight? No, the ball is in her court now. It pretty much has to be. She has to be the one to make the next move. Why? Because that's the way she's indicated she wants it, and if I love her, I have to respect that.

There is literally nothing I can do. That's her wish and I can honor it, but it's so painful. Nothing hurts me quite like having no control. There is nothing worse in all of life than being powerless.

Except maybe waiting.

But I'm not powerless; I have the power to rebuild this church. I'll be honest, it feels good to see progress. It feels good to see the product of one's own hands. I think back to my college days when I worked construction jobs. I was good at it. There was one brief moment when I thought about ditching philosophy and becoming a general contractor. Really there was. I can't think of two more different extremes. I wonder now what my life might have been like.

I throw parties and invite all the egghead-types, but my only true friend is Kevin—down-to-earth Kevin, who knows about football and not Intersectional Feminist Theory. Maybe I really was meant for something different.

I think about the people who might have lived in the homes I built. I picture traveling in the future a hundred years and finding houses I helped to build still standing.

And I think about Emily.

I am tempted to turn my car around and return to the church. I'm discovering there's a fatal flaw in my plan to distract my mind from her: the two-hour drive. All day at the site I didn't think of her. *Did I just call it the site? Old habit.* For twelve hours I felt powerful and in control, but what does it matter if those feelings just store up and assail me all at once? I didn't escape these demons; they were just waiting for me in the car the whole time.

I've been listening to Christian audiobooks. Every time they say something crazy, I think, *I could never be Christian and therefore never be with Emily.* But then when they say something that really makes sense, I think, *Okay I can do this. I should call Emily right now.*

I've tried listening to music, both my new Christian playlists and my old secular ones. Nothing. I turn the volume up for the music to lift my mood, but it's like that scene where Luke doesn't know the Force yet and he can't quite lift his spaceship out of the swamp.

I finally get home, and it's even worse. I'm so worn out from such a long day that I collapse in bed with all my clothes still on. I turn out the light on my nightstand and I… lie awake. I stare at the ceiling. I can't sleep. My muscles are aching and I'm exhausted from all day in the sun. I need some restorative sleep more than ever, but still it eludes me.

I can't stop thinking about her. I check and re-check my phone just to make sure I haven't missed any messages. I am well aware that if I do nothing and wait for her to call me, she likely never will. But I'm also aware that if I call her, it means I have no respect for her and can't truly claim I love her.

Still I think I might call her. Because doing nothing is too painful.

I reason with myself. If she loves me, she will call me. If she doesn't love me, calling her will accomplish nothing. If the only way I can get her to see me is to act like a persistent salesman trying to hit his boss's quota, what kind of connection are we likely to have? Do I really want a relationship built upon a clever sales pitch?

Isn't that kind of what she was trying to tell me about God? Interesting.

I can't badger her. I can't talk her into it. All I can do is love her, stay open, and wait for her heart to change.

Was this what she went through waiting for me to come to Him? Poor girl. It's really painful feeling so powerless and with no end in sight.

Chapter Forty-Two

I get to the church late because I had such a horrible night. My muscles are tense. My shoulders are stiff. And my lower back is killing me. My body isn't used to manual labor anymore and a lot has changed since I did this in college. After just one day of work, my body feels like it's eighty years old. I hardly get anything done all morning.

This is stupid. Why am I doing this? What on Earth possessed me? I decide to work inside today and begin to sweep the hard wood floors behind the pulpit, but every move I make hurts—not my body so much as my heart. Apathy engulfs me. Suddenly I don't know why the dirt and the grime is better in the dustpan than on the floor. So, why am I sweeping it? I don't know why it's better for my lungs to expand and contract. I don't know why it's better that my heart remains beating. So, why am I doing anything?

I freeze because I have no purpose to move left or right, forward or backward. I have no purpose at all, nothing to strive for, and nothing to look forward to. The broom falls out of my hand. A pathetic amount of floor has been swept.

I feel a connection with this church. There's simply too much work to be done, and I just don't want to do it. I feel an overwhelming urge to just lie down in the filth. I want to live out the rest of my time as a rat and curse the people who say it's better to be human.

"I'm going to have to take those pews out," I actually mumble to myself. "I'm going to have to take those pews out when I remove that carpet." There's too much to do. I can't do it. It's not possible. I take a quick look at how the pews are attached. There's a way to remove them but it's not immediately obvious to me.

I turn and walk out. Just like that. I started on a whim and I quit on a whim. *Why?* Because I'm a ridiculous person. I get in my car and drive.

There's a liquor store I pass on the drive over here, and I pretend I don't know that's where my car is taking me. I pull to a stop in the parking lot, almost between the lines. I grab the door handle and I think about it. I remember reading when Emily grabbed the door handle of my car, and I imagine how my whole life depended on her not opening it.

Emily.

The most pathetic protestation of a heartsick adolescent crosses my mind, *If she just knew how much I was suffering, then she'd want to be with me.* I immediately push such foolishness out of my head, and scramble hard to gather some dignity together.

"I *do* want my heart to beat." I hope this talking to myself out loud bit is not becoming a habit. "I *do* want air in my lungs." That's about all I can say definitively, but perhaps it's enough to build on.

I turn my car back on and hit the gas. Having freshly decided I want to live, self-preservation propels me far from the liquor store. I'm lonely and heartbroken and unemployed. I can't sleep. I can't act. If I throw alcohol into this tinderbox, the whole thing might likely go up in flames.

Instead, I turn the car to the hardware store. I pick up some heavy-duty trash bags, a face mask, some lanterns, some batteries, some PVC pipe fittings, and 250 feet of NM cable. I have no idea how it got so late. There isn't much sunlight left in the day, and on top of my miserable mood, I add the fact that I've gotten nothing done all day.

I know the perfect job for me right now, gutting the drywall. I literally begin by punching a hole in the wall. I have to tear this place apart, I must strip it down until there's nothing left but the bare minimum required for it to continue standing. Then rebuild. There's an analogy in here somewhere.

I work until late and I realize it's time to leave, but I just can't face another long car ride, followed by the dreaded moment of trying to fall asleep. I check to see if I have missed any calls or any texts from Emily. *Nope.* The light coming in through the windows is gone, and I have to switch on my lanterns. I tell myself I just want to finish the part I'm working on. And I do.

An hour later I reach a stopping point. All the drywall has been removed in just the sanctuary. The tall ceilings make this job harder than I would have thought. I look out at the section still left to be done behind the pulpit and I just don't want to do it. But I don't want to head to my car, either. I have to admit I'm afraid. I fear being alone in my car. I fear being alone in my bed. I check to see if I've missed any calls or any texts from Emily. *No.*

There is an impressive number of trash bags filled with drywall in the sanctuary. In fact, I reached the end of the box. I have no idea when trash is picked up around here, but I know I have to get them out of my way.

Inside the church, the floor is covered in dirt, leaves, broken glass, rodent droppings, and now drywall dust. My ankles are starting to itch.

An hour passes and I start a new box of trash bags for the moldy insulation between the studs. It's disgusting and I wish I had a Shop-Vac, but the hardware store's been closed for hours. I refuse to quit working, despite pain in my muscles, despite pain in my shoulders, despite pain in my back. All of that is preferable to pain in my heart. I check my phone. *Nothing.*

Another hour passes. She hasn't called. I can't bring myself to head to my car. I can't bear to return home to my bed. The liquor store is closed.

It's too late to head home anyway. It's 3 a.m. I would only get there after 5 a.m. I didn't think this through. I came to a moment where all I wanted to do was to keep working, so like a child, I did only what I wanted to do in one moment with no regard for the next.

I know what I am doing though, there is no deluding myself. I am afraid of a future, so I avoid it. I have the unique ability to analyze the foolishness I'm engaged in, while continuing to engage in it. At least I hope it's unique. I wouldn't wish it on anyone.

The truth is, there's only one reason people ever do anything: they believe the alternative is worse. I'm going to work until I drop, because leaving my mind free from distraction is currently my biggest fear in life.

Time is merciless. After what felt like maybe ten minutes, I discover it's somehow after four. This plan is unsustainable. I've reached the end of me. I'm reduced. My muscles have given all they have to give. But I have no options. I am trapped, trapped in a pointless plan, pressed up against a humiliating barrier of human frailty. I have no chance for success. No chance for relief. I can't imagine an outcome that could free me from my horrific fate of loneliness. I can't imagine much of anything. My muscles are cloudy and my thoughts are aching. No... wait... my muscles are confused, and my thoughts... my thoughts are getting...

Chapter Forty-Three

I'm watching Emily.

I was right about one thing: she will be beautiful until the day she dies. She will be beautiful even if she lives to 969.

The fine wrinkles around her eyes have become bold. Bold is good. She's never returned to her pre-pregnancy weight, no matter how hard she tries, but the extra pounds look good on her. Her long eyelashes are gone. The baby must've really needed them because they disappeared from Emily's face, and a short time later, showed up on his. Fair enough; I still get to see them around.

Emily still has a supernatural blush, and she turns it on for me now. She must've known I was just thinking about her beauty.

"Stop it," she says.

"Stop what?"

"Staring at me."

"Never."

She rolls her eyes and looks down at the baby. She says, "How can you look at me, when you have something as beautiful as him in the room?"

"I could never explain it to you," I tell her.

Actually, I am grateful for the baby because he represents the best chance I have to tell her. I say, "The way you look at the baby, and the things you feel, that's what it's like for me when I look at you."

She doesn't believe me, because I talk too much.

I suddenly wish I didn't go on and on all the time. I wish this one truth about how she overwhelms me was the first and only thing I'd ever said on the matter.

"I think he's sleeping now," she says.

"You want me to put him back in the crib?" I ask.

"No, I've got him."

I roll over on the bed so I can watch her wrap the blanket around him.

It's the middle of the night, so my eyes close against my will. I muscle them back open, but they close again.

The next thing I feel is comfort surrounding me. After she tucked the baby in his blanket, she came over and tucked me in as well. She is forever a mother.

Chapter Forty-Four

I wake with a start. I feel... warm and comforted.

I open my eyes and see a cockroach. This one's alive and he seems to be studying me. I'm on the floor of the church in the center of the aisle. I must've fallen asleep right in the spot where I collapsed from pure exhaustion.

I literally worked myself unconscious because I was afraid of leaving my mind undistracted, but then what happened the second I fell asleep? *Yep. Of course, I dreamt of her. Of course, I did.*

I close my eyes again and pull my blanket in tight.

My mind is still mostly asleep and I try to remember the dream. Let's see, we had a baby, and—

Wait... what blanket?

I open my eyes again and am shocked to discover I have a blanket over me. *Emily?*

I've reached my nadir. I fell asleep at rock-bottom but woke up being carried by the kindness and grace of a stranger. My mind sorts through everything the blanket could mean—the most important of which is that I'm not alone. It only takes me a second to conclude Emily's not here and the idea is impossible. But I know this kindness is *Emily*, no matter who's face I might find.

I hear something, so I try to listen. It sounds like whispering. It sounds like... *praying*. It's coming from behind me so I roll over in order to wrench my head around. I see a man kneeling at the front of the church. He is kneeling deep with his forehead against the ground, before the broken cross. And he is desperately praying.

What's this? I muse. *My first parishioner?*

He's obviously trying to pray quietly in order not to wake me, and he's obviously the one who covered me with a blanket, so I have no reason to be afraid. I investigate the blanket; it's baby blue color is comforting. It's clean and fresh. That means he came here, saw me and went home for the blanket. That means he lives nearby.

He hasn't heard that I'm awake yet. I try to rise to my feet without making a sound, but a broken piece of glass prevents that.

He turns his face toward the sound and quickly makes his way to his own feet. I see him wipe the tears from his eyes. He does this in order to properly engage with me, not to hide them. He doesn't seem to be embarrassed in the least.

The two of us stand there, early in the morning, in a rat-infested church, and evaluate each other. Neither of us know what to say. I look down at my own clothes. He probably thinks I'm homeless. Why else would a man be lying on a floor that's covered in filth and feces? I look around the room. Most the drywall has been removed. There are brushes and rollers, some new and some covered in dried paint. There is a paint tray with a liner of dried azure blue. A pair of thick dirty work gloves rest on the edge of a pew next to an empty box of black garbage bags. None this is typical behavior for a homeless man—or a man who has a home. *What must this man think of me? What must he think I'm doing here?*

Wait a minute. What am *I* doing here? What is *he* doing here? I was here first. What kind of man is this? Who comes to an abandoned church just to pray? Maybe he's the homeless one. I study his clothes now—*squeaky clean.*

We are still just staring at each other.

I already discovered he's local, so I wonder if he once attended this church. I clear my throat to ask, "Was this your church?"

He looks away. "No," he says quickly, then adds, "I used to be a part of the congregation."

I nod.

Suddenly I realize that I don't know where my phone is. My hand reflexively checks my pocket. I pull it out and hit the home key. It's dead! Without saying another word to the man, I turn and run out of the church.

Chapter Forty-Five

I plug my phone into the car and wait for it to collect enough juice to power on. *Agonizing.* Finally, I see some life as my phone begins the process of restarting. *More agonizing.* After what seems like an eternity, my phone lets me check for new texts. Nothing. I check for new voicemails. Nothing.

I know it normally takes my phone half an hour to fully charge with the car battery, so I sit and stare at it. Nothing else to do. I figure by the time it's done charging the strange man inside the church will be done with his prayers and probably—hopefully—be long gone.

I am curious about who he is, but not curious enough to miss a call from Emily.

Being trapped in my car alone with my phone is a dreadful position for me to be in. I want so badly to call her. I know my heartache makes me incapable of clear thoughts right now, but seriously, I am a *professor.* I am rational. I am reasonable. I just need to show her that. I can do this.

While the phone is charging, I make the very wise decision to send her a text. Texting has several tactical advantages. First, it's non-threatening. Second, and most important in my circumstance, it can be proofread. Half an hour is plenty of time; I can read and reread it to make sure I really want to send it.

I type:

> *I am willing to be the man you want.*
> *You knew I was atheist the day we met. And more importantly, you knew I was lost. I was selfish, egotistical, and depraved. And certainly not a virgin. You saw this and agreed to spend time with me anyway. Not because your standards are low, but because you saw something redeemable in me. On the day I was baptized, I proved you right.*
> *Against my will, I reverted to that man: still depraved, despite the work you did, but also still redeemable. Please, don't leave me in this place. Your my best hope. I no longer want to be the man I am. You have shown me a more excellent way.*

I check and re-check this text. I scan it for anything crazy or desperate or bitter. I like that I ended with a little Paul, the Apostle; but in the second to the last line, *I no longer want to be the man I am,* I change *am* to *was.* I think that's pretty smart. I also change *Your my best hope* to

You're my best hope. C'mon, Professor!

After the third read, I'm ready and I hit send.

Ouch. It physically hurts. This is such a painful moment because I just restarted the clock. I stabbed a small wound in my heart. This is dating in the modern world; to send a text to a girl is to remove part of your heart that will not be replaced until you receive a reply. I'm cursing myself for the recklessness and...

I hear a ping. *Hey! That was fast!*

I read the merciful text as one in the desert drinks water. It reads:

Everyone is redeemable. Jesus can change you into the man you want to be. He is your best hope.

I instantly type back:

Will you be there when it happens?

I hit send and wait. This time there is no merciful ping. I type out:

Will you be there and forgive what I did?

I hit send. I add:

Please?

I hit send. I add:

Please!

I don't hit send. I delete it all and type out again:

Please?!

I delete it again and leave it alone.

I rest my forehead against the steering wheel. Now it hurts more than if she'd never replied to begin with, because now I know she is there, available, read the text, and isn't replying anyway.

I look at my phone and see it's charged. I haven't seen the man exit the building, but I forgot to watch for that. The old Ford Taurus in the parking lot, which is obviously his, is still here.

I make my way through the door in a foul mood, not anxious to speak to anyone. But I remember he brought me a blanket, so I decide to be cordial.

I thought I might catch him praying again, but he isn't. The first thing I see is that he has swept the tile in the lobby and finished the job I started on the hardwood behind the pulpit. I see the blanket he brought me folded and placed on a pew, which has also been cleaned. He now has some pliers in hand and is working on detaching the pews from the ground. He seems to have figured out how to do it pretty quickly because he has a couple of pews completely detached. I'm impressed by that. I also notice the pliers didn't come from me. He must've brought more than the blanket from home, and he must've thought ahead. I watch him work for a minute, and he doesn't see me, so I turn and walk out.

In a storage area connected to the lobby, I find an extension ladder. I decide I'm going to work on the roof. The roof looks pretty good. It's not leaking, but is missing shingles, most of which I was able to retrieve from the yard.

The roof is so peaceful, I actually take out my earbuds. This is like walking a tightrope without a net, but surprisingly I don't think of Emily. The sunshine feels good on my arms, and the breeze up here is nice. I think about nothing more than the job I'm doing, and for a moment I remember what it's like to just be me.

After working up here for a few hours, I start to wonder more about the mystery man. Is he here to stay? Do I have a helper now, or something? I try so hard to be aloof, but the suspense of this mystery is driving me crazy. I could have just asked him. *Why did I find it more important to be rude to him?*

From down below, I hear an engine start. I look down to see it's the old Taurus. The mystery man is behind the wheel and I watch him pull away.

I laugh to myself. *Well, it's over now.*

Only about twenty minutes pass and I hear the Taurus pull in below me. I lean over to watch. The man gets out of the car holding two fast food bags in one hand and two large drinks in the other.

He sees me looking down at him and calls out, "I didn't know if you prefer Coke or Pepsi..."

I can feel my stomach lurch.

"...so I got you Dr. Pepper."

I'm instantly impressed. *Good man! God's providence.*

He heads inside and I climb down to join him. Inside on one of the few pews that has been wiped down so far, I find him sitting with a rectangular hamburger wrapper spread out on his lap.

I see a sack and a drink a few feet from him, obviously left for me. "Thank you," I tell him and have a seat.

The two of us sit and eat together like two guys who have known each other our whole lives. In other words, we don't say a word. He finishes his hamburger before I do, so he asks, "Who are you?"

"No one of consequence." *Princess Bride.*

He lets this go and moves on to the question he actually wants answered more, "Why are you doing this?"

I shrug. "Bummed out about a girl."

The man laughs hard from his belly.

I smile. It does sound funny.

I am a bit surprised when he says, "Yeah, I guess you don't have to tell me."

Something occurs to me now, something so obvious I can't believe it's taken me this long to realize: he *is* the pastor.

I try to study his face to find out if this was the man who helped my mom change a tire so many years ago. His apparent age seems to fit, but of course I can't remember a single detail about the man's face.

When I asked him if this was "*your* church," I only wanted to discover if he had attended it. His answer was basically, *No, I attended it.* Anyone else would have answered that question, *Yes, I attended it.* Only a pastor would have read a question of actual ownership into the word *your.*

So, I know he lied to me, and I'm curious as to why. I ask, "Do you know what happened to this church?"

He nods.

"What happened?"

"The pastor here let everyone down," he says boldly. His eyes gaze over to the pulpit where he used to stand before his flock. "He let us all down."

I clear my throat, impressed by his lack of equivocation, even if he's using the wrong pronoun. I ask, "How?"

He glances over to get a quick look at my eyes, but then looks away. He says, "He ran a good and virtuous church filled with *good religious people.*"

I heard the tone in which he said, g*ood religious people.* I think I partially understand.

He continues, "It was his third year preaching. He was awfully young for his position. And one day he wakes up and discovers that he doesn't truly believe in God." He frowned.

"Really?" My cat ears turn up.

"He should have stepped down, of course, but he liked the attention. He liked the authority. And what else was he going to do with a seminary degree? So, he convinced himself, God or no God, what he was doing was still good. He was still teaching morals and good behavior. What's the harm in that, right?"

He turns to look at me even though I swore the question had been rhetorical. I shrug. "Yeah, that sounds okay."

"But it wasn't. You see, goodness, brings with it pride, pride brings judgment, judgment brings resentment, resentment brings malice."

"So goodness brings malice?" I ask attempting to follow his train of thought.

"Absolutely."

Hmm. Maybe this guy's not the pastor after all. The poor old man's confused.

"See, you need a second pill to combat the side-effects from the first. You should run like mad from someone who is teaching only morals, virtues, and standards, if they don't also preach acceptance, love, and forgiveness.

"And by the way, you should run faster from someone preaching only acceptance, love, and forgiveness, but no morals, virtues, or standards. There's simply nothing in the world more dangerous than teaching half the Bible."

I roll my eyes. *Yup, sounds like a pastor after all.*

"So, after about ten years of teaching only standards and virtue, his congregation was full of the meanest, proudest, SOBs you've ever seen. He decided it was time to start preaching about acceptance and tolerance, and love and community. But that only made it worse!

"We began to hate anyone who could not love as well as we could. We excluded anyone not inclusive enough. And we could not tolerate those who were intolerant. So, what God means for good, man uses for evil.

"So, the pastor realized there was no such thing as goodness on the whole of the Earth. Mankind is just a mule, and no matter what good stuff you put into one end, it all turns out the same on the other."

I rub my forehead. *This guy's sermons must have been life-changing,* I muse. But it occurs to me that I *did* just see him praying. He had to have turned back to God at some point, and I see an opportunity to find answers of my own. I say, "Well, so what's the solution?"

He smiles like the Cheshire Cat, and now I wish I hadn't asked.

He says, "The answer is in Ephesians 2:8-9, 'For it is by grace you have been saved, through faith—and this is not from yourselves, it is the gift of God—not by works, so that no one shall boast.'

"When man tries to earn his salvation, he only likely becomes worse. But when he knows, not just salvation, but all good things are from God, then there's nothing to be proud of. When he accepts that Christ died on a cross for him—and but for that he is nothing—the only appropriate response is humility and gratitude. And humility and gratitude are life-changing."

I consider this. "Perhaps," I look out on the broken church. "But, that story still doesn't explain what I'm seeing."

He nods. "There was a tornado." He must've seen how my head jerked to examine the building one more time, because he quickly corrects the thoughts I am thinking, "It didn't hit the church. But when catastrophe struck, the town was tested. A tornado came and ripped through the town totally obliterating some properties, but at the same time, leaving others completely intact.

"As far as the damage to this church, it was total. Oh, it spared the building, but it ripped apart the congregation. It seems the sanctuary had a strong foundation; the congregation however was built on sand.

"You ever want to see what effect a tragedy can have on a church filled with *really good people*? You're looking at it.

"No one came together. No one lent a hand. Not one of the *religious* was there for the others when they needed it most. The gossip came out. Rumors started flying. Accusations. Back-biting. And in the end, our elegant façade was blown clean off and underneath we were ugly. In the end, we were left with nothing except clarity. We weren't the people we'd claimed to be. We had no love for either God or people. We had failed the test and no one could pretend otherwise.

"It took about eighteen more months, believe it or not, but there was no stopping it, the church fell apart. And without the church as the backbone, the whole town fell apart. People who had lost their homes in the storm, and many who hadn't, decided to cut their losses and make a fresh start somewhere else.

"We closed the doors to this place, the only church in town, twelve years ago. Some people were able to forgive the pastor. Most weren't."

"What about you?" I ask, already guessing the answer.

"What about me?"

"Were you ever able to forgive... the pastor?"

He shakes his head.

"I didn't think so."

"I'm not sure I'll ever forgive him."

"Isn't that a little harsh?"

"You tell me. We counted on him to lead us. That's a responsibility. We gave him our money, our time, our loyalty. That's a sacred trust. We gave him access to our sons and our daughters."

I turn my head to look away.

He catches my reaction so he repeats the line forcefully, "We gave him our *sons and daughters!* We trusted their minds and their hearts to him, and he abused his power. He filled their heads with poison. Poison. And why? Just so he could feel more puffed up. Just so he could feast off their blind allegiance? I think in the end it was only ever about his ego."

I shift in my seat. I think this hamburger is turning my stomach.

He continues, "No, it was worse than that. It was vanity. He wanted to call his side good and the other side bad. And although he claimed to be so certain of his own opinions, he never felt safe, never felt valid, until he could convince as many people as possible to side with him. It wasn't an innocent mistake. He misused his intelligence—a beautiful gift God had given to him—and misled people for the sake of his own vanity, his own desperate insecurity. So, you tell me if I should forgive him."

I shake my head. I whisper breathlessly, "No, you should not forgive him."

He continues to stare at the pulpit as if he's envisioning that smart and charming preacher. He says, "Try to imagine the moment you discover that everything you've ever done with your career had been a lie. Try imagining the pain of discovering that there is real truth in the world and you had spent your whole life leading people astray, people who had counted on you for answers." His eyes turn to look straight at me. They are filled with regret. He says, "That's a fate I wouldn't wish on my worst enemy."

I swallow hard. The man's eyes are nearly full with tears and I can feel mine starting to sting.

I stand up abruptly, breaking our connection. I say rudely, "Too much chit-chat." I shrug heartlessly. "I don't really care what happened to the church; I just need to get back to work."

Chapter Forty-Six

I didn't talk to the pastor again after that. I didn't thank him for lunch. I tried to avoid him entirely. And at the end of the day, I hopped into my car and left without warning. I didn't even say goodbye.

My foul mood is at least partially because of the car ride home.

I am halfway through it, and surviving, when the C. S. Lewis book I was enjoying comes to an end. I can't explain the feeling. It's like I'm suspended from a rope and am watching each individual strand break and unravel one by one.

I grab my old phone with urgency, as if I fear the silence, as if silence is an open door to painful thoughts. I open the music app as fast as I can, select my Christian playlist, and hit play.

To my surprise I recognize the song. I look back at the phone. *I selected Christian, not Christmas, right?* Upon further thought, I would never have created a Christmas playlist, because I only first met Emily in January. Somehow this song got downloaded to my phone—most likely by me—in the middle of summer.

When I get to the lyrics, I'm surprised I know every word. But I don't really. It's only at the end of one line that I magically discover the next line in my memory. I have to wait for the music to carry me, then each word seems to come to me the moment just before it's sung.

O holy night! The stars are brightly shining,
It is the night of our dear Savior's birth.
Long lay the world in sin and error pining,
Till He appeared and the soul felt its worth.
A thrill of hope, the weary world rejoices,
For yonder breaks a new and glorious morn.

This mysterious recall can't simply be explained by growing up in America. Growing up in my hometown, I was exposed to songs about Santa over Jesus, ten-to-one. It can't be explained by my past Christmases. Of course, I've heard it my whole life, but I've never once intentionally listened to this song. I can only imagine I put this song on my phone—during the summer—and listened to it again and again and again. Enough times that I internalized the words. But why?

I immerse myself in the music and I receive a vision. It feels like déjà vu, but I know exactly what it truly is: a *memory*. It's a memory provoked by the music.

I immediately pull my car over to the side of the highway. I rewind the song and close my eyes. I listen intently all the way to the end. Nothing. I rewind the song again. I try to employ the power of will I had practiced with such devotion while clothed in the shower. I try to clear my mind and summon the memory.

I hit the back arrow again and play. And pray. "Please God, let me see this." I turn the volume up so loud in the car I can feel the music through the seat. I close my eyes.

Fall on your knees! O hear the angels' voices!
O night divine, O night when Christ was born;
O night divine, O night, O night Divine.

The choir bursts into a crescendo with voices so overwhelming it causes my tired speakers to rattle.

Then I see her. *Emily*. She is in my arms and our faces are a mere inch apart. This song comes on and I tell her, smiling, "Looks like your shuffle included your Christmas playlist."

She shakes her head and starts to blush. "I like Christmas music." She doesn't say anything more but starts to chew on her lip slightly.

I wait, still holding her.

She frowns, shrugging girlishly. "I think, if music is beautiful, and honors the miracle of Jesus, then I'm going to listen to it anytime I'm in the mood for..." She shrugs again. "...beautiful music which honors Jesus."

I listen to the music. I like it. "Which song is this?"

"You don't know this song?" she asks.

I shake my head. "I mean, I've heard it obviously."

"It's my favorite. It may even be my favorite song ever."

I close my eyes to listen. Discovering it was Emily's favorite instantly makes the song worthy of my reverence. I listen to the words, as if I had never heard it as a child. And I am genuinely hearing this song for the first time.

Truly He taught us to love one another;
His law is love and His gospel is peace.
Chains shall He break, for the slave is our brother;
And in His name all oppression shall cease.
Sweet hymns of joy in grateful chorus raise we,
Let all within us praise His holy name.

I see the first Christmas, the glorious birth of a baby. I see two-thousand-plus Christmases since, worldwide. I see billions exalted in worship and I'm glad the Western world is ordered how it is. For once in my life, I don't want to detract a single speck from the Christianity in our society, and more than that, I want to stand in the way of anyone who does. Powerful like a king but fragile like a baby, I'm compelled to protect it.

When I open my eyes in my memory, I see Emily watching me. Her face is more majestic than the music, and she doesn't know it. I see genuine love in her face, but I see something else too. She's conflicted. It's as if she stands before a pool and dips her pretty toe in. She doesn't dare dive in head first, but she longs to be refreshed. She wants the feeling of weightlessness, surrounded and lifted up by my eyes and my embrace and my kiss.

It's a beautiful look on her. In fact, it's the most beautiful sight I've ever seen in my entire life.

Surprisingly, I'm a gentleman. I don't push her with my words, nor tempt her with my smile, nor dare her with a slight subtle lean forward. I'm content just to soak in her beauty.

My eyes are only on her, but I get the impression we are in her room. Emily is only ten years younger than me, but her room still has a teenage feel to it. Vague impressions of childish decorating tickle my memory: ponies and posters and pink. We are definitely alone, it's definitely late and the room is definitely dim. And this Christmas song is playing in the middle of summer.

Her face phases from white to red. The music swells and she takes the plunge. She leans in and kisses me.

Christ is the Lord! O praise His Name forever,
His power and glory evermore proclaim.
His power and glory evermore proclaim.

I am overcome, then and now, with everything that has been so tragically missing all my life: a sense of the *holy*. It's a sense of the sacred, coupled by a deep longing not just for the sacred, but for there to actually be something in this life which is sacred. It's a completely new ecstasy for me, and I feel it cleansing my soul.

Was this really the moment in which I had accepted Christ? The memory I'm receiving doesn't contain that information. Did it happen in a flash of revelation? Or was it just the catalyst? I still don't know.

The sight of her face is clear and vibrant. The feel of her lips, the smell of her hair, the taste of her mouth, it all feels very real to me. It's a vivid and powerful memory.

Ironic. I had been fearing silence, but it is music which betrayed me.

But I'm not sad. I'm not tormented by this memory; I'm overjoyed by it. When this church is built, and I am ready to stop distracting myself, I will let the idea of life without Emily enter my mind and it will hurt. It will hurt. But this is a woman I am honored to have kissed. I've recently learned the proper value of memories, and this one is first-rate. This one is heavenly.

Kevin said no one gets any memories back, not one. But here I just did and I am grateful. I know with this memory I will never be the same.

Headlights shine into my mirrors, then pass. I take a moment, on the side of the highway, in the middle of the night, to acknowledge that life is beautiful. I bow to its joy. I bow to its sorrow. I'm in awe of its depth. I am glad to be alive. And I'm glad a woman like Emily exists in the world. I'm glad that her smile exists, and her eyes exist, and her heart. I am glad I got to see them. And I'm glad that I love her, even if I can't have her. I am glad that I love her, even if that love hurts me. Because it is *right* to love her.

I rewind the song again and try my best to relive it.

Chapter Forty-Seven

The next day I pass the liquor store again. I'm thinking about heading inside. I'm thinking about blowing this whole thing. I hate the pastor. His story gave me pause, but so what? At least I was trying to educate my *flock*. What was he trying to do? I was trying to get young minds to think. He was trying to get them to stop thinking. Big difference. If you think our stories are similar, you're wrong.

Regret everything I've ever done in my entire career? No. That doesn't describe me. *Nope.*

I eye the liquor store again, now safe—relatively safe—in my rearview mirror.

I don't like him. In fact, for some reason, I can't stand him. I suddenly want to undo all the work we've done. I want to burn the whole thing down. I didn't start all this just for him. I didn't start all this to have some silly helper who thinks we're going to bond. I hope I never see him again.

I pull into the church parking lot and notice the trash bags have been picked up. I scan the area for the guy's car, but I'm alone. *Good.* Now I can get some work done.

I'm all the way on top of my ladder, painting the newly repaired eaves when I see some movement down below me. A red Honda pulls into the parking lot and two young men step out. I'm not sure where they came from, but they're definitely dressed more small-town than big-city. I decide they are not worth climbing down for.

I turn back to my work and wait for the inevitable. They'll call up to me with something brilliant like, "Looks like you're fixing up the church." I sigh. But I hear nothing.

They both look around. I'm not sure they've seen me yet. To my surprise they let themselves in. Now I wonder if I'm being robbed. I make a mental list of all the tools I have lying around in there and their approximate cost.

I sneak over to the broken stained-glass window. I lean my head in and sneak a peek through the missing part. The *Mission Impossible* theme runs through my head, unbidden.

Inside, I spot them going through my supplies. Confident that I'm being robbed, I hit pause on my earbuds. I'm about to holler down at them when I notice their idle movements are nothing like thieves. I watch as one of them grabs a crowbar. It's not the most expensive thing in the place, but I guess a petty crook would be naturally attracted to a crowbar.

The raised area surrounding the pulpit had become water-damaged due to the broken window above it. The pastor had begun the difficult job of tearing it all out yesterday, and to my surprise these two seem like they want to finish it. Apparently, they've come here to help, too. I continue to eye them in order to get a good idea if they know what they're doing.

When I'm satisfied with what I see, I withdraw my head from the broken aperture and get back to work.

The three of us work through lunch without stopping. Occasionally I hear them down there and no doubt they hear me, but we don't introduce ourselves at any point. The first actual encounter we share with each other happens when the tall one walks out and asks if I have a nine-pound hammer.

"No," I tell him and they both get into their car and leave.

When I see them again, they have a menacing hammer with them. They're also toting a circular saw, a table saw, some light stands, and a generator. From the looks of the tools, they are returning from their home, not the hardware store.

I am still working on my eaves when the pastor shows up again. He's brought more supplies, and this time he has a woman with him who I assume is his wife. Truth be told, I plan to be inaccessible all day because I have a strange suspicion he'd want to shake my hand. I let him see that I see he's here, but instantly turn my head back to my work. To my surprise, the two men—who no doubt know the pastor—give him an equally cold welcome.

I've got to hand it to him though; despite being completely ignored, he and his wife settle in and get straight to work inside the church.

I miss dinner and don't even notice. It's late and the two young men have already left. The pastor's wife also left, but he stayed behind. It's just the two of us left in the church, both working our separate tasks, both with our heads down.

I hate for things to go unsaid. I know that's the exact precedent I've set myself all day, but I wasn't playing games so much as I was just feeling antisocial.

I decide I definitely need to mess with him.

I can see he's finished the frame for what will be the stage area. This would be a perfect stopping point, and out of the corner of my eye, I can see him furtively glance over at me. He looks around, looks at me, then looks around again. I refuse to look at him, so he starts to haul piles of wood boards in. With each group he hauls in, he plops them down, stretches his back, then looks over at me. He is hoping to make a connection, but I refuse to help.

I finish wiring the outlet I was working on, and again I see him glance over to me expectantly, so I immediately begin to wire the next outlet.

This started with me trying to deny him an easy chance to talk with me, but it has become something else. We have a competition now. *The little twerp wants to be the last to leave. Like that would prove something!*

There's simply no way I will let that happen.

He finishes bringing in the wood and begins to hammer them in.

I finish wiring all the outlets and begin running wire up to where the lights will be. This requires a ladder and that separates us even more. I evaluate the old wiring to determine the number of lights there had been. I could still be working up here well into the morning.

A few hours later he has every board nailed down. It's good work. Again, he looks up to make a connection, and again I refuse to look at him. He sighs and opens up a can of wood stain.

This is childish, but we sure are getting a lot done.

His phone constantly chirps. I can see the irritation on his face as he constantly has to put down his brush to pull it out of his pocket. No doubt it's his wife texting him, telling him to stop being stupid and just let me win.

I look at my own cell phone and frown. No one at all cares to be a check on my stupidity.

This goes on until 2 am.

Finally, he finishes one section, and I see him raise his lanky body off the ground. The joints crack in his spindly legs and he lets out a small groan that he'd meant to hold in. Perhaps I wasn't competing with him; perhaps I was testing him. If so, he passed. He's definitely a trooper.

I remember the swiftness with which he swept in to help my mother, and I climb down from my ladder at last.

Sensing the opening, he moves straight over to me. With no preliminaries, he says, "I'm sorry I don't remember you. Were you a part of this congregation?" He's still trying to figure out why I started this whole project.

I say, "No. I sure wasn't."

"Have we met before?"

I shake my head. "We are strangers to each other."

"So why? Were you called by God to do this?"

He had already asked this question, but the answer's still the same. I shake my head.

"Why this church?"

This time I give a slight nod. I say, "I have been in this church before."

"When?"

"Twenty-eight years ago."

The number shocks him.

"My mother and I had a flat tire just outside that door."

His eyes are searching. "Well, you must've been a little kid... I... Yes, I..." He trails off.

He can't say what he wants without betraying the lie he told. I decide to help him out, "I met the pastor here that day. I'm sure he'd probably remember."

"Yes, I'm sure he would."

"I'm sure the pastor must've thought, *What a blessing for them to break down right outside my church!*"

"Yes," he replies eagerly. "He must've."

I continue, "My mother was leaving my father for good that day. We lived in the city. We'd been driving for two hours when my mom got a flat... right on that road out there."

His eyes light up. "Well, perhaps it was a greater blessing than he thought."

Again, I almost nod. "And inside this sanctuary, at ten years old, was the first time I talked to God. I prayed—I guess I prayed—for God to change my mother's heart, to turn around and go back to my father."

Mixed emotions show on his face. He is definitely intrigued by the idea that his church played such a role in a stranger's life. He asks, "Well, did God... comfort you?"

I think he almost asked if God answered my prayer, but he understands how many prayers don't get answered—at least not in the way people want. "I don't know," I lie. I suddenly don't want to continue on with the story.

"Did your mother and father ever get back together?" Curiosity compels him.

"Yes."

"And, was it... that day? Did she go back to him after you prayed?"

I look down. "She did."

He is delighted and can't understand why I delivered the news so understated.

I say, "Now, I guess I'm hoping for another miracle. I'm hoping for a girl to turn around and come back to me."

There's a spark of recognition in his eyes. He hadn't believed me when I said all this was about a girl. He says, "Well, the church is still here. Have you tried asking God the same way you asked before?"

I shake my head.

"Do you mind if I ask him?"

I shake my head again.

He bows his head and closes his eyes. He says, "Dear Heavenly Father, I don't know all the details. I don't know this man who sits beside me, but I know he's a good man. I don't know who he is, but I know who *You* are. You are a God of rebuilding. You are a God who restores. If this good man's life is in need of rebuilding, I know you can rebuild it. If these two young people are meant to be together, please bring them together. Let them forgive if there's anything to forgive. Let them both forgive and also ask forgiveness. Give them the courage to love deeply, without resentment, without holding onto the past, and without fear. Just as this church appears to be receiving a second chance, bring him a second chance as well. For this we pray in the holy name of Jesus, Amen."

He raises his head, unable to tell mine had never been bowed. I can't believe it—it must be the fumes from the wood stain—but I do say, "Amen."

He asks, "It's late. How long of a drive do you have ahead of you?"

Dang. That's what I get for messing with the old man. It's going to be almost morning by the time I get home.

He sees the answer on my face and asks, "Why don't you stay in town with us tonight. We have a spare bedroom already made up for you."

I shake my head, playing the martyr.

"Are you sure?"

I nod.

Chapter Forty-Eight

It's day five and I arrive at the church to discover there's already a crowd milling about. They're all dressed simply and appear to be from the town. The new arrivals look confused and out of place. None of this appears to be organized. The best that I can tell, people just seem to be showing up on their own.

I see the taller man from yesterday giving instructions to a group of ladies in their late forties. I sense a body walk up beside me and I turn to see a stocky man wearing denim overalls. It takes me a second to realize it's the police officer from the first day.

He says, "Looks like the retaining wall needs to be replaced. You know about them?"

I nod. "I'll be able to handle that. Do you know a place nearby where I can get some concrete and some plywood without spending too much?"

He points to a rusty pickup apparently weighed down with supplies, and says without inflection, "Right over there."

This makes me smile. I challenge him back, "You know anything about stained-glass?"

He laughs and shakes his head. "I got a guy. He says he's coming tomorrow."

I smile again.

He says, "What's the AC look like?"

I shrug. "Well, there's obviously no power to the place so I don't entirely know, but I managed to check the ducts. Visually, they look good."

Some more people pull up into the parking lot—a young woman and a man. Their faces are glowing in excitement as if they just stepped out of their car for a beach vacation. The woman looks at me and asks, "Who's doing this?"

"Looks like we all are," the cop answers for me.

"Who's in charge?" the man asks.

I point to the tall guy and say, "Go talk to that guy over there."

Almost immediately after that, I see three more cars roll in—a young man, an entire family, and even a young woman by herself. The latter walks up to me and says, "What's going on here?"

"I guess everyone's coming together to fix up the church," I say.

I can't describe the look in her eyes. "It's about time," she says.

I like this girl.

"What can I do?" she asks.

"What *can* you do?" I counter.

She shrugs. "I've never tried."

I just smile and say, "Come with me."

As the day goes on, more and more people arrive wanting to help. I've never seen anything like it. Some show up with supplies ready to go, but some saunter in just like that lady, asking, "What's going on? Where do you need me?"

After lunch, I stop just to watch everyone. It amazes me to see so many people come together. Some clearly had to take time off work to be here. A good number of them don't even know the first thing about construction.

The crowd seems to be dividing itself naturally into two groups: helping hands and supervisors. The number of supervisors—those who know what they're doing—is shocking, and the quality of the work is impressive. *Man, never underestimate country folk when it comes to building stuff.*

Chapter Forty-Nine

It's day six.

I pull up to the church after my usual two-hour drive. My body can't take much more of this. I have been working all day long and suffering through four hours a day in the car to boot. It's all worthwhile just to fall asleep the second my head hits the pillow. It's vastly preferable to doing nothing all day and tossing and turning all night thinking about Emily. Preferable, but not a long-term strategy.

When I reach the church, I discover I'm not the first one here, not even close. Someone must have arranged for a dumpster, and it seems to have claimed the last remaining spaces in the small parking lot. It's absurd, but I actually have to exit the parking lot, unsatisfied, and park nearby on the street.

The pews have all been removed and are in the front lawn. I look around for a roll of carpet and don't see any. I suppose they must be expecting it soon.

There's now a welcome committee standing at the door. When the lady sees me walk up she says, "Welcome," as if it were my first time stepping foot in the place. "There's still work left to be done. If you need tools, we have them. If you're not sure what to do, or how to do it, you can ask one of the men with the orange vests."

At least they didn't try to give me a name tag.

I nod like a dummy and stagger past the threshold, bewildered. It's standing room only. The room is filled with the sound of power tools and swinging hammers. There are bright flood lights in the corners of the building where the window light falls off. I count one, two, three more generators. I look up to see the cop's friend is replacing the stained-glass window as promised.

The carpet is already in and nailed down. Things are moving fast now. A few of the men are starting to bring the pews back in.

People are busy taping and sanding and painting and caulking and cleaning and polishing when more people show up. Some ladies set up a card table and laid out cold cut sandwiches. There's a spread of finger foods like it's a party. The cookies are almost gone, but no one's touched the vegetable tray. There's a cooler filled with bottled water and juice boxes. There's a couple of kids running around here. I see one baby in a stroller. *This is ridiculous.*

I remember I have to install the light fixtures so I turn to discover three men already working on it. Okay. I decide I could just polish the brass, but I check every pew and find that job is done. I could help bring the pews in, but there are three men carrying each end. I could help secure them to the ground, but there are seven women waiting on each pew to be brought in. All of them swinging socket wrenches. There are more people here than jobs to do! The welcome committee lied to me.

I see two high school kids routing the edge of a wooden railing. They're passing the router from right to left. I walk over to stop them, but I hear a voice from behind, "You're doing it wrong." I turn to see the cop. He steps past me and proceeds to show them the correct way.

Okay. Good... I guess.

I remember the built-in bookshelf in the lobby. Surely that hasn't yet been done. I step into the lobby and discover that it has. And it's already loaded with books.

I shuffle my feet. I check my phone. These people have completely taken over. I've got mixed emotions about all this. I turn around to take it all in. I turn around again.

This is completely absurd, I'm just spinning around in circles.

I check my phone again to make sure Emily didn't just try to call.

I look around for something I can do, something I can build with my hands. There's nothing. *Maybe I should ask someone in an orange vest,* I tell myself sarcastically.

I check my phone again. The problem with cell phones is they always display the time. I happened to catch a glimpse at 11:56. It was 11:56 last time I checked. That means I actually checked to see if I had missed a call—which, by the way, would have produced a loud ringing noise—twice in one minute.

What have I become? This isn't a life.

I feel a dark cloud descend on me. It's the thoughts of Emily I'd been using manual labor to avoid. Unbelievably—and unbearably—I check my phone again.

With so much noise in here, it could've rung without me hearing it.

There's a fascinating psychological phenomenon that happens in people awaiting bad news: at a certain point, the bad news becomes less feared than the wait itself. The situation is changed by tension. At some point, they will even welcome the bad news if it means the suspense is finally over.

I would rather she say goodbye now than to continue to wait for a hello.

I am standing frozen in the lobby thinking about Emily and saying goodbye, when I look up and see a painting. The surprise of seeing this beautiful piece of art stops my spiraling thoughts in their tracks.

Beautiful? No, it's exquisite.

It's a depiction of Christ being brought down from the cross. The Redeemer's body is limp and broken. A team of men are handing Him off, one to the next, while a small group of women stand off to the side and weep. One man is pressing the side of his own face to the non-pierced side of Jesus. The look on that man's face is one of perfect heartbreak and unguarded love. It's desperate and yearning, but at the same time, not sad. The man appears to be drawing life straight from a body, which currently has no life in it. I'm mesmerized. It's as if, even in that moment, even at that point of the story, the man felt a stronger need to worship than he did to weep.

The painting stirs something in me. The richness of the colors, the striking details of the faces, and the intense emotions are so elegantly and powerfully conveyed. I'm awestruck the artist was able to show the depth of each subject's distinct personality. I'm impressed with the fact that—in not just a painting, but a printed reproduction of a painting—so much raw humanity can be conveyed through a single image.

And it must be a reproduction, because an actual painting this inspiring, this brilliant, would cost thousands, possibly millions, or maybe tens of millions depending on the artist and the time period. It looks to be in the style of the old Italian masters, but a lot of artists have imitated that style since. I'm disgusted with myself for not knowing who painted this.

I claim to know about art, but I can't even guess the century this painting came from. I am one of a dozen people on the planet who can tell the difference between Casimiro's Detritus #12 and Detritus #13, but about this *real* masterpiece, I know nothing.

It didn't require phony courage to create the image I'm looking at, it just took *talent*.

I am convinced that it's the greatest painting I've ever seen in my life, and I'm reminded of something the world seems eager to forget: the power of real art. The painting makes me feel joy, and empathy, and heartache. I feel a deep connection with the subjects. The painting makes me love all people in the world. *A painting does that!* It makes me want to find the people I've hurt, all the way back to the second grade, and just tell them how sorry I am. And Emily! It makes me want to grab Emily and wrap her in an embrace and padlock both my arms. I want to tell her, "I belong in your arms and I don't want to live another second outside of them. *I'm not afraid anymore.*"

The painting has given me courage and I grieve for the time I've wasted. How dare I celebrate phony artists when there is real art in the world! When there's such genuine beauty, I cry for the time I spent passing along a counterfeit.

I take a photo of the painting with my phone. I said the painting has given me courage; I should just text the image to Emily. It's of her Savior, after all. If she likes the painting, and I like the painting, we will at least have that.

But my heart grows faint when I see a detail in the painting I missed before. Off in the background stands a man by himself. He's separate from the rest, observing the whole scene, feeling nothing at all. The look on his face is a most-expertly captured expression of brutal indifference. The contrast between him and the worshiping man is striking. *What is he doing there?* Why did the artist paint him?

I know why, because the artist was a genius. Rude. Very rude, but a genius.

The more I look at the man in the background, the more irritated I become. *Look away!* I scream in my head. *Move along, this scene is not for you!* The more I stare at this man, the more I can't look away myself. The man is me of course. He's a Casimiro fan who has accidentally happened upon real art and feels nothing. It's obscene for him to look on at such a moment and keep his face so piggish and placid. *At least have the decency to look away!* He's been given a fortune of pearls yet remains a swine. His heart doesn't break along with the others. He doesn't grieve or surrender or worship along with the others. He doesn't belong. He just... He... *He just shouldn't be there!*

I know what I have to do now. Yes, the painting has given me courage, but it is not the courage to text her. I raise my phone, right there in the lobby of the azure blue church. I watch its face for a second, giving the governor a chance for a last-minute stay of execution.

It's silent.

I navigate to Settings... Phone... Options... Block Calls... and then select her number. It's labeled *The Girl I Can't Forget.* I highlight her number and click OK.

Completely block all incoming calls and messages from The Girl I Can't Forget?

I click Yes.

And it's over. Just like that. Everything's over. The girl I fought for and searched for, and tried so desperately to remember, doesn't want anything to do with me. She doesn't need me. I release her to go find a better man than I. No one needs me. This church doesn't need me anymore either. I don't belong. I can't let my indifference ruin their worship.

I leave quietly, unnoticed by anyone but the girls at the door, both of whom tell me to have a wonderful day. I stagger out to my ultra-depressing Prius, slide into the driver's seat, and start the engine. But I have nowhere to go.

Wait. I have somewhere to go, of course I do: the only other landmark I know in this town.

That's where a guy like me belongs.

Chapter Fifty

I pull my car to a stop in the still-crowded church parking lot. The engine is making a new noise and the steering wheel is starting to shake when I hit speeds above thirty. Why do I continue to drive a totaled Prius when I have a brand-new Jag? *It's just what I'm comfortable with. It's just what I'm used to doing.*

The sun is low in the sky. When I started drinking it was directly above us. When I step out the car, my mind asks, "Should I return to the church now that I'm drunk?" I will have an answer to that one when I reach the sanctuary. I am carrying a bottle of Johnny Walker Black, still in its brown paper bag, *hobo-style.* It's nearly empty.

I also bring in a cooler of my own. I make my way to the front of the church and set down my cooler next to the one provided by the *Busybody Society.* I open it up so people can see its offerings: bottles of ice-cold Blue Moon and Shiner Bock.

A few people realize I'm drinking and proffering alcohol, but no one gives it much consideration. I find a place to sit with my back against the wall, my butt on the ground, and both forearms slung across the tops of my knees. My brown bag dangles from the tips of my fingers as if to say, "What are you going to do about it?"

But no one does anything about it. No one bothers me. I look around for the pastor, but I don't see him anywhere. He must've stepped out.

A boy with shaggy hair, about the age of my students—former students—comes to investigate my cooler. He digs around for a bit until he discovers it has only beer. I can tell for a minute he is thinking about cracking one open. Finally, he grabs a juice box from the other cooler and gets back to work.

I reach into my pocket and pull out the cigar I bought at the liquor store. I light it right there in the sanctuary.

I stop to consider my lighter. It was the one I used, being a total jerk, the first day I made Emily run out of the room crying.

I don't know what's wrong with me. Alcohol has stopped working. This is the third time I've been truly drunk since I took the Premocyl, and not one of those attempts has brought me a single ounce of elation.

The art I used to like no longer interests me; my old music no longer moves me; and not even alcohol can provide me any release, just frustration.

I've reached the end of me. I can't remember who I was. Nothing I've tried to do provides me joy anymore. *Forget joy; I'd settle for just some stimulation of any kind.* I am lost. My foundation is cracked. I've been rejected twice. A part of my mind was stolen from me. And I'm living secondhand.

I know that I no longer *have* to be Christian. Emily is gone. That door is closed. But I admit I still wish I believed. It's like this church: I don't have any real reason to want to see it built, but I can't seem to stop since I started.

It's like a puzzle to me now. It's like working on a puzzle that once you start, it has you. It owns you. You are under the puzzle's control until you figure it out.

I shake it off. *No. I am in control. And this Christian experiment is over. The Christian thing I was trying to do ends right now.*

Then why am I sitting in a church?

Augh. I press my cigar out right on the brand-new polished wood. I stand up and grab a paint brush. Embracing my heretic within, I grab a near-empty can of exterior latex—the *precious azure blue.* I dramatically step to the section of wall behind the pulpit like I own the place; I'm starting to believe I do. There on the newly painted beige wall beneath the cross, where vile graffiti had already been removed, I write in large blue numbers:

7

I can feel the eyes on me, watching me destroy the job they'd worked so hard on.

I paint a zero and another zero. I can feel the faces turn toward me as I work. I don't have to see their expressions, I can guess. *Meek Christian women.* Each of them composing the things they'd say to object, if they had the courage.

I write another zero, and another, and another. I hear audible sighs and whispers, and it confirms for me these people are completely at my mercy. I may even have just heard a tongue-cluck, but that's only because what I'm doing is the most audacious thing they've ever seen a man do in their entire cloistered lives.

When I finish, the wall reads "7, 0 0 0, 0 0 0, 0 0 0."

I step back and motion to it. I watch the old biddies look at each other, look at the wall, look at the bottle I'm still holding, look at the paint I'm dripping on the floor, look every which way but in my eyes. One brave lady has the courage to ask, "What's that for?"

"That is the number of people your God has sent to Hell last century alone."

I hear a few of them gasp. One or two of them turn their backs on me and get back to work. They make sure to let their opinions of me be known via their facial expressions but say nothing.

The brave lady asks, "Why did you write it there?"

"Why did I..." I feign indignation. "Lady, I just told you your God has condemned seven billion people to an eternity in Hell and you're worried about the wall?"

One of her friends grabs her arm and pulls her back to the job they were on.

It hurts my heart. It's the lonely feeling that's haunted me my whole life. No one ever wants to debate me. No one wants to hear me rant. No one wants to talk about what I want to talk about. No one wants to sit front row in the audience of my intellect.

"Don't go," I slobber. "Aww c'mon." I turn away from them and open my body language up to the room at large. I yell, "These are the facts. This is the record. Jesus did not come to save us from the wrath of the devil, but from the wrath of God."

No one says anything. I challenge. "Will someone here take me on? You people aren't eighteen! Seven billion souls in one century!"

I'm excited to see the young man with shaggy hair approach me from my right. His eyes want my attention, so I turn to face him. He clearly has something he wants to say. *Finally, a worthy challenger.*

He says, "That's where I know you from. You're Professor Larson, aren't you?"

I drop the brush and my shoulders slump. I hadn't given my name to a single person here. It's not that I'm ashamed of it. I guess a part of me hoped that if I went long enough without using it, it would just go away.

He continues, "I took your class... well, uh, for a few weeks. I was there the day they... let you go." He's not trying to be coy, only friendly.

I say nothing to the boy but give him a tepid nod. I slink back over to the spot where I was huddled and continue to drink alone.

I take a swig from my bottle and watch the docile Christian women fret over the numbers on the wall. One of them picks up the paintbrush I dropped, while another one has a roll of paper towels and is searching for a way to get them wet. Before long they at least have the hardwood floors looking like nothing just happened.

Okay, I'm starting to like them a little.

Chapter Fifty-One

The *Flibbertigibbet Committee* is consulting about what to do with the mess I made of the wall when the pastor finally bothers to show up. I imagine he might have been out looking for me. I see a cluster of clucking hens gather around him. He looks at me, looks at the number I wrote, and looks back at them.

Finally, he puts up both hands to hamper their animated remarks and makes his way over to my part of the room. He's walking straight at me—*busted*—but he takes a slight detour first, toward the coolers. He reaches into the *good* cooler, the godly cooler, and pulls out a small bottle of milk.

He sits down next to me and leans against the wall, mimicking my pose. We've got all the self-satisfied demeanor of two blue-collar laborers in a Norman Rockwell painting. He is slinging his quart of milk like it was a jug of the hardest moonshine. He takes a long swig—straight from the bottle—for me to see. He's got a sense of humor, I'll give him that.

He looks down at my cigar and the burn mark it left on the floor, but only because it catches his eye. He allows me to see no emotion over it.

The milk he's drinking softens my heart, and I remember the first time, the actual first time, we met. Still I am ready to battle. I'm ready to smash the first ideas to come out of his pious mouth.

He says, "I was that miserable preacher."

I say, "Well, duh."

He laughs. "I thought you probably pieced that one together. I'm sorry I didn't tell you that first day... I... Well, how can I explain it? I wanted you to like me."

I look at him to see if he's serious. "Why?"

"Why?" He laughs again, but there's no viciousness in it. "I just had a feeling."

"A feeling about what?" I prod.

He gives me a face that can be best translated to: *You really don't know? How could you not know?* He motions to the rebuilt church and everyone working, and informs me, "You're the best thing that's happened to me in years. You're the best thing that's happened to this town in years. You brought these people the hope they were needing, the hope I had failed to bring them. You showed us how badly the people in this town have been wanting to come together, all of us secretly waiting for someone else to go first... then you were the one who did."

Okay, I'm not going to smash that.

"Yes, I was that preacher. And yes, I do remember you and your mother. The Bible says, 'Do not neglect to show hospitality to strangers, for thereby some have entertained angels unawares.' That day when Mary and I invited you in and offered you a break from the cold, we had no idea we were in the presence of an angel. I did so few things right back then, but the hospitality I offered a stranger that day was the most important thing I've ever done, because that stranger was an angel and he returned to save my church."

I actually blush a little—must be the Scotch.

He continues, "This town has come together in the exact way we failed to before. A second chance! A second chance and this time with new leadership. You gave us the opportunity to do right what we once did wrong."

His eyes begin to rapidly fill with tears as emotions from the past twenty-eight years flood his mind: shame and regret and redemption and glory. "Thank you! Thank you for what you've done. You are an angel sent from Heaven to us. You re-wrote the ending to my story. You gave this entire town a second chance. We won't let you down. I promise you right now that I won't let you down. Thank you, sir. God bless you. May God richly reward you for the good you've done here and the hope you've brought to this town."

Well this sucks; I came looking for a fight. I put up a hand, trying to get him to stop. I see the ladies are pretending to work, but really just keep turning to watch us.

"Why did..." He struggles to push out the words caught in his throat. "Why?" His mind strains to focus. His wet eyes look at me. "Did God send you here to us? Did God tell you to build this church?"

My heart breaks for the guy. I shrug. "No," I tell him.

"But..." His eyes are searching. "But He must've."

"He didn't."

"But, tell me, are you sure? How can you be sure?"

"There is no God." It comes out sounding far more like an interruption than it does an answer, and far louder than I intend. I see some of the faces in my periphery turn and steal another glance at us. And I'm not finished there. I spit, "I'm an atheist. I'm not a blessing. And I'm damn sure no angel. This man who's the best thing to ever happen to this town is an atheist. An atheist."

At first his face is shocked, maybe even appalled, but then it softens. He looks out across the people there, coming together, grasping for hope, then looks back at me. He says very slowly, but quite deliberately, "Nah."

"Nah?" I scoff. "I know what I am! I'm an atheist."

"Nah," he says again, this time quick and casual, as if I had just asked if he wanted mushrooms on his pizza.

"Dude! You can't just..." I trail off. "You're really..." I feel my anger rising, and I also feel... a little dizzy. I put my fingertips to my brow, my nose cupped between my hands. I breathe deep and try to get the room to steady. I want to punch this guy.

I inhale and exhale a few breaths and I... start laughing.

The pastor starts laughing too. And we both just sit there and laugh until I forget why.

I look over at the ladies, still sneaking glances at the two of us. They're more confused than ever.

I tell the pastor, "That girl I'm lovesick for, she says she'll be with me if I can only believe in God."

"Then do."

"It doesn't work that way."

"Why not?"

"Because we don't choose our beliefs. We arrive at conclusions based on observation filtered through reason."

He nods. "I understand."

I laugh, then take another swig of Scotch.

He, in response, takes a swig of milk. He says, "But that philosophy... that doesn't get you where you want to go. It doesn't help your situation. Really, it's not your friend here at all."

"So?"

"So, why are you holding onto it so tight?"

"What?" I scoff. "Ideas are either true or not true. I can't decide what's true based on whether it's helpful to me at the moment"

"Sure, you can," he says blithely.

I just stare at him, trying to discover what percentage of his words are in jest.

He makes a show of looking over both shoulders, and says, "Oh c'mon. I won't tell."

I laugh again.

His tone gets serious and he says, "Let me tell you what I've seen. I've seen a man look at all the evidence, consider all his *observations* and filter it through *reason*, and decide there is no God. Then I've seen another man make the same observations, and also apply reason, and have his reason tell him there is a God. I've even seen one man conclude one way one week and conclude a different way a week later. How do you explain that? I've known men smarter than me who didn't believe. But in every one of those cases, there was a man smarter than him who did, and a smarter man who didn't, and a smarter man who did, and it goes on and on. So, in my mind, I've determined that reason isn't the full story, and somewhere in their minds—somewhere in all our minds—there must be a choice being made."

"Hey listen man, fine with me. I *want* to believe, okay? I'm trying to believe."

"You really want to follow Christ?"

"Yes."

"No, you don't."

"Yes, I do."

"I know a way you can do it."

"Tell me."

"You don't want to hear it."

"Yes, I do."

He says, "Well it's easy…"

I lean in. I look deep into his eyes. With no more light coming in from the windows, the electric flood lights are not enough to light the whole room, but they provide nice accent lighting on the side of his face.

"The answer is in the Gospel of Mark. A rich man asked Jesus how he could inherit eternal life. Jesus answered, 'Go and sell everything you have and give it to the poor, and you will have treasure in Heaven. Then come, follow me.'"

"You're kidding, right?"

"See? Told ya you didn't want to." He smiles.

"That can't be your advice."

"That was *Jesus' advice*," he corrects. The pastor looks at me and shrugs meekly. He says nothing else. He sits here quietly as if he had just given a long oration, as if he had pontificated on everything he knew about the Bible and simply had nothing left.

I look away. I'm thinking about just getting up to leave. *This is ridiculous. Right when I was starting to like him!* My mind searches desperately for a way to nullify what he just said. I wish to erase this conversation, and that passage of scripture, from my mind.

I reach for reason, my old trusted cudgel. "Wait, wait. You follow Christ. Have you given up everything you own?"

"Well, Christ doesn't want you to give up everything you own. He wants you to give up what you are worshiping instead of Him. For the rich man it was money. But for me it was something else. And for you it is probably something else completely."

I stay quiet.

"Is there something you know you're holding onto? Some place you've been searching for life outside of Christ?"

I sigh. "There was stuff I had tried to hold onto. But it's already gone."

He nods solemnly but says nothing.

"I have nothing left to hold onto," I insist. "Sell everything I have? I don't have anything! The bank's gonna take my house and my Jag, then all I'll have left is a totaled car, and a courageous painting."

He looks at me funny, but it isn't the strangest thing I've said today.

I continue, "I got nothing. What moths can eat, they ate. What thieves can steal, they stole. I literally have nothing left."

He nods again. "It sounds like you have been humbled, but that's not necessarily a bad thing. Some people are only able to let go when half the work's already been done for them. But some people feel their supports slipping away and it only makes them hold tighter to that one thing."

"What *one thing?*"

"The one crutch you will never let go of." He watches me expectantly.

I shrug. "All my life, I've felt that my logic and my intellect, my chalkboard, my zeros, and my slavish devotion to *reason*, were the only things that made me special. They were the only things for which I was worthy of being loved." I swallow. "So, what can I not let go of?" I search for an answer—actually search for an answer—and I laugh.

"What?" the pastor asks, seeing that something has just occurred to me.

I confess, "Every friend, every family member, and every girlfriend I've ever had would all expect me to say logic, reason or intellect right now."

"But you don't think so?"

I shake my head slowly.

"Then what is the real answer?"

"Control."

The pastor whistles. "Whew! Now we're getting somewhere."

I think some more. I turn to look straight at him and say, "Okay."

"Okay?"

"Okay, I'll give up control."

He looks at me dubiously.

I tell him, "You're looking at a man who gained the world and lost his soul… but then lost the world."

His eyebrows tick up. "And you believe Christ can help you?"

"Y-yes." *Short pause, not even sure he noticed.*

"And you are ready to give up control?"

Oops, long pause.

He smirks and says, "All your life you have used reason as your excuse. You have blamed it for your choices. You have pretended you're restrained by it. While the truth is, you just don't *want* to accept Christ. Even now. And the reason you don't want to is because you know he's going to ask you to give things up. The reason you don't want to is because you know—a part of your mind knows—He's going to ask you to change everything about your entire life."

I look away. "So, wait a minute… what about you? What was your one thing you couldn't let go of?"

"Can't," he corrects me.

"What?"

"Can't," he insists. "I haven't fully let go yet. I'm still struggling.

Jesus helps. He helps me every day, but *my* one thing... it's really a tough one."

"What?" I ask.

"Control," he says.

I laugh again.

"The world is a puzzle we have been working our entire lives to solve but haven't quite finished. The more it frustrates us, the more we are its prisoner. And any progress we ever make just brings us false hope. Then Christ comes around and says, 'There is no answer; the puzzle can't be solved. Now, put it down and follow Me.'"

He continues, "So, I'm begging you, let go of the world. Do you really love it so much? Has the world done anything for you to earn that love? Stop struggling. Stop working so hard to earn the love that has already been freely given. Let go. Release control in order to gain true freedom. Put the puzzle down and rest."

He could tell I was thinking about it. I tell him, "I had just given myself the analogy of a puzzle that I could not put down, and it was for the excruciating effort of trying to convince myself to believe."

"Put that puzzle down, too. Especially that one."

My face shows strain as I am trying to bring the analogy back to real life.

He sees my face and tells me, "Picture a Chinese finger trap. You're stuck because you're trying too hard. Just relax and go with it."

"Relax and go with it?" I challenge.

He laughs and shrugs. "Yeah."

"That is..." I shake my head. "I don't think that'll be enough to get Emily back."

His eyebrows furrow and I can see surprise flash in his eyes for a moment. It disappears just as quickly, and he looks over to my zeros and asks, "Do you realize I never did get your name?"

"James Larson," I tell him.

"*Professor* James Larson?" he asks.

"You've heard of me?" I'm a little surprised.

"Yes, I've heard of you." He shrugs it off. "I've seen you on YouTube."

I don't detect either approval or disapproval.

"Can I ask you just one more thing?" he asks.

"Sure."

"If you knew for certain you would never get the girl, would you still want to be Christian?"

I start to speak, but he interrupts before I can even make a sound.

"Tell the truth," he stresses.

I take a second to look into myself and discover the truth. I look him straight in the eye. I shake my head slowly and deliberately. I say,

"Yes."

He laughs. "Not going to answer me, huh?"

"I said yes."

"That's fine. You can think it over. It's a big decision."

"Dude, I said yes."

"Well, before you answer, I want you to consider this…"

I laugh.

He looks over at my zeros and continues, "Because…you know…" His voice has become quite serious. "It's going to be even harder for you, Professor, *even harder* because you know better than anyone how mercilessly Christians are mocked. All the venom you once doled out onto Christians will be doled out onto you… by men who were once your peers, by men who once admired you, even envied you.

"Are you strong enough to withstand that? The world will ridicule you, and there'll be nothing you can say to dissuade them, no defense they are ready to hear. So, their accusations will go undisputed, and simply put, *they will think you're stupid.* And it will be impossible for you to convince them otherwise."

I swallow hard.

"Are you strong enough to withstand all that?"

"No," I tell him, honestly.

He frowns and says, "I was afraid not." It even looks like he will stand up to leave.

I say, "But I still want to be Christian."

He looks me in the eye. "Why?"

"Because when I came to find the church that had played a pivotal role in my youth, I found it completely violated… and I wept." My eyes are filling with tears simply revisiting the memory of just a few days ago. I try desperately to blink them away. "I sat down in that pew over there and I knew something beautiful, something more than a building, was lost."

He asks one more time, "Was it God Who told you to rebuild this church?"

I try to look him back in the eye but continue to blink away tears. "I think it was."

He smiles. He says, "Romans 10:9 says, 'If you declare with your mouth, 'Jesus is Lord,' and believe in your heart that God raised him from the dead, you will be saved.'"

I don't know what to do with that.

"Will you repeat after me?"

I'm apprehensive, but I say, "Okay."

He bows his head and says, "Lord, I still have a lot of questions, but I suspect I always will."

That's pretty benign so I repeat that.

He says, "But what I do know is that I have been living only for myself up until now."

Hmmm. That's pretty on the money, so I don't mind repeating that.

"And I confess it isn't working."

Whoa. This one floors me. I pause, not because I don't want to repeat it, but because I can't believe I haven't figured it out until now. If anyone had ever asked me the simple question, "Is what you're doing working?" I would have obviously said yes—reflexively so. But is it really? How could I honestly say it is? I think of all the time I've spent trying to escape, but escape what?

I'm always running. I'm always searching for the next high, the next *distraction.* I accepted long ago that's what I had to do. I gave up on trying to remove the pain, I simply found a way to live *around* the pain. And I did all this so long ago, I don't even notice it's there. Unless I stop moving. Unless something happens to jolt me from my rut.

I can hear him shuffle. I'd forgotten he's waiting on me. He says, "If you're not ready—"

I look at the brown bag I'm holding, look at the zeros that defiled the finished wall, wipe a few tears from my eyes, and say, "I'm not ready."

I don't know why.

Chapter Fifty-Two

I'm alone again. What has it been, an hour? Two hours? I've gotten into the godless cooler, and I made a pretty good dent in it, too.

I remember the pastor saying goodnight, I think. It's hazy. He offered to drive me back to his place, of course. I told him I'd stay here until I was good enough to drive. I haven't yet broken that promise. *I'm still here, aren't I?*

I've moved over to the steps by the altar, the perfect place to sit and drink. I realize I don't have a charger to plug my phone into, but that doesn't matter anymore. I'm not waiting to hear from anyone and there is no one for me to call.

My mind has been running through everything the pastor said and seems to keep sticking on one thing, "I've seen you on YouTube."

I remember the video of me I started while at the Baldovini Gallery, but something about it made no sense: it was the new me—my hair was short and my face was bald—but I was giving the same speech I always gave. How does that add up?

I grab my phone and navigate to that video. I scroll to about the place I had stopped, and hit play:

"...who had lived in the last hundred years, that means somewhere around four billion will make it or have made it to Heaven. That means the number of people who have gone or are going to Hell is somewhere around..."

I draw out 7, 0 0 0, 0 0 0, 0 0 0.

"Keep in mind," I say somberly, "this is just one century."

I hold up a hand and say, "But wait." I turn back to the chalkboard and erase the seven to draw a six. At the first zero I add a little tail. I do this slowly and deliberately, and I angle my body so that my class can monitor my progress in real time. I draw another tail on the next zero and another tail on the next. Then I draw another tail on a zero, then another, then another. After the comma, I draw another tail on the zero. I draw another tail. As I draw the final tail on the final zero, I step back to see the number I have written and my chest swells with gratitude and worship.

The number I have *now* written looks like this:

6, 9 9 9, 9 9 9, 9 9 9.

I say the same line I always said; "That last change is because of me." Still looking at the number, clearly moved by it, I add, "Jesus tells us in the Gospel of Luke there is joy in the presence of angels for just one sinner who repents. Can you imagine—out of so many? Can you imagine a God who rejoices just for me?"

I can hear the students shuffling in their chairs.

I turn to face them and say, "Hell is real. Hell is serious. Hell is separation from God. You have all come here looking for answers, but there is only one answer. You've come here asking questions, but there is only one question in all the universe that matters: Do I accept God, or reject Him?"

The person who is recording this video is in the back of the room, so I am able to see the heads and shoulders of other students sitting in front of him. One of those students pulls out his cellphone and starts recording as well.

I continue, "The truth is we don't know who goes to Heaven and who goes to Hell." I motion to the chalkboard and reiterate, "We don't know... and frankly it's none of our business. 1 John 4:8 says that God is love. 2 Thessalonians 1:6 says that God is just. I will leave the fate of souls on Earth up to a loving, just God to handle. I have faith he will make each decision based upon his unfathomable wisdom and limitless goodness.

"So, there's just one thing we need to understand about Hell: the people who go there are no worse than you or I. And the people who go to Heaven are no better. Our afterlife existence is not a system of reward and punishment. People don't go to Heaven if they're good and Hell if they're bad. They spend eternity with God if they accept Him, and they don't if they don't.

"So, let's be clear, people don't go to Hell when God rejects them, they go to Hell when they reject God."

Two more students visible in the frame pull out their phones to record video of their own.

I am aware of this, but continue anyway, "Sin separates us from God and we don't have the choice not to sin. We are incapable of reconnecting with God on our own, but God, in His mercy, provided us a way.

"That way is Jesus Christ.

"I used to make a point to say the F-word in class. I thought I was such a rebel, but I had no clue what true rebellion really is. There's only one true message of rebellion against the world, and it's: *deny yourself and take up your cross daily and follow Me.* There is only one message so iconoclastic that it obliterates all the accepted wisdom of this world, and it's the Bible. I used to say that the F-word was the most powerful word. I was wrong. In fact, recently students have stopped showing any reaction at all. No one cares about *Fuck* anymore; it's meaningless. I used it for years, and it never once got me fired." I swallow hard. "You want to cause trouble; you want to see reaction in people's faces; you want everyone to pull out their cellphones and start recording, try dropping the word *Jesus* during class.

"*Jesus* is the most powerful word. I could say *Heaven* and *Hell*, and I could even say *God*, but when I say *Jesus*... There is power in that name."

I turn my face to look straight into the camera recording this video, the camera which started recording before all the others, and say, "Jesus is the Way the Truth and the Life. No one comes to the Father except through Him."

It is a strange thing to hear my own voice speaking this way, see my own mouth forming these words. I look good. I look confident and happy.

"But isn't that exclusivist?" a girl in the front calls out. She happens to be one of the few not filming.

"No. God our Savior wants all to be saved and to come to a knowledge of the truth. How is that exclusivist?"

"Aren't there many ways to get to Heaven?" someone else yells out.

"Isn't there truth in all religions?" another voice attempts to get in on the conversation.

The original girl from the front speaks up again, "You're saying only Christians make it to Heaven, not Muslims, not Buddhists, not Jews. That's exclusivist!"

"No. Not at all. It's like saying that salvation is a room, and it has only one door. Who can go through the door? *Everyone.* Not one bit exclusive. However, however, there will invariably be many who choose not to enter the door. They will protest..."

Here I start role-playing both sides.

"Why won't you let me in the room?

"I will let you in the room. The door's wide open.

"I don't want to use the door.

"Then I guess you won't get in the room.

"So, you're telling me that I can't get in the room simply because I refuse to use the door?

"Well, I guess that is what I'm telling you.

"Then they will become bitter, and their bitterness will cloud their thinking, so much so that this argument will actually make sense to them: *Christianity is exclusivist because they only let people in the room who walk through the door.*"

Someone calls out, "Can we choose to do something we are incapable of doing? And is it justice to punish someone for failing when success was never an option?"

The me on the video doesn't seem to recognize that as my own argument I make every year. He says, "No, no, you're not listening. That's a faulty premis—"

He's interrupted. Another student heckles, "So, God drops us into a maze, but you expect me to praise him for giving us a map? God throws us overboard, but you expect me to worship him for throwing us a life-preserver."

The me in the video surely recognizes my own words now, words that had been bandied about on campus for so long that the student in this video probably doesn't even know the source.

It's written all over my face: I look crestfallen as I realize I am stepping on the landmines I myself had laid. No, worse. I am protected in the loving arms of Jesus. The *children*, they are the ones left stepping on the mines. Christ has given me a new life, but the innocent and naïve are left paying the price for my mistakes. The pain is so evident on my face that even the crappy camera phone can pick it up. I am derailed. I appear completely at a loss when the video cuts off, leaving that last frame frozen on my devise.

A strange feeling comes over me. I am dumbstruck by the devastated look on my own face. It is a look of such powerlessness and regret, it can only point to one thing: I'm looking at a man who doesn't have to imagine what the pastor had said to me. "Try to imagine the moment you discover that everything you've ever done with your career had been a lie. Try imagining the pain of discovering that there is real truth in the world and you had spent your whole life leading people astray, people who had counted on you for answers."

I see the pain of that regret on a man's face, and that face is my own. I click off my phone and the screen goes to black.

So, now the choice is clear; following Christ does come with a cost: that pain I just witnessed. The choice is clear: accept Jesus and dive headfirst into that heartache and regret, or cling desperately to my puffed-up arrogance, which insists I am right and lets me hide from regret, safely in my own superiority.

Okay. I've made the choice.

I turn my face to look behind me, toward the cross. Turning my body around completely at the top of the steps basically puts me on my knees, so I give in. I am literally on my knees now.

Eventually I lower my head and close my eyes too.

God, I kneel before you unfinished. All I know is that this side looks better than that side. All I know is it would be a crying shame if I were to stop now.

Still before the cross, I ask the Lord for only one thing: Emily.

I offer God my simple syllogism: I want to be more like Emily. Emily wants to be more like Christ. Therefore, I want to be more like

Christ.

That's my five loaves and two fishes, God. Can you do something with it?

I lift my head and open my eyes. I feel… How can I describe it? A peace? Still. I feel still. I feel like myself, but a different myself. It's a truer me. It's not the me pursuing a girl. Not the me teaching my class. Not the me deep in philosophical thought. Not the me chasing down drunken elation. Not the me shamed by my own lustful acts. Not the me somehow obsessed with rebuilding a church. It's as if the last hour, month, or year of my life can't reach me, and next hour, month, or year of my life doesn't matter. It's the me I am when I first wake up—that moment of bliss before my mind reloads the incessant script sleep had paused the day before. It's what it feels like to merely exist.

And for a moment, I just enjoy being alive.

I say to God, "I think I'm ready now."

I continue the pastor's prayer by myself. With my head still bowed, I say, "God, I know what I'm doing isn't working. I'm tired of running. I'm tired of working so hard. I'm tired of thinking. I want to rest. I want You to take away my pain. I want You to take away my fear. I want You to take away my regret—what I did to that precious girl, what I did to all of them. I'm sorry. I thought I could do it on my own. Lord, I can't do it." I have to pause because I don't want to turn into a blubbering mess. With focus and grit, I steady my voice, "Thank You for my mind. Thank You for my logic, reason, and clarity," I say with a voice unwavering. "Lord I'm done letting them separate me from You. I'm done using them as an excuse. You want control, You can have it. I surrender. I give up. Please enter my heart. Please have Your way with me. My way didn't work." I laugh. "My way was a miserable failure. Can You make me into someone else? God, I do still have questions, but I'm willing to accept You died for my sins. I'm willing to accept Your ways are bigger than mine. Your logic is bigger than mine. I may never understand everything, but I'm ready to trust in You. Can you take this broken man and make him whole? I'm ready to—"

I throw up right there on top of the steps.

It's a disgusting mess and I don't know what I'll… I feel faint. I roll over to my back. I'm lying supine at the front of the newly-pristine, and re-desecrated, church. The room is spinning and… I feel…

Chapter Fifty-Three

I'm dreaming of Emily again. I'm at the altar of the church. I hear the doors at the back open and I turn to see. There stands an elderly man. His arm is linked with a young girl. She is an angel. No, she is a bride. The two of them walk down the aisle slowly, matching each other step for step.

The room is filled with swelling organ music. The melody fills my ears and my mind and chest. I recognize the piece. It's Vivaldi's "Spring." I know it by heart, yet I've never heard it played so sweetly.

As they get closer I get a good look at the bride. There is a natural blush on her naked face, and I can't help but notice her beauty one more time. I study the flawless skin of her face. Flushed and florid, it stirs something eternal in me. And yes, something godly.

Yes, she is an angel; she's my Emily, and today she is my bride. Her father is escorting her down the aisle to deliver her to me.

She wears no veil, because her veil had been torn.

A sound must've stirred me. I open my eyes and discover I am not standing. I am not wearing a tux. I am no groom. I am passed out on the floor of the church, and I'm drunk. My hair's a mess. There's slobber on my face and alcohol on my breath. There are a couple of empty bottles right by my head, and a puddle of stinking vomit.

I'm wretched. Unworthy of an angel. My eyes search the room. The father is gone and there are no attendants in the pews. No music can be heard. This is clearly not my wedding day. But Emily is still as beautiful as a bride.

She is carrying one of the candles from the front and its light gently caresses her wondrous face. She's heading toward me slowly and I am so unworthy. I'm unworthy of an angel so pure. All I can think about is how I hurt her. I want her to go. I remember the dark shadow of my dream long ago and I remember the words I shouted. "Stay away from her. Leave her alone. She is happy. Just leave her be."

She sees that my eyes are open and looks deep into them. She lowers her heavenly body to her knees before me and places the candle down by us. She uses a wet towel to wipe my forehead and cheeks, mouth and lips. It's so comforting that my eyes fill with tears.

She watches my tears silently. Her face is filled with a grace that could only come from Christ. She runs her fingers through my hair and I want to tell her how unworthy I am.

She turns her body to the vomit on the ground and for some reason she has a dustpan. Just as I begin to wonder why she has a dustpan, suddenly I no longer have to guess. To my utter horror, she takes the wet cloth and the dustpan and begins to clean up the vomit. I try with all my strength to move. I order my hands to reach out and stop hers, physically stop her from demeaning herself. But somewhere there must be dissension in the ranks. My body does not obey. I muster all the force of my will, and I feel the room spinning. I feel like I'm falling and my eyes shut tight.

When I open them again, her sacred hands are still busy cleaning my mess. The voice in my head cries out in desperate indignation. *Stop. Stop! Don't. Not after what I've done. Let it be. Stop the injustice. Not you, my virgin angel. Not for me. Run from me. Don't.*

But the only thing my weak breath can push past my lips is, "No." She doesn't respond.

I want to confess to her my wretchedness. She knows now anyway. I want to drop the act. She needs to see the depth of my depravity. All of it. That is my vomit, and its smell is what's inside me—the only thing inside me—just a horrible rot. I want her to know how undeserving I am of her, so she can understand it, accept it, and then she can walk away. She will leave me but I will have come clean. No more pretending. No more hiding.

She draws her sacred face nearer to mine and, in the dim light from the candle, I can see her ineffable blush. To me it is salvation. Her face moves closer and I am confused about what she's doing. She's leaning in toward me. Does she wish to tell me a secret? She leans her face closer still, and suddenly I can feel her mouth against mine. It's the sensation I remember from my one retrieved memory. The injustice of this kiss is almost more than I can bear.

She stands up, now high above me, and I still yearn to confess to her my desolation and demand that she flee.

I do open my mouth. But I only utter two words, two simple words that sum up our entire story; I say, "I surrender."

She smiles at me. "I'm ready to believe you," she whispers, then her pretty lips pucker and she blows out the candle.

Chapter Fifty-Four

I wake up... I feel redeemed. It's day seven.

I've woken up disoriented after many a bender. This is not the first time I've had to piece together the things I did while drunk. I've said, "Oh no, did I really say that?" and "C'mon, did I really make out with her?" but never have I said, "Wait, did I really ask Jesus into my heart?"

That is a first, and if not for the fact that I once woke up missing seven months of my life, I'd have to say the strangest ever.

Does a conversion still count if it's made while drunk? Was my first act as a Christian really to throw up in a church? And what was up with that dream? Was it a message from God? Was it meant to be symbolic?

If so, the symbolism is crystal clear, and right here and now I reaffirm my commitment to an awesome God.

I open my eyes to discover my puddle is gone. I'm again covered in a warm blanket. There is a glass of water and a bottle of Excedrin by my head. The unimaginable kindness of this gesture is not lost on me. I know I'm in a place of acceptance, love, and forgiveness. There are no *good religious people* here. If this is what grace is, I want more. I want to be a part of it. If this is following Christ, count me in. I rejoice because I know these people will not blow the second chance they've been given. This is going to be a vibrant, living church.

I look around. No one's in the sanctuary. I notice the painting of Jesus being lowered from the cross has been moved into here. It's actually now hanging below the large cross, covering my zeros like a Band-Aid covering a waiter's piercing. Someone must've moved it this morning. They probably got tired of seeing my zeros, because it's a strange spot for a painting. No one could actually want the painting there. It must have been the best temporary solution.

Good, because I don't want to see them either.

I'm curious where everyone is because the clock on the wall says it's almost 2 pm. The vegetable tray table and the godly cooler are gone. I look around. My godless cooler is gone, too.

I hear a noise outside and I stagger to my feet to investigate. I push through the front doors of the church and discover a crowd of people on the steps and in the parking lot, a far bigger crowd than I've seen here before. Some of the faces I recognize, some I don't. I discover the pastor and his wife without much searching. I walk over to them and ask, "What are all these people doing here?"

"They're here for the ribbon cutting," says the pastor. He has a peculiar grin on his face and he's watching my eyes. He takes a quick look behind him.

"Ribbon cutting? Shouldn't we wait until the church is finished?" I ask.

He looks behind him again and back to me. He replies, "It is finished."

I turn my head to see what the pastor keeps looking at. Over the pastor's shoulder I see the angel of my dreams.

It's Emily, all glowing and otherworldly as ever—a pure and radiant vision of hope for the godless!

She steps swiftly over to where I am standing. I'm wondering what she could possibly be doing here, but all I can think about in this moment is her arms. I make a study of them, glued to her sides. No embrace is offered.

"Dr. Larson," she addresses me like she's my student.

"Emily," I address her like I'm her professor.

Her eyes dart over to the pastor and then back to me. I almost laugh at what Emily says next, "Can we speak in private please?"

The pastor leans forward and insists. "You two can use the sanctuary. No one's going in yet."

I try to play it cool, but I practically run inside the church hoping she can keep up, impatient to hear what sweet Emily possibly has to say and to discover what she's doing here.

Once inside I walk straight to the candle she was holding in my dream. It's lined up in its correct position as if it had never been moved, but as I suspected, the wick is black. All these candles are brand new, but there is evidence that this one, and only this one, had been lit. I say, "That wasn't a dream last night, was it?"

She smiles and shakes her head. "My father doesn't know it, but I stopped by here first once I got into town."

"Did you mean it when you said you're ready to believe me?" I ask.

"Did you mean it when you said you surrender?" she counters.

I look straight into her eyes and say, "I have never lied to you." *Except for that Olive Garden thing.* "Wait…" I say out loud. "Wait… your father?"

She's watching my face intently. She's judging my acting ability. She wants to know what I know.

I stumble on helplessly, but with obvious sincerity, "Your father… the pastor… the pastor is your father?"

"Did you know?"

I shake my head. "No, I honestly didn't know."

"I've never mentioned this church to you. Not once," she said affirmatively.

She should know. I shrug. "I wouldn't have remembered anyway."

She smiles and her eyes begin to fill with tears. As good as her word, I can see she believes me. She put her hand to her mouth and her tears fall, first the left then the right. Probably she's remembering her prescient words about God wanting us together. It was her father's church I had been rebuilding the whole time. She's no doubt already heard the whole story from her father, how I prayed in this church at ten years old, how the idea for me to fix it up could only have come from God.

And she believes me. She doesn't assume I followed her or hired a private investigator somehow. Amazingly, she recognizes this moment for what it is: providence.

A God who relentlessly pursues.

I try my best to stand straighter. No respect I can show her is enough. We step closer to each other but don't touch, almost as if there might be a bright, brilliant spark when we meet, an arc between her heart and mine. Tears fill my eyes too, and I stand in awesome wonder at the glory, the beauty, and the majesty of this moment.

It wasn't the miraculous sign unfolding before us that made my knees tremble, it was that I suddenly saw for the first time all the miracles I had overlooked before.

God had told me to rebuild the church. Of course, it was Him. Sometimes from the cleft of the rock, you can see God only after he's passed by.

But I wasn't rebuilding the church; God was rebuilding me. And leading me back to her. And leading me back to Him.

I say, "It was God I spoke to at ten years old, in your father's church. My exact words, the first words I ever pleaded to God were, "*Make her turn around.*"

She smiles.

Emily had said if God wanted me in her life, He'd make it happen. He did. Amazingly, He had put me in her life twenty-eight years ago. I can still remember the image of that woman's swollen belly, and it fills me with the overwhelming feeling that life is sacred and God is beyond our ability to imagine. I say, "God had inexorably entangled our lives from a time before you were even born."

She flings her body into mine and she holds me so tight. Her forehead is on my cheek and my tears are in her hair. Her breath is on my neck and my heart is in her hands.

And I know *again for the first time* that our lives are in His hands.

"You told my father you wanted to become Christian, even if we could never be together..." She trails off, but it is clearly a question.

"I did," I tell her. "I mean, I will. I mean, I am." I shrug off my own stumbling answer and offer, "I'm still a little hungover."

I instantly regret saying it, but to my amazement, she laughs.

It was in that laughter that I find the acceptance I've been searching for my whole life. That sweet, kind, heavenly laughter is an angel wiping the face of a drunk. It is a pastor draping a clean blanket over a filthy intruder. It is waking up to water and Excedrin when I deserve neither. It is my first step in coming clean and my first taste of God's sweet grace.

I can't get enough of it and instantly tell her, "I walked into the shower with my clothes on."

She laughs again and says, "Why Professor, you're a wreck!"

I look at the spot she found me on the floor, and say in disbelief, "You cleaned up my mess."

She shrugs. "You cleaned up my father's mess."

I can sense she wants to kiss me, but I offer her my hand. She takes it and the connection is real. She looks at it for a moment, as if just the hand of her beloved is a source of awe and wonder, then she places it palm-first against her heart.

My joy is complete. My heart has been rebuilt. I breathe in deep and say to her what I've never once said to a woman. I tell her, "You were right. You were right about everything."

We lean our foreheads together and I just take a second to bask in the grandeur and the sweet majesty of admitting I was wrong. I can't believe I've lived this long without knowing this feeling.

When we step back out of the church, the crowd erupts in a raucous applause. I pretend I don't know it's for me, but the timing is not coincidental. The pastor must've made it known to everyone who had started the whole thing. Emily grabs my hand and I am reminded of the day we showed up to that first party together. I had become a hero in her friends' eyes in her absence. And now I've done the same thing with her hometown. God sure knows what He's doing.

Speaking of friends, they're all here: Alyssa, Sophie, Brandon, Sherry and Karen. I'm about to go speak with them when the pastor, *Emily's father*, approaches. Emily and her father nod to each other, and she smiles. No other explanations are in order. They had the whole morning to compare notes on "the man who I'm in love with but can't remember he's a Christian," and "the mysterious man who came to fix my church."

Nothing more needs to be said. They've both seen God orchestrate the impossible before, in His time and in His way.

There really is a ribbon, and Emily's father hangs it across both front doors.

He stands before the crowd and projects his voice. He says, "I want to take this opportunity to tell you I'm so sorry I let you down. I want you all to know that I was never qualified to be the leader of this church.

"But this town needs a church, so we're going to re-open these doors. I want you to know I have no intention of leading you. If you trust me, I would still like to be your pastor, but I promise you today, Jesus Christ will be the leader of this church. We will look to none other than

Jesus to direct our lives, yours and mine. So, that being said…" The pastor grabs the scissors and opens them. He positions them over the ribbon to cut it. This is just an act and he isn't fooling anybody.

He pretends he'd just thought of it, and he hands the scissors to me. I nod and accept the scissors and cut the ribbon. It's a strange custom, but it's beautiful. It's all about a new start, a new beginning.

Emily hugs my bicep and her father tells me, "Michael has something inside he wants to show you."

I dutifully follow. I'm trying to remember which one is Michael. Was he the cop? I'm not sure I've even met a Michael.

We step into the sanctuary and I don't see anything different. After all, I was just in here. In fact, I woke up here.

The pastor nods to the young man who recognized me yesterday, my former student. *I think he must be Michael.* Taking their cue, Michael and his friend grab the sides of the large painting underneath the cross, the one covering up my drunken graffiti.

I feel my heart contract as I figure out what they're doing. I can't help but cry out, "No, please leave it!"

They don't listen and begin to lift the large painting off the wall. "Don't!" I cry.

But they do, and to my surprise my graffiti is gone. I was dead-to-the-world half the morning after all; that was plenty of time to remove it. Now, what I see there in its place nearly brings me to my knees.

If I wasn't sure about being Christian before, I am now. That young student truly had been in my class that day, or he saw it on YouTube, or both. That shaggy-haired kid must've worked all morning— and he did a magnificent job.

On the wall behind the pulpit, beneath the towering cross, are ten perfectly stenciled numbers, painted in azure blue. It reads:

6,999,999,999
Luke 15:10

The whole thing is painted with perfect crisp, straight edges, and is to be a permanent addition to this great church.

I am humbled. At no time before this moment had I fully considered everything that me being Christian actually meant. Never before this moment had I been able to nestle into Jesus like a chick beneath His wing. Never had I pressed my cheek to His side and drawn life from Him. I realize my whole world has changed. I accept it. I surrender control. I accept Him. I'm prepared to live no longer for myself.

I am baptized in gratitude. I am immersed in humility. I am picturing a story more grand than I have ever pictured life before. I see now that I've spent my whole life waiting in line for execution. And the members of that line—all of them doomed—acted nothing at all like lambs led to the slaughter or sheep before the shearers. That line was loud and proud, boisterous, irreverent, and braggadocious. And I was no different than them.

But by some miracle, I felt a tap on the shoulder. I heard a gentle voice, faint among the mocking and the cursing, asking me to step out of line and follow Him.

And for the very first time in my life, I care about those left in line.

Life is a bigger story than I had ever imagined, and that story is heartbreaking. Life is glorious, tragic, and incomprehensibly *big*, and I was a fool every second in which I pretended to have a handle on it.

I recite the verse to the crowd from memory. "There is rejoicing in the presence of the angels of God over one sinner who converts."

Emily's father looks at me and smiles. "Very impressive. It's *repents,* but close enough."

I laugh. "Close enough."

She squeezes my hand.

Overwhelmed with community, acceptance, love, and salvation, I lack the ability to care about being cheesy—in fact, I may never feel embarrassed again. Remembering the snarky rejoinder I once gave Emily, I start to sing. I've never been a great singer, but with a voice full of simple, naïve joy, I project:

> Jesus loves me, this I know,
> For the Bible tells me so...

Emily smiles at me and members of the crowd join in.

> Little ones to him belong.
> They are weak, but he is strong.

I watch Emily's eyes fill with tears again. *What can I say? The girl likes cornball.* They were the same tears she cried the day she ran into my car. They were the same tears that started this whole thing in my classroom. But really, they're not at all the same. These are tears of joy and could only best be described with one word: *triumphant.*

I know because they're in my eyes too.

> Yes, Jesus loves me.
> Yes, Jesus loves me.

I can't get more lyrics out because Emily plants a kiss right on my mouth. The crowd cheers.

Emily's friends in the crowd cheer because they know half the story. Emily's parents cheer for the same reason. The rest of the crowd just cheers for two people kissing. They know nothing of the story; it's enough for them just to see undiluted happiness on display. They understand well enough; two people have found love at the rebirth of a broken church.

Chapter Fifty-Five

There is one more thing I have to do, and it has to be tonight because it's been too long already. I drive with Emily to see Dimples. We take the new Jag. It's a beautiful machine.

In the car outside, Emily tells me, "Take your time. I don't mind waiting."

"You didn't have to do this," I remind her.

"I want to be here for you. I want you to know I'm right outside waiting."

I exit the car and she rolls down her passenger-side window to yell one last thing. "Don't eat or drink anything she offers you!"

On her front step, I ring the bell. And wait. I hear faint movement inside and I know she has already looked through the peephole at me.

She's either deliberating on whether she wants to see me, or she is making me wait as a negotiation tactic. The wait makes me uneasy. I don't know exactly what the dynamic will be. It has been nine days since I proposed and only seven days since I broke into her house and stole from her.

To me it feels like much longer because I have relived my missing life via my own words, helped rebuild an entire church, and reunited with both my new love and my True Love. But it also kind of feels like just yesterday. I imagine it feels even stranger for her.

The other question of course is if and when she found out I stole back my journal. How often do people go into their guest bedrooms? I don't know.

My questions are answered the moment she opens the door. She is visibly drunk.

"You stole from me!" she barks.

I remain calm. "That's a bold charge for you to make."

"What are you doing here?"

"I came to return your stuff," I say as I hold up the bottle of Premocyl. It was the same line she had once given me.

Her face hardens and I reproach myself. Even though it was clever, I told myself I wouldn't say it.

I add in a more pleasant tone, "I just wanted to check on you."

"I don't need you to check on me."

"May I come in please?"

"No." Her voice is still cold, but I see her face starting to warm.

I ramp up my most sincere charm and say, "I really just want to talk."

She slams the door but not in my face; she actually slams it open. The door bangs against the wall in the entry way as she turns her back on me to head inside. I enter and inspect the wall for damage. The home seems to be okay, but I can't say the same for the homeowner.

I follow her in and discover her place is even more of a mess than the time I broke in.

She says, "Sorry 'bout the mess, but I guess you've already seen it."

"Yeah, sorry about that."

She is drawn back to her drink and I wander into her kitchen behind her. Before she can take a sip, I step over to her. I take the glass slowly from her hand with no sudden moves. I pour the alcohol down the drain and fill the cup back up with ice water.

She doesn't protest, but she pouts and folds both arms over her chest. I lean the small of my back against her kitchen counter to face her.

Suddenly she says, "I don't care what name you called me."

Her attitude's changed, and I don't know what to say.

"I mean, I know I never introduced myself. And, to be honest, it's my fault for giving you the Premocyl."

"Yes, it is," I say firmly.

"I know. So I deserved it." Her whole face changes when she smiles. "It's poetic justice really. Can't we just forget about it? Can't we just forget about all of it?"

She could've picked a better turn of phrase.

"I've done enough forgetting," I retort.

She laughs, even though there was no humor in my tone, and she *knows* it wasn't meant as a joke. She says, "You're so funny." She turns to open her cupboards and asks, "Let me pour you something."

I laugh, but not for the reasons she might think. "Nothing for me, thanks."

"Oh c'mon." She slams the cupboard, but obviously didn't mean to. "I just want things to go back to the way they were. Can't we just let things go back to the way they were?"

"The way they were, or the way you *told* me they were?"

"The way they were that Friday night." She means the sex.

I swallow a lump in my throat. "No, I don't want things to go back to the way they were."

"I am sorry I gave you the Premocyl, okay? It was stupid. I was just hurt. I guess I wanted you to feel what it was like to be rejected. I guess I figured my only chance to get you back was for you to forget about…" She trails off.

"Emily?"

Her eyes turn cold.

"I don't want to forget about Emily."

"Well, you're a loser," she snaps.

I understand what's happening. There's been a battle raging in her head over me, the real feelings she had for me and the hope for us to be together versus the very real anger she still has toward me over being rejected. I interrupted that internal battle when I knocked on the door. Both sides are still vying for victory, only now it's external.

She continues, "You're a... why would I want you anyway? Why would I waste my time with you? You're a..." She keeps searching for what to call me, but her anger is freezing her mind up. "You're a... You're *an idiot!*"

"That word doesn't hurt me anymore," I say calmly, but falsely.

"You're so stupid. You think you're smart but you're not. You let some girl talk you out of everything you once loved. You bought into all her religious crap. I mean how dumb do you have to be? That's pathetic! Path-et-tic!" She leans into my face and drags the word out mockingly.

I realize there's little point talking to her while she's this way. I decide I just need to say what I've come to say. She needs to know that the battle inside *my* head has been resolved, and she needs to hear from the side that won.

I say, "It is over for us. It has to be. We can't go on, but I want you to be okay. I want to help you."

"I don't want your stupid pity."

"It's not pity," I insist forcefully. I smile and shake my head. "I know you won't believe me, but I have to speak the truth. The truth is that I care more for you than you could possibly imagine."

"Shut up."

"And I want you to find happiness—"

"Don't! Don't do it!" she shouts before my sentence is fully finished.

"Don't do what?" I honestly don't know what she wants me not to do. I see her clench a fist with her right hand.

She hisses, "By God, I'm warning you, don't do it."

I'm still confused, but I laugh. "God is actually what I wanted to talk to you about."

Her eyes transform. The anger behind them goes from red hot, bypassing white, and straight to blue. Both her fists are now clinched and she begins to rock back and forth on her feet. I should pick up on these warning signs, but don't.

"I know what I have said about God in the past, but something has happened to me, something joyous, and I—"

"Don't you dare!" she shrieks.

"—I want you to have the same joy."

She lands two hard palm slaps against my face before I can stop her. I grab both her wrists, but her left hand is able to grab my hair and I can't dislodge it. We struggle and she pulls my head by the hair hard to one side. I am bent awkwardly in half trying to keep my balance and disentangle her grip from my hair when I feel sharp pain through the knuckles of my other hand. She is biting that hand trying to free herself from my hold.

I let go.

More blows land on my face, ear, and shoulder. A wave of pain rushes through me and it's hard to keep my temper in check. I attempt to overpower her. I don't want to hurt her, but my only hope is to restrain her. I receive many more blows before I am able to spin her and step into the space behind her back. She no longer has a hold of my hair, none still left on my head anyway, so I can finally get my arms around her.

She struggles a moment or two, but it's clear that she can't break my grip. "What the…?" I shout by her ear, clueless to what set her off.

I can feel her body relax as she gives up the fight. My body, without waiting for my orders, relaxes to. The second it does, she slams her head back hard into my nose.

Blood drips down the front of my face and my lip is split.

I step back to avoid a second attack, but it doesn't come.

She turns around trembling. "You stole my cross!" she yells with a voice that sounds more bull than human.

"What?"

She jabs an accusing finger straight at the top of my chest. "You stripped it off me and put it right onto you."

I reach up to touch the cross I'm wearing.

"I spent years looking up to you, and you didn't even have the decency to remember me!"

Okay, yeah, now I can place her face. "I remember you, I remember you," I insist impulsively. I just hope it might make her happy to hear it.

But it's too little too late. She continues to wail, "I know about Christ. I know about joy. That's what you took from me!"

My heart sinks. I have no defense.

She continues without pause, "You took it from me and put it right onto you." She keeps shouting. "You took it from me and put it right onto you! So, don't you dare… Don't you *dare* judge me for not having it! There's my cross." She's still pointing. "Looks like you have it now."

I've never seen so much suffering as I'm seeing before me. I've never seen a woman so lost. I'm surprised by how much true love I feel for her, and how her every tear—now that I've heard exactly what I've done—weighs painfully on my heart.

I vow, deep within my heart, and in the span of a nanosecond, that I will do anything for her if it means I could help. She is right. She is right. I am wearing her cross. I first tore Christ away from her, then judged her for not having Christ. And apparently, I did it *twice*.

I reach up to touch my fat lip. I poke at my own nose. It hurts just to touch. I say, "This conversation… this *exact* scene has played out before, hasn't it?"

She doesn't answer but her eyes dart over to the bottle of Premocyl I foolishly left on the counter.

I should run to beat her to it.

She must have anticipated that, because she herself ran the few feet it took to reach the bottle. She opens it and pours its contents straight into her mouth. I take a few uncommitted steps toward her as she grabs the glass of water I had poured.

I know I could stop her, and I probably should, but I can't help but think about the vow I just made. I know the fear and confusion that she will feel tomorrow. But all I can think about is the pain that she won't. I understand, as she does, that there will be other pains, but this pain will end. Come what may, *this pain* will end.

God help me, I do nothing. I allow her to swallow them all.

She finishes the bottle and collapses to the floor, crying.

I step over to her and place an arm around her. She instantly turns to embrace me. I begin to lift her up and she uses the last amount of strength in her body to assist me. But then it's gone and she falls slack in my arms weeping. I reach down and scoop her legs up as well. I carry her weightless body in my arms like a bride and make my way to her bedroom.

I lower her down on the bed and pull a blanket up around her. As soon as she is covered she turns away from me, facedown, out of sight.

She begins sobbing and I'm certain she will lie here crying until she loses consciousness. I try to think about what I could say to her, but I know she'll never remember it anyway, and my mind just can't come up with anything that is profound, or appropriate.

I'm watching a life fall apart. I'm watching a woman come undone, a woman I care about. I study what little of her face I can see as she sobs uncontrollably. With no great epiphany about what to say, I decide to say what I know to be true—perhaps the only thing in this moment I know to be true. I stroke her hair to let her know I'm still here. It's such a strange moment. Her loss of memory will render it all so unimportant, but I must go with the truth because somehow I feel like it's more important than ever. I feel like it's the end of time. Oddly, I feel like it's the last thing any boy will say to any girl. I say, "I love you."

Her cry quiets a bit and she whimpers, "I love you, too."

I turn and walk out.

On the way out, I can't help but notice a wire basket by her door which contains some letters ready to be mailed. I take a quick look at the name above the return address: Ruth Blevins.

Ruth. Her name is Ruth.

Pain strikes my heart when I remember the story of the little girl, perhaps the *one* part of everything she told me that is probably true.

230

Chapter Fifty-Six

I was a predator. I think of all the faces, the real lives. They were someone's sons, and someone's daughters. They were my prey. I preyed on their innocence and inexperience.

I see their faces and I hope they're happy today. I hope there were other influences in their lives. I hope that someone wiser and stronger came along after me.

I hope they've just outgrown me.

And I hope it didn't take them too long.

I think of Ruth. The thought occurred to me as I watched her take the Premocyl: I wish there was enough for her to erase ten years. I wish I could take her back to before she gave me that cross, before she walked into my class, back to when she still had faith.

It pains me to think of how I used them. It's not just that I corrupted their young minds, it's that I did it to feed my own ego. It was never about liberation. It was about pulling them down into the quagmire I was in. I claimed to be so certain of my own opinions, but I never felt safe, never felt valid, until I convinced as many people as possible to side with me.

It was and is always about vanity.

I sided with the mean against the merciful and I called that brave. I sided with the people who try to destroy their enemies, and against the people who pray for them. I sided with the Rottweilers against the kittens, yet somehow thought I was so courageous.

I marched in lockstep with the dominant philosophy of our time and I called myself a trailblazer. I became what every teacher, professor, reporter, author, and celebrity told me to be, and I called myself a dissenter. I was a Synchronized Nonconformist. In fact, I was their captain.

I built my monument so high, to distract from the fact that what it represented was so low. Just vanity. Nothing more complex or lofty or venerable than that.

But it doesn't take great genius to get the rebellious to rebel. It doesn't take sagacious powers of persuasion to convince a child to satisfy his most immediate urges in the short run. *You're on top. You're in control. If it feels good, do it. It's better to receive than to give. Do unto others what they have done unto you. And above all, pretend loudly to love thy neighbor as thy self.* This is all I ever convinced them of, nothing more than their errant hearts and this fallen world had already proclaimed. I convinced them of nothing. I never once inspired anything new. It is so much easier to muddy the water than to purify it. If an immaculate linen touches a soiled one, the former is transformed while the latter appears unchanged.

It is only now that I grieve for what I've done—God's perfect justice at work—because it is only now that I realize how precious those young minds were. Pure water. White linen. It is this type of purity that, once lost, can never be brought back. How dare I touch them with my blackened hands? How dare their parents, as well as our once-great institutions, hand them blithely over to me? Couldn't they see my hands were filthy?

But that purity *can* be brought back. I spoke wrong. With man this is impossible, but with God, all things are possible. Jesus can bring that purity back. Christ alone can fix the damage I've done. Christ can clean faster than we can tarnish. Christ can purify water faster than we can muddy it. Jesus can remove the black stain on your heart and remove the zero from your permanent record.

People will follow you if you're smart. They will idolize you, worship you, and put you on a pedestal, because you are smart. But you will never get them to do the one thing that matters: let go. Prepare a vacancy for Christ. To get people to truly do that, to truly make a change in their lives, you must love them. A smart man can change someone's mind, but only Jesus can change their hearts.

Emily tells me I couldn't have stolen souls from God; He doesn't allow it. John 10:28 says, "And I give eternal life to them, and they shall never perish; and no one shall snatch them from my hand." I hope that's true.

I watch as the street lights pass from the front to the back, but the shadows they cast move from the back to the front.

I can feel Emily rest her palm on the back of my hand, trying to comfort me.

Romans 8:38 says, "For I am convinced that neither death nor life, neither angels nor demons, neither the present nor the future, nor any powers, neither height nor depth, nor anything else in all creation, will be able to separate us from the love of God that is in Christ Jesus our Lord."

I sure hope it's true. When I marvel at the work He did to reclaim me, I believe every word. Even after I was given Premocyl, things were different inside my head. Things that once excited me and that made sense to me—like Casimiro's work—no longer did either.

Perhaps He will do the same work for Ruth. I pray it is so.

We pull up to Emily's house. I put the car in park and leave the engine running. She asks, "So, what are you going to do now?"

I laugh. And then sigh out loud. "I guess, I've got to pick up the remaining pieces. Well, at least it seems I have friends now." I smile, then add sincerely, "I'd like to get to know them."

"You'll love them."

I tread carefully, "And, of course, I'd like to get to know you better."

232

"Oh, you'll *really* love me!" she says.

I laugh. "I think I always have."

It's uncomfortable.

"I guess I need to—"

"I love you, too," she blurts out. "I'm sorry I didn't say it at the party. I do love you."

I squeeze her hand so tight, and I feel my eyes fill with sweet wonderful tears of joy. And I know this sounds strange, but I feel this moment is just too beautiful to ruin with a kiss.

Fortunately, she doesn't think so. She leans in to kiss me.

It doesn't feel strange. It just feels right.

It makes me think of something. I ask, "When were you in my shower?"

"What?"

I'm an expert at perfect timing. I quickly add, "I'm not saying we were in it together or anything. I figured you just used it or something. Maybe you came straight to my place from somewhere else. We decided to go out, but you needed to shower..." I trail off when I see the confusion on her face.

Finally, I remember I took a photo. I pull out my phone and ask, "When did you write this?"

She looks at the photo and starts to laugh—her fingertips shoot to her mouth, just as I had described it in my journal. She says, "Oh you're going to be sorry you showed me this!"

"Why?"

"Because that's not my handwriting."

"Well, then who else could have..." *Oh, I guess it does kind of look like my writing...*

She continues to laugh. Her entire head turns red, not just her face but her ears and neck and collarbone.

I scoff, "Really? I drew a heart and everything?"

She smiles lovingly. "Such a romantic!"

Now I'm the one blushing. I try to change the subject, "I still need a job... and I have no idea what I'm going to do."

"Oh? I wasn't sure if you would decide to work."

I look at her funny. "Well, I need to work," I say oddly.

Now she looks at *me* funny. "I just thought because of Casimiro..."

I'm so glad she pronounced it the non-pretentious way. Plus, she's so stinking pretty. "What about him?" I ask.

Now she *really* looks at me funny. "Are you... wait, you don't know?"

"Know what?"

"Seriously, how is it that you don't know? Casimiro? That's the guy who painted your painting, right?"

"Yeah..."

"Wait, how could you not know, if even I know?"

I'm amused by her stall tactics and while laughing insist, "What? Know what?"

"He died."

I immediately stop laughing. "Oh," is all I can say.

The news hits me strange. I had spent so much of my life loving Casimiro. I am amazed by how much I am still touched by his death. And even if I can no longer stand his work, and probably agree with him on nothing, that was a human being who died and... honestly, I close my eyes and say a quick, silent prayer for his soul.

Emily is still watching me, there is an expectant look on her face and I am not sure what reaction she is expecting and—*Oh!*

"Oh," I whisper.

She reaches out to squeeze my hand.

234

ELEASHA POST SCRIPT

"I think I am going to tell the buyer about Jesus."

"You should."

"Can I somehow get to interview him first? I want to interview him, and if he actually likes the painting, I won't sell it to him."

She laughs.

I have been Christian for a few weeks now. It's not quite what I thought it would be. When I think of the sheer magnitude of God, Heaven, and Christ's sacrifice, all my problems seem insignificant. When I try to fathom the unfathomable scope of eternity, all my problems seem insignificant. Even when I just consider the beauty of spending my days here on Earth with such a soul as Emily, all my problems seem insignificant.

Yet somehow, I still have problems and they don't seem insignificant.

I am finding it difficult to keep my mind focused on what really matters, in fact if I were to twist Dostoyevsky's line one more time, I'd have to say: One *lifetime* of bliss... Why isn't that enough to last a *moment?*

It's not poetic, but it's true. It's how our minds seem to work. It's as if the one thing we're specially designed to do as humans is to forget the eternal and focus obsessively on the ephemeral, to turn toward the darkness and away from the light.

I've spent so much of my life wanting to be a great and inspiring teacher, but I am discovering that what followers of Christ need most is not to be instructed but *reminded.* What we need most is someone to perpetually turn our heads back, turn our heads back, turn our heads back. This is not nearly so glamorous.

I turn in my seat to look behind me. I pan the whole room.

"Is she here?" Emily asks.

"Not here yet."

Emily checks her watch. "You still think she'll come?"

"I sure hope so." There is more meaning in my statement than even Emily could interpret. From the moment I cowardly left Ruth alone in her bed, there has been one image I haven't been able to get out of my mind: the gun in her nightstand two feet away. I know the pain and confusion of emerging from a Premocyl stupor. I know the desperation.

I look over my shoulder again. I check my watch. *It's too late; she should be here by now!* I desperately long just to see her dimpled face, just to know she is still alive.

The auctioneer approaches his podium. It is the same man I originally bought it from. He addresses the crowd, "Good evening ladies and gentleman, and welcome to the Baldovini Gallery. Thank you for joining us tonight for this exciting and yet somber occasion. We are honored here tonight with the opportunity to display and auction some of the most important works from the recently deceased master, Fran Marco Ambrosio Casimiro. Casimiro is largely considered to be one of the preeminent..."

I tune him out.

Where is she?

I look at Emily. She can see the lines of worry on my face.

She turns to look over her shoulder. "I think that's her," Emily exclaims.

This time Ruth is alone. Her shoulders are slumped; her eyes are bloodshot and her face looks utterly devoid of hope. Her dimples lie stagnant from disuse.

I stand up immediately and wait for Emily to stand. Emily's eyes dart over to the front where the auctioneer is doing what he does best. She says, "Right now?"

I glance over at the young man, then back to Ruth. "Right now," I nod.

I walk straight toward her, with Emily in tow. We get surprisingly close before she notices us.

She has just walked in so we are well positioned in the back of the room. We can hear the distant sound of the auctioneer throwing out numbers at an alarming rate climbing higher, ever higher.

Finally, Ruth spots me coming toward her. Her face changes. First it shows shock, then the dimples come out.

"Professor Larson?" she asks.

I pause for the briefest of seconds, as if trying to remember her name. I point at her and smile, "Ruth Blevins?"

"Yes," she says happily. "I'm surprised you remember me." Her eyes dart down to my hand that's holding Emily's.

"Ruth, I would like to introduce you to Emily. Emily, Ruth. Ruth, Emily."

Ruth smiles and extends her hand. Emily ignores the hand and brings Ruth in for a hug. "It is an honor to meet you," Emily says.

Straight to the point, I say, "Ruth, the truth is, I am so glad to see you. I have something of yours that I want to return to you." I reach behind my neck. "You gave me this about ten years ago, and I never should have accepted it."

Her dimples disappear and she looks down at the cross. She is clearly uncomfortable and she says, "No, I don't... I don't need it."

"I want you to have it."

She pulls her hands to her sides like she doesn't want to touch it. As if to grant me permission to keep it, she says, "It's not worth anything."

I smile. "It is of infinite worth."

She looks at me confused. In the background, we can hear the bids slowing down.

"Twenty-four million, do I hear twenty-five million?"
"Twenty-four million, five-hundred thousand, do I hear twenty-five million?"

Emily steps in. "Hey we have a group of friends who we get together with all the time. We have barbeques and bonfires; we go to concerts and stuff. Just a great group of people from our church who try our best to love and serve each other. We'd love it if you'd come out with us sometime."

"*You* go to church, Professor Larson?"

It was clear from her tone that the *you* was in italics. I frown. "I know what I said to you before on the matter, but I was wrong. I took this from you," I extend the necklace one more time, "and I would love the chance to give it back."

Ruth looked at me, then at Emily, then at the cross.

I am holding Emily's hand, mere feet from the woman who tried to tear her away from me. She is the woman who drugged me, violated me, lied to me, and tried to keep me from my Savior. But, looking at her now, I feel nothing but love. I hold the cross in my hand and I know it was I who wronged her.

She is fragile and human and precious. I see the blush on her cheeks, the awkward way she shuffles her feet, and the heartbreaking way she keeps looking back at our clasped hands. She hurt me, but she was lost. I hurt her first, but I was also lost. I tell myself this isn't about my guilt, and I know it *shouldn't* be about my guilt. *But I feel like if I could reverse the damage in just one heart...*

Mainly I just want her to be happy. I want her to take back her cross. Literally and figuratively. I long for the day, with me beside them, that Emily pulls back Ruth's hair and clasps it around her neck once and for all. And God shows the world once again that His children will not be taken from His hand.

Ruth says, "No, I'm sorry. I don't want it back."

My heart sinks.

I can see that she is uncomfortable. She begins to turn her shoulder. I know if she does, she will not just walk away from us, but out of the building and back to her car. She says, "Well, it was nice—"

"It's still there, you know," I interrupt her.

"What is?"

I tread carefully, but not timidly. "If you had ever felt peace and contentment in the presence of God, it's still there. If you've ever felt impressed by people's genuine love, not just for God, but for each other, it's still there. It's all there waiting just for you."

She hesitates. Obviously, her own words are able to resonate.

I add. "I'm talking about joy. It's the type of joy that once you see it, I just know you'll want to be a part of it." *Her own words.*

In our mutual silence, we can all hear the young auctioneer wrapping up.

"Twenty-five million, do I hear twenty-six million? Do I hear twenty-six?"

"Twenty-five million, one-hundred thousand, do I hear twenty-five, five?"

"Twenty- five million, five-hundred thousand, do I hear twenty-five, eight?"

"Twenty- five million, six-hundred thousand, do I hear twenty-five, eight?"

I turn for the first time to see the painting being auctioned. *Yep, they started with mine.*

But that's not what I came for. I know I can get through to this girl. I know that Jesus can reverse the damage done by my *philosophy and empty deceit,* if I can just convince her of one thing, the truth I uttered when I was at my intellectual nadir, my least articulate: *This side looks better than that side.*

"What do you think," Emily asks her, "will you come and see?"

"Twenty- five million, eight-hundred thousand, do I hear twenty-five, nine?"

"Do I hear twenty-five, nine?"

I hold my breath.

"Going once, going twice, sold to the man on my right for Twenty-five point eight million dollars."

I hear the knock of the auctioneer's gavel, but I watch only Ruth. Ruth smiles and says, "Sure, I'll come."

I can't help but throw my arms around her. I say, "That's the best news I've heard all day."

COMING VERY SOON FROM B.K. DELL:

September 2018
How to Stop a School Shooting: a Novel—a Celebration of Love, Youth, and Sacred Life.

January 2019
Bullies—the Continuing Saga of a Child Activist (Novel)

May 2019
The Shroud of Turing—the Clash of New Age Tech with Old Time Religion (Novel)

Note to Reader:

I hope you have enjoyed reading my second novel. If you haven't read Mead Mountain, please check it out.

It was the AMAZING REVIEWS that made Mead Mountain a success, so please:
Love this book? Please leave a five-star review on Amazon.
Hate this book? Come find me on Facebook and let's talk about it.

This book was published by Authoritative, a small start-up from Texas, without the assistance of the large New York firms. You can help support this novel, and those to follow, by spreading the word about the work we are doing. Those of you on Facebook, please join my fan page: Facebook.com/AuthorBKDell, and invite your friends to join. Mention this book on your wall and share a link to BKDell.com. If you run a blog, please mention me on your blog. Come find me on Goodreads.com; friend me and click to become a fan. Amazon and Goodreads are the best places to leave a five-star review.

Of course, the most helpful thing you can do is tell your friends and family, face to face, how much you enjoyed this book.

Please visit BKDell.com for updated links to Facebook, Goodreads and more.

Please check back often for new titles coming soon!

God bless you!

Made in the USA
Middletown, DE
05 July 2018